SWIMMING WITH PIGS

LAURA & ALAN HOLFORD

LEM Black Publishing

For our special beloved mums
Edith & Heather
who we lost too soon and
will be forever remembered.

To our dear friend Anselmo

Thank you for hosting our
book launch party

Love and best wishes

Laura & Ste

CHAPTER ONE

'This has been more than seven years in the making. Finally, Project Orpheus has progressed from a dream to reality. Today, we are gathered for the launch and inaugural sailing of our majestic ship Destiny Celebration.'

It was a proud moment for Andrea Kennedy, the CEO of Destiny Cruise Line, and the overarching parent company Destiny Luxury Group. It was her principal project since taking over the company from her father, Seamus. She wanted the most technologically advanced cruise liner on the planet; after all, this was a global enterprise. She wanted it crewed with the finest in the industry. She wanted to showcase this naming ceremony to the cruise family, that Destiny was the market leaders who could attract the most eligible clients. The Destiny Celebration was that liner. The choice of her close friend Michelle d'Vere as the godmother of the ship was the natural choice. Their respective fathers had been best friends for life, almost like brothers. Andrea and Michelle had grown up together but drifted apart when university had called. After a decade apart, their paths had crossed again, and their lives entwined once more. Since Andrea's separation from her estranged husband James, Michelle had been a confidante, as she had been in those formative teenage years. This was Andrea's way of rewarding her friend.

Andrea addressed the crowd on the dockside. 'To share this proud moment with me is the chosen godmother of the ship, Mrs Michelle d'Vere, whom I have asked to name this vessel on its maiden sailing voyage.'

Michelle, with the lever for the champagne bottle release in her right hand, called out in an exuberant voice, 'I name this ship Destiny Celebration.'

The bottle swung through the air at great speed and smashed into the hull. It resembled the thunderous crash of an Icelandic glacier calving into the water. The liquid explosion confirmed its success. Michelle breathed a deep sigh of relief, matched only by that of Andrea. Smiles and loud cheers echoed around the faces at the dockside. Flashbulbs from cameras at different angles lit up Michelle as she appeared to relish at being thrown into the limelight. The couple of thousand inaugural passengers clapped with delight before heading for the gangway to the fanfare of the ship's band. Order and decorum had bypassed everybody. Andrea laughed at the chaos unfolding before her eyes. The tickertape rained down from the skies above. She desired to cherish the moment as a source of joy for many, and she wished their travels to mirror that. Once onboard, she knew everyone would be a captive audience, and things would settle down. Andrea could not join in on this debut itinerary as her father had recently been taken ill, but she felt confident that Michelle would be the ideal ambassador.

Michelle grabbed her husband Theo's hand and mouthed, 'Thank you,' to Andrea, turned away and walked towards the gangway. Until a few months ago, Michelle had no idea this would be the start of her 10th wedding anniversary celebration.

Upon completing the swirling turns of the gangway, Michelle and Theo reached the entrance to the ship. There to greet them was the ship's Captain, Nico Stavropolous. A native of Santorini with the ocean running through his veins. The youngest captain across the Destiny fleet, but highly regarded by his peers for his levelheadedness and attention to detail.

'Welcome to our most magnificent Destiny Celebration.

A true honour to have you both aboard. Your majestic home for the next two weeks. May I introduce you to your dedicated suite butler, Jose deSousa, who will take you to your elegant stateroom within the Utopia suites. Just to inform you that the Captain's Welcome VIP cocktail party will be held in two hours' time in the Illumination Lounge. No rest for the wicked, Mrs d'Vere!'

'Apparently not,' she replied.

***

Jose proceeded to the nearest lift, inserting the pass allowing privileged access to the Utopia suites deck.

'Awaiting your arrival, I noticed the high excitement amongst the passengers. Rest assured that "Destinations," the daily newsletter, contains all the details for the party, ensuring that all the passengers will be present. There will be an eclectic mix of guests attending as this is an exceptional sailing.'

Jose escorted the d'Veres to the Concierge Lounge and introduced them to the host Henrique Suarez. 'Ma'am, we have arranged for your luggage to be transferred to your suite. Jose will unpack for you whilst you relax here. Champagne?'

She replied, 'Why not?'

Theo interjected, 'We have a long day ahead, darling.'

Michelle detected Theo's frosty tone. Not for the first time that day. She questioned why he wanted to be there and her own choice of how to spend her time. He had once again only just returned from a photographic assignment abroad. The spark was diminishing with every exploration he undertook. She had no actual interest in his profession. He was a much sought after professional photographer, perhaps one of the most revered in his field. A hint of jealousy maybe after being on a level pegging at university together. He was the star that shone the brightest out of the two of them. To hell with it. This was her day. She will have that glass of champagne. In fact, why stop at just one? She had stared at the bottom of many a wine glass during her time spent alone. Did Michelle support Andrea or vice versa? The look in her eyes told Theo she was going to be stubborn. He could not wait for the suite to become available. Michelle, once a stunning beauty, now faded in front of his eyes and heart, despite her glamorous appearance as the newly appointed godmother.

Henrique interjected their inner thoughts with, 'In partnership with Jose, I am here to make sure you have a wonderful cruise. This extends to any shore experiences you may wish for me to arrange on your behalf. An itemised brochure is available on the coffee table in your suite. We can guarantee exclusive access to many sites and even private tours as part of your privileged status.'

That prospect was far from Michelle's thoughts. Within thirty minutes, Jose returned to announce that their suite was ready for their enjoyment. He placed Michelle's second glass of champagne on the silver tray alongside Theo's sparkling water and proceeded to their suite. Opening the dramatic oak veneer door, he ushered them in. It was an opulent display. Separate walk-in wardrobes either side of the main entrance with a marble bathroom each beyond. Jack and Jill bathrooms were not befitting the butler suites. There was a large living room with a classic dining table that God forbid could seat eight. The room was adorned with three separate floral displays, leaving an exquisite perfume of roses and lilies. Michelle pushed open the internal double doors to reveal a luxurious king-sized bed with an infinity hot tub looking out over the veranda. Soothing classical instrumental music was playing through the Bluetooth speakers throughout the suite. Jose, with one call of "Robyn," activated the voice control. Michelle smirked at Andrea, choosing her late mother's name for such a command. Not too dissimilar to how her mother was always calling out "Andrea" when she was a petulant child. Jose turned and left them to relax in their surroundings.

'Can I give this a go?' asked Theo.

'Of course, sir. Ask it anything you want.'

'Robyn, play jazz funk music.'

Without hesitation Robyn replied with 'Playing jazz funk music.'

After a couple of seconds, the speakers were softly playing out Theo's request. Michelle rushed to freshen up before heading to the Illuminations Lounge, but first, she had to complete the mandatory lifeboat drill as required by maritime law. The seven short blasts and one long blast, watching guests adorn a life vest and blowing the damn whistle. Not much use, she thought, in shark-infested waters 100 miles from civilisation, but it was a ritual she had to endure with sarcastic thoughts or otherwise. Marine emergencies were a natural leveller. Hierarchical privileges, as seen during the Titanic era, no longer existed. All this was on top of her priority of trying to rebalance the continued rocky status of her own marital relationship. The cracks resurfaced, but she preferred to keep them hidden from view. Not her most triumphant moment. This was her day, and she wanted Theo to accept it. For once, she was the shining star in their solar system.

She returned to the living room to follow out Jose, and as he reached the door, he turned to Michelle and said, 'Sorry, one more thing.'

Jose reached inside jacket pocket and pulled out an embossed envelope addressed to Michelle. 'For you.' He handed it over and closed the door behind him.

Michelle used her perfectly manicured nails to slide under the lightly glued down envelope sleeve. Revealed inside was a brief letter from Andrea.

Dear Michelle,

I'm so sorry that I can't join you on this special occasion. I want you to thoroughly enjoy your time onboard. While I appreciate your enthusiasm for becoming the godmother, it's important for me to emphasise the potential stress and high expectations that accompany the role. As a small token of my gratitude, I have arranged for you to have unlimited onboard credit for the use of your husband and yourself. The one exception I have had to make is regarding the "Aquamarine" jewellery boutique. I wanted to leave jewellery for other passengers to purchase. Please order anything you wish. I have instructed the Food and Beverages Director to ensure that any purchases made using the Onboard Credit (OBC) are not charged to your stateroom account. I have also organised for you to have daily use of the "Oasis" spa and the "Tranquillity" solarium and pool. You already look like a million dollars, but I want to ensure we do everything we can to keep you that way!

Enjoy!

Andrea

***

'Ladies and gentlemen. A warm welcome to this special event; the inaugural Captain's Welcome Party. In our eyes you are all VIPs and we are honoured to have you aboard,' boomed the Cruise Director Oliver "Call me Olly" Jenkins over the microphone. 'Without further ado, may I introduce to you the Master of the vessel and his senior officers. All are here to help you "Cruise towards your Destiny", which is the motto of our company.'

A round of enthusiastic applause greeted Captain Nico as he took the microphone and introduced the members of his senior management team. Except for the absent First Officer, from Chief Engineer to the Director of Housekeeping, from Food and Beverages Director to Executive Chef. Each strode up onto the low stage to raucous applause. The clinking of champagne glasses paused, replaced by repeated requests for more from all corners of the lounge.

Standing back from the stage but mingling amongst the throng was Jack Shaw, the Head of Security. A sobering position that did not merit a mention in the introductions. He was there to add his presence to the white uniformed staff, creating a certain ambiance. Passengers relished the chance to ask condescending questions to the service staff at their beck and call. Captain Nico interrupted his thoughts by introducing his next revered guest.

'May everyone please raise a glass and toast Mrs Michelle d'Vere, who joins us onboard as the godmother of this vessel. This will be followed by a few words from Mrs d'Vere. Everyone please "The godmother"!'

They reciprocated the call to an even louder clanking of glasses. The ensemble was growing less attentive as the speeches rambled on. The second and third glasses of fizz on empty stomachs were starting to take effect.

'Thank you, Captain Nico. I am deeply honoured to be appointed as an ambassador for the Destiny Cruise Line. To be made the godmother of this wonderful ship is a dream come true beyond my wildest imagination. My thoughts and wishes go far beyond this inaugural sailing, as I will forever more be associated with this vessel. My heart and thoughts will go with every sailing regardless of whether I am onboard. I believe this is my legacy to the vessel and all those who sail upon her. The cruise line has invested heavily in making this the best vessel at sea. Their reputation goes before them. They have the smartest technology and, without doubt, the most professional crew to ensure the safe and secure operation of this ship. That unique combination will ensure you have an enjoyable journey and an incredible experience. Please join me in a toast to the ship and its outstanding crew. "The Destiny Celebration and its crew"!'

Jack raised his glass of grape juice. He had multiple reasons to abstain from drinking. He carried the responsibility of randomly breathalysing five staff members every week and organising disciplinary proceedings against any personnel found to be intoxicated or causing trouble. Two separate events lead to the same unfortunate outcome for the recipient.

The company's image was as important to the vessel's safety. Any adverse publicity was detrimental and frowned upon. If that happens, the PR machine at HQ in London would go into overdrive. Destiny's mantra of "professionalism was non-negotiable" was integral to every chapter of their cruise line staff manual. The personal consequences of not abiding by the rules were draconian but widely known.

Jack looked around so that he could identify guests with whom to mingle. He wanted to avoid the monotony of repetitive question-and-answer sessions with familiar faces. His mind went back to a previous cruise on the sister ship Destiny Jubilation and the unforgettable Mr and Mrs Morgan-Brown. Never a couple more unworthy of possessing a double-barrelled name whilst trying to perform above their social status. They took delight in telling anyone how they had progressed up the cruise company "Aventurine" loyalty scheme over the years. The scheme name was based on a precious stone to reflect their strap line "How precious your loyalty is to us as returning customers".

The Morgan-Browns knew every level that was represented by the five oceans of the world, in reverse alphabetical order: Southern, Pacific, Indian, Atlantic and Arctic. They were aware of the qualifying requirements and benefits for the next level, including the number of days or cruises needed. Every conversation they had with another passenger appeared to start. "And are you an Arctic member as well?"

As "Arctic" members, Jack thought to himself how ironic if they abandoned the Morgan-Browns on an Arctic excursion! They could irk you with a single question. But wait. Could his eyes be deceiving him? Was that the Morgan-Browns? There, quite close to the port side stage steps, were the couple. Their unmistakable dated clothing style resembling something collated together from a charity shop pre-cruise. The smell of mothballs gave no reason to doubt the real possibility that their stylist was carrying out a charitable act to adorn them with the latest donations to the shop. He had to avoid them at all costs. They never forgot a thing. He looked in the opposite corner towards the rear of the lounge in the starboard direction. It was also close to the 'Staff Only' exit. Jack noticed a couple with their backs to the stage, laughing with each other. He was indescribable in a dark suit, but she stood out as she was carrying one of the flashiest cameras that he had ever set his eyes upon. Before he could make a beeline towards them and the relative safety of descending below deck, he heard the unmistakable shrill voice of Connie Morgan-Brown, with a sharp tap on his shoulder and the accompanying musk. How could he have dropped his guard? How painful the next twenty minutes would be. Twenty minutes of his life that he could never get back. They cut their conversation short by the appearance of First Officer Dani Lawson.

'I don't think you've introduced us, Jack?' she smiled encouragingly.

Jack wished he could save Dani's life like she had just saved his, but their history had prevented that to date. She used the same words the last time she saw him on a previous cruise, talking to an eligible member of staff in the crew bar. The irony was not lost on him. He was not expecting to see Dani there as she had deputised for Captain Nico on the bridge, but since he had taken over the ship's command after the speeches, she was released to join the party. Jack felt the close supervision of Dani. He believed it was professional, devoid of personal bias.

Out of the corner of his eye, he spotted the official Ship Photographer Lesley Richards mingling amongst the ensemble, taking unchoreographed photo shots. He noticed that as she approached and snapped the couple in the starboard corner; they looked at the photographer and parted in different directions. She tried to say 'Hello' to them both, but they had already separated. The woman left the lounge with her face lowered, while the man confidently scanned the room and surroundings. He smiled charmingly at the photographer and acknowledged her as she said, 'I admire your work,' but he casually walked away through the crowd towards the front of the stage where he took a stance alongside Michelle d'Vere.

**

Jack had followed the man's journey as he steered his way through the crowd. From Jack's experience, he could tell from this man's body language that potentially he had something to hide. His posture as he moved was like a chameleon camouflaging in a new environment. Jack knew that the advanced sophisticated technology on the ship included the ship's photographer having facial recognition software that had the capability of being interfaced with the ship's security CCTV and embarkation photos. Someone could therefore trace images back to individual cabins and suites. The ship's photographer saved time by not needing to ask for cabin information or distribute numbered receipts. Instead, the photos would be accessible in your personal portfolio within the electronic gallery. If you were from different cabins in the photo capture, it would appear in both portfolios. The technology advancement of the IQ in-suite TV meant you did not need to go to the ship's photo gallery to view, print and purchase the shots, as they were available to select and purchase at your leisure from your own lounge. Your onboard account for charges was also available to enable you to keep tab of expenditure as the cruise progressed.

His thoughts wandered to his day-to-day chores. He had his twelve members of staff to manage. All of them, recruited from Gurkha backgrounds, had experience in high-end security. They grasped the concept of the chain of command. Jack liked detail, but not boring trivia. He had enough issues with working out the security detail for each port from arrival to departure, as well as the rich tapestry of incidents that a cruise can bring. Each day was unique, much like in his previous careers. Before he knew it, the lounge was in full bright lights. The customary signal indicated the abrupt end of the event, prompting everyone to move on. Subtle as a brick, but it worked. With the passengers dispersing before the crew, Dani seized the opportunity to talk to Jack.

'How's your day been, Jack?'

He replied sharply, 'I was wondering when you were going to appear? Hopefully, this cruise will be more "plain sailing" than the last one.'

Jack turned away before she could reply.

***

That evening, Captain Nico had arranged for a private VIP dinner at the Chef's Table. A secluded environment for the top dignitaries onboard. The spacious round table facilitated intimate conversations without raised voices. To one side, the harpist played mellow songs in front of a mock fireplace. The faux flames provided a backdrop to add a sense of drama and illumination. Captain Nico had placed Michelle beside him. As an alternate male and female arrangement, Theo was seated between Michelle and First Officer Dani. The other two guests at the table were the ship's doctor, Smita Patel, and one of her medical team, nurse Nathan Williams. Since the sail away was scheduled for 11pm to coincide with a fanfare of fireworks, Dani could participate in the hospitality activities. Because of their "Arctic" status, the Morgan-Browns found themselves amongst the select few. She gripped the gold embossed invitation in her hand. Connie showed it to the Maître d' as she entered the room. She clung to it, determined to display it in her cabin for the room steward to admire during the rest of the cruise. The senior crew occupied the rest of the twelve-seat solid oak table, except for one man, Mr Gonzales, who was impeccably dressed in a rather dapper shiny silver suit and paisley cravat. After the introductions by the Maître d', the Executive Chef and Head Sommelier introduced each course and the chosen wine pairings that complimented each other. Somewhat embarrassingly, Cecil could not help himself in asking for a top-up with each glass. Connie did nothing to stop this faux pas. Out of misguided courtesy, everyone else at the table remained silent.

'How uncouth,' Michelle whispered to Theo.

He did not care as his thoughts were elsewhere beyond the velouté amuse-bouche.

'Are you a "Arctic" member Mr d'Vere?' enquired Connie.

'I'm afraid not. Although my wife is the ship's godmother, strangely enough, this is my first cruise. My work often takes me far away, which, of course, gives Michelle the opportunity to enjoy the luxury of taking cruises alone, allowing her to be pampered and relaxed.'

'What's your business?' asked Cecil.

'I'm a freelance photographer. Luckily, my hobby doubles as a business, allowing me to travel worldwide. The cruise line has invited me to perform the duty of a guest speaker on one of the sea days this week. I'll let you know that the subject is one of my favourite locations, the Galapagos Islands. The home of the Blue Boobies.'

'Mr d'Vere!' gasped Connie.

'Sorry, let me elaborate. It is, in fact, the home of the Blue-Footed Boobies, a unique and beautiful bird. There are also Red-Footed Boobies, so don't be offended if I refer to the contrasting Boobies in my talk. It's all part of the humour level I use to enhance my presentation to keep the audience awake and interested. You'll have to come along and listen to my other "titbits"!'

Cecil giggled in approval, or as he thought to himself, 'tittered'.

Theo reminded himself that he cannot mention he was leaving half-way through the cruise for an assignment in the Florida Everglades, as Michelle had sworn him to secrecy. She did not want others to know, presumably, he thought, because it may cause concern to senior crew members why her husband had to leave so soon after joining. Theo thought it would be better to be open and honest in advance, so it did not come as a revelation, but Michelle had been so insistent when she asked him. Maybe she had a surprise in store for him. He did like surprises.

As the beetroot cured salmon gravadlax was served at the table, the gentleman in the shiny suit lent forward over and said, 'Bravo Mr d'Vere. Bravo. The Maître d' didn't fully introduce us, so kindly let me introduce myself. I am Hugo Gonzales, the Sculptor in Residence for Destiny. My dear friend Andrea Kennedy has approved of my Sculpture Studio concept. The first for this cruise line. Absolutely pioneering. I'll be holding demonstrations during this voyage, with certain pieces of artwork being made available for auction on the final sea day. All net profits are going to the Destiny Charity Foundation, of which I am a patron. You must come along to "Sculptures by Hugo". I'd love to have you pose as a muse sweetie,' giving a knowing eccentric wink and sly nod of the head.

Theo brought his wine glass to his lips and took a slow sip to gather his thoughts and replied, 'Well, that's not an offer I get every day, sweetie!'

Connie turned to address Dr Patel and asked her about her role on the ship. She was a veteran of the cruise industry, having originated from the historic port of Cochin in India. Destiny recruited her from another cruise company. She saw this as her last contract before her well-earned retirement.

'It's a funny business being the ship's doctor. At first, there is little demand, but as the ship moves, so do the passengers. Some abuse the drink packages at an alarming rate. A rate their bodies can't handle. One might say it's too much of a good thing. Some people are not accustomed to the movements of a ship during bad weather. They may feel unsteady. Unprepared individuals may require sea sickness tablets or a pressure pad to relieve their symptoms of nausea. For others, it's worse. The next thing we encounter is to treat the more serious injuries from slips or falls. With each passing day, workloads can frequently grow. Cruises can range from serene pond-like voyages to, let's say, choppy experiences.'

'Yes, we've seen both ends of the spectrum in that respect. Haven't we Cecil,' agreed Connie.

'You have, sadly, other implications dependent on the age and mobility of the passenger demographic. On previous cruise ships I've been on, the mortality rate sometimes reached one person per week. Some passengers have pre-existing illnesses and conditions that increase the risk of an unfortunate outcome. I understand why some people may want to book possibly their last holiday on a cruise ship and believe they will enjoy that. However, there may be consequences. We cannot provide x-ray services for those who fall over, so we transport them to a nearby hospital. There are also occasions where we decide a guest receives more critical medical care than we can provide, which means leaving the ship and being transferred to an onshore medical facility at the next available port or at great expense via a helicopter medical emergency evacuation. In that situation, they and their family may not return to the ship. As for those that think it's only a bit of high jinks in getting drunk, the worst of them could require short-term monitoring by us which is a serious inconvenience to a small medical team with a limited bed space,' Dr Patel highlighted in a serious tone.

'Well, I hadn't thought about it so much. Do people actually die on the ship?' asked Connie, looking horrified.

'They do indeed, hence the four mortuary fridges located discreetly in the crew area,' replied Dr Patel solemnly.

Nurse Nathan took a deep sip from his wine glass whilst maintaining his stare on the polished silver cutlery set in front of him. Unusually for him, Nurse Nathan found himself lost for words and did his best to conceal it.

'Gosh, that is a revelation. Any sound advice?' asked Connie.

'Yes, quite simply have adequate medical and health cover insurance if you want to keep your house!' responded Dr Patel.

Nurse Nathan recovered himself and raised the atmosphere across the table with a funny anecdote of a time he mistook the notes on a medical record and nearly mixed up an endoscopy and a colonoscopy. It was fictitious but lightened the mood. Nurse Nathan questioned whether Dr Patel was revealing excessive confidential information to someone who was just a passenger, not a crew member. Could Connie's discretion be relied upon? It's not the sort of statistics or information he would like to hear being repeated along the ship's corridors or over a balcony as idle chit-chat. Nurse Nathan had a significant amount of professional respect for Dr Patel. They had agreed on a rota where Dr Patel, Nurse Nathan, and Nurse Kenny Williams equally shared the on-call time 24/7. Kenny was currently covering on-call so that Dr Patel and Nathan could enjoy the Captain's dinner.

Not before too long, the chef presented the saddle of aged venison, accompanied by roast potatoes in goose fat and vibrant green savoy cabbage.

'I heard you mention the Galapagos Islands, Theo,' interjected Captain Nico.

'It's somewhere I once went on holiday with my family only a few years ago. My highlight was the interaction of the marine iguanas together with the sea lions and Sally Lightfoot crabs. A kaleidoscope of colours lying across each other in a raw environment. The wildlife is so trusting of humans. Fascinating. Without spoiling your presentation, Theo, what are your personal highlights?'

'A difficult one,' he replied. 'Each island is unique and offers something different. For me, it's the unfettered access we have through our close co-operation as professional photographers with park rangers, all of whom are native to the Galapagos or Ecuador. Their conservation efforts span the islands and oceans, safeguarding marine life. It's not just about what you can see, but also what lies beneath.'

Connie sprung into life and said, 'That sounds more like the title of a horror film than a remit.'

'That's closer to the truth, Connie, than you realise,' recounted Theo. 'Seeing bits of micro-plastic strewn across the beaches where the turtles come to lay their eggs is indeed a devastating sight. We encourage visitors today to spend even as little as thirty minutes of their time collecting plastic fragments off the beaches. We need to go much further than that, but I'll leave the rest of my thoughts on the subject to the lectern in the Kennedy Theatre during my onboard talk. As one artist to another, you must come along, Hugo?'

'Awesome. Of course, darling,' he responded.

The mix of exquisite desserts and cheeseboard concluded the meal as the conversations ended.

'That's one of my earlier pieces over the mantlepiece behind the delightful harpist,' gestured Hugo.

'So how much is it worth, then?' enquired Connie.

'You can't put a price on beauty, Connie. I'm sure that's something that Cecil says to you every day, my dear!' said Hugo, looking across to Theo with raised eyebrows.

'Absolutely,' said Theo.

Cecil was engrossed in the wine list, calculating the cost of the excessive amount he had consumed tonight, grateful that it was complimentary.

'Your dress, Connie, is that Coco Chanel?' cheekily enquired Hugo.

Cecil glanced up from the wine list and slurred, mocking the brand name "St Michel or something like that," associated with a popular department store.

Caught in the moment, Connie asked of Theo, 'What do

you do for thrills?'

'Good question,' he replied.

'I'm a bit of an adrenaline junkie, but that can take various forms. When out photographing wildlife, I enjoy the thrill of the hunt and then the ultimate capture. We often have to stalk our target over long periods of time in order to capture the perfect photograph or film. To accomplish that, I can either lie prone or with my elbows tucked in, completely still, like an assassin with a rifle. Unlike an assassin, when I shoot the intended target, it lives on!'

Changing the subject, Michelle felt duty bound to say something to others around the table rather than purely engaging only Nico and Dani in private conversation about the expectations of her godmother role.

'Cecil, what are you looking forward to on this journey?'

'The excursions. Although I enjoy being on the ship, I also like to explore when I get the chance. We haven't travelled that much around the Bahamas and the Caribbean. Captain, as I have a walking stick. Do you think I'll be able to get priority disembarkation when visiting ports on this cruise?'

'I'll leave that with my guest relations team. Dani can speak with them on my behalf. I'm sure we can arrange something,' said Nico.

'Yes, Captain,' replied Dani resignedly.

Her smile resembled a grimace. How many times had someone with a walking cane approached her, seeking priority assistance? Many were deserving, but not all. The "benefit stick brigade" as they were sometimes known. Once you rushed them through onboard, you watched them head to the buffet whereby the stick became obsolete in a Lazarus miracle moment. They replaced the stick with sharp elbows and the ability to balance a heaped tray with the walking stick perched in the crook of their arm, hanging like a useless appendage. It was never in use again until there was a queue for a free cocktail at a captain's gathering or a stampede for seats in the theatre. Should there be a book signing by a guest speaker, they would be at the head of the scrum like a rugby hooker playing dirty tricks to gain an advantage on the referee's blind side. Bless them, she thought. The flash of the Maître d' flambéing the Crêpes Suzette brought Dani back in to focus. The performance distracted the rest of the table. Food theatre at its best.

'How about you, Connie? What are you looking forward to?' asked Dani.

I'm fascinated by astrology, and there's a talk about it during the cruise. I'm excited about the Poetry Workshops, a new activity for sea days.

Cecil gazed at Connie in confusion, unaware of her interest in poetry. 'She reads me my daily horoscope from the paper every morning. I then feel pressured to conform to it for the rest of the day,' grumbled Cecil.

'I love to guess other people's star signs,' trilled Connie.

'Give me a few days and I'll see if I can identify you by your zodiac signs.'

'Good luck with that!' said Michelle, somewhat sarcastically.

Cecil picked up on the tone of voice and cautioned, 'Beware what you wish for. She's rather good at it.'

***

The delectable meal came to an end. Another hour remained before the sail away fireworks. Michelle was expected to attend the opening night at the Kennedy Theatre and then be on the deck for the fireworks extravaganza. She believed that after these commitments, she would be able to finally retire to bed. They had reserved a theatre box for her overlooking the stage and stalls. There were two seats set aside, but for Theo, the Fortuna Casino was calling. It did not open until the ship set sail and reached international waters, but he wanted to walk around the ship and the outer decks beforehand to familiarise himself with the layout and grab a bit of fresh air. Being artistic did not mean he necessarily liked the theatre. He felt too claustrophobic in rooms with doors closed, sat with numerous strangers. Private dining was his limit. Being a free spirit, he did not like to be confined to a seat.

During his stroll around the ship's promenade, he passed the still closed shops, including the Aquamarine Boutique. Due to tax and duty regulations, they had to wait until the ship reached international waters before they could open. A dazzling tanzanite and diamond bracelet in the window display caught Theo's attention. The obscured price tag lured Theo to lean closer to the window. The observant shop assistant could not help but notice Theo gazing with an obvious interest. She was an expert in seducing unsuspecting gentlemen into parting with their money for beautiful, yet expensive, gifts for wives and partners. The shop assistant mouthed encouragingly 'Hello' through the window from within the shop. Theo smiled and mouthed 'Later' to her, then walked away, glancing back at the bracelet in the window.

Theo also was not a gambler per se, but did like the thrill of the game of chance played to an audience. He enjoyed the one-on-one against 'The House'. Supported by the cheering masses, he felt like a gladiator in the arena. No-one ever watched casino tables and hoped the house wins. For no other reason, it seemed like a win-win situation.

**

Michelle glanced at her watch multiple times in the theatre, aware of the time constraint. She anticipated the house spotlight would illuminate her taking a seat in the box. A warm light round of applause echoed around the room. She could not hold up the cast and guests, as the next event would be the fireworks display as they set sail. Destiny's team had meticulously organised ahead of her embarkation her tight schedule of appointments. The pressures described in Andrea's letter were proving to be accurate. Michelle's stress levels were rising. Her face displayed an expectant smile, though her thoughts told a different story. She could not wait until she was able to retire to her suite.

***

The amphitheatre setting of the casino, with its marble columns, gold leaf etchings and imposing carved alabaster busts, just added to the gladiatorial challenge. Looking around, Theo tried to guess which ones were created by Hugo. Did any resemble Hugo's previous lovers, he wondered, and if so, which ones? Male or female? Theo's favourite game was playing at the roulette table. No introductory lessons for him as he had his tried and tested numbers and lines. No looking at the previous draw history for him. Numbers have the potential to repeat continuously. It's not about the past, but about the future. Not playing the "High Roller" tables where the mood was more subdued and serious, lent itself to the open tables having a more relaxed yet dramatic atmosphere.

As Theo continued to scan the casino, he noticed that there were at least 5 blackjack tables, a lucky spin machine, a lotto draw, half a dozen various forms of poker tables, and approximately 100 gaming poker machines. There were extra-large television screens to display sport channels with raised seats to play poker games at the sleek black quartz semi-circular bar with cocktails to dull the sense and reactions. The gleaming surface of the bar reflected the bartender's appearance. To replicate the feel of Las Vegas, there were no mirrors or clocks. The gaudy patterned carpets allowed guests to wind their way through the tables and slot machines. The whirring, jangling, clapping, cheering, bells ringing, roulette ball spinning combined with the many slot machines created a constant cacophony of white background noise. A kaleidoscope of colours rotating and flashing attracted gamblers towards certain machines. The slot machines were covered in neon lights and buttons to encourage placing further bets. The glittering pendant lights suspended over the tables highlighted the concentrated faces of the players.

Theo, skilled at detecting gamblers' gimmicks, could spot the signs - mirrored glasses, caps, earplugs, even hoodies - used to hide their poker faces. An exceptional player, with a focused gaze, intuitively knows when to make the right call. He could see that the players onboard this ship replaced these items with more elegant clothes with their suits and dinner jackets and the occasional ballgown and were enjoying the escapism from ordinary life. There were still the traditional gambling styles of flicking chips, tapping tables with cards and discreetly turning the cards to avoid anyone else seeing its face whilst gazing at the sleight of hand manoeuvres of their opponents. As he approached one of the roulette tables, he saw the players literally willing their favourite numbers to win on the nose.

'How's it going Spartacus?' came the familiar-sounding voice of someone who knew him well. Without a camera in her hand, Suzanne Harrington sat to his left at the end of the roulette table.

Theo glanced sideways, careful not to show any sign of recognition to the casino staff. The croupier's badge indicated her name as Ji Lin. A petite looking lady with almond-shaped eyes concentrated on the entire table, gamblers and observers. Some players searched for weaknesses in staff and systems to exploit, gaining an advantage over the casino. Every little helps, right? Ji could not relax and observe others away from her table, with the Pit Boss, Janik Stoicov, strategically positioned behind the croupiers to assess everyone and everything. Janik observed not only the guests but also the casino staff, assessing their performance and interactions with clients. Familiarity can breed contempt. "Never bite the hand that feeds you" was a regular part of Janik's pre-cruise staff briefing. It was a long and lonely flight home if they kicked you off the ship at the next port.

Theo and Suzanne's familiarity went unnoticed by those around them, except for Janik. Nothing unusual, he thought, as life upon the high seas brings an unusual mix of people, both above deck and below deck. 'Flirtatious' was the first devilish word that came to mind but was countered with the angelic "Who am I to judge?". Looking around the other tables, no one was showing a potential spark like this couple. Did the absence of wedding rings hold any meaning in today's world? One to watch, he thought, out of curiosity, if nothing else. Their relaxed body language suggested a close acquaintance. Both Theo and Suzanne put forward their cabin cards to request chips against their individual stateroom accounts. Janik noted their separate stateroom numbers on the computer and different surnames. He was familiar with the d'Vere surname, but he did not know Theo. He noticed Theo was staying in the Utopia Suites, which high rollers often frequented. Theo was not a name he recognised from his high roller list or one that he had seen before on other cruises. The demure $200 amount they both wanted against their respective stateroom accounts did not make them high rollers by any stretch of the imagination. That was croupier tip money to the cardsharps. How Theo, with his right hand, reached over and placed ten chips on the same numbers, made him query what kind of player he was. His method was repetitive and reserved, with a likelihood of having just lucky numbers. He was not reacting to the draw history as some players do. Rarely touching or moving his stack of chips, he had them neatly laid out in piles five high on the right side. Janik noticed him placing them in the same sequence and numbers using his right hand. He drew off any winnings to the left and did not reuse them. Janik thought this was a strategy to harvest something from the gamble with minimal risk. Gamblers chase money, hoping to defy the odds that the house always wins. Theo, he thought, was not this kind of player. Janik noticed him looking around at the supporting crowds for encouragement if he won "on the nose". He observed that some of his numbers were identical double digits such as double zero, eleven, twenty-two and thirty-three. He also played one chip on the 19-20-21 street, but then also placed five chips straight up on the number twenty. When Theo waited for the small white roulette ball to lose momentum and settle on a number after its revolutions around the mahogany wheel, he flicked a spare chip between his right thumb and fingers. Janik noticed Suzanne had a different approach. Although she laid down half the amount of chips each time with only five, the numbers and areas she bet on were a more random scatter gun approach. Unable to reach the far end of the table, she passed chips to Theo for placement. She would not use the croupier to assist her like many other players would.

Over the next two hours, both of them experienced mixed fortunes. Theo was the only one who had to reload his chips, since he was betting double the amount without winning at the same rate. His only triumphant run came when the theatre emptied and crowds flocked to the casino. Theo's consecutive wins on the roulette wheel caused shrieks and attracted a larger crowd to the table. However, the even louder clapping and screaming from the craps table drowned out the cheers. He did not enjoy the craps table. The rules were hard for him to follow, and it was way too boisterous. He felt there was a false atmosphere around it. People back slapping like they were your best friend when you rolled the numbers they want, but that faux friendship did not necessarily last that long. The stateroom account was taking a bit of a hit, but he had had worse days. It was not time for ordering his favourite Sweet & Smoky Rob Roy to celebrate. He hoped that time would come around soon, but lady luck needed to change. Janik had the option to increase the house profits by raising the table limits for both maximum and minimum, but acknowledged that the crowds around the tables were dwindling without others joining in at spare seats to fill the table. Taking what he could in these early hours of operation rather than alienating the guests, making moderate profits. Some money was better than no money.

***

Michelle returned to her suite. She had slipped her black high-heeled shoes off and was rubbing her sore feet when she leaned forward to the coffee table and picked up the shore excursion brochure. She flicked through the pages in search of something spectacular with which to enchant Theo for their imminent anniversary. There were excursions to suit every taste and ability. They ranged from animal sanctuary visits to scuba diving, from guided tours in town to helicopter flights over secluded islands. She called the Concierge, Henrique, on the phone and requested if there was anything bespoke.

Henrique went through some of the high-end experiences and suggested one of his personal favourites. 'Can I highly recommend to you the beautiful "Swimming with pigs" tour. For absolute privacy, we can arrange for you to be provided with a speedboat. You can then take yourself to a private island owned by the Destiny Luxury Group. We will anchor the ship about two miles away, as the day I have in mind is a tendering day for all other guests. Once the other guests have disembarked, we'll bring the speedboat from the island and leave it tethered to the ship for you. The speedboat pilot will return to the island by other means, leaving you with the speedboat for your exclusive use. We will provide you with a picnic and snorkelling equipment. You can travel to the island in the afternoon.'

'This sounds interesting. How does the excursion work?' asked Michelle.

'Guests can swim with pigs during a two-hour morning shore excursion. Island-dwelling pigs love swimming in the sea. It's a sight to behold seeing these lovely friendly creatures keeping their heads and necks above the water as they paddle. You can either stay in the boat or join them in the sea.

Professional animal handlers have a dual responsibility to care for the guests, as well as the pigs and marine life. The handlers will supervise guests during feeding time. I can schedule your outing in the afternoon, after the island excursion guests have returned to the ship. We can leave the beach unattended for just the pigs. We will give you some animal-friendly food for them to be fed by yourselves.'

'What sort of things do they eat?' enquired Michelle.

Henrique laughed in response. 'They eat absolutely anything, but we'll give you some carrots. It is quite easy and safe. A peaceful and intimate setting, just for the two of you. We can offer you a one-night stay at our prestigious Destiny Bahamas Hotel, where you can experience the same luxury as on the ship, extended to the island. It would be a romantic escape for you both. They have secluded beach huts so that they separate you from the other hotel guests. The huts have dedicated butlers who cater to your needs. They can set up and serve dinner for you in your hut without even disturbing you in the other quarters. Alternatively, you could stay in one of the luxurious suites in the hotel's main building. Providing this service would come at no cost to you. Would that suit you?'

Throughout, Michelle's astonishment grew as she listened intently to how far Destiny was extending their courtesy to her. 'Yes, that sounds wonderful. Can I leave that in your capable hands?' Michelle asked.

'Of course, madam. Leave it with me. Since this is a treat for your husband, I'll keep it a secret and communicate only with you. I'll leave an envelope with all the instructions with your butler, Jose, for personal delivery to you.'

Michelle thanked Henrique and replaced the phone in its cradle. She headed towards her built-in wardrobe, undressed, and hung up her outfit. After slipping into a towelling bathrobe, she ran a warm bath with relaxing bath salts. She soaked herself for twenty minutes before drying herself and heading to her bed to get some rest. It had already been an exhausting day.

***

As the casino lacked clocks, Theo was oblivious to the passing time. The complimentary drinks for those working the tables had been flowing as much as the time flying. The malt whisky on top of the wine pairings was starting to break down Theo's guard.

'Another drink, sir?' asked the bar waiter, standing between Theo and Suzanne.

'Make mine a double malt whisky and she'll have a G&T,' said Theo, gesturing towards Suzanne.

'Single please,' she added.

'Just how I like my women,' joked Theo, not realising that his every word was now being picked up by both Janik and Ji. Suzanne put a finger to her lips and shushed Theo.

The bar waiter looked over to Janik, who nodded in approval of the complimentary order. The couple appeared to him to be merry but not intoxicated enough to intervene in their drinks order. Janik had to maintain the integrity of the casino and the company. Allowing drunks to gamble was a big no. Janik observed Theo's fortunate turn of luck as he racked up a series of wins, ending the evening ahead.

Realising that his guard had now dropped, Theo sobered up and cancelled the drinks. Instead, he pushed his remaining chips across to Ji to check-out. 'That's enough for tonight. It's been a long day. Could you write a note for the cashier? I'll quickly grab some late-night snacks.

Theo swung his legs around in order to get up from his seat and took a couple of steps towards the covered sandwich platter. He lifted the clear plastic cover but inadvertently dropped it on to the china plates. There was a distinctive clunk that was a pitch above the ambient noise levels. A few heads turned, then returned to their usual position. Is anything more crucial than the next spin on the five-cent slot machine? Surely, it was just another passenger who had not quite found their sea legs? 99% of the casino would think that, except for the couple sitting at the poker slots.

'Isn't that Theo?' whispered Connie to Cecil, peering around the tall edge of the slot machine.

Theo had not noticed the couple enter the casino after the firework display. Complimentary night-caps for those on the cheapest slot machines were a trick the Morgan-Browns had exploited on many a cruise. They did nothing to draw attention to themselves upon recognising Theo. The opportunity to snoop on such a prominent person was a real treat. Theo returned to the table and collected his cashier receipt to cash in. He gave a couple of chips to Ji in a gesture of appreciation.

Suzanne cashed-in with a humble return, leaving not enough with which to tip. She apologised to Ji, who said, 'No, it's not a problem. Better luck next time. Good night.'

Janik bid them both a good night. Theo and Suzanne headed off towards the bow end lifts, leaving the casino glitz behind them. Cecil and Connie shared a silent gaze.

***

The cabin door closed. Suzanne turned to Theo and passionately kissed him on his lips. Theo did nothing to stop her. 'Thank you for inviting me onboard Theo. Are you sure Michelle doesn't know?'

'She won't find out,' confirmed Theo. 'She has been oblivious for the past three years, so nothing will change. We have to make the most of this week as I'm leaving the ship in seven days, and you'll still be on here whilst she is onboard. Don't worry, your paths won't cross. The chances of two people crossing paths on a ship with two thousand passengers are slim. She will circulate in different circles to you. Destiny will work her into the ground. This godmother role will be like a millstone around her neck. When I leave the ship, just keep your head down and I'll see you on our next assignment together. I've got big plans for us, but I need to sort things out. A pending divorce won't be a surprise for her when it happens.'

Suzanne kissed him again and started to remove his tuxedo jacket. From experience, she deliberately did not wear perfume so as not to contaminate his clothes. Theo reached behind her and switched off the lights.

CHAPTER TWO

The lights were off. Theo walked over to the king size bed, pulled back the pure Egyptian cotton sheets, and laid his head on to the two duck feather pillows. He turned to face her as her breath brushed against his cheek. The air blew back a lock of his dark hair.

'How was your luck at the casino?' asked Michelle. 'I was wondering how late you were going to be coming back.'

'Not now Michelle. It's been a long day!' he retorted.

***

The sunlight broke through the extreme edges of the golden velour bedroom curtains. It stung Theo's eyes as he rolled over to see the empty pillows alongside him. He heard the shower running in one of the bathrooms. He wandered over to the other bathroom to find Michelle has already moved his wash kit and shaver into the cut-glass cabinets, mirroring the arrangements at their home back in London. Like Noah's Ark, everything came in twos. Two wash bags, two electric toothbrushes, two razors, and so on. Pre-meditated packing by Michelle. This had been the case for the past four years. Ever since, they had moved from the quiet country house on the edge of the New Forest to a more compact house in a cosmopolitan area of central London. More becoming of Michelle's taste and not to the liking of Theo. Michelle attributed Theo's lack of input to his frequent foreign assignments. She had engineered, having the house evaluated whilst he was away. Coming home to find three estate agent evaluations on the kitchen table was a surprise. He normally liked surprises, but not that one. He remembered that when the house went on the market, Michelle would use the old estate agent trick of having the smell of freshly brewed espresso coffee emanating from the open planned kitchen diner. How she loved the smell of a strong, black, unsweetened coffee. So much for the home building ideal of taking a chocolate-coloured Labrador for quiet walks across country fields. It did not help that they never bought a dog. The turning point did not occur when Michelle and Andrea reconnected in London, but Michelle changed soon after the move. The few times Theo joined Michelle and Andrea for lunch or dinner at one of the many central London Michelin-starred restaurants, everything appeared cordial and dandy. Andrea's husband, James, rarely joined them as he also spent a lot of time abroad on business, like Theo. Although Andrea was not the catalyst, she influenced Michelle to some extent. Something was bubbling in the background; however, he could not put his finger on it. He had little time now to dwell on it, as he had to get ready for the day.

Jose had already arrived and laid out a modest breakfast on their balcony table whilst Theo had been in his bathroom. He could see the breakfast layout through the patio window. Although the contents were not to his liking, Michelle had likely completed the order slip and left it on the door before going to sleep. It was not on the stateroom door handle upon his return, so he had not reviewed it prior to its collection. It was yet again another trick of Michelle's in showing her disregard and indeed disdain for Theo. Anticipating a frosty breakfast, he was in no position to say a thing.

From the balcony, Michelle called out for Theo to come and enjoy the spread. Michelle was sitting in her towelling bath robe having just finished her own shower. She had applied no makeup, as she was due in the spa. Her skin still had a healthy glow, in which she took great pride. She sat patiently at the table, scrolling through emails on her phone whilst she waited for Theo to join her. To save time, Theo swiftly donned Bermuda shorts and a loose sweat top. He took a seat at the table opposite Michelle.

'Sweetheart, you look divine. Mind if I join you for a selfie? Move along so the sun isn't behind you,' suggested Michelle.

Theo shuffled his metal chair around ninety degrees as Michelle dragged her chair alongside him. She took a seat and held out her phone in the traditional selfie-taking way.

'Smile then, darling,' she demanded.

Theo broke into a slight grin with his head upright. Michelle turned her head so that her forehead was leaning against his face. The click confirmed it had captured the photo. A quick check of the screen confirmed for her it was good enough. Theo set about selecting a few breakfast items and added them to his plate. Michelle remained in her seat alongside him.

'Isn't this cosy?' quizzed Michelle.

Theo did not answer. What game was she playing? Sometimes, he could not understand her. Trust was mutual, but it had been clear for a while that neither trusted the other. He had not trusted her since they first met at university all those years ago. He still found it a bit of a mystery how they even ended up getting married. It was of Michelle's instigation. The leap year tradition allowing women to propose on February 29th. He could not resist the moment and lacked the strength to say no. They now celebrated it, in name only, on the 28th of February. How significant is a day's difference, anyway?

***

Michelle had yet another busy day ahead. Michelle, inspired by Andrea's words, headed straight to the Oasis Spa to kick-start her day. Before attending to the other guests, she could unwind and enjoy some pampering herself. She was already getting the measure of what her role entailed. For now, she wanted to set aside her feelings, or lack thereof, for Theo. He could take his wretched camera and snap away for all she cared. She did not care if he was leaning over the balcony photographing a dolphin and fell overboard. She had little time to spare, as the spa manager would expect her. The stateroom door slammed shut behind her as she shuffled down the corridor in her embossed white towelling robe and matching slippers. She never felt comfortable walking around the public areas of a ship in what she considered a state of semi-dress. Fortunately, the suites were located close to the spa through a restricted access corridor.

On arrival, the spa manager greeted Michelle, who introduced her to her dedicated beautician, Maisie Laine. 'Maisie offers a range of complimentary treatments we'd like to provide for you. Today we would like to start gently with a head and shoulders massage in our dedicated salon. We're usually busy at this time of day, so you might have to share the space with other passengers. It's rather ad hoc, but we often have a rush of interest in the first few days because of our promotions scheme we advertise in the Destinations newsletter, along with bespoke leaflets and spa tours.'

Maisie ushered Michelle through the opaque doors to the salon. There were three faux-leather treatment chairs. Michelle chose the one furthest from the door so that as a worst-case scenario, she would only have one other guest alongside her. She was relieved that she could retain her towelling robe for the duration of the treatment. Undressing in front of strangers made her uncomfortable. Maisie was talking Michelle through the 30-minute treatment programme and started the fingertip massage of her forehead when the gentle creek of the opaque door caught her attention, along with the images in the mirror. Accompanied by another beautician was Connie, wearing an identical towelling outfit.

'Oh my, what a lovely surprise. Good morning, Michelle.'

'Yes, what a lovely surprise. Good morning,' she responded in an acidic tone.

Connie took the adjoining seat whilst waiting for the 30-minute electrolysis treatment for the removal of some wispy facial hairs around her top lip.

'We saw your husband was enjoying himself in the casino last night. The star sign Aries is often associated with the competitive streak of gambling, but funnily enough, I don't think he's Arian judging by the first impressions he gave me,' disclosed Connie.

'Really?' replied Michelle.

'Well, from what I've observed in the short time I saw him at dinner and in the casino, he exhibited the signs of someone who was, erm, maybe a Gemini,' said Connie with a ponderous facial expression.

'Please explain,' said Michelle with an inquisitive voice.

'Well, where do I start? First, you need to know a bit about the astrological chart, but I won't bore you with all the details. It's so complex for a beginner to understand. A Gemini male can be quick-witted, they can be quite charming, intelligent in both conversation and academically. Ruled by Mercury, we classify the Gemini constellation as an 'air' sign. According to Roman mythology, amongst other things, Mercury was the god of travellers, games, and storytelling. Does any of that sound familiar?'

Michelle was aghast. 'Very interesting, Connie. What do you want to know?'

Connie grinned with glee and said, 'With that reply, I take it I'm right? You can help in answering just a few questions. His academic background?'

'Theo and I met at university whilst both studying at Oxford,' replied Michelle.

Connie nodded. 'And what did you read?'

Michelle rolled back her eyes and in a more mellow tone answered, 'I read Sociology and Psychology whilst Theo studied Geography and Sociology. We had some common interests, plus we overlapped at tutorials.'

Connie pursed her lips in concentration. One because of Michelle's reply, the other due to the electric current pulsing through her upper lip.

'Did you fall for his charm?' she asked encouragingly.

'Who wouldn't back then? He was very handsome and could captivate an audience with his storytelling,' whispered Michelle.

'Travelling? Games?' asked Connie.

'Well, his father had been a member of the government's Foreign and Commonwealth Office and worked in junior ambassadorial roles at various embassies around the globe, before he went in to banking in the city. The family travelled together, moving on every couple of years. At university he won colours as a rugby player. I saw him play a few times back then. To be honest, I'm not sure who was chasing whom. He had rugged good looks even then, and I didn't want him getting hurt. He used to joke that he would play amongst the backs rather with the forwards in the scrum, as he didn't want cauliflower ears. The number 8 used to call Theo "Pretty Boy" until one day he got the ball kicked in his face, that resulted in a bloody nose. Thankfully, it didn't break, but he gained a lot of respect for continuing to play with cotton wool stuffed up his nostrils.'

'Interesting,' said Connie.

'Can you just confirm his birthday for me?'

'Yes, it's the 20th of June,' stated Michelle.

'Oh!' exclaimed Connie. 'That's on the cusp of Gemini. It's the last day of the date range. Although associated with someone in the middle of the date range, his display of Gemini traits on the last day of the sign indicates a strong character. I advise you to manage those traits, especially charm.'

'What makes you say that?' enquired Michelle.

'Oh, just my observations, dear. Just my observations. But let's not dwell,' replied Connie. 'Please keep still Mrs Morgan-Brown as I need to be accurate with the electrolysis,' interrupted her beautician.

This comment brought the conversation to an abrupt stop. The session soon ended for Connie, and she left with a shrill, 'Enjoy your day,' aimed at Michelle. Exiting the salon, she walked with a confident stride, casting a triumphant look over her shoulder. Michelle was left to finish her own treatment. That last comment played on her mind.

***

Dani and Jack exited the daily morning Senior Management Team (SMT) meeting. She was reading the last couple of pages of notes from the meeting in her A4 sized red day book. Captain Nico, metaphorically speaking, ran a tight ship during the SMT meetings. They were always only one hour in duration. Nico headed the table, and everyone sat in the same position during each meeting. If their deputies needed to attend in their absence, they all knew where to sit. The ship's management team positioned themselves in order of seniority to the left of Nico. The invitation to speak at the meeting on any given subject was always in a clockwise direction. It only ever went out of turn if Captain Nico invited someone else to speak. Dani as First Officer minuted the meeting, allowing Nico to concentrate on the issues at hand. Following the meeting, she always headed to her office behind the bridge to type up official minutes before Nico checked them for onward transmission to Destiny HQ in London. Andrea, as CEO, awaited them at all times of the working day. She had a keen interest in the comings and goings of the ship. Andrea could handle the minutiae. She also received daily reports from across the Destiny empire, but her full focus for now was on the Destiny Celebration.

'Our reporting on the first day at sea went according to schedule. Nothing of note for you to report back, Dani,' said Jack.

'It's early days and I wouldn't like to jinx the rest of the voyage. Personally, I would have liked a longer sail-out practice voyage before this one. It was risky having no full practice sail, even for three or four days. We could have taken a shorter trip with a smaller capacity for friends, family, and travel agent partners. I'd feel a lot more comfortable if we had challenged the systems before going full steam ahead with an inaugural sailing,' Dani mused.

'I guess that's why the top brass back at London HQ get paid the big bucks. Best you get those typed up and I'll catch you for a coffee later. I'm still curious about Captain Nico's mention of a surprise he has planned for us later in the cruise. I'll see you soon.'

Jack and Dani both headed off to their respective separate offices. Dani only had half an hour in order to compress an hour's worth of meeting blurb into a written report.

***

Meanwhile, Theo headed back towards the Aquamarine jewellery boutique. He had his eye on the tanzanite and diamond bracelet in the window display. Before he could return to the boutique, he had to cash in his reasonable winnings from the previous evening at the casino. He had his receipt in his trouser pocket. They were still at sea, so the casino desk would be open. He only needed to skip down three decks. He entered from the stairwell. Only when you turned the corner did you hear the slot machine bells and the roulette wheel's metal ball swirling. The familiar cry of "No more bets" being drowned out by the winning cheers from the various cards and craps tables. Although it was still early morning, the tables and slots had been open all night. There had been a turnover of staff from last night, so he saw no familiar faces.

He hoped he had been discreet in his actions, but he recalled cancelling his drinks order and loudly dropping the food cover. He approached the casino cashier's desk and handed over the credit slip from the roulette table.

'Would sir like this credited back to his onboard account or paid in cash?' the cashier asked at the kiosk.

'Cash please,' came back Theo's confident reply.

The cashier exaggeratedly counted the cash, mimicking a croupier at the tables, impressing the pit boss and cctv cameras. Whilst they counted his winnings out in front of him, Theo could not help but notice the dark cctv camera domes overhead that he presumed were centred on the cashier's position. This triggered him to scan the entire casino ceiling, searching for the other camera positions. They were everywhere. He couldn't see any blind spots. All the domes looked the same. With their black smoked glass, you could not tell which way the cameras inside were pointing. He avoided appearing too curious, fearing that it would draw the attention to him, and they would challenge him. Theo thought his behaviour now would appear suspicious to any onlooker, let alone security. He then reverted his gaze to the cashier's hands whilst trying not to look too conspicuous. Did he blend in while tracking the camera domes, or did he stand out? It was that human instinct again. Not that he had done anything wrong, but he felt guilty at just staring. His mind drifted to last night, when he left the casino with Suzanne. Was he caught on camera? Pull yourself together, he thought. Who would bother monitoring him on CCTV? He wasn't planning a heist or anything. Theo had not seen a single dollar counted out by the cashier. He thought, should I care? Not really, as the camera domes did the job for him. Thank god for the cameras, he thought.

With the dollars pocketed in his casual jacket, he climbed the stairs up a single level to the shopping arcade. He joined a few others perusing the Aquamarine window displays. Thankfully, most other shoppers positioned themselves behind him in the walkway, looking in the opposite direction at various sale items laid out on covered tables, while sales assistants engaged guests to force a sale. The usual array of port memorabilia, ladies' fashion items, cheap jewellery and modest priced watches were arranged close together. He used the reflection of the shop window to monitor if anyone was looking at him, but he appeared to have gone unnoticed. The bracelet he wanted was still available. Its beauty was unmistakable. He had to gather the courage and inquire about the price. Upon entering the shop, his eyes confirmed for him just how bright the lights were shining. The sparkle from the diamond jewellery alone was overwhelming.

Unmistaken in recognising his tall, confident stance and athletic build from previously looking at the window display, 'Can I help you sir?' asked the shop assistant, before continuing 'Oh, I recognise you from last night. You were looking at the window display. I have the chance to say 'hello' to you. Hopefully, you won't run away this time? My name is Jenny-Mai Chong, and I'd love to show you close up anything you are interested in.'

Theo replied, 'I didn't realise I was that recognisable or memorable, but now you have my attention. Maybe there is something you can help me with?'

'Certainly, sir,' she beamed.

'The display,' said Theo, gesturing to the centre of the main window, 'has a lovely bracelet. Is it unique or is there more than one? I only ask as I'm interested in maybe buying more than one.'

Jenny-Mai replied, 'It is unusual to have more than one of the same design, however, the work by this designer is very popular and therefore we have signed exclusive rights for its sale and distribution.'

She reached into the display cabinet and brought out the tray containing the bracelet, and placed it carefully down on a glass top display unit with a soft lint-free cloth alongside it. Jenny-Mai lifted the bracelet and placed it down on the cloth. She rotated the cloth a few degrees so that the diamonds in the setting caught the bright shop lights and, therefore, sparkled more.

'What I can reveal to you is that we do stock more than one sample of this piece. We hold a backup of popular items in stock and introduce them after the cruise leg concludes and most passengers have disembarked. Like the stateroom stewards who change the bed linen and towels between guests leaving and arriving, here in Aquamarine we restock the displays with our most popular items, amongst other things. It helps prevent the original recipient from seeing someone else in an identical piece of jewellery. That's unlikely to happen if we only put out one per cruise. I know we have a second identical bracelet in the stock safe.'

She excused herself and went over to speak to the manager for their authority to bring out the second sample. She returns within a couple of minutes with the second bracelet and places it alongside the first one. The beauty was obvious. She then placed the first bracelet around her own wrist in order to showcase it. She also rotated her wrist in different directions so to once more catch the overhead lights in order to exaggerate the reflections.

'Beautiful!' exclaimed Theo. 'Really beautiful.' With his acquired casino winnings in folded notes still burning a hole in his trouser pocket, he asked, 'Can I pay cash for them both?'

There was a moment's pause when Jenny-Mai replied, 'I'm afraid not, sir'.

Theo asked, 'Ok, how about on my credit card?'

Jenny-Mai took a deep breath and said with a shallow sigh, 'I'm sorry, sir, but all ship purchases have to be made against your individual stateroom account. It's how most ships operate across the cruising family.'

Theo considered the implications. Michelle had her

onboard account that had a huge credit on it from Andrea, whereas he had his credit card placed on file for his expenses.

'I'll take both, please. Can you gift wrap them separately for me?'

Jenny-Mai glanced up and asked, 'Two important women in your life, sir?'

He replied, 'Two important wrists more like!'

He laughed to play down the suggestion. Did she mean something like wife and daughter or wife and sister rather than wife and mistress? He reassured himself that he didn't need to make light of it, defusing his own paranoia. Maybe just agreeing to the question would close the topic.

'You are right. It's common for people to have more than one important person in their life. Parents and siblings are so important to us all,' agreed Jenny-Mai.

After all, discretion was important in high-end jewellery sales, she thought.

***

Whilst they still occupied Michelle in the spa, Theo took the opportunity for a pre-arranged catch up with Suzanne over coffee in "Delicio". Upon arrival, Theo noticed that most seats were occupied, but he spotted Suzanne sitting at a small table for two. He walked over to join her as a waitress placed down two coasters on the table and asked for their orders. Suzanne had her quintessential pot of English loose-leaf tea. Theo indulged in a latte with a caramel biscotti on the side. A shot of brandy in the coffee was tempting, but he had to keep his wits about him.

The overarching sound of a loud, penetrating voice of a high-pitched server from the Philippines drowned out the soloist playing on a pristine white piano in the atrium. The pianist's oval name badge unmistakably identified her as a member of staff amongst the guests. There was a continuous contest between the high register notes of the piano being played and the server's voice at the adjoining bar as passengers confirmed their cocktail orders. Overhead, the recessed lighting offered a mellow and comforting ambience. Deep mahogany shelves between thick glassed windows and the chairs and sofa double seats. As the guests reclined against plump cushions, one could hear their stifled yawns because of jetlag. Other guests talked, snoozed, listened to their own music, read library books, watched passersby and hovered for a vacant seat. Some individuals sat in a relaxed trance, carefree and oblivious. The cappuccino and gold-coloured wallpaper with a recurrent chocolate leaf motif on the ceiling adorned the lounge. A cruise induced therapy.

Within moments of the pianist completing his repertoire, two violinists appeared, both wearing black and gold sequinned dresses, and stepped on to the low-level stage. During the brief interval, the automated coffee lounge music faded out on the arrival of the new musicians. They simultaneously tuned their antique instruments and applied resin to their bows ahead of their performance, enhanced by a backing soundtrack. Onlookers shuffled and rearranged their chairs to face the stage in appreciation and began foot tapping in time to the haunting melody. Their technical skill and ability entranced the audience. The spotlight beams hit the chrome railings, creating a blinding light for some people. Every twist and contortion of the synchronised violinists caused shards of light to gleam off the sequinned dressed like a flashing lighthouse guarding treacherous rocks. The passengers that walked through paused at the low railings to admire the performance. Some patrons could be heard to huff and puff loudly in annoyance as their views became blocked. Their indignation stirred the consciousness of the obstructers, who moved on with acceptance. The captivating performance reached a crescendo, interrupted by incessant coughing. It raised whether Dr Patel needed to be summonsed for a medical emergency, as the server observed the guest whilst polishing a crystal wine glass. He was ready to pounce if necessary to perform initial first aid. Fortunately, the need subsided.

Cecil had gone unnoticed, sitting on his own facing the other way, reading a broadsheet newspaper that the Concierge had arranged for bespoke printing off over the internet. Being unable to control the urge, he earwigged their conversation from behind his paper. Theo and Suzanne across the way were talking about the forthcoming presentation. The PowerPoint required a few more tweaks. Theo wanted to incorporate some photos that Suzanne had taken on their joint Galapagos assignment. They spent the next twenty minutes discussing at length the finer points of their presentation, including camera settings, focus, filtration and exposure.

Cecil lowered his paper, turned around, and mischievously interrupted them. 'You two lovebirds look busy,' with a suggestive smirk.

'Mr Morgan-Brown, you're clearly preoccupied with our discussion on wildlife and the events of last night,' Theo deflected, concerned about the revelations of the past twenty minutes.

Cecil raised a broader grin in acknowledgment. Happy that Theo had even recollected having had a previous conversation with him.

Theo said, 'We were about to discuss the effects of climate change on vulnerable wildlife and a potential forthcoming ecological disaster for mankind. Any thoughts on the matter, Cecil?'

Realising that he would be out of his depth on such topics, Cecil folded up his newspaper into quarters, sipped the last dregs from his teacup and declared, 'I'll have to leave that to you two experts. Fascinating topic. I look forward to your presentation. I must excuse myself as bridge classes are about to start. Good day.'

Theo nodded and smiled. Suzanne half smiled and raised her teacup to her lips to hide her shock and amazement at being interrupted by what to her was a complete stranger. Theo waited for Cecil to stand up and slip away. He glanced at Cecil to ensure he had moved on.

Theo turned to Suzanne and said, 'Don't worry. He's quite harmless. Last night, I spoke to him at the dinner table out of obligation. It's the way he talks. I'm sure he means nothing by it. Look at the time! It has tapped on. No wonder my second coffee has gone cold. Let's go, as I need to talk to you privately in the lift.'

Suzanne hastily packed up her notebook and made sure she had her memory card of photos from the Galapagos with her, as Theo would need them downloaded to his laptop for the presentation. She handed the memory card across the table to him for his use. They both got up and headed towards the adjacent elevators. Suzanne pressed the lift call button and waited.

Theo said, 'When we get into the lift, close your eyes, as I have a little surprise for you.'

The ping of the lift's arrival broke the conversation. The doors opened to reveal no-one else inside. What they both failed to notice in their fixation with each other is that these were the atrium glass elevators. The waterfall back drop could be quite mesmerising. Suzanne closed her eyes and stepped in, gently guided by Theo. As the doors closed, Theo reached inside his jacket and removed a gift-wrapped box from within. He slipped it into her hand. 'Open your eyes and see.'

Suzanne opened her eyes and unravelled the wrapping, revealing a sparkling tanzanite and diamond bracelet. Suzanne hurriedly pressed a button on the elevator to go to the highest deck, wanting to savour the moment before someone else called the lift. As she pressed the button, she gazed up at Theo to look him in the eye. Their bodies squeezed against each other, with her arms naturally curled behind him. She pressed her lips against his and kissed him as her spare hand tenderly brushed against the nape of his neck.

'Thank you,' she whispered as the lift ascended.

A surge of sensation shot through his nervous system, causing the hairs on his neck to stand on end, reminiscent of the excitement he craved but lacked in his marriage.

***

Upon leaving the spa, Michelle returned to her suite to get changed into her day clothes. She noticed a flashing light on her bedside phone, which notified her of a voicemail. She listened to the recording. It was Olly, the Cruise Director. He asked to speak with her and to page him upon her return to the suite. He had another favour to request from her. Michelle paged Olly, who in return appeared at her suite door within a few minutes.

'Michelle, I desperately need your help tonight. Captain Nico has had to deal with a medical emergency onboard. One of those dreaded Code Bs, as we call them. He's therefore unable to be a judge in the theatre tonight on the "Mr & Mrs" game show, which brings the house down. Would you be able to step in and be a panel member?' Olly ended the question with a grimacing face that would befit an emoji.

Michelle felt she had no option. 'Of course, I'll help Olly. It sounds fun.'

'Great,' said Olly.

'Can you spare 15 minutes to accompany me to my office on the first deck? I would like to talk you through the questions I'll be asking, and you'll be judging on. I can help script you some funny one-liners, so you don't freeze when giving your critique.'

Michelle's hope for an hour of solitude vanished in an instant. 'There's no time like the present, Olly, so let's do it. Remind me again where your office is?'

'It's tucked away behind the Delicio Café, which can be a blessing or a hindrance, depending on your coffee addiction.'

Michelle made sure she had her room keycard and closed

the door behind her. They strolled to the elevator that would take them down to Olly's office. Olly called the lift, and it arrived from below. The doors opened. The lift was empty. Olly stepped in, pressed the first deck button as he walked to the far end of the lift. It was common courtesy to leave ample space in the elevator for others who may join on the way down. Michelle followed him in and stood face to face with Olly as she looked out of the glass elevator. Olly was facing the lift doors as he always liked to see who may join him so that he could be proactively courteous and professional, as becoming of a Cruise Director. Everyone liked to say hello to him. As the elevator descended, Michelle heard the distant rush of the waterfall for the first time. She had found herself too distracted before to have even noticed that these were the perspex atrium lifts. The drop from the Penthouse suites deck to the atrium floor was ten decks. It was a slow speed lift which was designed to not hinder progress through the ship, but to enable an enhanced passenger experience for the prolonged admiration of the cascading waterfall into the tropical garden setting below. The lift descended as Olly carried on talking about the show. Within moments, the one-way conversation became nothing other than white noise in her ears. Michelle's attention shifted from Olly's words to what she saw through the 180-degree clear windows. It was not the rapid flow of the waterfall, or the moss and ferns draped down over the rockery façade. It was the sight of an identical perspex lift ascending opposite from the atrium floor. From her vantage point, she observed a woman kissing a man who resembled her husband. She felt nothing. She said nothing. At that moment, she experienced total shock.

CHAPTER THREE

Theo exited the lift and headed towards his Penthouse Suite. Suzanne remained in the lift and returned to her own deck. After the excitement of opening her surprise gift, her thoughts turned back to her real priorities for the day.

She reached her cabin and accessed her laptop. It contained her diving schedule and safety manual for protocols on entering the aquarium tanks. Suzanne was to be the first person ever to photograph marine life inside a real onboard aquarium. During the official opening, she would be in the tank, demonstrating how marine life and humans can co-exist.

Destiny Cruise Lines had pioneered the first ever "Aquarium at Sea". An innovative piece of marine engineering. It was an undersea marvel for guests to witness such an intimate marine encounter. The project took years to develop because of unsuitable and unsustainable prototypes. The complexities were colossal. Incorporating a living aquarium within the confines of a vessel that could encounter any sea conditions that nature threw at it.

The mechanics of placing a sizeable aquarium where every cubic metre of water weighed a ton, safely into what is a floating hotel, was a remarkable piece of engineering. It incorporated the best architects, shipbuilders, marine biologists, oceanographers and interior designers. It was cutting edge.

On this scale, it was unique, and the result had stunned

everyone. A marine environment containing various fish that could cohabit together yet remain viable in the long term was the ecological goal. The engineering dynamics were one thing, but it also had to embrace the practicalities of an active marine auditorium whereby guests could interact with the habitat and embrace marine culture.

They positioned the aquarium in the centre of the ship, below the lowest atrium deck but for two entire decks. Its low central position would stabilise the ship when at sea, which would maintain the equilibrium of the aquarium. Stretching from floor to ceiling, it spanned the entire width of the ship. It held lectures on the lower deck, which doubled as an auditorium. The aquarium surrounded the auditorium on both sides, extending to the deck above.

The audience was at the centre of an immersive show resembling a marine snowdome. By day it was an educational lecture theatre. By night, they transformed it into a sensory specialty dining venue. Beyond the main aquarium tank sat other smaller enclosed tanks that featured different marine life from the oceans around the world, in keeping with Destiny's mantra of global inclusivity mirroring the passenger loyalty scheme.

In striking contrast to the other tanks, they had filled one of them with fragments of plastic to showcase the severe danger of how ecologically damaging any waste created by humans was to the ocean environment and marine life. The chilling didactic message of the imminent ecological disaster inflicted by mankind. The concept aimed to combine practicality and information with an elegant restaurant experience, featuring a sumptuous dinner menu that excluded fish and marine life.

Suzanne reminded herself of the protocols within the aquarium tanks as there was a complex system for filtration, nitrifying bacteria, and the removal of toxic waste. Blocking outlets and inlets could have a fatal impact on marine life. It was critical to know where she could operate in the tank.

She had to check all her diving equipment as well, including the dry suit, face masks, and the oxygen tanks. She had her hair kept short yet feminine so as not to entangle with equipment and to ensure a clear peripheral vision through the mask. Suzanne prepared her waterproof camera and lens so that she could take still photography and videography during her dive. Once Suzanne was satisfied with the readiness of her sophisticated camera equipment, she left her stateroom and took the lift to the staff access-only room above the aquarium tanks. She mentally and physically prepared herself for the dive.

***

Upon returning to his suite, Theo noticed that the voicemail light on the bedside phone was still illuminated. He listened to the message from Olly to Michelle and deleted it in order to turn the light off. Theo always found them distracting. The bracelet for Michelle was still in his pocket. He removed it and hid it inside a pair of his formal black shoes. That will remind him to present the gift to Michelle before the Gala Night dinner. Feeling somewhat lethargic already from two days on the cruise ship without physical activity, he changed into his gym kit and headed to the fitness centre, leaving a note on the side.

CHAPTER FOUR

Michelle returned to the suite after Theo's departure to the gym. She switched on the 'Privacy' light at the suite door. She flung herself onto the bed and lay there motionless. Did her eyes deceive her? It was a momentary glance, but Theo was unmistakable. Facing the other way, the female was unrecognisable. There was an embrace. There was a kiss. Was there passion? Theo was undeniably attractive, but would he give in to the advances of a stranger on the ship, considering their brief acquaintance? If it was not a stranger, then who was she? She wore trousers and had short hair, giving her an androgynous look even without seeing her face. This person wasn't someone she would have imagined Theo being attracted to. He was a manly man who had a curious eye for attractive women. He would be charming and debonair if a pretty and flirtatious woman engaged him. She had occasionally witnessed such encounters, but they were dismissed as potential rivals. Michelle had a strong inner core and knew how to win back Theo's attention. She could when she wanted out-flirt anyone, oozing her own sex appeal. Her passion would know no bounds when the mood took her. It was a brief kiss she saw in a glass elevator, visible to everyone. Was Theo foolish enough to take such a risk? Her mind continued to race, and she was struggling to think. Her heart was racing, but for all the wrong reasons. She needed to calm down and get her heart beats lower. Michelle reached across for the remote control and noticed Theo's note saying he had gone to the gym. She picked up the bedside phone and called down to the fitness centre reception. She informed the receptionist that she did not want her husband disturbed so not to distract him from his fitness regime, but could anyone tell he was in the gym? The receptionist confirmed for her, and Michelle ended the call with thanks. Feeling relieved, she knew he was in the gym, not gallivanting around the ship chasing other women. She reclined on the bed and activated the TV's intelligence system. Michelle began navigating the options. She browsed through the entertainment, shore excursions, dining, spa treatments and guest information, before settling on the 'Onboard Account' information. Michelle just wanted to check the credit level set up for her by Andrea. She was used to seeing the account information only in her name, as previously they had assigned a suite all to herself. Since there were two people in the suite, they each had their own account for the cruise. However, she could access both by scrolling across. Upon reviewing her account, she noticed that the sub-total reset to zero after every onboard charge. She had no outstanding charges to her name, as Andrea had generously promised. She switched over to Theo's account to make sure that the generosity had been extended. As she scrolled down the page, she noticed they had also reimbursed the charges. They covered the cost of the drinks, but not Theo's withdrawals in the Casino. Despite knowing it was his moment of escapism, she remained unruffled. However, a few pages later, she spotted an unexpected $8000 entry for the Boutique. The amount was comparable to a significant item of jewellery. Well, it was after all their wedding anniversary this week, and Theo was not averse to buying jewellery for her. She could not let the cat out of the bag. She had to keep to herself that she already knew about the jewellery purchase and to appear surprised when she received it. It was undoubtedly going to be something stunning, since he had never spent that much on her in one purchase before. Her inner thoughts on the mystery woman were still swirling around in her mind. How could Theo drop his guard, finding himself in such a vulnerable position? Ensnared and cornered like hunted prey in a trap. He was so good at maintaining his personal space, yet he appeared pinned in with nowhere to turn. He had a controlling charm. She thought he had unravelled himself from this unexpected position. No doubt this other woman had forced herself upon him, and Theo would have been diplomatic about it to avoid causing offence. To distract herself, she searched for something to watch on TV. She recalled that there was an "Enrichment" channel that showcased forthcoming lectures. As Theo was to be guest presenter on his chosen subject of the Galapagos, she was intrigued to see what Destiny had used to promote him. She soon found the hour-long video that was Theo working on the Galapagos islands. She had not seen it before, as it was a recent film production of one of his expeditions.

Halfway through the programme that Michelle was watching, Theo returned to the suite from the gym. Upon entering the bedroom, he could hear his own voice. He recognised it was from the promotional video, as he had been involved in the programme's editing. As he pushed open the bedroom door, he could see Michelle lying on the king-size bed, propped up with the pillows, staring at the screen. Theo glanced back at the TV to check the progress of the program. The documentary featured Theo's presentation for 45 minutes, followed by a 15-minute behind-the-scenes look at the filming process on location. He recalled the film crew and naturalists involved in the filming, included Suzanne. Even though they didn't mention her name during the filming sequences, they would have featured her there and given her credit.

'Stop the video darling,' called out Theo, as he tried to reach the remote control on the bed next to her.

'I've got a surprise for you,' he exclaimed with a grin.

Michelle reached for the remote control and paused the video. Theo looked back at the TV and noticed it was 33 mins in with 27 minutes remaining. He breathed a quiet sigh of relief as he recoiled his outreached arm.

Michelle found the documentary interesting but said she would have to come back to it later.

Theo said, 'Sure. It took lots of patience to film the sequences and then edit the production.'

He turned to his wardrobe, opened the sliding doors and bent down to reach inside for his formal polished black shoes. Theo obstructed Michelle's view so as not to reveal his secret hiding place. He stood up, turned around and crouched over the bed, leaning over towards Michelle. From behind his back, he produced the gift-wrapped surprise.

'Happy anniversary, darling,' he said as he theatrically handed it over to her.

'I was going to give you this present just before we went to the Gala Dinner tonight, but I just couldn't wait to see your reaction.'

Michelle was too captivated by the present to look him in the face. 'Can I open it now, or should I wait?' she purred.

'Now's fine. Sure, please open it,' he replied.

With both hands she pulled at the pink bow and unravelled the crepe paper. Inside was an elegant, slim blue box. She lifted the lid and exposed a tanzanite and diamond bracelet sat on an arched cushion. She lifted it out of the box and held it up to the light. It sparkled in every direction.

'Theo. This is beautiful. It must have cost you a fortune?'

'Less than you think, my darling, but you are worth every penny,' he replied, whilst trying to look composed. Ironically, he was telling the truth. 'Anyway, I came straight back from the fitness centre, so I need to jump into my shower and freshen up. We have a busy evening ahead.'

He went to his bathroom, undressed, and showered. His preference for having the shower on as high a heat setting as possible meant the entire shower cubicle steamed up.

Michelle turned off the TV. She knew that when she resumed the programme later, it would remember the paused position, saving her from rewatching everything. Michelle gave Theo a few minutes in the shower alone. She could hear the shampoo bottle being popped open. Michelle knew that washing his hair was towards the end of his showering routine. She went over to her dressing table and removed her outer clothes before she slipped out of her black underwear. She strolled over to Theo's bathroom and pushed open the door. It was a mass of steam combined with the beautiful scent of jasmine. Through the misty lighting, she could make out the silhouetted yet unmistakable athletic body of Theo. She pulled at the shower door and stepped in, closing it firmly behind her.

***

Suzanne located her designated aquarium locker and changed into her outfit. The familiar sound of her bespoke diving suit as it snapped into place brought a smile to her face. It thrilled her to practise her underwater dive and began her orientation of the enormous tank. Her affinity for aquatic things was befitting, as she was born under the sign of Aquarius. Aquarians, amongst other things, were humanitarian and independent. Whether being constrained in a dive suit within an aquarium could count as being independent, she was at peace with nature. Finding the optimum angles to capture the exotic and beautiful marine life was what she did best. As she carefully lowered herself into the tank, she experienced a wave of excitement as she witnessed the first inquisitive shoal of fish swimming past. She knew her first public dive later in the afternoon had a dual purpose. She was not only there to capture stunning photos from within the tank for later printing and marketing sales, but she was also a backdrop for the aquarium's official opening. Captain Nico was due to cut the ribbon at precisely 3pm. She had less than an hour to prepare for the free dive before a staff debriefing and re-entry for the opening. Time was tight, but she remained unphased.

Panicking whilst in the water was not an option. The on-duty Aquarium Supervisor, Bruno, remained on the maintenance platform as Suzanne entered the water. After a few minor mask adjustments and tuning of the valves, Suzanne settled in the water and Bruno handed her underwater cameras. The filtration and circulation bubbles effervesced around her. Inquisitive shoals of fish swam close to her before darting away. The larger fish made a steady beeline for her before brushing past. When she conducted ocean dives, the marine life was visible some distance ahead. The relative confines of the tank meant her reaction time and the fishes' reaction times were much shorter. She had to adapt and control her movements more than she otherwise would. Suzanne did not want to cause shock waves throughout the marina. She was entering their world, not the other way around. Suzanne sank lower in the tank. She had already accustomed herself to the external layout of the aquarium, but now she had to interpret that external image into a reverse image when orientating her way around. The surroundings appeared distorted when viewed through a face mask, water, and thick glass. The tank had a high level of illumination, while the guest side was much darker. Aware of her high visibility, she had limited sight of the audience. She explored all the extremes of the tank and practiced an emergency evacuation with the aquarium assistant. A complete necessity if she was to be given the green light to dive during the opening ceremony. In the limited time before her next dive, she photographed and filmed marine life to assess the quality of her captures. She knew Theo intended to have signed prints available to sell as merchandise after his lecture. The prints needed to be of a high quality to encourage guests to purchase the inaugural commemorative souvenirs. Suzanne exited the tank and changed into casual attire before heading over to the ship's photographic studio to process some trial prints for her own exacting quality assurance.

***

Michelle was drying her hair whilst sitting at the dressing table when the telephone rang. She picked up the call and recognised Olly's familiar voice.

'Michelle, you won't believe this. The eye of a tropical storm is some 300 miles away to our starboard, but Captain Nico has some concerns for it as we are tendering at our port of call tomorrow. He has called a meeting at short notice, inviting select members of his staff to discuss options in the light of this storm impacting on the ship's operations tomorrow. The meeting duration is uncertain, as they can sometimes be lengthy. It is doubtful that he will make it to the aquarium's opening ceremony. I understand if you're tired of me asking for favours, but it would be a great honour for Destiny if you could perform the opening ceremony. Are you good with scissors?' quipped Olly.

'In my professional life, sometimes I've had to pull pairs out from between my shoulder blades. I have a saying that you need to be one hundred per cent behind somebody to stab them in the back! Of course, I'll perform the duty. What time do I need to be there?' asked Michelle.

'Ah, that's another thing, Michelle. Is twenty minutes' enough time?' he responded.

'Ok, it's pushing it, but I'll be there. I need to find a new dress for the Gala than what I planned to wear. I can't stay too long as I must return here to get ready for tonight,' she insisted.

'Don't worry Michelle, as the ceremony has to be short. As soon as we conclude it, we must then undertake its transformation into the specialty restaurant where, in fact, you will dine tonight. See you soon. Don't worry, I'll bring the scissors, but I'll make sure that I am standing beside you and not behind you!'

Olly rang off as Theo exited his bathroom with shaving foam on his face.

'Did I hear the phone ringing?' he asked.

'It was only Olly. He's asked me to open the aquarium at short notice. What an honour. It never stops,' she beamed.

Theo retreated into his bathroom and shut the door. He realised Suzanne would be in the tank. He needed to let her know. Near the mirror in the bathroom, there was a wall-mounted phone. He silently picked it up and tried to dial directly to her cabin. It rang unanswered. He believed she could be anywhere on the ship, as she had her own time and space apart from him. It was too late for him to warn her now. As he finished his wet shave, he could hear the opening and closing of a door in the bedroom's walk-in wardrobe. Theo's wardrobe contents were being sifted through, and he could hear the familiar sound of coat hangers sliding and jangling. Shortly after, he could hear a zip being pulled up. He patted his face dry and exited the bathroom. Sat at the dressing table was Michelle, applying her make-up. She was wearing a three-quarter length lilac coloured dress.

She stood up in it and asked, 'How does this look for the aquarium ceremony? I hadn't planned another change of outfit, as I wasn't expecting this. I think it will do.'

'Yeah, it's fine,' replied Theo, as he wandered over to his own wardrobe to prepare for the Gala dinner.

'The dress goes nicely with my new bracelet,' said Michelle, extending her arm to show it off on her slim wrist.

'I didn't expect you to wear that at this moment. I thought you would save it for the Gala?' he queried.

'Nothing like the present,' said Michelle as she strode towards the door. 'Can't talk, gotta run. I'll be back shortly.' She clutched a small matching purple handbag with her suite key card token and mobile inside and left the room.

After the door slammed, Theo grabbed the TV remote from the bedside unit. Switching it on, he then scrolled through to find the Galapagos documentary. Activating it gave him the option to continue watching from the last saved position or cancel to reset. He reset the documentary. He knew Michelle wouldn't return to it or see it as a reminder to continue watching. Anything to lessen the risk of her identifying Suzanne physically and by name.

***

Suzanne returned to the staff gallery above the aquarium, changed back into her dive suit and fixed her oxygen tanks. There was quite a din with the circulation systems running into the tanks from above, accompanied by an echo because of the confined space. It was only minutes now until the ceremony started. She looked at her waterproof watch and counted down the final few minutes, repeating in her mind the underwater photographic stages that she intended to complete whilst the show went on. On expedition, she often wore a full-face mask when snorkelling, and her scuba mask was very similar. It obscured her face except above the bridge of her nose and around her eyes. Her masquerade mask she had acquired for the Gala Ball later was the total opposite as it exposed her face but hid around her eyes. She heard the compere's muffled voice in the background. Suzanne checked her watch and calculated it was time to dive with her cameras. She descended with the apparatus on her back. Her initial focus was on finding the schools of fish somewhere in proximity to where she expected locating the ceremonial ribbon and the outline of Captain Nico. She snapped away with her camera at some of the rainbow-hued fish, in the exaggerated stance of a marine photographer. She could not hear it, but imagined there were gasps of excitement from the crowd watching. It was quite fascinating watching divers in action with all their apparatus. It brought back her own memories as a child on an aquarium outing with her late parents. They could easily become a talking point and star of the show. She lowered the cameras and swam to a specific point on the rocky backdrop where the ribbon would be.

Suzanne could make out someone in a light grey-coloured suit holding what appeared to be a microphone close to their mouth. She could not make out a merchant navy white shirt with epaulettes or the distinctive shape of the tall and broad-shouldered Captain Nico. In a light purple dress, a female figure held something glistening in her hand. They held the glistening object out near the perspex, touching a scarlet ribbon that adorned the clear screen in front of her. Suzanne drifted towards where the ribbon was to be cut at its lowest point. She wanted to position her upright body as close to the perspex as possible. Suzanne raised her camera to capture the moment from within the tank as a unique perspective of the event. She focused on her camera as she looked through the lens to pinpoint the scissors. Things were now a lot clearer. She spotted the poised scissors in an outstretched hand. She gazed beyond the hand, noticing something even more beautiful shimmering in the dim light. It was something she recognised, the sight of an identical tanzanite and diamond bracelet. She instinctively lowered her camera and recoiled backwards, using her hands in a circular motion like a swimmer does when treading water and propelling backwards. The bubbles effervesced around her as her breathing became more rapid and deep. Never claustrophobic, she felt the confines of the aquarium closing in on her. She looked up to locate the green exit light above and surfaced at the top. She broke through the water and removed her mask, taking in deep breaths of fresh air as she did so.

'Are you ok?' called out Bruno.

Suzanne paused for a moment and nodded. 'Yes, I'm fine. I surfaced as a precaution, thinking there might be an issue with the regulator. Just a moment, and I'll go back down again.'

In her own mind, she needed a few minutes to gather her thoughts and regain her composure. Was that Michelle she just saw? She wasn't sure, but how on earth did she end up with an identical bracelet? What were the odds of her having the same one? It didn't add up.

'The ceremony is done and they're preparing the area for tonight's festivities, so you don't have to go down again. You've done well. I understand the crowd enjoyed seeing your dive. Your ascension in a cloud of bubbles was dramatic!' exclaimed Bruno triumphantly.

Suzanne pulled herself out of the tank and looked down into the depths below. Normally she would look for the fish swimming in her wake, but this time she felt disconnected and somewhat hollow inside. Captain Nico's absence surprised her, but what she witnessed in those ultimate moments left her overwhelmed with shock and confusion. She needed to talk to Theo desperately, but first she had to get the captured photos processed. Giving them to Theo would give her the ideal opportunity to talk with him and to make sense of all this. She locked away her apparatus and headed to the photo gallery with memory disks in hand.

***

Having left the aquarium opening ceremony, Michelle scuttled to the spa. She was overdue on her scheduled appointment to have her hair styled for the Gala night. She checked in with apologies, which with her entitlements was unnecessary, but accepted. Her regular beautician, Maisie, conducted a manicure whilst the hair stylist worked on her hair. The salon was, as expected, very busy. Two seats down sat Connie, having a purple rinse hairdo. The chair between them became vacant, so Michelle invited her to move down to be closer, as she had something to ask her.

'Please help me with this, Connie. I value your thoughts on the astrological signs. I used to be indifferent, but now I'm seeing some truth in them. You previously mentioned the positive traits of Gemini. Could you also share some insight into their negative characteristics? Based on your experience, what should I watch out for?'

'Well.' confided Connie, 'I will temper my answer, as I

don't want to have you too concerned or delving too deeply, or else you'll end up looking for characteristics to match the broad realm of possibilities. Don't forget that they can vary depending on how central your birthday is to the star sign core, or to the contrary how far you are away from the strong centre and drawn towards the outer limits of the date range and closer to adjoining star signs. Factors like birth time and year can influence one's personality.'

'Ok,' replied Michelle in an exaggerated, slow voice.

'Now,' Connie continued, 'I take it that the reason you are asking is that of your husband Theo, so I'll err towards the more masculine characteristics. Things vary between males, females, and even children. Look for signs of being indecisive. They cannot express themselves emotionally and can be impatient as well. They can be over friendly and somewhat flirtatious. With a low attention span, they can be fickle. Mercury is the planet associated with Gemini, which may explain a rise or drop in emotions. It is the planet of communication, which means they can be excellent storytellers.'

'I'll stop you there, Connie. That's too close for comfort. Wow!' exclaimed Michelle. 'As you know, Theo has an enrichment lecture coming up soon. As for the other traits you've mentioned, I better hold my counsel on that. Thank you for the insight.'

Maisie was only momentarily behind the hair stylist in finishing with Michelle.

'I have to run some errands before dinner. Thank you once again.'

With that, Michelle eased herself out of the relaxing chair and removed the black cotton gown protecting her dress. She gave a wry smile to Connie and left the salon. What Connie said caught her off guard. She had a realisation that Connie was much better at assessing people than she had previously acknowledged. On her way back to her suite, Michelle intended to stop by the jewellery boutique. Striding along the corridors with purpose, within a few minutes, she was outside, gazing into the window display. The shop was quiet inside. She walked in. Michelle noticed two male members of staff talking to each other in the corner. She could not help but notice that the taller of the two kept his eyes on her as she meandered between the glass display cabinets. She paused at the tanzanite display. The trigger caused the staff member to approach her. His face broke into a smile the closer he got to her.

'Can I assist you with anything, madam? I notice you are looking at only the finest jewellery that we have, not only in our store, but amongst the stock we hold globally. Tanzanite is a wonderful and rare commodity. I can't help but also notice you already have a lovely tanzanite and diamond bracelet. How about earrings or a pendant to match? Dare I say it, maybe even a ring for the opposite hand?'

Michelle did not raise her head. She continued to scan the display. After thirty seconds, she looked up and dismissed his observant and wise suggestions, stating they weren't what she had in mind. 'I love my bracelet so much that I'm thinking of buying another for a dear friend of mine. How much should I expect to pay for something similar, if not identical? I need to budget accordingly.'

'Well, madam,' he said. Just the other day, I saw something identical in our stockroom. I can't recall seeing it over the last day or two, as we only check our inventory at periodic times. I can check our electronic system and see what the availability is for you.'

He moved over to a point of sales computer on the adjoining glass worktop. 'Yes, here we have it. We had two in stock, but they were both sold within the first two days of this cruise. Worry not, as we have exclusive rights to the design. We can place an order for you and have an identical one brought onboard the ship from our Bahamas flagship store before this cruise ends. I have the piece here on the computer as a picture, and it appears to be identical to yours. Would you like to place an order?' he asked, stepping up his sales patter.

'That's good to know, but what is the outlay that I am looking at for such a purchase?' persisted Michelle.

'Well, considering that we offer a thirty per cent discount on the recommended retailer's price, and we are also duty free, I would be happy to offer it to you at the same price as the two we had for sale, at four thousand US dollars. How does that sound?'

Michelle half-smiled, paused and said, 'Well, that is in the price range that I expected, but I need to give it some thought. Thank you for your time. You have been more helpful than you can imagine.'

'I'm glad I could have been of assistance. Please come back and see me within the next two days and I'll be able to secure this piece for you. No deposit is required. As with all purchases, we will place it against your onboard account for later payment. I will also provide you with a paper certificate of authenticity. We will also include a professional evaluation for insurance purposes free of charge. We will waive our usual fees on this occasion if the purchase is made before the cruise ends,' concluded the salesman.

'Wonderful,' replied Michelle. 'That is also very informative.'

She turned on her heels and moved towards the exit. The false smile dropped from her face. Her brow furrowed and eyes narrowed as she considered the implications of what she had just discovered. She headed back to the suite. Should she confront Theo with this? Should she bide her time? Who had the second bracelet? What did it all mean?

***

Theo was sitting waiting in his formal wear, minus the jacket. To prevent creasing, he would put it on at the last minute. The butler, Jose, had returned his shoes, polished immaculately.

Because they would be stepped on during the close quarters dancing at the ball later that night, how they looked wasn't Theo's primary concern. He was an untalented dancer, always tripping over Michelle's feet, even when he was supposed to be leading. Theo disliked formal wear because it felt constricting and was far from the khaki-coloured safari outfits he typically wore. He could hear the faint sound of the suite door lock deactivating by the use of a keycard. The suite door opened and in walked Michelle. Her face seemed less furrowed now, but she still had the look of someone distracted.

'How did the aquarium ceremony go?' he asked.

She walked straight past Theo and into the walk-in wardrobe. 'Fine,' she replied, as she slipped out of her lilac dress and into her pre-chosen burgundy ball gown.

'Your hair looks nice. I forgot you had a salon appointment until I checked the interactive TV calendar,' he said, projecting his voice to reach the walk-in wardrobe.

No response was forthcoming, only the sound of shoes being dropped onto the floor. Theo was unaware as Michelle desperately rummaged through his wardrobe, searching for the other bracelet, receipt, and certificates of authenticity and insurance. She heard his footsteps approaching from the living area, so she quickly closed the wardrobe doors.

'Are you okay darling?' he asked.

'Sorry? Erm, yes. I'm fine. I was searching for something, but now I can't remember what it was, so I'll look again later when I can remember. We better get going or else we'll be late for dinner.'

CHAPTER FIVE

Although early in the cruise itinerary, the Gala Night with the Masquerade Ball was always one highlight. The opulent dinner followed by a Venetian themed Masquerade Ball was a sight to behold. It was a sensual experience. They filled the dinner with colourful and fragrant food with an amazing array of delectable flavours and textures. The face masks were only worn in the ballroom. Each face mask was commissioned and hand made by Hugo at his studio. They distributed them to all the guests on board during the previous evening's turndown service. Both the men's and the women's half-masks were distinguishable from each other. The women's masks were golden and feline shaped, adorned with multi-coloured feathers, whilst the men's masks were ebony black, embellished with metallic silver to be mysterious. Hugo created a selection of masks in different colours to depict unique personality traits, such as mysterious and seductive, inquisitive and flirtatious. The Destiny Masquerade Ball was based on the 16th century Venetian traditional public festivities for the upper classes. They re-decorated the Destiny Celebration ballroom to represent a baroque style hall, which was the traditional setting for such gatherings.

Michelle and Theo took pre-dinner drinks at the Homage Cocktail Bar, next to the steakhouse and seafood restaurant named "Seasoned". The bar layout was not dissimilar to a Manhattan speakeasy bar. They festooned the walls and décor with mahogany panelling and maroon leather cushioning on the barstools and booth seating. Around the walls were picture-boards paying tribute to the creators of various world-renowned classic cocktails. Each told a personal history of the inspirations behind the drinks. It was a lesson to the modern world of mixology. On each table and bar top were cocktail menus describing both classic and modern interpretations providing a stylish mix of drinks. The phrase "Where mixology knows no bounds, where fusion meets infusion", was embossed on the front of the dark brown leather-bound drinks menus. All this resulting from painstaking corporate focus groups and PR analysis. The right blend of content, context and substance. The clientele had to be immersed in this synthetic environment, with the ultimate feeling of embracing nostalgia.

Michelle and Theo took a seat on adjoining bar stools at the far end of the bar. Slavic the barman proactively placed cardboard coasters on the cream and gold-coloured granite bar top in anticipation of a drinks order. In tandem asking, 'Madam, sir, what can I get you both to drink?'

Theo, knowing what he liked, ordered a sweet Manhattan on the rocks with no hesitation. Less sure was Michelle, who needed to scan the entire drinks menu. Befitting the environment, she selected a "Cosmopolitan", popularised once again by her favourite romcom. Even having made her choice, she continued to read the menu for modern interpretations of the classics. What was missing were the frozen drinks, as the corporate decision was for those to only be available at the pool bar because of the annoying decibels of the blenders in their making. The Homage Cocktail Bar was a relaxing environment with cool vibes. In the bar's corner there was a pianist playing jazz music, interspersed with relaxing melodies from the Rat Pack era. The music was subdued in order to encourage conversation. Because of its secluded location high on the ship, the bar was quiet, in contrast to other bars on natural thoroughfares on lower decks. It was the kind of place you had to go out of the way of to find. A few couples were arriving in dribs and drabs, moving away from the bar area and towards more dimly lit booths. Looking across the bar, they could spot the occupants of the other booths as they pointed at the picture-boards and discussed their merits. They briefed the waiting staff on knowing the cocktail menu inside out and trying to upsell to the more exotic modern cocktails on offer, coming in at a premium price. There was the smell of coffee in the air to promote the espresso martini, similar to the tactic used by homeowners when potential buyers wander around their kitchen during a viewing. A practice that brought back mixed memories for Theo. There was the unmistakable smell of burnt hickory used in the smoke guns when applied over aged dark rums. Displayed were tall glasses filled with colourful layers of alcohol, complemented by a spinning glass globe ball. The vision of the bartender shaking the metal cocktail container by his ear to a gentle rhythm. Cracking it open and the filtered pouring of the contents into a glass. The adornment of the glass with a variety of garnishes to complement the alcoholic contents. It all added to a sense of theatre. It was about feeling the senses of the body all around you.

'Cheers,' exclaimed Theo as he clinked his tumbler against Michelle's cocktail glass.

'Yes, cheers,' she responded in a flat tone. 'It's good to see you've made the effort tonight with your DJ. You keep stretching and twisting your neck like a giraffe,' she added.

'I hate this constriction. It's not me,' Theo reminded her.

He took a short sip from his glass and asked the barman Slavic, 'Can you add a little more bourbon for me, please? It's just my preference.'

'No problem, sir. I'm with you. That's what I think is the perfect pour. It's good to meet someone with the same taste. Ship's policy is for traditional pours unless specified. I'll make sure I'll get that right for you next time,' said Slavic, as he finished pouring the bourbon into the tumbler. He made a mental note to expect Mr d'Vere's preference for his return visit.

He completed the top-up with a flip of the bottle over the back of his pouring hand, replacing it back into the original line up position in a well-practiced slick manoeuvre. Glancing over towards the other end of the bar, Slavic could see another couple taking a seat on a stool. 'Excuse me,' he said, as he smiled at the new arrivals and moved away, leaving Michelle and Theo in solitude. Theo tried to remain upbeat while talking to Michelle, but he could still feel the undercurrent of icy coldness emanating from her.

'Is this godmother role getting to you? You haven't been yourself since we came onboard,' asked Theo.

'I'm fine,' said Michelle, as she paused for thought by taking a sip herself.

'It's a combination of things. Look in the mirror yourself. You've been distant. I know you have been wrapped up in your presentation and concerning yourself with it, but this holiday is in danger of turning into a bit of a nightmare. I'm not seeing you much whilst I'm being pulled from pillar to post with all the godmother engagements. We're both going to have to make more of an effort to find time for each other. One of our problems is that we don't know how to communicate with each other. This should be about our special anniversary, and not as a make-or-break holiday. We've had one reconciliation in the past. I couldn't go through another one, Theo.'

She tried looking at Theo into his hazel eyes, but he was doing everything possible to avert his gaze. That avoidance said so much to Michelle. Actions often speak louder than words.

'Are you listening to me, Theo? You are so fickle. You have the attention span of a goldfish,' she hissed.

'Of course, I am listening. That's what I was thinking, except for your unflattering assessment of me. You can be so cutting. It's just that you put some things into words much better than me. Remember, you were the queen of dissertations at university. Your grasp of the English vocabulary is far better than mine. A right little thesaurus, aren't we?'

Not liking the direction of the conversation, Theo took charge and suggested, 'We better finish these drinks and get ourselves down to the Aquarium. I'll let you lead the way.' He knocked his head back to take a large intake of his drink.

Michelle heard the ice striking his teeth. 'I am barely halfway through this, Theo. I can't just take it with me. It will make me look like an old soak walking around the ship with a half-finished cocktail,' said Michelle, snarling with no glimmer of a smile.

'Okay, take your time. It's that or you can just leave it,' he conceded.

'Bloody typical of you, Theo. Let's all play the tune to the beat of Theo's drum. Why the hell don't you put me first for once, Theo? We've had these discussions before. Do you remember what the marriage guidance counsellor said? You are so forgetful when it suits you.'

Michelle picked up her glass and downed her remaining cocktail in one gulp before slamming it onto the bar top.

The conversation had been at a reduced volume at close quarters, but the glass landing made Slavic's head turn in their direction before retracting his gaze.

'Let's not have another bloody episode, Michelle. I only took you back because you promised you would have no more tantrums. It cost us a lot of bloody money for you to have that private therapy. Money down the drain again. God, woman. You drive me to despair sometimes,' wrapped up Theo.

He stood up abruptly from his stool and went to head towards the bar exit. When he realised people were looking at them, he slowed down his pace and offered Michelle his arm. She gripped his elbow in a vice-like hold, raised her chin up, and walked out alongside him as if nothing had happened. To her knowledge, no-one could overhear the conversation. She felt she had to keep up appearances. She nodded acknowledgement at Slavic.

As Theo passed the bar, he said, 'Thank you. See you later.'

They had transformed the aquarium into a luxury silver-service speciality restaurant called "Creations at The Aquarium". A cellist and violinist played together close to the gourmet restaurant entrance. It set the mood as soon as guests joined the short seating queue for the designer-inspired restaurant. It added to the air of wonderment. Theo and Michelle patiently awaited their turn to be seated. Unlike previous seating arrangements they had participated in, this one was different, as there was an officer or dignitary assigned to each table rather than all the officers sitting together. The heads of departments were scattered throughout and available for questioning. Fortunately, most of the conversations were going to be skewed towards watching the fish swim around above the diners. The ladies in the queue were all wearing magnificent ballgowns. Some were already playing with the masquerade masks that were only intended for the ball later that evening. The temptation to flirt with its use was just too much for some. Michelle joined in the charade, but more out of wanting to hide behind the mask than to have any fun. They congregated the diners underneath the "Aquadome" tunnel to enjoy the canapes being served on silver trays with glasses of champagne prior to being seated. The chamber music radiated around the aquarium. A little noise could go a long way. Michelle maintained the charade now so as not to be noticed and drawn into any unwanted conversations. The Maître d' made a loud address, calling everyone to be seated. Wine waiters were on hand to take the guests' drinks and lead them to their tables. They asked the guests to give their names to the wine waiters and table waiters who checked their hand-held devices, which contained the seating plans. The tables only seated sixty select guests, with six per table. Four strangers were assigned seats with Michelle and Theo, alternating between male and female seats. Michelle had no other option than to put her mask into her handbag containing her mobile phone and keycard. Still, she was not smiling. Michelle ignored Theo when he looked over at her.

The Maître d' banged his gavel on a table and called out in a style befitting a Toastmaster, 'Ladies and gentlemen, Executive Chef Goran proudly presents a magnificent Gala Diner comprising his own creations, suitable for such an occasion. As you know, we acknowledge our setting this evening and the fantastic marine life surrounding us, so the "Creations at the Aquarium" restaurant does not serve any fish or crustaceans. To start your culinary experience, you will enjoy an amuse-bouche of leek and potato velouté with a chervil foam. Your appetiser is a delectable foie gras served on warm brioche toast, accompanied with a date and apricot chutney, and paired with a delicious glass of Sauternes. To cleanse your palete a coconut and lemongrass sorbet follows this before moving on to your main course of tenderloin of beef, presented with dauphinoise truffle potatoes and turned vegetables. A smooth glass of Argentinian Malbec is your Sommelier's pairing this evening. To conclude your banquet of exquisite dishes, we will serve you a chocolate bombe with hazelnut ice cream, and a light whisky cocktail. Enjoy these culinary delights surrounded by this theatrical spectacle. Bon appétit!'

They could hear the chatter of excitement and the toasting of glasses from around the restaurant.

The talk around Michelle and Theo's table soon started with belated greetings and introductions. The two other couples were known to each other, travelling from central Utah, USA. They both commented on how honoured they were to be seated with the godmother of the vessel. Michelle smiled for a moment in acknowledgement, with Theo looking on at her to see if her defences were finally thawing after the tempestuous last thirty minutes since leaving the suite. Michelle was still not looking Theo in the eye. When the side of various artisan rolls of bread arrived in two baskets at the table, one of the other guests asked if Michelle would pass over the butter dish. As Michelle picked it up and passed it over, the sleeve of her ballgown rose up her delicate wrist to reveal her new bracelet. One of the other female guests commented how lovely it looked on her.

Michelle said, 'Theo selected it for me. I like it as it's unique, isn't it darling?' as she turned to Theo and looked at him with a fixed stare.

'Yes. Yes, it is,' he replied, not knowing where this was leading. As he turned to look over his opposite shoulder in a vain attempt to catch the eye of the Sommelier.

'Theo is such a devil. I'm sure he charmed the salesperson in the boutique to such a degree that reverse psychology applied, and he agreed to pay twice as much as its worth just to secure it, hey Theo?' said Michelle with a false grin from ear to ear.

'Darling, you're the one with the psychology degree. You tell me?' he retorted.

'Oh, you two are a feisty couple!' exclaimed one of the two men.

'I like to keep him on his toes. He knows I'm just pushing buttons, don't you, sweetheart?' said Michelle as she nudged Theo, again with a fixed smile others could interpret either way.

Theo turned and looked over his opposite shoulder again and said, 'Excuse me, could we get some more wine over here please?' as he attempted to detract from the conversation into which he was feeling increasingly cornered.

'Michelle is an intelligent woman who likes to play these

little mind games. At the end of the day, I'm just a simple photographer.'

A bead of sweat rolled down his temple. He was fortunate that it was on the opposite side of where Michelle was sitting. He discreetly brushed it away as he raised his hand to attract the Sommelier's attention.

'Would anyone else like a second glass of Sauternes? I do like the sticky wines, as the Australians call them.'

'I'm sweet enough, thank you darling,' claimed Michelle.

When Theo swirled his wine and held it to the light, he liked to look at the legs draining on the inside of the glass, showing body and maturity.

'You do like legs, don't you, Theo?' Michelle sneered with an even broader grin.

'Oh, stop it, you two. You are such a couple of teasers. You make me laugh,' chuckled one of the other wives.

'Don't worry. It won't be long until she couples this up with my fondness for Blue-Footed and Red-Footed Boobies. As you are from Utah, you probably haven't seen the Red-Footed Boobies as they breed in Hawaii, and are only found on the US continent in California or Florida,' said Theo with a light-hearted laugh, turning to each table member as he explained his story.

All the other table guests laughed out loud as if to acknowledge the end of the somewhat tense exchange between Michelle and Theo. Capturing the opportunity, one of the other table guests changed the subject to Theo's love of photography.

Michelle said, 'You'll have to look on your stateroom TV and find the enrichment documentaries. Theo has one in the Galapagos. I can't tell you the whole detail, as I haven't finished watching it all yet, but it is a fascinating view into Theo's professional life. It's an insight I don't normally get to enjoy, as Theo is away a lot on location whilst I remain at home. I'm looking forward to watching it all the way through for myself, ahead of his lecture tomorrow if I get the chance.'

One of the male guests asked Theo to elaborate on anecdotes relating to a recent photographic assignment trip to Iceland.

Theo responded, 'I advocate as the best value for money for a future cruise would be to combine whale watching in Isafjordur and witnessing puffins up close on Vigur Island, which would also support the local tourism industry. For those using a mobile phone or a more sophisticated camera, a helpful tip would be to pack extra batteries or ensure that the chosen device is fully charged or equipped with a back-up power supply, which is now available because of the advances of modern technology. There is nothing worse than seeing a spectacular display of a pod of humpback whales as they somersault into the Icelandic fjord and then missing their individual flukes because your camera battery dies. A cautionary element, though, when booking an excursion in Akureyri to experience Lake Myvatn and the glorious Godafoss waterfall is that the prevalent blackflies are a real nuisance, but the views are so worthwhile. Research online before you go. Purchase a mosquito net for your head. Don't worry about wearing them. You may look odd, but so will everyone else. Another word of warning is to take a clothes peg for your nose to reduce the overwhelming smell of sulphur at the geothermal area of Namafjall Hverir close to the lake. The clothes peg reference is only metaphorical, of course. As they say, please don't do this at home. And if you love a bit of adventure, I can also recommend an exhilarating buggy ride along multi-terrain surfaces around the blue mountains. You'll pass wild Icelandic horses in varying shades of black, chestnut, bay and silver dapple with flowing thick manes. White, yellow, blue and violet wildflowers fringe the paths with conifers and yew trees. After you climb steep and rocky terrain, they will reward you with breathtaking 360-degree aerial views of mountains, fields, lakes, and rippling streams. It's an absolute playground for those with a sense of adventure. I'll tell you another time about the equally scenic Greenlandic discoveries that will await you on the world's largest island. The icebergs, the Northern Lights and much more.'

There were nods of approval from all around the table, except for one whom Theo could have predicted.

'Theo does like a sense of adventure when on assignment, don't you, sweetheart? Mind you, when the cat's away, the mice will play,' retorted Michelle.

Theo didn't bother in replying. The other guests stayed silent and continued to finish the course before the next arrived. Before too long, they concluded the remaining food courses, as was the intense questioning of Theo by the other guests. For once, Michelle allowed Theo to be the centre of attention instead of herself. It may have appeared that she had let the fish off the hook, but was she re-hooking the bait to catch a bigger fish?

'Ladies and gentlemen. That concludes your dining experience. It is now time to make your way to the Celebration Ballroom to join the rest of the ship's guests for the Masquerade Ball. Please wear your provided face masks and enjoy the mysterious and mischievous festivities on offer tonight,' announced the Maître d'.

Once again, there was the overwhelming sense of excitement from those present. Ladies rummaged in their clutch bags and handbags for their masks. The men searched their inner jacket pockets at a more relaxed pace with a slight air of reluctancy, whilst accepting the inevitable expectation of putting on their respective masks. Their transformation was hypnotic, with the mood becoming more mystical as the minutes ticked by. The light humour echoed along the corridor between the restaurant and the ballroom. Voices that converged from each corner of the ship into the ballroom only added to the congregational excitement. Women entered the dancefloor, with an arm outstretched to their partners. They each started swirling to a slow waltz tempo, whilst each found their own space, moving along in unison.

Michelle stepped on to the dance floor in her flowing burgundy ballgown. The dress fell into the shape of an ornate bell, with long sleeves that were draped at the elbow like sheer lacy butterfly wings. The waist was nothing short of being a corset. With her long, raven coloured hair pinned up in a chignon style, she looked majestic and graceful as she completed her first twirl. For that moment, she caught Theo's eye, and it reminded him of their early days at university. The formal graduate parties were something to behold, but even back then, Theo thought something was amiss, but he could never quite put his finger on it. There seemed there was a distraction in the background, but he could never understand it. That all seemed to change when they eventually got married. For now, she looked serene, but it did not fool Theo. What was not on display was her cold-hearted, calculating, and manipulative persona. Oh, how she had changed. Nothing that sudden, but over time there had been a transformation. For Theo, it was irreversible. It was like a snake shedding its skin after it had already grown a new one underneath. Her quips at dinner were the true Michelle rising to the surface like a python in search of its unsuspecting prey. She liked to tease at the best of times, but tonight was a stellar performance, even by her standards. He thought she would have been more gracious in receiving a bracelet gift, but in fact, it appeared to have galvanised her resentment even more so. The animosity between them was growing in front of his eyes. He knew she was playing a long game with him, and she appeared to have been giving him some clues along the way tonight. Theo knew that with playing games, Michelle would throw the rule book out of the window and play it her way. What the university had not taught her about psychology was not worth knowing. He found it quite creepy that her final dissertation at university was on psychopaths. She could be manipulative. Michelle could be callous. She could be impulsive. Could she be promiscuous? The little he knew himself about psychopathic behaviour was self-taught from dipping into Michelle's study material in their shared university accommodation and reading her draft essays. She had indulged in her studies like any top-grade student would, but to what extent and with what impact on her? Michelle could be a liar. She could often have a lack of remorse or guilt. The way she manipulated the conversation tonight during dinner was a prime example. She conversed with a superficial charm. These things were ringing alarm bells in Theo's mind. What was the defining line between academia and reality, and where was Michelle on that journey? Of the few characteristics that he knew of that were not evident to him in Michelle were ones of sexual promiscuity, emotional pain developing into violence, and ultimately reaching the point of no return. Her behaviour, as far as he was aware, had never stretched to that extent. When does an elastic band decide to break and how soon after it does, do you know?

The music continued to play, and the people danced. There was a rhythm to the ensemble of partners moving across the floor, navigating their path. The Cruise Director Olly appeared on stage in front of the ship's orchestra.

'Ladies and gentlemen, we will now dim the lights further and elevate the mystery. During the next song, you are all to switch partners and continue to do so for the next twenty minutes. It's our way of emulating the history of the Masquerade Ball and allowing you to meet new guests. Fear not. If you want to step out, then please take a seat at the side. When I return to the stage, you can all return to your own dance partners. Orchestra, please!'

The next waltz began as the lights dimmed. Everyone looked around themselves, putting their arms out to invite the next dancer to join them. No-one left the dance floor as everyone was enjoying the spirit of the occasion. Someone who was a better dancer than Theo joined Michelle, although any man on the dance floor could have earned that accolade. Ballroom dancing was not Theo's forte, but he could survive with the basic steps. His new partner was a more elderly lady who danced at a slower pace than others. This allowed Michelle to waltz away ahead of Theo, and off into the distance, being obscured by other couples and an increased tempo between the two of them. The average waltz lasts between one and a half and two and a half minutes. Not quite long enough to elope, thought Michelle. The three/four-time signature was uncomplicated. Theo, therefore, could concentrate on his footwork without embarrassing himself too much. With the next waltz came a change of partners. Theo held out his right arm, only to find it gripped as he felt himself being drawn closer with an arm wrapped around his upper torso and shoulder. The electric blue ballgown was flowing to the floor. His right arm pointed forward as if to lead. The female partner gripped his hand, with a bracelet sparkling on her wrist. He snapped his head to face his partner. The face mask could not hide the sapphire blue eyes and unforgettable pursed lips.

She said, 'Hello stranger! Care for the next dance?' as if Theo had a choice.

'Are you crazy, Suzanne? We need to talk. Meet me in the casino,' said Theo as he tried to ease himself away from Suzanne's hold.

'Not just yet, Theo. This is my dance,' as she held his elbow tighter and pulled him even closer in an intimate embrace as their midriffs rubbed together. 'I thought you'd be happier to see me. You're not feeling as happy as I would have expected. In fact, I'd say you are feeling a little, shall we say, down?' Suzanne replied.

'Not now. Be serious. Have this dance and then meet me at the roulette table,' hissed Theo. The next two and a half minutes felt like the longest in his life. On every pirouette he gazed over Suzanne's shoulder on the look-out for Michelle. He could see her about half the length of the ballroom away, now dancing with what appeared to be an older gentleman at a pace that was not catching up with Suzanne and himself. He had to maintain that space. By his own calculation, if this was the second waltz and it had taken five minutes for the first two, he would have about another fifteen minutes until Olly appeared to reunite the original dance partners together. That should leave him enough time to briefly talk with Suzanne. Suzanne's passionate demonstration was not in tandem with Theo's. The timing was off. The normal sexual chemistry between them was not there. She grasped this was not the time for innuendos. She felt the underlining frustration emanating from Theo's reaction to her suggestive embrace. The waltz was ending, and with the last few bars, Theo released his grip from Suzanne's left arm and pulled her off the dancefloor in a corner where there was an exit from the ballroom, before any other willing partners could grab his hand. On her high heels, Suzanne struggled to keep pace with Theo's long stride through the small crowd of people congregated around the periphery of the dance area. He felt the need to reduce his pace before the exaggerated departure drew any unwanted attention.

'Go ahead of me and I'll see you near the roulette table. Don't join in the game as I'll have no time to talk to you. Something strange is happening,' said Theo in a serious tone. 'Now go.'

***

Michelle was dancing with gay abandonment. Her thoughts were no longer on Theo, but on finding the original anonymous dancing partner. He had rhythm and a panache, holding her like she had never been gripped before. He also had a name badge saying he was a Dance Host. They gave volunteers a free cabin and food so that they could partner single dancers during lessons, tea dances and balls. He was the one she had eyes on now should the tempo move upbeat to a tango or cha-cha. The pairing wines were now pumping around her body and to her head with each swirl she made.

***

Suzanne stood between the roulette table and the slot machines. She wanted to look quite discreet, but her striking good looks and beautiful unblemished skin somewhat prevented that. Her only saving grace was the mask that was her only disguise. She was looking towards the games tables when Theo appeared alongside her. Before Theo could speak, Suzanne said, 'Nice bracelet, Theo. I see someone else has one as well as I saw it in the Aquarium from within the tank. What the hell is going on? I thought you said we are making plans for our future together?'

'Right. Ok. I'll explain,' said Theo, looking stressed. 'I said I have a plan, but I need to buy a bit of time. I bought one for Michelle to keep her quiet for now. Somehow, it seems to have had the opposite effect than I had intended on both of you. She's been acting strange. I don't know what she is up to, but I feel it is not good. I have been keeping up the charade so as not to raise her suspicions and cause an unpleasant scene. We need to cool this for tonight. I need to get my thoughts together and get through this presentation tomorrow. I have hardly any time until I leave the ship for the next photographic assignment. You need to stay on here until the cruise ends next week, and then we'll meet up again. I'm secretly meeting a divorce lawyer between the assignment and going back to the UK. Let me take a seat at the roulette table because it would be unusual for the staff to see me in here and not be betting if there was a spare seat. You just watch for now.'

Theo took a seat. He handed over his keycard to the regular roulette croupier Ji Lin and asked for $200 worth of chips to go against his room account. He had to spend the money quickly and return to the ballroom before anyone noticed his absence. Spending $200 for a cover story seemed to him a bit much, but worth it in the long run.

***

While enjoying the euphoria of the waltz twirl, Michelle heard Olly's voice coming over the microphone when the last few bars played.

'Ladies and gentlemen, that concludes the random dance. If you wish, you can either return to your original partners or continue dancing with those who still want to be randomly selected with an outstretched arm.'

Michelle felt the need to sit down. 'Thank you for the dance, but please excuse me,' she said to the charming dance host.

She turned and walked to the edge of the dance floor, where she expected to find some chairs available, but onlookers had taken them. She squeezed out between two seated people and towards the hallway. With her mask still adorned, she caught the lift to return to her suite. As a privileged VIP, her card would allow her to commandeer the lift and override other calls for it, allowing her an express journey. She removed her keycard from her handbag and inserted it into the reader within the lift, but nothing happened. Michelle pressed the button for her deck and the lift made its way. She reached her deck and went to the suite door. She presented her keycard to the door lock. There was a clicking noise acknowledging the card presentation, but the lock light flashed red instead of the green light she was expecting. She tried once more, but the same thing happened again. The door remained locked.

'Damn, I'll have to go to Guest Relations in the Atrium,' she said to herself. She retraced her steps and took the lift down to the Atrium. There she headed over to the smartly dressed lady at the Guest Services desk.

'Madam, may I help you?' she asked.

'I'm having problems getting into my suite. My card isn't

working,' said Michelle with a hint of frustration.

'No worries, madam. We can give you a replacement card. Have you had it next to a mobile phone?' she asked.

Michelle looked inside her clutch handbag and realised that the card had been resting next to her phone. 'Ah, yes, it has. Does that affect the card?' she asked.

'Yes, madam, it does. It's a common thing with magnetic strips, so don't worry. Because your card wasn't registering on the door lock, we put a freeze on it in case it was compromised or stolen. We have, therefore, also put a hold on your husband's card. We will need to replace it as well. I see on our system that just a minute ago he was trying to charge casino chips to his onboard account, but that, unfortunately, was just after we had placed a hold on both your cards. We can arrange for the Concierge to run a new card down to him immediately,' offered the helpful receptionist.

'Oh, don't worry about that. I'm due to draw the nightly Lotto game in the casino, so if you give me the replacement card, I'll take it to him myself,' replied Michelle.

The receptionist stepped into the back room and returned with two new key cards and handed them to Michelle.

'Thank you,' replied Michelle with a fixed smile and walked off towards the lift to the casino.

***

'I'm sorry Mr d'Vere, your card appears to have a problem, some kind of malfunction. I can't issue you any chips against your card at this precise moment. You'll have to go to Guest Services to have it reactivated,' said Ji Lin.

'Wait here,' Theo instructed Suzanne. 'I won't be long. I'll jog down the stairs to the Guest Services Reception and get this card sorted. In the meantime, order me a drink from one of the casino waiters.'

It took Theo only about 45 seconds to bound down the

stairs of the sweeping marble staircase, sliding down the gold effect banisters to reach the Guest Services desk. He recognised the ornate eye-catching bejewelled chandelier suspended above the foyer and headed over to the receptionist. 'Excuse me, I have something wrong with my key card. It won't work in the casino,' he stated, catching his breath.

'Oh, Mr d'Vere. I've just issued you with a new card. We had frozen yours because of a security issue. We gave your wife your new card only about 30 seconds ago. She said she would deliver it to you, as she was going to the casino now anyhow.'

A thousand thoughts started racing through Theo's head, but the overriding one was that Suzanne was standing next to his regular roulette seat. It was the only spare seat at the table and Michelle would see a sweet & smoky Rob Roy drink in Suzanne's hand and would put two and two together. That was where he should be sitting, only to see Suzanne there instead with his drink. He had to get back to the casino fast.

***

Michelle exited the lift on the casino deck. As the lift doors opened, she caught a glimpse in the opposite glass mirror of a tall man running down the adjacent sweeping marble staircase. It was too quick to recognise who the person was, especially as all the male guests looked so similar in dinner jackets and identical masks. She strolled into the casino, which was in full swing with many gaming machines and tables full of punters. Before she reached the roulette table where she expected to find Theo, Janik, the Pit Boss, stopped her in her tracks.

'Mrs d'Vere, you are early for the Lotto draw. Can I get you a drink and offer you a seat at the casino bar?'

The conversation was close enough to Suzanne that she could hear what was being said over the constant background noise. She instinctively turned around to see only ten feet away stood Michelle. Michelle had already removed her Masquerade ball mask, but Suzanne was still wearing hers. There was nowhere for Suzanne to turn.

'Madam, your drink,' said the waiter as he handed Suzanne a sweet & smoky Rob Roy.

'Thank you,' she replied as she took her Long Island Iced Tea and went to place it in the drink's holder at the seat that Theo had temporarily vacated. She handed the Rob Roy back to the waiter.

'I think I've ordered the wrong drink. Please take it back.'

Her dress sleeve rode up and partially revealed her tanzanite and diamond bracelet. The glint was unmistakable. It caught Michelle's eye. Suzanne hastily pulled down her sleeve to hide the bracelet, but it was too late. She snapped her head to see if Michelle had noticed, and the icy stare that she received confirmed her worst fears. Suzanne had to squeeze past Michelle and Janik to escape. She bowed her head down and took a couple of steps forward. As Suzanne brushed past them, Michelle called out, 'Wait' and went to grab Suzanne.

Suzanne shrugged off Michelle's loose hand grip on her forearm and accelerated with lengthy strides through casino onlookers and zigzagged her way to the far end. Suzanne twisted her right ankle in her high-heeled shoes, but quickly recovered. Her partial collapse caught the attention of several nearby guests, with one woman putting her hand to her mouth with a gasp. Janik did not know what was happening. He had inadvertently blocked any attempt Michelle could make to follow Suzanne. Michelle could not tell her features through the mask, but the view of the back of her head through the crowd, showing a long silver hairstyle which confirmed for her that this was not the same person she saw in the lift kissing Theo.

Theo appeared at the nearby entrance of the casino just in time to see a snapshot of Suzanne running off through the casino towards the far end. He retreated towards the stairwell from where he had just emerged, turned a full 180 degrees and swore an expletive to himself. Knowing where Suzanne's cabin was on the ship, he bounded up the stairs, taking two steps at a time, and headed to meet her to find out what had happened in his absence.

***

'Is everything okay Mrs d'Vere?' asked Janik.

Michelle had to gather her thoughts.

'Yes. Everything is fine. I thought I recognised that lady from the fitness centre. I think it was the lady I had borrowed some headphones from, and I just wanted to let her know I had not forgotten to return them to her. Do you know who she is?'

'I'm sorry Mrs d'Vere, I can't say I do. If I see her again, I'll let her know. She was by the roulette table, so maybe I'll see her there again. Would you like that drink now?' asked Janik, guiding her towards a seat at the bar.

'No. that's fine. I won't have a drink for the moment. Can we make the Lotto draw now as I need to check on something in my suite?' she answered.

***

There was a frantic knock on Suzanne's door. Not knowing who to expect on the other side, she put her eye to the spyhole. She could see Theo's head moving from side to side, looking up and down the corridor. She unlocked the door and let him in. He hurried through to the living area.

'I didn't see it all unfold, as I only caught the tail end of you running out of the casino. What happened there? Is your ankle okay?' he asked.

Suzanne was bent over, rubbing her ankle with her right hand.

'I think she saw my bracelet because of the way she then stared at me and tried to grab me as I raced out,' said Suzanne, becoming emotional as she wiped a tear from her eye and felt her throat tightening. 'It's going in the safe and it can stay there.'

'Okay. Okay, I understand,' said Theo, trying his best to

comfort her.

'Look, she doesn't know who you are, and she won't find out either. You had your mask on. She was only there to bring me a new key card. She won't figure this out. It's all coincidental. So, what if you have the same bracelet? She doesn't know I bought it. You could be anyone who's just bought the same one. It's an international store with other outlets on land and I'm sure on other ships,' he continued, trying to placate her. 'Let's just calm down a little and get ready for tomorrow's presentation. Have you got the underwater prints ready?'

Suzanne replied after a moment once she had collected her thoughts together. 'Yes. I have plenty printed off. There are five different fish in 4 by 6 prints. I've arranged with the photographic department to have each done in A1 size to pin on a board behind where you will sit for their autographing outside the theatre after the presentation. The Quartermaster will store down below 100 of your latest books that are also available to purchase and for you to sign. I have the help of a runner from the gallery to help me set up the table and display whilst you are conducting the presentation. I have a memory card with the five different photos and the book for inserting in your PowerPoint as the last few slides as you finish. You will find the file under the book name "In Focus – Beyond the Lens" on the card,' she concluded.

'You are a star, Suzanne. My Girl Friday, that also needs to encompass Saturday to Thursday,' said Theo in a comforting tone. 'I think I had better go. Just lie low for now. I'll see you tomorrow outside the theatre after the show. I'll take the memory card and download it,' as he pecked Suzanne on the cheek.

She looked forlorn and turned to look in the mirror on the wall. Suzanne could see the imprint of the masquerade mask around her eyes, which were now looking a little red and puffy. She looked back at Theo, but he had already reached the door and was opening it, ready to leave. He gazed back, gave her one of his winning smiles, and blew her an air-kiss. For a moment she raised half a smile, but Theo was getting restless. He was already gone, with the door closing behind him. She turned back to look in the mirror and removed the long-haired silver wig, putting her fingers through her short hair to massage her scalp and add life back to her locks.

***

Michelle had returned to the suite ahead of Theo. She still had his room key, as she had missed him in the casino. She was waiting for him to knock on the door once he realised his pass had been deactivated. The possibility of Theo not being able to get through the door without her assistance meant she could conduct a more thorough search of the wardrobe without interruption. Having seen the bracelet worn by the mystery woman at the roulette table, then surely Theo was not playing games again? Was it possible that there was a third bracelet sold unbeknown to the shop assistant? When she perused the jewellery shop on the launch day, there was only one on display. It must be a possibility that the bracelet was also available on an earlier sailing or even another ship in the fleet.

'Perhaps I'm dreaming this,' Michelle said out loud.

She thought to herself that it was only her having an affair. Their trial separation three years ago had not been the proudest moment of her life. They both attended marriage counselling in order to resolve their differences. The subsequent referral for her to meet a psychiatrist that she had reluctantly accepted and endured. The things she learnt about herself and the dark moods she encountered. Recounting her childhood and upbringing, along with the unexpected diagnosis of mild psychotic episodes. Was all this déjà vu? She wanted more evidence on Theo, to be sure. She could not move freely around the vessel, as she was so well known as the godmother. After all, everyone was there at the inaugural launch. She could walk nowhere without someone every thirty seconds blurting out her name and wanting to come over and chat. How could she keep tabs on Theo? She needed to befriend people. She needed her own spies who, unwittingly, could do her dirty work. The scene of the crime would have been the casino. After all, Theo went there every night until late and sometimes during the day in tournaments. He was drawing money from their onboard accounts. She could see that on the statement on the cabin's interactive tv. Michelle could cut out the middleman and go straight to the pit boss.

She knew Janik from one of her earliest trips with Destiny Cruises when she was sailing alone because of Theo being on a photographic assignment. Janik was only a croupier back then. She provided good customer feedback on his performance in the casino, which secretly, on that occasion, matched that in her bedroom. It was her take on customer satisfaction that they never ask you to complete during one of their surveys. It was a staff policy not to fraternise with guests. Maybe Janik would feel as if he owed her something, or even out of admiration. She could also stoop as low as to use her newly acclaimed notoriety to threaten to have him removed for anything she could invent. It reflected one of her favourite song lyrics where she got him there but could also put him back. Her only concern was that Janik was of a steely character. He had seen combat back home in his Baltic country. He was made of sterner stuff. Would she have to resort to her other seductive charms? It would not be the first time she would have taken such manipulative actions. An issue she had to overcome was how to contact Janik, because the casino was closed and tomorrow they were in port. The casino would not open again until five miles out of port and into international waters on the next evening. The nocturnal lifestyle of the casino staff meant Janik would be nowhere to be seen until then.

She picked up the phone and spoke to the Concierge, 'As I would like a lie-in tomorrow morning, can you advise me if there is a crew lifeboat drill in port?'

The Concierge Henrique confirmed that there would be an announcement at 10am to inform all passengers about the upcoming drill, which would involve only the crew and not the passengers. When the announcement was made, Michelle knew they would advise passengers to stay away from the drill but also encourage their participation if they wished, in order to add a touch of authenticity. She saw this as her opportunity to approach Janik in the hours before the casino opened again. It would not be unusual for the godmother to participate in the drill to show her support for the wider ship's crew, who often go unrecognised for their behind-the-scenes work. It would also not be amiss to have coffee in an open area with a staff member post-drill as several crew members use the public areas so long as they are identifiable as staff through wearing their name badges. She had to know more about the mystery woman at the roulette table at all costs. Theo had already booked an excursion through Henrique for the following day to visit a local Cuban community in order to meet one of the US visa visitation conditions for Cuba, where one of the twelve reasons was a one-to-one interaction to learn about their culture, interspersed with the wildlife. This would give her the space she needed. Henrique had a handful of interested passengers and had arranged a private small-group tour. As far as Michelle was aware, the group was a random collective of suites passengers. Surely Theo could keep himself to himself for one day? He had his presentation beforehand, so at least after that, he could relax and enjoy his excursion with no pressure. His mind and soul would be elsewhere, as most important to her, so would be his body.

CHAPTER SIX

Walking on to the stage of the Destiny Theatre, Theo acknowledged the warm applause from the audience. 'Ladies and gentlemen. Thank you for attending this presentation this morning. You may ask yourselves how can one hour be enough to describe "Wildlife – As seen through a lens", and to be honest it isn't. This is an insight into the wonders of photographing some of life's fantastic creatures. I'll be taking you from the fascinating Galapagos, through the wilds of Africa, and on to the magnificent National Parks of America. I also plan to include countries that kiss and embrace the Arctic Circle. It is a journey to all corners of the world that few people experience in a lifetime. I am fortunate that my passion for photography and my appreciation of nature, have blessed me with the opportunity to embrace the two together,'

Behind him was the first slide of the PowerPoint presentation showing the Galapagos trilogy of a Sally Lightfoot crab atop of a large boulder and a basking seal with a sea iguana lying alongside sneezing out salt from its nostrils. With the presentation underway, and the PowerPoint appearing to work well, Suzanne slipped out of the back of the packed theatre in order to set up the autograph and book signing stall outside. Now the audience was sitting and engrossed, she could work undistracted. She had to erect the pop-up display backdrop, as well as layout the glossy animal photographic prints and books ready for Theo to sign in front of the guests. The personal touch always went down well on such occasions.

'While I was onboard the ship the other day, someone asked me if I had seen the Big 5. My response was, which Big 5? Everyone thinks of the Big 5 as the pneumonic BRELL; namely buffalo, rhino, elephant, lion and leopard, from the savannah plains of Africa, however, give the following some thought. As a photographer, you need to be innovative. How about the other 5? For instance, we have the Ugly 5, the Pretty 5, the Small 5, and the Shy 5. That's just in the animal world. In the scenic world, you can have another Big 5. I think you can find them only in the state of Utah. They are the National Parks of Arches, Bryce Canyon, Canyonlands, Capitol Reef and Zion. Staying with the animals, let's look at those other groupings of five. The Ugly 5 being hyena, warthog, vulture, wildebeest and the Marabou stork.'

Theo pointed to a few men in the front row, 'Gentlemen, not the mother-in-law and her relatives as you were thinking!' to a tittering response amongst the audience. 'The Pretty 5 are leopard, giraffe, springbok, oryx and zebra, also known affectionately as a donkey in pyjamas,' as another laugh echoed around the theatre. 'The Small 5 are tiny animals that share the same name as the traditional Big 5. They include the buffalo weaver, rhino beetle, elephant shrew, ant lion and the leopard tortoise. Now I've got you thinking, can anyone name the Shy 5?' asked Theo.

There were mumblings in pockets of the theatre as people turned to each other to discuss. 20 seconds passed with no one calling out.

'I thought that might fox you, which ironically is the first answer. The group comprises the bat-eared fox, the porcupine, the meerkat, the aardwolf, and last, the aardvark. If you take nothing else away today, take away thinking broadly when speaking of nature. I have captured all these wonderful animals in my book, which will be available for purchase outside the theatre after this presentation. Incidentally, before I forget, photographs taken during the launch of the aquarium will also be on sale outside. I'll be happy to autograph any of the merchandise and answer your questions straight afterwards. Plug over, now on to the in-depth analysis of how my team and I undertake photographic assignments for documentaries, films and books. Let the journey of discovery begin,'

***

Suzanne had finished setting up the table outside, leaving a space for Theo to take a seat and sign autographs at the end of where the walk-up line would finish. She did not want the area to descend into chaos, with people swarming like locusts around the table. A rope barrier was capturing people along the left-hand side wall as they exited the theatre. Unlike her normal chaotic lifestyle, such occasions demanded decorum and organisation. She heard the thunderous applause from inside the auditorium which for her signalled the end of Theo's presentation. Looking towards the swing doors of the theatre, she noticed the first few people leaving. Some were heading straight out and passed by, no doubt aiming towards the next buffet. The look on their faces gave away the clue. Most people entered the roped area, where the gallery assistant held them just short of the table. Suzanne spotted a female who, out of the corner of her eye, was looking down at the table and had taken hold of one book for sale. The floppy brimmed hat and its shadow disguised the face.

'I'm sorry, but I need to let you know there is a queue forming for the book signing,' said Suzanne.

'Oh, that's okay,' Michelle said, as she leafed through the pages of her husband's book, intrigued to see what it looked like now that it had been published. Suzanne steadied her emotions and gulped in anticipation of imagining the worst. Bereft of anything to say in reply, Suzanne shuffled around the photo prints.

'He's a fine photographer, don't you think, Suzanne?' asked Michelle, gazing up.

'Sorry, have we met?' she answered, shivering at the sound of her own name.

'No, I don't think so. I just noticed your name badge. Although you look vaguely familiar. Do you work for the ship?' enquired Michelle with a spike in the question's tail.

Suzanne stumbled over her words. 'Umm, no, not exactly. I'm representing the author's company, "Never Lose Focus". I'm just trying to make sure this runs smoothly with the stall set up correctly, etcetera,'

***

The last power point slide was displayed on the big screen behind Theo, showing him in a pose with an albino Burmese python wrapped around his neck and shoulders. He was nearing the end of his presentation at the lectern and finished with, 'I look forward to seeing you all around the ship. Please come up and have a chat with me if you see that I'm alone. Twenty of you I know will join me this afternoon when I lead an exploration tour of the flamingos at the Reserva Ecologica de Cayo Coco in Cuba. It's an exhilarating location that is a must-see destination on this cruise, just off the Old Bahama Channel here. I'm sorry that we are limiting the numbers on this occasion, but it ensures we maintain the ecological balance in this protected area. I thank you all for your attendance and good afternoon.'

The audience showed their appreciation with thunderous applause, and soon they were decanting out of the auditorium. The waiting line was becoming more boisterous as the volume of talk increased. Suzanne was struggling to talk over the background noise.

Michelle asked, 'I can see you are busy. You don't mind if I take a copy, do you? Theo doesn't need to sign it. I would just like to take it away to appreciate the contents in peace. Is that ok?'

'Of course,' replied Suzanne, just relieved that Michelle

would soon leave and bringing her own racing heartbeat down with it.

'Thank you,' said Michelle as she clutched hold of the book and turned to walk away. Michelle stopped, turned on the spot. 'Oh, one other thing.'

Suzanne felt her heart skip a beat.

'Can you tell Theo not to be too long and that I'll be waiting for him back in our suite? After all, it is our wedding anniversary and I think the public has seen enough of him today!' Michelle exclaimed whilst winking suggestively with her right eye.

Before Suzanne could even acknowledge the request, Michelle once more turned on her heels and headed off. A migraine was forming across Michelle's temple, and she needed something medicinal to overcome it. She had not had these pains since she had finished the psychiatry sessions a couple of years ago. The pulsating pain had been getting worse over the last 36 hours. How she wished they would stop. They were bringing back memories of the emotional and physical pain she had endured before.

Suzanne took a sigh of relief and shook her head in disbelief at the chance encounter. Had she got away with it? Had Michelle rumbled her? Focus, she said to herself, as she stopped arranging the table and put her hands to her side. She could see Michelle walking away without looking back. Hopefully, that was a good sign. The power of Michelle's presence was something she was fearful of ever encountering whilst bizarrely being in awe when it happened. There felt something sinister in just the way she raised her head and stared at Suzanne. How she directed the brief conversation and the way that she had the last word. Her eyes held a disdainful look, whether she directed it at Suzanne or when talking about Theo. She felt as if Michelle was trying to portray passion in her words, but her soul was missing. She could now see for herself why Theo was cautious when he talked of Michelle, as there was callousness in her actions and manners. It was easy to find the worst in someone you disliked, but there was an inner feeling that Michelle was everything she feared and more. It was just that gut instinct. That woman's intuition. Did Michelle have that same intuition? It was hard to say. She seemed such a cold fish that it was hard to read anything else into her. Suzanne had seen enough with her own eyes to not want to probe any further. She needed to relay her thoughts to Theo in private, but when would they find the time? He was due off the ship onto the photographic assignment the next day and then she would not see him for some time.

Theo emerged from the theatre doors. There was some back slapping as he passed the line of patient onlookers. He approached the desk and smiled at Suzanne. There was an acknowledgment back, but without a smile. He took a seat, glanced up at Suzanne to his left and mouthed, 'You okay?'

She shook her head, bent down to whisper in his ear, 'We need to talk urgently. Michelle has been here and taken one of your books away.'

Theo raised his eyebrows towards his hairline in only a way that someone who had not succumbed to Botox could manage. Despite being surprised, he recovered himself, selected one of his books and turned to the first person in the queue, greeting them professionally with, 'And who shall I make this out to?'

***

Michelle looked through the bathroom cupboards in a desperate search for painkillers. Her prescribed medication had finished some time ago. She did not want to approach the ship's surgeon for medication as she had no desire to share with senior crew members her medical requirements. The thought of someone delving into her medical history would be painful. She entered the bedroom and phoned the direct line to Jose, the suite butler. Hopefully, he would be more discreet. She asked him whether he could find her some headache tablets or maybe something a little stronger? He said to leave it with him, and he would return to her soon. His unfettered access to supplies in the background would prove beneficial. Afterwards there was a knock on the door with the familiar sound of the keycard engaging. The combination of a knock and entry could only mean Jose. It was only as he entered the corridor that Michelle confirmed for him to come in.

'This is as strong as I could get,' he said. 'I recommend you only take two tablets twice a day. I'm no doctor, but please don't mix them with alcohol. Otherwise, it will be more of a sedative than a painkiller.'

He handed Michelle a small capsule of tablets. She popped off the lid and looked inside. There were approximately 50 small tablets inside.

'You can take these with water, but you must swallow them straightaway as they dissolve. They will effervesce in your mouth unless you down them quickly,' explained Jose.

'You are a star, Jose. Thank you. I need some peace and quiet now. Please, can you put the "do not disturb" switch on as you leave?'

Jose nodded in acknowledgment and strode out of the suite, carrying out Michelle's instructions as he did so. Michelle took two tablets and swallowed them down with no water. She could taste a bitter residue in the back of her mouth. How she would love a glass of Prosecco to wash the taste away. She headed over to the chaise longue to raise her weary feet. Nothing could be more relaxing for her than to thumb through Theo's photographic book. Despite his flaws, she still respected his professional accomplishments. She believed the book needed to prove it was worth his absence. The attention to detail and the sharp focus on the subject were second to none. The variety of animals within the scenic setting was something to behold. She had seen many photographic books before, but this elevated the contents to a new level. It was no wonder Theo had been under a constant barrage of requests to produce a fantastic portfolio for publication. Having viewed every picture at speed, she skipped to the index page to read his biography. It was a rather modest interpretation of Theo's background and accolades. She could tell Theo had penned it. It was typical of his style. It was his own description of himself that he would relay to new students he met at university. To him, the artist was the subject he was photographing and not the person behind the lens. She returned to the front of the book to skim through the "foreword", where an esteemed critic had written a very flattering description of Theo and his work. She then flicked to the back of the book once more to read the "acknowledgments" page, expecting to see some recognition of his "long-suffering wife", only to find something rather different.

It read, "This book would never have come to fruition without the help of my dedicated assistants in the field. Having to put up with my every demand, every whim and every tantrum. Knowing how I operate and understanding the demands of working in remote locations has been invaluable. You were there for me and I'm proud to be there for you, no matter what the future holds. You know who you are, but I may have to spell it out for you!"

Curiously, Michelle moved straight to the front of the book to the "dedications" page. There it recorded "For Suzanne and the entire Never Lose Focus team". Michelle slammed the book shut and threw it down violently onto the coffee table, knocking over the flower vase and the display.

***

The sales had gone well. Customers bought over 90% of the photos and books. Every punter had got what they wanted. It was only the "buffetistas" who had missed out, but that was of their own making. Suzanne placed the unsold photographs into storage boxes ready to return to the quartermaster. Theo did likewise with his few remaining books. A couple of books had been thumbed by curious onlookers, who had baulked at the price before putting them down again and scurrying off. They were easily identifiable as they were the same ones coming out with the "don't we have to be at the shore excursion presentation" excuse as they debate buying one before walking away. Theo tried his best to smooth out the creases, but it would never be a success. He could present a signed one to the end-of-cruise charity auction for the Foundation, with an unsigned one going to the ship's library for future passenger enjoyment. Hopefully, they would tag it to stop it from being pilfered. Modern tags activated a warning to the security department in case passengers ever removed them from the ship. The signs in the library next to the daily sudoku and crossword puzzles warned of the consequences. Content in his endeavours, Theo helped the gallery assistant to fold up the table. He reached inside his pocket and handed over a $20 note as a thank you. Although not a lot in western terms for a wage, it was proportionate to the cruise industry wages with a bit more on top. The assistant smiled with glee and wheeled away the sack truck of storage boxes to take behind-the-scenes. Theo deposited the two books in Olly's office behind reception, then headed over to the Excursion Desk to check that everything was fine with the arranged zodiac for the afternoon's exploration. Suzanne had already gone ahead of Theo to her cabin. Anticipating her visitor's arrival, she had already illuminated the "do not disturb" sign. She only had to wait a few minutes until she heard the coded knock at the door.

***

Michelle laid on the bed and turned on the TV. She still had to finish watching Theo's documentary. Michelle tabbed through the listings to find the programme. She pressed "ok" to start the programme and realised it was starting from the beginning again and not from the paused place. She thought this strange, but pressed fast-forward to the estimated position that she remembered from the last time she viewed it. There was not much of the programme to play through before the end. Nothing very remarkable appeared in the last few minutes as the programme faded into a finish and then came to life again with a "behind-the-scenes" director's mini-documentary into the work that makes such a programme. It was a ten-minute extra narrated by the director. The scenes included Theo in dialogue and working closely with a short-haired female in khaki clothing on location in various places, setting up camera and video equipment. Michelle reached over for a pair of glasses from her bedside cabinet. The face was not any clearer, so she paused the programme and crawled along the bed on her hands and knees to get closer to the screen. She thought to herself that there was a remarkable resemblance to the lady she had just spoken to at the book-signing table. Sitting on the end of the bed, she reached back for the remote control and rewound the programme to the start of the behind-the-scenes. She played it again, but this time looked closer at the interaction between Theo and this female. Both on second inspection looked to be working intimately with each other. There were often smiles and laughter between them, like how she again remembered being with Theo at university all those years ago in the throes of immature, youthful passion. This female significantly influenced how the filming on the set was carried out. Theo was obviously taking the final shots behind the lens, although not without this female looking through the lens first, ahead of most of the shots. Other people in the mini-documentary were performing a role, but not as intensely as Theo and this woman. The untrained eye might have missed this, but the observant onlooker could see a deeper connection beyond professional appreciation between them. Nothing overtly sexual, but definitely some kind of connection. Michelle let the video run its course to the credits in order to ascertain the full name. She scrolled down the list with Theo's name at the head of the credits alongside his pen-picture. The next name was for the "Locations Manager", Suzanne Harrington. Michelle again paused and looked at the pen-picture for her. This confirmed for her it was the same person to whom she had just been talking. A knot tightened in Michelle's stomach. She stood up from the edge of the bed and went over to the drinks cabinet and poured a large glass of still water. She picked up the tablets she had just taken, paused and put them back down again. Jose was quite strict in telling her to limit how many she could take at any one time. She felt a thumping migraine in her head, and now a nauseous feeling in the pit of her stomach accompanied it. She put the glass of water down, picked up the TV remote control, and sat on the end of the bed once more. The picture was still paused. She looked at Suzanne's frozen frame and studied her face. It was from on-location, so perhaps not the most endearing of shots. Although not the most beautiful looking woman, she had a glow on her face from working in a hot and challenging environment. There was no make-up, but with her hair kept short, you could see more of her face. The healthy complexion also enhanced her younger looks. Michelle discarded the remote control on the duvet, stood up once more and walked over to the dressing-room mirror. She took a dispassionate look at herself in the mirror. She did not recognise the face looking back at her. The mask of make-up could not disguise what lay underneath. She had lost the youthful looks in such a short time. The worry-lines across her brow told the actual story. She glanced over at the TV to compare herself to the picture of Suzanne. It took little to see why Theo would want to spend more time with the face on the TV than the face in the mirror, she thought to herself. But Michelle was still confused. Despite not finding Theo's jewellery receipt, it was clear from the onboard account and the shop assistant's statement that two identical tanzanite and diamond bracelets existed. She knew Theo had purchased them both. She had witnessed another woman in the casino wearing the other bracelet, but that woman with the long silver hair in the masquerade mask did not closely resemble Suzanne. However, Suzanne, in the documentary, and again outside the theatre, had definitely sported a short hairstyle. It made little sense to her. How many women was Theo playing-off against each other? Should she also feel some pity for Suzanne? Not bloody likely, she thought to herself. She looked across to the coffee table and saw the flower vase and its contents strewn across the plush cream carpet. The vase water had seeped into the carpet, leaving a darker area. She nipped into her bathroom, brought out a hand towel, and started dabbing the area. She put the ornate vase back onto the coffee table and rearranged the flowers inside. One had a broken stem, so she placed this over Theo's book. It had fallen open on his "biography" page with his pen picture. She continued to soak up the water spillage, but it took the need of a bath towel to make any difference. Michelle discarded both soaked towels on the bathroom floor, in the recognised international language of the need for both of them to be replaced by the room steward. She returned to the bedroom, walked past the still frozen TV picture of Suzanne, and over to the coffee table. She seized a bottle of still water, topped up the vase and replaced it in the centre of where it was before her little tantrum. Her attention returned to the damaged flower lying over Theo's picture. She picked up the flower stem between thumb and forefinger with her left hand. She stared at the beauty of the delicate gerbera flower head. Her mind could not help but regress into a child-like state. They had sectioned her for a short time in a rehabilitation centre during her psychological assessment because of her trial-separation. She had memories of sitting in the sensory garden picking at the flower petals. It was a time of solitude and sanctuary where she first felt the healing inside. She now sat once again with the thumb and forefinger of her right hand picking at each petal.

'He loves me, he loves me not,' she repeated softly to herself, with the detaching of each petal. As she rotated the stem, more and more petals succumbed to her vigorous plucking. The rhyme continued until the last petal with the words 'he loves me not' echoing in her ears. Her sour face now had a deeper frown not only across her forehead, but also in the puckered jowls around her mouth. No, it could not be right. Surely, Theo still loved her? She picked another colourful gerbera out of the vase and started the rhyme and petal-picking process again. Once more it ended with 'he loves me not'. No, no, no, she thought. This was not meant to be. Or was it that Theo and her were not meant to be? No, no, no, she thought again. Her heart rate was racing even further. She could feel each beat. The migraine pain was not showing any signs of subsiding. She scrunched the second gerbera and left it on the table. During her previous psychotic episodes a few years before, she had had similar thoughts that spiralled into a deeper and darker place. It was only because of the recommended twice daily psychiatric sessions that she had maintained a degree of sanity, leading to a gradual improvement in her condition. She sat there looking at Theo's picture, with sporadic glances at Suzanne's face on the TV. She instinctively turned off the TV to blot out the face. The TV screen had been frozen so long that even when it was powered off, Michelle could still see an imprint of Suzanne's face. She picked up the discarded petals from the coffee table, shaking with rage, scurried over to the TV and threw them at the screen with a screech of 'No!' The petals dropped to the floor below. Michelle returned to the book on the coffee table and snapped it closed. She left the book cover picture of a leopard facing upwards. Poignantly, could this female leopard change her spots?

***

An hour had passed as Theo laid there, twizzling his star sign pendant on the chain around his neck. He pulled the duvet off his partially covered body. He swung his legs around to exit the opposite side of the bed to Suzanne.

The passion had abated when Suzanne said, 'You never told me it was your wedding anniversary on this cruise. The more I think of you, the more I realise I know so little about you.'

Theo replied, 'It wouldn't make any difference for how you feel about me or what lies ahead for us. The timing of the ship's launch dragged me here. I doubt Destiny Cruises had considered my anniversary when deciding on the launch party. What matters most to me is how I get out of the trap I am in with my dignity intact. Michelle and I should never have got back together after the trial separation. For me, I did not mean it to be that way. I foolishly fell for Michelle's description of how she had overcome her demons and how she was going to become a changed woman. I just wanted to delve deeper into my work, which if I hadn't, would have meant we wouldn't be where you and I are today. It will break my heart to leave you behind on this ship. You're a sensible woman, but there is a grenade onboard that could have the pin removed at any time. I don't fear for myself, but I fear for you. You've just got to lie low for the coming week until I can see you again. Just focus on the aquarium work and keep yourself to yourself. When we are back together and have all the time in the world on our hands, I can fill in the blanks and tell you what you want to know. I've had a complicated life to date, but going forward, I want a less complex existence.'

Suzanne breathed a deep sigh as Theo stood up from the bed and gathered his abandoned clothes from around the cabin.

'I'm due off the ship in two days, so I doubt I'll be able to see you before I go. No-one is to know I'm leaving the ship as it's an agreement Michelle has with the senior management. They believe I will be here all of next week and it will disappoint them to see I've had to leave. She's going to wait until they've realised I'm missing before she tells them I've gone. The longer she has to concentrate on that, the less time she has to connect you to me.' He looked in the refrigerated mini-bar and pulled out two miniature bourbon whisky bottles and poured them into a tumbler. He dropped in a couple of cubes from the ice bucket and gave the glass a swirl. In just a couple of gulps, he finished the refreshing drink. Not his normal tipple, but there was no sweet vermouth available to concoct his favourite, Rob Roy. He put the tumbler on to the silver tray with the sound of the loose ice cubes clinking in the glass. 'A little Dutch courage for what lies ahead before I go!' he exclaimed. 'I'll have my phone on me whilst away. I've put you in there as "Steve" in case anyone nosy searches my phone,' added Theo. He walked back to Suzanne's side of the bed and kissed her on her bare shoulder. 'Nothing stupid whilst I'm away. Keep your bloody head down and lie low.'

In reply, Suzanne gave a wry smile with a gentle nod as she took a long blink with her eyes.

Theo pushed his hand through her soft short hair and ruffled it. He smiled back at her with their faces nose to nose. He pulled back and turned away.

'Phone me when you get to the assignment. Make sure you have enough charge on it,' she demanded.

'Sure. Speak soon,' he replied, as he pulled the door closed behind him.

***

Michelle had been stewing for the last couple of hours and had become increasingly agitated. As her headache subsided, her thoughts concentrated on Theo. She felt an elevated emotional rage inside, but her external appearance gave no clues. She picked up the phone near the dressing table and looked in the mirror as she contacted Henrique, the concierge.

'Sorry for the late request Henrique, but for the private excursion tomorrow, can you kindly arrange for an eloquent picnic to be placed on the boat? I'll leave the contents to you, but champagne is a must. In fact, make it a magnum of champagne if it's available? Also, some cold meats would be nice. If possible, please include rare roast beef, as Theo loves it. I'd like it to be a fusion picnic, so how does sashimi sound? I love tuna and salmon sashimi.'

'That sounds marvellous, Mrs d'Vere. A good basis for me to work on. Looking at our computer, I note that there are no allergies or intolerances to be considered. I'll speak to Executive Chef and ensure it's freshly prepared in the morning,' Henrique concluded.

The phone went down at Henrique's end, as Michelle placed the phone on the receiver. She stared into her own emotionless reflection and mouthed, 'Goodbye, Theo.'

***

Theo looked at his own reflection in the glass of the atrium elevator, using it to enable him to straighten his necktie. The lift bell pinged as he reached the Penthouse Suites deck. He exited and walked along the corridor, took in a few deep breaths in order to compose himself. Arriving at the door to the suite, he presented his keycard, but it did not work. By chance Jose, the butler, was approaching the suite with canapes. He witnessed Theo having a problem with the keycard, so opened the door for him.

Michelle was exiting her bathroom wearing a robe and drying her hair with a towel. 'Sorry I missed your presentation. How did it go?' Michelle asked Theo, with acidity in her tone, whilst ignoring Jose.

Sensing the tension and so as not to interfere, Jose placed the canapes on the side and left diplomatically.

'It went well. As a bonus we sold a lot of merchandise.'

'Great. I grabbed a copy of your book at the theatre entrance. I've read it already. It's very insightful and thought provoking,' Michelle described in a more warming tone, as she turned away, still rubbing her hair dry. She turned back towards Theo and walked over to him as he was removing his jacket and tie. As she stood near him, she could detect the aroma of whisky on his breath. 'It smells like you've been celebrating your success already, but I can go one better than being sat in a bar seeing out the day. To celebrate your success and our anniversary, I've arranged a little surprise for you. Tomorrow they anchor us close to the private cay owned by Destiny. I thought it would be a great opportunity for us to spend some quality time together, alone. I've organised a two-day trip out to the cay on a private speedboat. Knowing you like snorkelling, I've arranged for you to swim with pigs. It's a take on a similar well-known excursion on the Exuma islands that has existed for several years. This one, though, is a private trip just for the two of us. No outside interferences or snoopers. What happens on the island stays on the island, as they say. Afterwards we can take the speedboat to the Destiny hotel on the neighbouring cay where we can stay in their luxury penthouse suite for the night.'

Theo was relieved at the realisation that he had got away with his extended absence. 'Wow! That's some excursion, but you know I am going on an assignment in two days' time, and I need to pack?' he asked matter-of-factly.

'That's no problem. You pack in the morning, and I'll arrange for the butler and concierge to transfer your luggage to the hotel. It will be in the hotel suite, ready for you to take with you the following day. All you need to do is pack an overnight bag. You won't need much in the sense of clothes. Just relax and I'll take care of the rest,' reassured Michelle.

'That sounds good,' said Theo, as he looked concernedly at the discarded flower petals on the carpet. 'What happened here?' as he gestured with open palms at the petals.

'Oh that. I was pulling them off the stalks and was going to throw them romantically over our bed cover when I stumbled and dropped them on the floor just before you came in.'

She turned back towards the full-length mirror, continuing to rub dry her long black hair to the tips. She looked at Theo's reflection, still in deep admiration of his looks and physique, but now with a feeling of emptiness inside. It was his personality that she detested so much. She pulled her robe tighter. She no longer wanted him to see her bare flesh. Theo retreated into his own dressing area and changed into a safari outfit suitable for the afternoon's exploration, for which he was the assigned guide. He reappeared to say goodbye. She exuded a slight smile, but it was now all for show. She realised Theo had withdrawn his love and the journey could only go in one direction. His destiny was in her hands.

CHAPTER SEVEN

They awoke in the morning to the motion of the ship pitching and rolling from side to side. The floating white cotton-wool clouds in the azure Caribbean sky had disappeared. The stateroom view now displayed an inky, black sky. Despite the unsettling weather, breakfast was already being served in their suite when Captain Nico announced over the tannoy. 'Ladies and gentlemen. Good morning and apologies for the interruption. Many of you last night probably felt the ship rocking a little more than normal. This has been because of the approach of the tropical storm "Josephine", which is out of season. As a result, we slowed the speed of the ship down to 9 knots in order to allow you a comfortable night's sleep as far as is in our control. Consequently, we will not be at our anchor point for another hour, but fear not, as the swell will dissipate shortly, and in good time for our tendering process. Enjoy the entertainment the ship has on offer for you this morning and listen out for further disembarkation announcements from our talented Cruise Director, Olly. Thank you.'

Jose entered the suite and started cleaning down the breakfast table.

Michelle announced to Theo, 'I've got an appointment at the spa. Why don't you use the time to pack your belongings and camera equipment into your main suitcase and leave it in the walk-in wardrobe? I've left your empty overnight bag on the bed. There's a luggage tag on the bedside. Be a sweetheart. Fill it in and attach it to the bag.'

Michelle then went over to her walk-in wardrobe and slipped into a loose-fitting blouse, three-quarter length jeans and her pair of luxury towelling slippers, ready for her pedicure and manicure.

'I'll be gone for about an hour. Don't feel rushed, as we have loads of time. We won't be going ashore until the morning tour is back from the island. I've arranged for our excursion to be a private affair so that we are left alone.'

Michelle looked at her watch and realised she had to get a move on to fit in enough time in the spa. She scurried to the door and left.

***

Theo was never comfortable at packing bags, either for going away or for his return home. He scratched his head and wondered where to start. Bottom line was it all had to go in his luggage, as he was not coming back. Packing for an overnighter was much easier as it only meant smart casual attire, toothbrush and underwear. He had his regular snorkelling clothing for what was, for him, a casual affair. He did not have to wear the most up-to-date brand version, as this excursion would not be filmed for the world to see. This was 'day-off' wear. He could get by with swim shorts and a T-shirt to wear on the speedboat. Theo would not even bother with footwear normally, as post-snorkel he expected to be off to the hotel with his overnight bag containing his other possessions. The ship's regulations demanded footwear outside of pool areas. This made him think otherwise. He had a selection of snorkelling equipment at his disposal from which to choose. There were the regular goggles with a separate mouthpiece tube. Then there was a new full-face mask with an integrated air tube that they had given him to trial. He was involved in the original prototype design and was now, a few years later, asked to review the current version and see what improvements he could make. This gave him the ideal opportunity to test the provided kit. Michelle was never one for snorkelling herself, so it was pointless asking her opinion. It wasn't her bag. He finished packing his overnight bag first to make sure he had enough clothes to survive until he saw his suitcase again in the hotel; at which point he would repack again if necessary. He was wary about having his specialist photography bag go with the suitcase to the hotel, but he implicitly trusted the Destiny staff both onboard and land side at the hotel to look after his belongings. It wasn't so much the value of his camera kit, but more of the total inconvenience should anything happen to it. He followed Michelle's instructions and left the packed suitcase and camera kit just outside the walk-in wardrobe for later collection and transfer. He double-checked all the drawers and his bathroom before then adding the luggage tag to his overnight bag. As a guarantee, he filled out a second tag and affixed it to the suitcase.

***

Michelle knew she had tucked up Theo with the chore of packing. She sat back in the spa chair, pleased with herself. Everything was going according to plan. Maisie had already completed the pedicure and was now halfway through the manicure. Michelle had chosen the deepest red nail varnish, which was even more striking given her naturally pale complexion. For once, Mrs Morgan-Brown was not there to oversee the treatment. Some mild relief at least as she thought to herself, this is my time now. She remembered she had to see Olly to let him know she was going to be off the ship overnight. Michelle could not go any faster, as the lacquer still needed to dry. She still felt relaxed as her time was her own and she had to remain focused on what she had planned for the next couple of days. Theo's destiny was in her hands, manicured or not.

'How much longer, Maisie?' she enquired.

Anticipating that Michelle was looking to expedite her departure from her clutches, Maisie brought over a drying machine to accelerate the process.

'Not long now. Just a few minutes,' she reassured

Michelle.

Within ten minutes, the process was over, and Maisie brought the reclined chair back to an upright position. Michelle thanked Maisie and made her way out of the spa to Olly's office.

***

Theo thought of phoning Suzanne's cabin from the suite phone, but he was concerned that Michelle would redial the number. He realised he could call Suzanne first, then afterwards contact Jose with a fictitious question. He picked up the phone and called Suzanne. It was picked up after just one ring. 'Suzanne?' he asked.

'Yes, speaking,' she replied.

'It's me. Listen. I'll be leaving soon, but just stay on your guard. Michelle's been far friendlier than normal. I just don't trust her. I smell a rat, but then again, maybe I'm just being paranoid. She's so relaxed today that it's unnerving. Maybe she's just happy not to see me again for the rest of the week. I don't know. It doesn't make that much sense to me.' He sighed into the mouthpiece.

'Don't worry yourself,' she replied, taking charge. 'It may be seven days until I see you again, but you'll come back safe from the assignment, and I'll stay low as you've asked me to. Now get off the phone before you get caught.' Suzanne blew him a kiss down the phone and said, 'Go. Take care. Remember, I love you.'

Taking the initiative and to ease the pain she felt inside, she put down the phone before Theo could reply. Theo shook his head from side to side and replaced the handset. He paused before he picked up the handset again to speed-dial Jose, the butler, to request the needless ironing of a shirt that he pulled back out of his suitcase as a prop.

***

Olly was busy on his laptop writing his speech for the next

televised morning programme that plays on loop in the cabins. He glanced up and through the open office window blinds he espies Michelle approaching. Without a knock on his ajar door, Michelle walked in and leaned over Olly sitting at his desk.

'I hope this is not an inconvenient time to talk?' said Michelle. 'I need to tell you something, but I don't want everyone to know. It's my wedding anniversary and I'm taking my husband away for the night off the ship. Unfortunately, I won't be available for any godmother obligations. I hope my absence won't be felt too much, but I need some time to myself for privacy. I hope you understand, Olly?'

'Absolutely. No problem. You enjoy yourself. Where on earth are you going for privacy? We are pretty much in the middle of nowhere!' laughed Olly.

'I've been clever. I remembered my good friend Andrea talking to me about the other subsidiaries of the Destiny Luxury Group. She told me about the equally luxurious hotel chain she has created at locations across the world. Near to here, she bought a private island and developed the site. They only opened it earlier this year, but she recommended I should visit it sometime. Now is the time. Secretly, in the background, I've organised this treat.'

Olly had a surprised look on his face. He raised his eyebrows and looked at her from the corner of his eyes. He did not say a word.

'Well, I must be on my way, as I have other things to do before I leave. I'll let you know when I'm back onboard.'

She straightened herself from her stoop and headed out through the door. She strode from behind reception and towards the lifts without a backward glance.

***

Theo heard the cabin door mechanism unlock. Knowing there was no knock accompanying it, he realised it must be Michelle rather than Jose. He had only just chosen the shirt he was going to hand to the butler as a pretence following his phone call to Suzanne. He scrunched the material in his hands.

Michelle noted Theo looked a little furtive and eyed him. He avoided eye contact as he continued to check the shirt for creases.

'I have called Jose to iron this shirt before we disembark,' Theo explained.

'Ok, I am all set after my spa treatment, and I also caught Olly to let him know about our anniversary celebration. I am going to visit "Serenity" up on the sun deck so I can enjoy a bit of escapism before the ship becomes too busy after this morning's excursion. I am looking forward to experiencing this area of peaceful solitude before the mad rush of guests returning to the buffet queue.'

Michelle picked up her wide brimmed, light blue floppy hat plus her oversized tortoiseshell sunglasses and headed to the door. She called for a lift, stepped onto the tempered glass flooring and pressed the sundeck button. She noticed the art deco lights and then arched her neck to look up at the ceiling to admire her own reflection, like a narcissist. As the lift doors opened, she noticed the number of vacant sun loungers with large striped towels and discarded books. No doubt reserved by the same passengers who were enjoying early excursions and standing in line for their buffet lunch. A bugbear of fellow travellers. She exited the lift and meandered through the maze of empty sun loungers. There were some pasty looking individuals, and some who were various shades of crimson coloured skin from their overindulged sunbathing. The different poses included lying face down with a small towel covering their heads or just laid back to ensure complete tan coverage. The assortment of passengers sporting farmer's tans on their arms and legs bemused her. Some of the older couples still insisted on wearing white vests and long socks with their sandals. She was relieved to arrive at the narrowed entrance to "Serenity". A member of staff guarded it in a manner similar to a nightclub bouncer. She was aware from reading the brochure that it contained approximately 25 sun loungers to reduce the number of occupants. Boris was very professional and attentive. He greeted her with a smile that showed that he recognised her as the godmother and guided her like a famous film star to the best location via the sandstone pathway. He explained how she could order anything she desired and fully enjoy the experience.

They left her to ponder the food and drinks menus. She could look and explore the area in more detail in her own time. White masts overhead against a less than perfect azure sky encouraged a peaceful sailing ambiance. The recycled bamboo furniture with lightly striped vanilla and cinnamon-coloured seated pads was surprisingly comfortable. The assorted cushions were forest green and Dijon mustard yellow. There was a low clipped yew hedge surrounding the excluded area and tall bronze ornamental pots containing coloured succulents, including an aptly named x semponium called "Destiny". Large green and bronze ferns were used to flank the sun loungers to add an exotic feel to the design. The stencilled fern motif on the panels completed the look. The slatted false walls allowed the sea breeze to filter through and provide natural ventilation. Overhead, she heard the mellow guitar music, and the water flowed like a waterfall in the background from the hot tub encased in larch slats with yacht varnish to preserve its colour. More water flowed from the adjoining external shower used by guests to remove any trace of sweat beforehand and chlorine after bathing.

She noticed the endless supply of refreshing cool water with the essence of both cucumber and citrus notes being available and poured herself a long drink. As she sipped and savoured the flavour, she decided not to order an alcoholic cocktail because she needed to keep her wits about her. There was also a bowl of assorted fruits and separate dishes of pumpkin and sunflower seeds placed beside the interactive television. She found a pair of Bluetooth black headphones in a sleek ebony box so that she could avoid disturbing the tranquillity of other guests. On a small round wooden table there was a selection of miniature bottles of lotion and moisturisers to use post-dip. Aromatherapy scents wafted across from the masseur table. She also detected a fine mist from the discreet humidifiers. The white flags flapped in the wind behind the Captain's bridge. The unmistakable smell of funnel exhaust fumes competed with the other scents. She heard the approach of the waitress wheeling her trolley containing delicious and healthy food options and accepted a small complimentary plate. After admiring the surrounding arc of large double rectangular windows which split the distinct horizon of the cloudless sky and the deep blue sea, she closed the curtains to create her privacy cocoon, but deliberately left a narrow gap to watch the passing activity. She gazed around the swimming pool and spotted two attractive men of different ages who were holding hands and were engaged in a deep conversation. They were the epitome of toned fitness and sported all over tans that could be the best she had ever seen.

Michelle finished her small plate of perfectly hulled strawberries accompanied by another iced drink. She repositioned herself on the shaded sun lounger, which was covered in a Destiny branded towel. Michelle allowed her head to rest on the cushion. She sensed the slight vibration because of the ship's movement. Soon her eyelids felt heavy, and her thoughts drifted away to the sound of the expert guitarist playing melodic chords and the rocking of the ship. The shadows moved and danced as the sunlight flickered between the overhead masts as the ship changed its course of direction. After a brief deep sleep, she was stirred by a small yellow bird which flew into the clipped yew hedge. She heard it begin its unique melodic birdsong. She checked her watch for the time and realised that she needed to return to her cabin in order to make the final preparations for the excursion and her carefully orchestrated plans. There was no room for error.

***

'Attention. Attention. This is a crew announcement. Shortly, we will undergo a crew emergency training drill. Temporarily, we will suspend guest services. The lifts will be out of order during this exercise. Passengers do not need to respond to this drill. It is for training purposes only. Standby for the sounding of the emergency alarm. The internationally recognised emergency signal of seven short blasts and one long blast of the ship's whistle and alarms. Standby,' came the call over the ship-wide tannoy.

It was a drill announcement Jack must have heard over a hundred times. As a key member of the ship's management team, he had responsibility for planning the events, monitoring their performance and debriefing for the Captain. He varied the drills to test all areas of response. Mindful of not disturbing the paying passengers' enjoyment of the vessel, he still had to incorporate different areas of the ship, both public and crew side. This time it was a simulated fire scenario in a crew-quarters with injuries. They put the crew personnel to the test, as were the systems for hose deployment and the correct functioning of the watertight fire doors. God forbid they would ever have to use them for real, but as the Boy Scouts say, "Be Prepared". Dreaming up new weekly scenarios was far more exciting for Jack than the mundane tweaking of shift rosters and creating fall back plans for security screening if there was an electronic systems failure. The problem with having such high-tech systems aboard was the increased chances of electronic gremlins and having to revert to manual. He was the master of the "What if's". Always thinking outside the box and thinking the unthinkable.

***

Michelle returned to the suite. As she entered, the unmistakable presence of Jose by his silhouette was clear for her to see in the walk-in wardrobe. She saw him holding up a wooden coat hanger and draped off it was a crisply ironed shirt. She heard the shower running in Theo's bathroom. The joyful whistling from the cubicle was competing with the rush of water. Although she detested his whistling as she considered it a relic pastime, the melody was quite pleasant in tone. Without announcing her arrival, she walked deeper into the suite behind Jose's back.

With the acute hearing of a predatory animal and the flexible neck-turn of an owl, Jose glanced to see Michelle out of the corner of his eye. 'Good morning. I will leave you in peace once I have helped Mr d'Vere to pack, ma'am.'

Michelle nodded and replied, 'That's fine. I'm glad you are here, as I need to just check we are all set for leaving the ship. Is everything packed?'

Jose, as sharp as a button, went through the checklist in his mind with the added detail that would pacify Michelle. 'Certainly. Shirts and T-shirts, trousers and shorts, numerous socks, black slip underwear, trainers, shoes, jackets, everything, ma'am. Once the last tender of the morning is back from on shore, I have arranged for a tendering pilot to bring over your chartered speedboat. As we are anchored overnight with a full day here tomorrow, you will have plenty of time to relax and enjoy the amenities of the Destiny hotel. The marine office on shore is happy with the insurance coverage. They reviewed your nautical qualifications and confirmed that they met their requirements. The speedboat is all yours until an hour before we need to set sail.'

Michelle grinned to herself. 'I need to thank my father for that. He was a qualified marine pilot and instilled in me the skills of boating from an early age. How did you manage with my picnic list?'

'That was no problem, thanks to you providing me in good time with your list of delicacies and drink selections. Although there are fifteen common sizes of Champagne bottles available on the ship, the largest one we have in stock is a Jeroboam, which is equivalent to four bottles. It will come with its own chill box. You'll know which one by its weight!' Jose exclaimed.

'I know what you are thinking, Jose with me driving the speedboat. It's more for Theo's enjoyment than mine. He will be the beneficiary. Do still put two glasses in there though so that we can toast the occasion.'

Jose nodded, 'Of course. On the culinary side, your choices are heavy on the protein front. As requested, we have packed a lot of sashimi and raw fillet beef carpaccio. I've balanced that with a mix of healthy bulgur wheat salad and asparagus spears, together with boiled quails' eggs and celery salt. Is ma'am content with my selection, or is there anything I could add for you?'

Michelle stared up at the cabin ceiling for inspiration. 'Is there any overproof vodka available, maybe with some orange juice? And how about some crudites as well? I fancy slicing them myself to the thickness I like, so if there are some fresh chunky carrots and a sharp knife, that would be useful?'

Jose hesitated for a moment but did not want to draw Michelle's displeasure, as his role required him to fulfil the wishes of Destiny's guests. 'If you can give me a few moments, I'm sure I can rustle that up? I'll make sure we add them to the picnic hamper, ma'am. Now, if you would kindly excuse me, I'll get that underway. I'll return for the bags and conclude their transportation to the hotel.' Jose smoothly did an about turn and exited the suite.

With the brief conversation over, Michelle detected the shower had finished, making the whistling even more prominent. True to form, Michelle leaned over to the bedside phone and dialled the most recently called number. Even though he had just left the cabin moments earlier, Jose answered.

Michelle said, 'Sorry, just one more thing. Can I have a

fresh mint Greek yoghurt for the crudites?' She replaced the receiver. She frowned to herself with disappointment.

'Theo, I'm off to the crew drill to show my support. I won't be too long. I'll see you back here.'

***

'No, no, no!' Jack shouted out aloud, as he studied the live CCTV system remotely. 'Starboard side, you idiots, starboard. What are they doing down there on the port side? They're 30 seconds away, but by that time the ship would be up in flames. For God's sake, get a grip.'

The drill was not going to plan. He could feel his heart beating and his pulse racing. To disorientate the emergency fire crew, he had them spun around for 20 seconds before they had to find the mock fire. It mimicked them flinging themselves out of bed in the middle of the night. They could not complete these drills at night as it would be too problematic with the ship full of passengers who were retiring to bed. The smoke canister had added to the confusion. The impact upon them was supposed to be proportionate to the realities of the emergency they could be dealing with, but the ineptitude shown was outside the boundaries of acceptability. I've seen nothing like it, he thought. At this rate, they would have to call this an outright failure and do it all again in the next few days. He could not call a halt to the exercise, as it would be obvious to the other crew involved that there was a failure and those responsible would be identifiable. The company's ethos was to learn from such mistakes and move forward. Never look back. Not on the same wavelength as Jack's, but he was Destiny through and through. He lived and breathed the corporate message. It was not his position to challenge it. Others above his paygrade make those decisions. He was there to enforce it and provide feedback. Jack could always advise, but the bottom line was to accept decisions made and sell the direction to those below him that he could influence. He also knew the contempt some of the drill staff would have towards the senior management on the ship and himself when they later announced they had to do the whole fire emergency drill again. Another day, the crew would have their precious downtime interrupted. Time they would never get back. Fools, he thinks. Damn fools.

***

Michelle had been wandering along the decks where the crew have been performing their drills. She had been giving the impression that she was encouraging the staff in their drill exercises. In reality, she was hunting for Janik. As he was a mid-level supervisor, she was sure that she will find him in charge of something during the drill. She meandered between the muster stations and finally found him with a fluorescent tabard and clipboard in hand. The "Supervisor" baseball cap was a giveaway. The call over the tannoy instructed all crew to stand down from the drill and return to their normal duties. Janik directed his two remaining assistants to remove the muster station signs and return to their duties at the casino. Now left alone, Michelle approached him.

'I wonder if we could have a quiet little private chat, Janik. Maybe at the coffee shop.'

'Mrs d'Vere, I can talk with you about official matters, but I'm in no position to hold "private chats" with any passenger, no matter what their position onboard.'

'Come, come Janik. I'm sure you can find five minutes for me. I need to know who that lady was in the casino. It would be in your best interest if you helped me with that.'

'What do you mean by that Mrs d'Vere?'

'Please Janik, you can call me Michelle. Do you remember when you used to call me Michelle before?'

She leaned forward and whispered into his ear. 'Do you remember being this close to me and whispering my name into my ear when you weren't allowed? Now we wouldn't like your bosses to find out about that, now that you have risen to the dizzy heights of casino manager, would we, Janik? Just one name and we can forget about this.'

Janik paused for a second and looked at Michelle with his steely blue eyes before he pulled himself away from her.

'Ok, I have a name, and that name is Mrs d'Vere. That's who I know you as, and that is how it will remain. Don't threaten me, Mrs d'Vere. Passenger confidentiality is important to the Destiny Luxury Group, but even more so, it's doubly important to Janik Stoicov. The Stoicov family is a proud family. Rich in values. I knew you when I was a lot younger and somewhat impressionable, but I have grown up a lot since then. I've seen the torture of war. You don't compare to the hurt and suffering I have been through. You don't scare me. My faith and belief are strong. When I walk the narrow alleys of my hometown of Sibenik, I seek salvation in front of the statue of the Virgin Mary in the Lourdes Grotto, alongside the church of St Lawrence. I reflect, pray, and meditate. It clears my mind and conscience. Afterwards I sip a coffee in the monastery gardens above the grotto. The only time I will be physically above our blessed Lady. All other times she is above me, looking down and guiding me, like she is now. I suggest you do as I'm about to do. Walk away.'

With that, Janik turned and walked away. He removed his fluorescent yellow baseball cap and tabard as he did so. Janik secreted them in a cupboard at the muster station, then carried on towards the casino. He did not look back.

Michelle laughed out loud. First a soft laugh that gathered momentum to such a degree that two passing passengers turned their head towards her. Michelle walked in the opposite direction to locate a lift back to her suite.

The earlier mention of Storm Josephine drew in echoes within Michelle's thoughts. She moved towards the thick silver and turquoise-coloured curtains shielding the balcony doors. She pulled them back along the runners to reveal the lace net curtains. Pulling those back parallel to the outer curtains enabled her to have a clearer view outside. The sea conditions were not as calm as first thing this morning. There was no landfall with which to compare the movement of palm trees, but she could tell with her nautical training that the swell on the sea was just that bit frothier. She could see the first of the ship's tenders returning from the morning's excursion. Unwavering to her with her strong sea legs, she did not think that would be the same for everyone on the tender. She switched on the smart TV and searched for the ship's weather channel. Most passengers would only ever focus on the outdoor temperature and the likelihood of bright sunshine or rain. Few ever focus on the wind speed and sea conditions, even on a tendering day. They thought that the sea parts like it did for biblical Moses in the Red Sea. She noted the forecast was for winds of up to 26 knots, very much on the brink of small boats or tenders remaining a viable option. The decision by the First Officer earlier in the day to allow passengers off by tender in the first place forced the hand of the Captain to allow the tenders to return to the ship. As the tenders were also the ship's lifeboats, it was imperative that they all return as to allow for enough lifeboat coverage for all crew and passengers. For a moment Michelle thought all her plans would be blown out of the water, literally. She had to convince the Captain to let her go ashore and return tomorrow. Michelle heard the buzz of an electric toothbrush emanating from Theo's bathroom. She realised that she only had two minutes to make a call. She knew the number for the bridge and made a direct call. The Navigator answered. In the background she heard a heated discussion between the unmistakable voices of the Captain, and another she took to be the First Officer because of the topic. She asked if she could have a moment to speak with Captain Nico. After a brief pause, Captain Nico came on the phone. The Navigator had forewarned him that Michelle was on the line.

'Captain, I need to ask a favour. I've made detailed plans

to leave the ship to go ashore this afternoon and overnight. The tenders are returning to the ship. I was planning to leave after the last one pulls alongside. Would that still be possible?'

'Michelle, the sea conditions are getting choppier by the minute. We must be prepared to stop operations immediately after the last tender arrives back. The storm will not hit us directly, but it is close enough to cause us some discomfort tonight. By tomorrow morning, the storm will have passed, and conditions will quickly improve. Can your journey not wait until tomorrow morning?' asked Captain Nico.

Michelle was expecting this suggestion and retorted with, 'Perhaps we can compromise. How would you feel if I was to depart just prior to the last tender returning? That way, I have departed during your window of operation on my own navigational course, and I would not, technically, be under your responsibility. I wouldn't be a burden to you. I don't know if you know of my nautical qualifications, but I am licensed to operate in these sea conditions and even during hours of darkness. Please, I intend to finish an excursion I have planned within an hour of leaving the ship and, by any means, be safely within the sheltered private marina of the Destiny Hotel within an hour and a half.'

'Michelle, if I said yes, then it would be against my better judgement. My legal obligations to you and my moral obligations to you may be two different things, but they are two things I would not usually separate. Your request drives a stake through me. Legally, I cannot stop you. I can only advise you. You are making your own judgements based on your own wants, needs and, importantly, what you think are your abilities. I am not one to judge. If you wave a piece of paper in front of me, who am I to question those who have professionally tested your maritime capabilities? You understand if you leave under those circumstances, then on your head be it.'

There was a momentary silence. Michelle drew a light

sigh loud enough to be heard on the phone line. 'Captain Nico, I wholeheartedly accept your honest advice and thoughts on this delicate subject, however I am a grown-up woman, and I don't take the decision to ask you lightly. I have considered the risks against the rewards and on balance I would like to go ahead with my intention of leaving the ship this afternoon. Thank you for your understanding.'

'Very well Michelle, I will give instructions to security to allow you and whoever you will be enduring this adventure with, to depart the vessel as you have described, and I look forward to your safe return tomorrow.'

The Captain hung up the phone and called Jack's ship mobile to instruct him on the agreed arrangements.

'Captain, I will oversee their departure and see if I can persuade Mrs d'Vere to reconsider her journey.'

Theo exited his bathroom with the towel wrapped and tucked in around his waist. His hair was still damp, but he did not mind. He knew he would swim in the sea sooner than later. Theo put on a light-weight unbranded blue T-shirt and similar casual swimming shorts. He would spend most of his time floating on top of the water, enjoying the marine life whilst snorkelling. It was not a fashion parade. He was not wearing socks, just a pair of laced white trainers. Probably the most popular and common brand on the planet. They would dry out if they got wet. He had already packed his suitcases, along with his camera bag, for filming later, on assignment.

'Have you got everything together and ready?' questioned Michelle, from the cream chaise longue.

'Yeah, I'm ready. The suitcases are by the bed. My camera bag is on it,' clarified Theo.

'Look, you race ahead, and I'll meet you at the disembarkation point down on deck 3. I'm just waiting for the last couple of nails to dry. Can you be a sweetheart, and on the way down, pop into the florist and put a hold on my fresh flowers until I'm back on board later tomorrow?

That way, they'll look fresher for longer upon my return. In the meantime, I'll call Jose to take the bags down,' instructed Michelle whilst blowing furiously at her painted fingernails on both hands.

'I thought you just had a manicure at the spa?' called out Theo from the bedroom.

'I did, but I just re-read the excursion notes and it explicitly says not to wear red nail varnish because it negatively attracts wildlife,' Michelle explained.

Theo replied he would do as she wished, and he would catch up with her at the gangway. With no sense of urgency, he departed from the cabin and went on his way.

Michelle gave it 10 seconds. She pushed herself up off the chaise longue and moved over to the bed. She lifted Theo's camera bag off and hid it under the bed. 'He won't be needing that anytime soon,' she said aloud to herself. She reached over to the bedside phone and contacted Jose. She informed him that the bags for the hotel were now by the bed and ready for the arranged transfer to the hotel, instructing them not to be loaded onto the transfer boat until Theo and her had left for the excursion on the speedboat. The reason was that there was a surprise in the bags, and she did not want Theo to have the chance of seeing it. A plausible excuse, but a total lie. She did not want Theo to see that his camera bag was not there. She collected her belongings and proceeded to the gangway.

Michelle arrived at the gangway with her blue floppy sun hat and favourite sunglasses. She was, of course, recognisable to Jack, who was now controlling the security screening together with the disembarkation and embarkation duties. This was not only because he had two security staff in isolation because of the norovirus, but he was on behalf of the Captain about to try to dissuade Michelle from leaving the ship. Theo was there already, awaiting Michelle's arrival.

'Mrs d'Vere,' said Jack. 'They have docked your speedboat alongside the gangway pontoon for the last ten minutes. Since that time the sea swell has already increased. The waves are already lapping against it. It's already looking like it's going to be north of Beaufort force 5. That's quite choppy. Are you sure you want to set off in these conditions? It could get worse before it gets better.'

'Mr Shaw. No doubt Captain Nico has put you up to this. I appreciate yours, or his concern, but I've faced much worse. It is now or never if we are ever to see the pigs swimming,' retorted Michelle.

'There is always next week,' stated Jack, but Michelle responded with, 'But then again, it wouldn't be our 10th wedding anniversary. It's no fun then. Anyhow, where's your sense of adventure? We'll be fine, but thank you anyway.'

'I did not mean to be discourteous, but the safety of our passengers is paramount. In that case, can you please touch out both of your keycards, so the records show you are off the ship?'

Theo and Michelle clicked their respective cards on the system, which would record their extended absence.

Jack thought he was acting resolute, but Mrs d'Vere appeared to be built of carbon. He had done his best, but she had the final say it appeared. Jack beckoned for the speedboat to be brought forward to the middle of the pontoon. It was the first time Michelle had set eyes upon it. It was a formidable beast. Gleaming white. It was of exceptional beauty. Eight seats for a two-seater occupancy. A powerful 300hp engine to the stern, with a reserve smaller fallback engine alongside. The sound of them ticking over was impressive by itself. The acrid smell of ethanol fumes in the air announced the engine's presence. A loud gurgling noise from the underwater output only just drowned out the creaking of the compressed buoys between the two crafts. Michelle was looking forward to experiencing its performance. It was bobbing up and down on the swell like a seal. Theo looked a little concerned, and Jack even more so. The wet ropes became taut and squeezed the boat against the pontoon.

'Give me a hand down please,' demanded Michelle as she moved towards the side of the speedboat. With the forearm to forearm grip, they helped her down. Theo remembered the drill to getting on a boat from his exploration in the Galapagos Islands, where it was a daily ritual to clamber in and out of rib boats.

'Sit down, Theo. You're making the place look untidy,' quipped Michelle.

Theo had a bag across his body that contained his snorkelling kit. There was now no exact rhythm to the speedboat pitching and rolling. He just had to go with where the movement took him. One of the docking crew jumped on to the boat to receive the light brown wicker picnic hamper Jose had collected from the galley. Despite the warnings from the crew member handing it down, the weight of it shocked the docker. He fell back but steadied himself at the last moment before he would have hit the speedboat deck.

'What's in here? A dead body!' he joked.

Michelle snapped her head around to look at him. She frowned but stayed silent. She just as quickly rotated her head back and looked over the small glass shield between her at the controls and the bow of the speedboat. A couple of seconds later, she turned to the crew member and shouted, 'Are you still on here? You are putting us in danger. I need to pull away so, for God's sake, get off, man.'

The crew member accelerated his exit from the speedboat and onto the pontoon. He sharply pulled his trailing leg out of the way before she could trap it between the two vessels. A close call, seen by Theo all too often. Michelle increased the revs on the speedboat as the ship's pontoon crew pushed her away. It didn't take long for her to pull away.

'We'll see you tomorrow,' she yelled over the engine noise, and without a second glance, increased the engine output enough to take the front of the hull out of the water.

Tomorrow? thought Theo to himself. She must have been excited by the moment and forgot that he was not due back on board now because of his assignment. He was already getting a bit of an adrenaline rush as the speedboat crashed in to every third or fourth wave. A rougher ride than he had expected, but safe all the same. Michelle, for all her other faults, certainly knew how to master a boat in these conditions. He would give her that.

'We're going to go swimming with pigs,' declared Michelle loudly over the sound of the 300hp engine. 'Or, to be more precise, you'll be swimming with them. I'm staying on the boat. I'll observe. That's enough for me. We can enjoy the picnic once you are back on board, having enjoyed your snorkelling. Stay in the water as long as you like. That will give me more time to prepare it for your return. I understand that drinking Champagne before snorkelling isn't the best feeling once you take in your first accidental gulp of sea water.'

'You're not wrong there. The tourist boats in Cancun, Mexico entice you on to their two-hour snorkelling tours with the lure of bottomless beers and cola. You want to see the colour these people go when that happens. I don't think there's a word invented yet for that colour of green,' elaborated Theo.

Michelle emitted out a polite laugh, but only she realised at that moment just how false that appreciation sounded. The island that Michelle was heading for was out of sight of the ship, just on the edge of the horizon. Destiny Celebration had moved just that bit further away from the cay where the pigs lived, once the morning excursions there had returned to the ship. They moved the ship closer to the island, where most of the afternoon excursions would be based, to prepare for after-lunch afternoon disembarkations for guided tours. This was an inconvenience for Michelle, but it helped her with what she had in mind.

Before long, the cay was coming into sight. Being a low-lying island with virtually no trees, and only diminutive growing compact shrubs. She approached from the windward side; however, the pig beach was on the other side, the leeward side. That should guarantee a much smoother sea and steady anchoring. The ship was anchored in the dark blue sea, which they had left behind. They progressed towards the island. The sea was getting distinctively lighter and clearer, and more the recognisable emerald waters. The balmy, warm breeze seemed to envelop them. Rounding the headland, they both saw several different coloured pigs on the beach. Some were much larger than others. It was a sight to behold. You could even distinguish some of the different pig families by how the piglets were close to the sow. There were some with random black and white patches. Some had a pale pink coat; very much like the generic description everyone had in their mind that they associate with the 'pig' word. Some were laying down with others literally trotting around. There were no other signs of civilisation to the naked eye. Signs of manmade items were dotted around. Blue butts, which might have once held pig food, were found discarded. There was a hand-built low reed shelter to offer the pigs some shade on what would otherwise be an unshaded landscape. There was a hollow excavated area on the beach that appeared to be a mud bath. What was a bit of a surprise to Michelle was that there were no pigs in the water! She presumed they just soaked and paddled in it all day. She cut the boat's engine to an idle as she drifted in on the tide towards the shore. The colour of the water had been for the last few minutes a turquoise blue but now changed to clear water. She saw the rippled sand under water, and upon closer inspection, could view the sea creatures. Michelle went to drop a light anchor over the hull and as she did so she saw what was quite unexpected for her, three or four stingrays. She recalled they had a spike just below where the body and tail meet, and that they could be deadly. Her recollections of the facts were not that proportionate. Yes, there had been deadly encounters between stingrays and man, but the number of fatalities for man was, in fact, miniscule. She then glimpsed a sea turtle. What a gracious creature. Serene and a wonderment to anyone who saw one swimming in nature. The attempts to protect and preserve them were legendary across the globe. Here was one right beneath her boat. Shoals of smaller fish swam around, and then Michelle spotted something she had been half hoping to see, but it astounded her nonetheless. The sight of sharks. For her, they had only one notoriety. They were killers. The stories that they could smell a single drop of blood from a mile away. Their rows of razor-sharp teeth. A fear instilled in man, and for a good reason.

Theo was already swishing his hands in the water. Michelle thought that very brazen but did nothing to stop him. If he wanted to annoy the fish, and especially the sharks, then let him. They both saw the first few pigs wandering off the beach and towards their boat. The closer they got, the bigger they looked. Quite menacing, with a significant presence. That had some balance, but Michelle was thinking just how mean they looked close up.

'It's time for that snorkel, Theo,' she called out to him. He was already ahead of the game. Theo had removed his training shoes and was in swimming shorts and a T-shirt. He pulled apart the opening of the string bag, which contained his snorkel full-face mask. The string bag allowed it to drain and dry easier post usage, and ready to go back into storage. Theo clipped the breathing tube into the top of the face mask. He checked the float ball was within the tube and it was moving freely up and down.

Michelle was not paying that much attention, as she had undone the straps on the wicker picnic basket. After all, a snorkel mask is a snorkel mask, right? Theo prepared the inside of the mask by spitting a small bit of saliva in to his four fingers and rubbing it on the inside of the perspex screen. Michelle had seen other snorkellers and indeed other divers do this with their masks, so knew it was time for Theo to descend into the water. Michelle removed her floppy hat and large sunglasses. She wanted to see clearly what she was about to do. Theo positioned himself on the side edge of the boat. If he was scuba diving, he would proficiently roll backwards off the side of the boat, allowing the water tank to break the water's surface. As a snorkeller, he preferred to just slide forward off the boat as he was going to land on the shallow floor beneath, whilst holding his mask with one hand. He wriggled his bum to get himself in the right position whilst holding on to the outer ropes. Happy with his position, he steadied himself once more for balance. Michelle had got the boat perfect with no roll. The full-face snorkel mask was sitting over his forehead and hairline. With both hands, he pulled the face mask down over his face. He tugged any stray strands of his hair from around the mask rim and ensured it fitted tightly. Theo made a minor adjustment to one strap. He was now seconds' away from plunging into the ocean. His bare feet felt the water, which seemed quite cool, but in fact he knew that by the time his body temperature acclimatised, it would feel like a warm bath. Michelle was crouching on the floor with the picnic basket open. The twisted second strap was more difficult to open than the first one. She did not panic. This was not the time for alarm or to change her mind. She reached into the hamper and found the Champagne's cool box. She pulled out the bottle. There was condensation on the bottle and around its neck. She grabbed a white napkin and wiped the condensation away. She took a tight grip on the bottleneck and had it pointing upwards. It felt as heavy as she expected. A couple of times, she relaxed her slender fingers and re-gripped the bottle. Like a tennis player making a serve, she drew the bottle back behind and over her head. Theo made the final adjustments to the mask, giving it a little twist from side to side until he was comfortable. He stopped his drill to kiss the Gemini pendant on its silver chain. It was his personal good luck ritual he always performed before he entered the water. He then raised up both hands to the side of his face, next to his eyes. It blocked his peripheral vision, but he did not need that again until he was in the water. Michelle positioned herself behind Theo, and at a distance, she estimated that should she swing the bottle, it would catch him on his head.

'This is for you, Theo,' she announced in a calm and controlled voice.

Theo turned his head about ninety degrees to his right to see what Michelle had for him. He did not have time to see what it was. With all her might, Michelle squeamishly squeezed her eyes shut and swung the Jeroboam bottle like a tennis volley at the net. The brutal force of the impact caught Theo squarely on the temple to render him unconscious. He instantly dropped like a stone landing face first in the water. No sound emanated from Theo. Within moments, his still body was tossing in the water. His feet dragged along the floor bed, breaking the sand ripples as he drifted. Theo's shorts had filled with air in the same way they do when you jump in a swimming pool. His head was face down, with his arms outstretched to the side. There was a trickle of blood from the side of Theo's ear that dyed the water, destroying its otherwise perfect crystalline appearance. A similar but heavier stream of blood appeared from his right hand. The severity caused a slick of bright red blood to appear on the water's surface. Its distribution was getting wider by the second. Michelle wasted no time. It was legendary that pigs ate anything. She had planned for this, and they would help her with the disposal of Theo. That there were also sharks present was an added bonus. The scenario had worked out perfectly and, in fact, better than she had expected. She unwrapped the cling-filmed plates that contained the special food requests. The whole carrots she genuinely ordered to feed the pigs were now redundant, but she might as well throw them in the water now, to whet their appetite. In went the raw fish and very rare beef carpaccio. The sharks were playing right into her hands. Before long, Theo's limp body was attracting the attention of the pigs, stingrays, and the sharks. As ruthless as she was, Michelle could not stop and watch what she expected was about to happen. She pulled up the anchor, returned to the driver's seat, started the engines up and put it in to forward. She faced out to the open sea and sped away. The speedboat's wake behind her pushed Theo's body in towards more approaching pigs that were walking into the wash. His body was ebbing and flowing on top of the sea, getting forever closer to the shore. In this heat and sun, Michelle thought his body would not take long to completely disappear.

CHAPTER EIGHT

Michelle cut the revs on the speedboat engine as she guided it into the private marina of the Azzurro Cay Mirage Hotel. She brought the boat to a standstill. Michelle had in the last thirty minutes since leaving Theo in the water, time to gather all her thoughts. She felt as if her heart rate was returning down to normal, but she was still feeling clammy. Was it the humidity or was it the nerves? Probably a bit of both. She extricated the high-proof vodka from the hamper and poured it over her hands, rubbing them together. They were bloodless anyhow, but she wanted to be sure. She soaked a cloth napkin in the same vodka and wiped down the Champagne bottle from top to bottom, replacing it into its own cool box and sneaked it back into the hamper. She fiddled about with the two clasps and got them secured. Michelle ran her fingers through her dark silky hair, and put her favourite blue floppy hat on her head, accompanied by her trademark sunglasses. Looking at her own reflection in the smart dials set into the perfectly polished yacht-varnished fascia. She was content with her appearance. Increasing the boat speed from idle, she glided into the marina of the Destiny owned hotel. She gathered together Theo's day bags and her own tote bag containing some essential items, including her clutch bag, and prepared them for collection for when she moored the boat. Michelle reached inside Theo's day bag and removed his mobile phone. She reached over the side of the boat and released it into the depths of the ocean. The hotel staff, aware of her due arrival that afternoon and having tracked her via the security CCTV, proactively sent a bellboy out to greet her. Her cool persona disguised anything untoward about having happened. With caution, she navigated the low revs and docked the boat next to the cream marble boardwalk. The boat remained unaffected by the strong winds in the marina's shelter. It was steady enough for her to throw a mooring rope to the bellboy. With the engines on idle, the bellboy pulled it forward a few feet and secured it to a mooring pole with a round turn and two half hitches knot. Michelle turned off the engines, left the day bags in the boat well, and started her gradual ascent of the short steel ladder, treading carefully as she stood on each interlaced wooden step.

'Welcome to the Azzurro Cay Mirage Hotel, ma'am,' greeted the bellboy with a welcoming smile.

She handed him the speedboat key and demanded, 'Have those two bags in the boat transferred to my room, along with that hamper there. It's quite heavy and there's nothing of you, so please be careful. I don't want to see them floating out to sea from my balcony.'

The bellboy wasted no time in descending into the boat and getting onto the small walkie-talkie hanging off his belt to ask for some more help from the desk. Although the blood orange sunset was creating an attractive glare off the water, its effect was diminishing by the minute. Michelle insisted on keeping on her large-framed sunglasses. With a small black clutch bag in her hand, she strolled towards the marina-side entrance to the hotel. The doors were as decorative as all the doors aboard the Destiny ship. A gold-coloured, framed door with smoked glass that you could just about see through. She could make out the vague silhouette of a member of the Concierge desk wearing traditional doorman dress you would find at any top-class hotel around the world. Not a unique design Destiny could lay claim to, but becoming. They pushed outwards the door towards her to coincide with her arrival.

'Good afternoon, ma'am.' The formalities just kept

coming. She ignored the individual and walked straight on through to the foyer. The marble floor design continued from outside to inside, in a seamless transition. The lobby was very well lit with a modern chandelier, festooned with filament bulbs, glowing a golden orange colour. One difference she could tell was the air conditioning at work. So cool compared to the humidity on the sheltered boardwalk outside. The reception counter up ahead appeared to be carved from one continuous piece of dark mahogany. There were Tiffany lamps at each receptionist position. There was no separate line for suite guests as there were ample open positions for all guests to be received and dealt with in a brief time. The corporate use of high-grade technology allowed the receptionists to identify guests registered on the booking system as they approached the desk.

A lady of West Indian heritage looked up from her screen and gave a beaming smile to Michelle as she approached. Her bright white smile against her dark complexion made the greeting feel even warmer.

'Good evening, Mrs d'Vere. Welcome to the Hotel. Your main suitcases arrived ahead of you from the ship and are already in your room. I hope you had a pleasant trip from the ship. The sea has been a little angry this afternoon.'

'It has indeed, but I'm all the better for it. You need to be tested now and then to keep your wits about you,' she replied.

'As per your request, we have assigned you a penthouse suite on the top floor, without a butler. However, should you require anything, then please call down here to reception or go through one of your suite's TVs. It really is no different to the service you have experienced already on the Destiny Celebration. The Destiny Luxury Group believe in synergy.'

'Good to know,' answered Michelle.

In the background, two bellboys rushed to the foyer towards the lifts with the two day-bags and the heavy hamper. They entered the lifts and disappeared out of sight.

'Here is your room card. This card will cover all expenses incurred during your stay in the hotel and its surrounding grounds, bars, and restaurants. I have two messages for you. The first is from Ms Andrea Kennedy, our CEO, who also warmly welcomes you here today and hopes you have a wonderful time with us. To help that along, she has instructed us to absorb all your expenditure. The hotel is yours. Please enjoy the facilities we provide and don't worry about any cost. She absolutely insists on spoiling you and she tells us she won't take no for an answer!'

'Well, that is welcoming news. The next time I speak with her, I will indeed thank her for her generosity. What was the second message?'

'The second message was for me to inform you that your husband, Mr d'Vere, is currently on the hotel's private golf course.'

Michelle showed no emotion or surprise. 'Is he indeed? I wasn't expecting that.'

'Looking at our systems here, if he is with his assigned golf buggy, he is at present at the 13th hole. On my reckoning, he should be back here within 90 minutes or at latest by sunset,' clarified the receptionist. 'He has already been to the room and assigned his own keycard.'

'Thank you for that. I look forward to his return.' Michelle put the keycard into her clutch bag and headed towards the lifts. An observing bellboy, in anticipation of her arrival, headed over to the lifts to summon one. Right on time, one pinged on its arrival and out stepped the original two bellboys, who were returning to the Concierge lectern. The new bellboy held the lift door whilst Michelle entered. He instructed her to tap the room key card token against the panel so that the lift could take her to the correct floor. Being a Penthouse Suite guest, it would override anyone else trying to call the lift. She would therefore have an express service like onboard the ship.

The extravagant privileges just never stop coming, she thought to herself.

The smoked glass walls of the lift enabled her to look at her own reflection. Her heart was racing now, either out of fear or anxiety. She reached the top floor and exited the lift. It was eerily quiet, as if no other soul existed. Her suite was at the end of the corridor, taking up the corner of the building. Upon approaching the suite door, the door handle went from looking like any other door handle to glowing green around its periphery. The proximity of her keycard activated the unlocking mechanism. All she had to do was turn the handle to enter. She rotated the handle a quarter of a turn and walked into her room. The opulent suite was of a substantial size. Not too dissimilar to her suite on the ship. It had two large bedrooms, two elegant marble bathrooms, a dining area and a sitting area. The corner had patio doors on two sides, opening up to a spacious sandstone patio. There was an outdoor dining area on one side, and two luxury padded recliners on the other. From either side, you looked out over the ocean and the extensive gardens and challenging golf course below. The two suitcases forwarded on to the hotel from the ship were standing upright alongside the wardrobe, with day bags placed neatly alongside a canvas fold-out wooden stand for ease of unpacking. They placed the hamper on a side unit next to one of the televisions, with a convenient black minibar fridge underneath. She inspected the rest of the suite. Upon inspection, she observed that someone had used one of the spacious shower cubicles. There was the distinctive scent of men's deodorant. A blue and white electric toothbrush was standing up next to the washbasin, alongside a small travel bag that contained a razor and shaving gel. She went back to the main bedroom and saw one of the wardrobe doors was only partially closed. She pulled open the door to see an unrecognisable, medium-sized tan coloured designer suitcase. A change of casual clothes was hanging up on a couple of coat hangers together with a suit carrier, leaving another thirty or so coat hangers clanking together on the rail. That high-pitch noise annoyed her, even more so when on a swaying ship. Being on dry land tonight, they would not interfere with her sleep pattern.

She returned to the balcony and looked back out again across the impressive panorama of the privately owned golf course. The natural light was fading now, following the warm orange sunset. Evidenced by the automated lighting system around the complex, illuminating the lamps a few at a time. Even the balcony lights had come on with a soft glow. Looking below, she could make out that there was a single golf buggy parked about 50 yards away next to a building that she took to be the Clubhouse. She could make out a solitary figure walking back towards the hotel. Long meaningful strides bringing them ever closer. Michelle returned to inside the suite and closed the patio door behind her. She went over to the bedroom dressing table and removed her sunglasses. Michelle looked at her reflection in the mirror and ran her fingers through her hair to even it out. She heard the unlocking of the main suite door and the unmistakable sound of it opening. Michelle took a couple of steps and entered the living room, where she had a direct line of sight with the suite door. She pressed a button on the wall that closed all the curtains and shutters. The door was being closed by a man, about six feet tall, of an athletic build. He was wearing a collared navy-blue golf shirt, matching blue straight-legged golf trousers and smart brown leather shoes.

Michelle quipped, 'I was told that Mr d'Vere was here. It looks like I'm not mistaken?'

'Indeed, you are not Michelle,' he replied with his trademark grin.

'I've missed you, Spencer. Thank you for coming.'

'I've missed you too, Michelle,' he said as he walked confidently towards her. He gripped her right hand with his left hand, and with his right hand, he reached around the back of her head and pulled her towards him. His fingers lightly brushed through her long, dark, silky hair. They passionately kissed and embraced. With Michelle's left hand, she used her forefinger to run it down the side of his neck. She reached down to the front of his T-shirt and undid the two buttons around his neck. With both hands, she slowly untucked his T-shirt from within the trouser belt line. She took a grip of the T-shirt hem with both hands and lifted it over Spencer's head. The T-shirt turned inside out in the process and caught on a chain and pendant around his neck. Spencer used a spare hand to hold on to the chain and untangle the precious medallion. He had the medallion from such a young age and cared for it dearly. Michelle tossed the T-shirt to the floor towards the wardrobe. She pushed Spencer on to the bed. They slowly undressed each other whilst they continued to kiss each other on the lips and around their necks. It was only a short time before they were on top of the sheets making love.

***

They both laid back under the Egyptian white cotton bedsheets, with shoulders resting against the two luxury silk pillows, and their heads against the tall velvet burgundy headboard.

'Where's Theo?' asked Spencer.

'Your brother is on one of his assignments. I don't know when he'll be back, but it won't be this week,' replied Michelle. 'In fact, I've got a bit of a surprise for you. I'm glad you enjoyed your golf this afternoon. You'll be able to play again tomorrow morning following breakfast, but after that we can't stay here.'

'I thought we were going to be together for the entire week?' questioned Spencer.

Michelle was slipping naked out from under the bedcovers and walking towards the wicker hamper basket. She undid the two fiddly straps on it.

'We are going to be together, but not as you thought. I thought we would have a bit of extra excitement and play a little game. For the last week, Theo has been on the cruise ship. People are expecting to see him back onboard tomorrow, and I don't want to disappoint them. I'm taking you back to the ship with me tomorrow afternoon. You are going to pretend you are, Theo.'

'You are kidding me, right?' questioned Spencer.

'I'm deadly serious. I'll brief you on who the people are onboard who know or met Theo last week. You just need to keep your wits about you, and it'll be a breeze. Don't panic and everything will be fine.' Michelle reached into the hamper and pulled out two crystal champagne flutes.

'I'm sorry that this isn't chilled, but I didn't have time to take it from the cool box and put it in the minibar fridge. I brought it from the ship so that we can celebrate properly.' She undid the foil wrapper and cork guard on the Jeroboam bottle of Champagne. Even under control, it still prematurely popped and effervesced everywhere. She placed the bottleneck into the glasses one at a time to catch the contents. Regaining control of the pour, she topped each of them up. She held on to one glass and, with her right hand, placed the other into Spencer's left hand. In anticipation of this, he had pushed himself into an upright seating position in bed.

She proposed a toast, 'To us, fantasy and fun.'

Spencer replied, 'To us.'

They clinked the two glasses together in unison and both took a sip. Michelle more so than Spencer. She took Spencer's glass out of his hand and placed it down on the bedside table underneath the Tiffany lamp. With her glass, she poured it over his chest and down his smooth torso as she licked it off him and tenderly bit his nipples. Spencer slid himself back down into a horizontal position as the Champagne reached his inner thigh. Michelle worked her way down his body as Spencer arched his body in reaction to her every movement. The intensity of their passion was building with every passing moment. Before long, they were both lost in time. Michelle twice more reached over for the champagne bottle to douse Spencer again. Her lips could not work fast enough to contain the bubbles oozing off his body. She thought nothing of using the champagne bottle that had been used to knock out Theo, and then consuming its contents with his brother Spencer in such an erotic way. She was as cold as the chilled champagne itself.

A couple of hours later, Michelle came round from her snooze with Spencer. She rested her head on his naked chest. He was laid back, resting his own head on the soft eiderdown pillows, with shallow breathing barely audible. As Michelle pulled her head away, Spencer's eyes slowly opened, and he looked down at her, raising a gentle smile. 'Are you serious about us going on to the ship?' he asked.

Michelle took a moment to sit herself up and reach for a silk bathrobe supplied with the suite. Sitting on the edge of the bed facing away from Spencer, she looked back at him over her right shoulder and with no facial expression says, 'Of course I am. I've thought this all through. As long as you follow my explicit instructions, it'll go without a hitch. You'll have to put everything I tell you to memory. You can't take any notes,' she emphasised.

'That's going to be tough. I'm not renowned for my memory. I can hardly remember a birthday or people's names. Especially if they mean nothing to me or they can't help me progress in life. There are so many wasters out there. I need a drink on the back of this,' said Spencer as he reached down beside the bed for his blue polka dot boxer shorts. He stood up to put them on and then walked over to the minibar. He pulled together the components for his favourite spirit drink and poured it out. The first drink he consumed in three mouthfuls before he poured out a second. 'I'm ready. Tell me more.'

Michelle took a seat on the sunken sofa in the living room area. She beckoned Spencer over to join her on the sofa. As Spencer made his way to the sofa, he commanded the intelligent speaker system to play music. Within seconds, it filled the suite with lively rock music playing through multiple speakers. As Spencer took a seat on the sofa, Michelle called out for the music to stop, which it did in an instant.

'Hey,' Spencer retaliated.

'Listen, you will need to concentrate. You can have as much music as you want later. For now, listen to what I need to tell you.' Michelle then meticulously outlined life onboard the ship and what to expect. She named the key staff members onboard and their roles and how they would engage with him. Michelle informed him of those who Theo met on the ship, as well as those he already knew on the ship from working with them on previous cruises. She explained how they must re-board the ship, bringing no attention to themselves. She had identified a way that they could go through the ship's security without triggering any alarm bells. Spencer would be perfect for this. She had Theo's ship security pass, and they would utilise that. After over an hour of briefing, Michelle felt she had imparted as much useful information as she could and that they were all set for the next day. Throughout the briefing, Michelle tested Spencer and was satisfied with his memory retention. She was sure that it would all become even clearer for him when he met these individuals in person, whereby he could then put names to faces. Content with what she had achieved with Spencer, she turned to the nearest smart speaker and commands, 'Play music'.

Spencer smiled at Michelle and leaned over to give her a passionate kiss, whilst the noise of swirling ice in his tumbler was then drowned out by the onset of the random playlist.

***

'Hey, Cindy-doll. Any chance of a nightcap over here?' shouted out one customer, rattling his near empty glass.

'Billy, you heard the bell ring over 30 minutes ago. You know the drill. That was last orders. You've gotta be gone, Billy-boy, or else I ain't going to have my conch or lobster for tomorrow's guests. You need to be out at sunrise, bringing my haul in. And as for you Leroy, you need to get out of here too. You've gotta be sober when you sail those paying guests onto my beach tomorrow lunchtime. Stop that grinning Leroy, I'm not your mother or wife!'

Cindy Boscoe ran a tight ship at her beach bar. A mile down the beach on what the locals called "Pig Island". During the day, it served tourists looking for a bit of paradise under pale blue skies and palm trees. By evening, it was the casual bar that the few island locals and nearby fishermen and guides would use to relax. Officially, it was called "Flora's Retreat". The locals had their own nickname for it, "Snooters". Not so much a take on the internationally renowned "Hooters", but more famous for its pigs and snorting drinks than raunchy servers. The local tradition of snorting a shot of local over proofed rum up your nostrils, a "Snooter", certainly helped to bolster the nickname and the bar's notoriety. Cindy hated the tongue-in-cheek slang name, but she was as tough as they came given the salty dog clientele, who were more than happy to grace the small wooden hideaway building. This was not just her bar, it was also her home, and had been for longer than fifteen years. Having worked up the ladder for over 26 years from a Hospital Corpsman in the US Navy Medical Corps, she had retired as a Naval Surgeon, yet the sea was still her calling. The beach bar was as close as she could get to marine mother nature.

'Come on, boys. Drink up now. I've got to be up at dawn to feed those pigs. Fair is fair.'

Without further delay, Billy and Leroy downed the remains of their bourbons and eased themselves out of their rusty bar stools and did their best to take steady steps.

'Good night, Cindy. Sweet dreams,' called out Billy as he waved goodbye with his spare hand, glancing back over his shoulder. Billy accidentally clattered with a table, but kept himself upright as both he and Leroy held onto each other in a brotherly embrace. They encouraged each other to take the next step in their daily, well-rehearsed routine.

God help us, thought Cindy to herself. Luckily, they were both wise enough to have brought their bicycles with them to the beach bar and not a motorbike or boat. They had obviously pre-planned to have a skinful but worked out their transportation needs ahead of time. Not that everyone thinks that way, as you would never see a police officer patrol the island. It could exist in its own right without too much external intervention. Everyone knew everyone. If things happened, it just got sorted. Never any fuss. Never any fury. Let bygones be bygones was the island mantra.

Cindy watched the two companions get astride their bikes and pedalled away along the narrow track. They swayed from side to side until they built up a bit of momentum to go in a straighter line. The only light illuminating their way was the moonlight reflecting off the glistening sea. In minutes, they were out of sight. Their laughter and singing diminishing to Cindy the further they cycled along the lonesome track. She knew they would be safely home within twenty minutes or so. Cindy could only imagine the reception they would both receive as they staggered through their front doors to be greeted by their respective spouses. She was confident that they would recount the tale on their next visit.

There was no locking up routine to complete as there were never any thefts reported on the island. Everybody looked out for each other. She packed away the fresh food produce in the single fridge, but as a deterrent to the local auspicious wildlife. The pigs never ventured as far as the shack, as they were content with their man-made shelters a mile down the island. Cindy was one of the volunteers who ensured that they had a healthy existence with daily provisions of food and fresh water. The delivery of fresh water was essential, as otherwise, the pigs may have been tempted to digest sand if they became too dehydrated. It would not be the tourist attraction of Pig Island if it was not for the existence of content and adorable pigs. She considered them as her extended family. Potential suitors came and went, but she never found that special one. She had been married to the Navy for too long, but she would not have had it any other way. Valuably deployed in battlefields across the globe. She knew she had done her time saving life and limb. Now her focus was on other things. Cindy had her bar. She had her locals. She had the resident pigs. Cindy finally had her peace. She enjoyed the emotional love she had found on the island. Physical love would have to come and find her. Her travelling days were done.

Every morning, like clockwork, she jogged out along the ridge of the island to the pigpens. The cinnamon sunrises were spectacular, and she felt at home with the cappuccino froth as the turquoise waters lapped across the sugar white beach. The white pearly sands encircled this exotic oasis, and the lush tropical greenery of mangroves and coconut trees with its surrounding crystal-clear pristine waters made it her own personal paradise. She fed the pigs and spent a little time with these porcine creatures before she jogged back barefoot along the sandy, silky shoreline. It was her private time for fitness, her selfless animal welfare dedication and her solitude away from everyone else on the island. Time for bed and not a moment too soon. She entered her top floor bedroom and turned the key a half turn. The warm sea breeze passed through the room, which provided the perfect temperature and humidity to aid her sleep.

CHAPTER NINE

The sun had risen over the peachy horizon. The air temperature was rising. Theo's body had landed on the beach. With the current making progression along the shore, his body was now some 200 yards away from the pig enclosure. His full-face mask still covered his face. Dried, congealed blood stuck his hair to his scalp. With the warm turquoise waters ebbing against the ivory-white beach, he was now left on the high tide line, with the water washing about eight feet below his body. He was lying face down.

***

Cindy awoke without an alarm as her inner body clock was automatically tuned to 6.30am. every morning regardless of the amount of sleep she received overnight. She reached for her matching dove grey sports bra and loose-fitting running shorts. The colours were admittedly not very interesting, but it stopped the various insects mistaking her for a flower. Despite her advancing years, she still had kept her athletic build by exercising daily. Nutritional eating and avoiding processed foods were very helpful. A lean and mean fighting machine. Her aspirations to join the Navy Seal recruitment programme arrived too late as it was only in development a few months before her departure. Tide and time could wait for no man, or indeed woman. She applied some sun protection lotion with insect repellent. She went downstairs to swig some refreshing water from the fridge and ate a small ripe banana.

As ever, she had options, but she set off on her

more regular route along the upper ridge towards the pig's shelter. She had incredible views across the peninsula from her elevated position. The local fishermen delivered food and fresh water to the pig enclosure twice a week on their rounds of the island. The local vet visited monthly to check on the pigs and had confirmed their good health the previous week. Cindy arrived to hear the pigs snuffling and rootling contentedly in the undergrowth. They kept the litter of baby piglets in a separate pen and were excited and squealing as they heard her footsteps. A drift of larger multicoloured pigs huffed and puffed as they navigated their way towards her and nudged her to prepare for their daily feed. She located the whole carrots in a covered container and handed the tip of each one to the pigs and they responded by grunting with satisfaction. She also poured out some fresh water from the full large blue recycled plastic barrels to keep them hydrated. Now that the piglets had been weaned, she started feeding them a balanced diet of corn, fruits, vegetables, and other food scraps. The piglets appeared thrilled with their snacks. She stroked and patted all the pigs and piglets one at a time as they finished their meals and in return; they oinked and grunted in appreciation, rubbing themselves against the outside of her legs. She enjoyed their company for a while. There was no rush at this time of day.

She left the contented animals to rest and seek shade until the tour boats docked. The tours were self-regulated by the fishermen and tour guides with no set timetable. There were two to three boats at a time, with five or six on certain days. Occasionally, you would not see a soul. She ran back to the bar, but this time via the water's edge. Cindy loved her early morning run along the beach. She felt the soft sand under her feet and the cool wash reached up her shins, which allowed her to free her mind from all her thoughts and worries. It was an easy way to suspend time and create space. As she listened to her own footfall and breathing, she settled into a steady, comfortable pace. The sand was dense because of its saturated wetness, making it easier to run on. Now and then there would be a dry crest where it made it feel you were running through treacle on the powder-soft sand.

Up ahead, she noticed a human body lying down with his head appearing to be slightly drooping to one side, coming to rest against a large boulder. They appeared to have been washed up or were resting against it. Despite finding it odd, she remained calm. This beach, like others in the Bahamas, was not privately owned below the high tide mark. She picked up her pace for the short remaining distance. As she closed in, she did not recognise him, but presumed he was an international visitor from one of the B&Bs catching some early sunshine before it became too intense. As she continued to jog closer, she noticed his pale complexion and that he had what appeared to be a full-face snorkelling mask. In a matter of seconds, she noticed blood on his scalp. Her naval medical instincts took over, and she ran towards him with more urgency. He was along the tidal mark, which meant it has washed him up to this point after all. She reached him and dropped to her knees and gently lifted the face mask to above his hairline whilst cradling his neck with her other hand. With her hand beneath his neck, she used her fingers to feel along his vertebrae. She could feel there was warmth to his shaded neck skin. A good sign. She looked at his face and chest for obvious signs of life. Cindy put her ear close to his mouth and, with her turned head, looked along the line of his chest. She could feel a faint breath against her cheek and saw his chest rising and falling, albeit at a slow and shallow rate. More good signs for a start.

'Hey dude, wake up. Come on man,' she called as she tapped the side of his face with a little more impact with each pat.

She continued her medical assessment of him. She used her hands to feel over his limbs and body. His torso was easy to race over with him just wearing shorts. No bones were obviously sticking out and nothing displaced. The only sign of blood was around his temple. Carefully parting his hairline, she noticed a two-inch-wide cut reaching down to the scalp. Skin in this area of the body was delicate and thin and could easily open, leaving an appearance worse than it may be in reality. She had seen a lot worse in the theatre of war, but this was no battle zone. She was uncertain about a fracture in the cranium or its surroundings. There were signs of tissue damage and swelling in that immediate area. His head bore the signs of impact, either from something he struck or something that struck him. Having been taught by her life experiences and training, she kept an open mind. The patient could share that with her. With a lack of CCTV cameras and no witnesses rushing to share what they saw, the deserted part of the island offered no evidence. The congealed blood showed that this occurred over thirty minutes ago. It had happened some time before. Several hours, possibly. Unless he was on a nocturnal swim, this guy has been here since yesterday.

'Come on man, talk to me.' With another gentle tap on his face, Cindy tried to arouse his senses, but this time, each slap had a little more gusto than the last.

He remained silent, followed by a groan. He coughed and coughed even deeper again. His right hand instinctively removed the mask from his head. He was dazed and confused. What had happened? Where am I? The only thing he knew was he was alive, but how? He lay there, not moving any further. Who am I? He had no memory. He tried to roll over on to his front and closed his eyes as the intense glaring sun shone brightly onto his face, but he felt a resisting forceful grip on his upper bicep. He coughed again and then retched. Theo pulled himself into a sitting half-upright position. His head was pounding. He reached up, and it was tender by his temple. Theo slightly opened his left eye and saw a patch of dark red blood on the back of his hand, but had no way to confirm how he looked. He could only presume he had some kind of head injury. How did he get it? Confused, he tried to make sense of it all in quick time. He remained oblivious to the presence of others. His blurry vision prevented him from focusing on anything more than a few feet away. Theo looked down at himself. He was wearing shorts. He had a snorkel face mask.

Cindy relaxed her grip on him so that he could freely move, but she was there to control his movements enough around his head that he cannot cause himself any further harm.

He could barely see the large boulder. Had he accidentally banged his head on a rock? Nothing made sense. He had a dim recollection of pushing away some pigs whilst floating in the water, and the feel and sight of shark dorsal fins passing under the flesh of his stomach. He felt an overwhelming sense of fatigue and drifted off into a semi-conscious state.

'Oh, no you don't. Stay with me Marine.'

Who is that? Who am I? he thought. Marine? He made another attempt to open his eyes, this time trying to open both of them. Trying to see who was talking to him, he attempted to turn his head to the right. He could feel a hand move on to his right shoulder and his neck being cradled for support.

'Hey, don't move. You're okay. Don't move just yet. Relax.'

Above him, he could discern the outline of a face. He focused on the lips as they moved. Was he hearing right? The voice sounded calm and feminine. Was he in a dream? Was it a mermaid?

'Thank you, ma'am, but I've got to go.' He tried to put his right arm underneath himself to push up. He attempted to rise but fell back onto the sand. 'Argh. Jesus.'

'Well, he can't make it today, Marine, but he's sent his guardian angel,' Cindy replied.

'Marine. Am I a Marine?'

'Well no. That's a force of habit of mine. What's your name? I'm Cindy.'

He could not answer. Who was he? 'I'm sorry. I don't know. God, my head hurts.'

'Although God isn't here, I'm confident he's watching over us. That's a cute accent you have there. Are you a limey? A Brit?'

'Am I? You tell me, love,' Theo raised half a grin.

'Look, the sun is getting up pretty quickly now. In about thirty minutes, if we stay here, we're going to fry. Because of the lack of shelter, it's best we go to my shack just down the cove. I can check you out properly back there. After cleaning it up, I can stitch the wound on your head.'

'You'll do what? You'll do nothing of the sort. Cindy. Cindy, was it?'

'Well, it looks like you can remember some things like my name. That's a good start. Look, I may not be a practicing doctor now, but I was a Naval Surgeon. I'm pretty used to patching up our military personnel with flack firing overhead. I'm sure you won't be too much of a problem with only coconuts overhead, although they'll probably kill you before I do. There are not a lot of medical services around these parts. That's why they call it paradise, but it comes at a price. The local fishermen are forever getting a fishing hook stuck in a finger along these shores. Who do you think they approach first? You got it. Auntie Cindy.'

She continued her examination of him before she checked his balance and ability to stand and walk. She asked him how many fingers she was waving in front of him, but she detected that his vision was too fuzzy to focus and answer. His lack of total understanding and the answers he had already given showed he had a temporary loss of memory, varying from medium to long term. Short term appeared to be not too bad as he had remembered her name, but he did not even know if he was British. She hoped for his memory to return, but understood there was no specific timeframe. Everyone was different, depending on the physical and emotional trauma suffered. The brain was a complex organ. He winced as she conducted a closer examination of his forehead and scalp for any indentation and presence of deep cuts or debris, which could confirm a serious impact. A severe blow to the head with a heavy or sharp object can cause the brain to hit one side of the skull and rebound to the other, causing a contrecoup. It was possible that he had also sustained whiplash injuries to his neck, although he was not bringing that to her attention.

It was difficult to judge at this stage whether he was a victim of a violent attack or just a nasty accident. She checked his forearms for signs of defence marks, like bruises or abrasions. There were none. Since there were no defence wounds, it appears he was caught off guard and not anticipating an attack. This could imply that he had hit his head in an accident. Nothing ever happened on the island, so it couldn't be the former. Despite his pallor, she could see that he was handsome, estimated mid-thirties and of strong athletic build and, to her knowledge, not one of the regular fishermen crew. She checked him thoroughly for any other visible injuries as he murmured. She decided she needed to coerce him to a standing position.

'Okay, let's give standing up a go.'

As a walking casualty, she felt his full weight against her. She guessed his height to be around 6ft as he was not capable of standing up. The shack wasn't far, but she would have to exert all her strength to navigate him through the terrain, avoiding obstacles and keeping him from wasting energy by stumbling. Once at the retreat, she could attend to his head injury. The retreat had an extensive kit for treating minor injuries, as day visitors often got a little too adventurous and fishermen sometimes caught their fingers. She was very experienced and confident in her abilities to execute surgical sutures from her previous vocation and now her island life.

Cindy would report him missing to the police and cruise ships if she confirmed he wasn't a fisherman or a B&B visitor. Prior to its arrival, she had been informed through local news and extensive advertising that a large cruise ship would visit the island on its debut voyage. Time was of the essence to aid his immediate recovery and to find him some longer-term help. Somebody must be missing him, she thought.

The walk along the shore was a slow one, but as Theo found his stability, he also discovered an inner strength. Yes, he felt exhausted. Yes, he felt immensely hungry, but from somewhere he was finding an inner energy and survival instinct.

'If I'm allowed to say this from purely a medical point of view, you're quite fit,' quipped Cindy.

'If I'm allowed to say this without causing offence, from a male point of view, you aren't doing too bad yourself,' responded Theo. They both smiled. He thought to himself that he was feeling better already. His throbbing head told him otherwise. Cindy was using her arms to support Theo's torso as they walked along the firmer sand. She swapped alternate sides every few minutes to give each of her arms a rest. She was proud of her athletic physique, but a man of Theo's build took a great deal of strength to support.

Cindy knew the island like the back of her hand and therefore gave him a countdown to how far it was to the shack, as they slowly progressed. For Theo, every step was a blessing. He felt awkward being so vulnerable and relying on a total stranger for his salvation. With the sun forever rising above the horizon, his sight was becoming less strained. Just ahead, he spotted a wooden building nestled in a secluded setting.

'I guess this is home?' he asked.

'Yep. It sure is. It's home and a lot more.'

Sun loungers dotted the beach, followed by benches and

tables leading up to the shack. Theo didn't settle for the first seat he saw, as Cindy had a specific place in mind to take him. They passed the volleyball net, comfortable light blue lilos and a collection of mismatched, colourful hand-painted chairs that rested on casual tables for eating conch fritters and lobster rolls. They climbed the two wide wooden steps on to the main concourse and the bar itself. She manoeuvred him between the tables and chairs and through the gap in the serving hatch. With her inner leg, she kicked open the door and took him through to a room with "Private" on the door. It had an adjoining bathroom facility which gave her the supply of fresh and hot running water she needed. He continued to mutter and mumble under his breath. As she had expected, the brief journey has taken its toll. She settled him onto the old brown leather settee. Theo laid back, allowing the rear of the settee to take the full support of his arched back. She located her medical bag within a tall cupboard which contained all her sterilised equipment and go-to supplies. There was even a defibrillator on permanent charge sat on the shelf above. A charitable donation from the local doctors' surgery on a neighbouring island in recognition of Cindy's medical expertise and triage service. If you don't receive proper medical care before reaching a facility, the chances of arriving alive are lower due to long travel distances and time.

'Ok now. Let's have a closer look. No moving. This might hurt just a little.' She once again concentrated on the cut to his temple, as that seemed to be the only obvious injury and would account for his unresponsiveness when she first came upon him. She carried on distracting him by talking to him during the examination. Ouches and hisses accompanied each touch.

'Since you can't give me your name, we'll make things even more informal by giving you a name. In this part of the northern hemisphere, if you come into contact with the authorities and you don't have a name, they'll name you John Doe or sometimes just plain old Joe. Now, you have a choice.

John or Joe? Being a Brit, I would say you have the voice of a John, but the physique of a Joe. A tough choice, hey?'

John or Joe? What sort of choice was that? Neither rang a bell nor even sounded anything like what he would imagine he was really called.

'Joe, I guess,' he replied.

'That settles it. Joe, it is then,' she said as she never averted her gaze from her fingers on the wound. She wiped the area with the gauze she had dipped in a saline solution. He gave a little wince.

'Oh, come on now. Be a brave boy. Th's just the skin around the cut. I'm trying to get that dried blood off so I can stick in a couple of stitches. Glue and tape won't hold this baby. Do you want me to put you under for the next bit?'

'You can do that out here?' he asked incredulously.

'Oh, of course not, Joe, but at least you appear to have your wits about you enough to realise I can't.'

He realised with a gloomy outlook that the upcoming part might be more painful, and he needed to brace himself. Cindy's sympathy and empathy were only so deep. He thought she had some fortitude behind the pretty exterior. Time to be a man.

Cindy was meticulous. She had her trusted method of firstly looking at the debridement necessities. Was there any dead tissue to remove? Critical if to prevent infection and rot. Luckily for her patient Joe, there was not. That simplified things. She could carry on with the clean and stitch. Against popular myth, sea water was not good for cleaning wounds. It contained a lot of germs, especially in warm sea water. Being in water for a while didn't aid the open wound; instead, it hindered its healing process. There was also the added concern that no insects had embedded any eggs in the open wound whilst he had lain unconscious on the beach. Nothing looked obvious in there, so it was full steam ahead with the best possible outcome, a sutured wound. She decided on four interrupted sutures with a vertical mattress suture. She did not bother patient Joe with the minutiae. It was five stitches as far as he was concerned. Let's keep it simple and not overcomplicate things, she thought. That was all he needed to know for now. He would need them in place for seven to ten days being on the scalp, or until a surgeon would need to perform a more severe procedure. Let's not hope so, she thought as she applied a little local anaesthesia to numb the affected area. In a matter of minutes, Cindy accomplished her work on Joe without causing him any more discomfort.

'There you go. All good for now.' She handed him a couple of over-the-counter pain killing tablets for the discomfort in his head.

'You need to rest. I have two rooms upstairs. Sit where you are and then later, we'll move you upstairs when you feel you can walk or crawl up the stairs. You make that decision, as I won't be able to catch you if you fall, big boy. In the meantime, I'll make us a brew. Tea right Limey?'

'Yeah, tea. Does milk and no sugar sound right?' he asked.

'Sounds right to me. It looks like you can recall some things. Taste it and let's see if you screw your face up?' she smirked.

Cindy returned with two mugs of tea along with a couple of croissants from the bread barrel.

'Let's try you with a little something to eat. I can get you some jam or cheese and tomato to go with the croissant. What would you prefer?'

'I'm more of a savoury man, so let's go with cheese and tomato.'

His decisive answers were becoming even more reassuring for Cindy. All these simple questions were being used to analyse him further. He knew more about himself and was expressing it well. Since taking the pain killing tablets, he was not complaining of head pains. She faced a dilemma: let him rest or subject him to a traumatic journey to a distant hospital, risking additional strain and harm. She went back to her medical supplies cupboard and returned with a simple electronic blood pressure kit running off AA batteries.

'Now you are a bit more relaxed, let's just check out that blood pressure,' she applied the straps around his upper left bicep and started the machine. It increasingly constricted around his arm, feeling the bite with every passing second. The audible heart rate beeped and after what felt like an eternity, the pressure was released. The display showed the results. 122 over 85, with a resting heart rate of 81. All were slightly high, but considering what he had been through, all at an acceptable rate.

With his eyes wide open in the dappled room, she examined his pupils. Both were the same size, and as she shone the handheld light into each, they contracted and expanded as expected. He traced the path of her finger in all directions. There was no straw-coloured liquid coming from his ears, showing he was not leaking fluid from around the brain.

'Are you on any meds that you know of? Statins, diabetes related, ulcer, or anything at all? I can't see any injection marks on your body that indicate anything intravenous.'

'Not that I recall,' answered Patient Joe.

'Okay. Let's keep you here for now under close observation. It would take hours to get you to a hospital. Let's keep you stable and evaluate from there. I'll phone the surgery and advise them what we have and take it from there. I'll also have to inform the police authorities in case someone has reported you missing.'

Cindy walked to the office desk, then sat at the small dining table with a notepad and pen. She drilled down on some details.

'I need you to be open and honest with me with all these

questions. Please say you don't know, or you can't recall if that's the case. Don't make answers up to please me. You got it?'

'Yeah, sure.'

'Is your name coming back to you?'

'No, not at all,'

'Your last recollection?'

'Um, I recall seeing pigs and sharks. They were close to me. Through the mask I thought the water around my head was cloudy, sort of diluted blood colour.'

'Well, that would be consistent with your head wound. I can't fathom how you could have banged your head underwater on Pig Beach. The nurse sharks are only harmful if you wave your hands in front of their eyes and they can become aggressive. It's a pristine sandy beach. If you could see, then it was daylight. As the blood on your scalp had dried and matted and sunrise was only shortly before I found you, I believe this happened sometime yesterday. You've got no ID on you, so you can't be from that far away. If there was no boat on the beach, how did you get here?'

'I don't have the foggiest.'

'Okay. Maybe you walked to the beach. Perhaps you're staying at one of the rental properties further back on the island?'

'Not that I recall.'

'What about the hotel on the nearby island?'

'It doesn't ring a bell.'

'Around the bay and out to sea, there's the new cruise ship anchored since yesterday. Are you anything to do with that? A passenger or even crew, maybe?'

'I really don't know.'

'You aren't wearing a wedding ring, so I guess you aren't married, or maybe you are and don't wear a ring. Can you recall a special person in your life?'

'Not at the moment.'

'I notice you have a necklace on and a pendant on it. That's a sign of the Zodiac. It's the sign of Gemini. Does that mean anything to you?'

'No ma'am. Nothing.'

'When I was taking your blood pressure just now, you were twisting the pendant through your fingers. It looks like it means something to you.'

'Maybe so, but I can't bring forward why that would be.'

'That full face mask we left back on the beach. That's a sophisticated piece of kit. Do you snorkel a lot? I mean, you also weren't wearing a buoyancy aid. To me, that's someone who is confident in the water and are comfortable with it.'

'I remember panicking a bit in the water, but I put that down to seeing blood and sharks at the same time. I think there were stingrays, too.'

'Sure, I understand. Anyone would instinctively feel that way, but those sharks would never harm you. That close to the shore here, we only have reef sharks. They are extremely docile. We wouldn't recommend to the tourists that they hand feed them, but the tour guides do, in fact, feed them in the shallow waters as part of their tour show. People naturally fear them, but guides understand the low likelihood of attacks. As for the stingrays, they swim around the legs of the tourists as they feed carrots to the swimming pigs. They are pretty harmless, too. If the stingrays feel threatened, they may use the barb near their tail as a defence mechanism. However, such instances are as rare as finding rocking horse poo. And the pigs are no worse. The tourists think the pigs only get food when they feed them a carrot. The volunteers always ensure they care for and feed them, ensuring they never go hungry, especially when tourists are absent. Handheld or floating carrots are more of a source of amusement for them than a reliable diet. Some myths we leave with the tourists for the mystique, whilst others we banish as an education. It depends on an individual's receptiveness, whether we tell the truth or embellish the myth. I hate to break it to you, but Santa Claus doesn't exist, but we don't tell everyone that, do we?'

'He doesn't! Damn,' Patient Joe exclaimed with a wry smile. 'That's a good analogy, I guess.'

The cognitive recollection by Patient Joe that he knew of even Santa Claus was another positive sign for Cindy. Things were going well, but there were many gaps to fill. She had her fingers crossed for gradual improvements.

'I've tired you out a bit with all those questions.'

'No, not at all. Thank you for asking,' he replied.

'Let's get you upstairs to rest for a while. I also need to get the bar and things set up for today's guests. Rest in my bedroom for now. I'll set up the spare bed later.'

Gingerly, he rose to his feet, but now with a bit more stability. He held onto the back of the settee while taking his first few tentative steps. It was an immediate right turn and up the rickety wooden open-tread stairs. Straight ahead, he pushed the ajar door and entered Cindy's bedroom. There was a hint of femininity, albeit subtle. It was an eclectic mix of ornaments and memorabilia. There by the window was a sparse dressing table with the minimum of makeup. He imagined the natural light through the window illuminating her face as she sat in front of the mirror. There were only a few knick-knacks on display, mainly nautical. In a small alcove, there was a military emblem that caught Theo's attention. It was a vertical pin with wings at the top and two symmetrical snakes wrapped around the pin. He looked at it for about twenty seconds.

'That's my Hospital Corpsman insignia. My small homage to the distinguished men and women who serve and protect our navy personnel.'

'Impressive,' he said, as he gazed intently at a portrait photo of a young Cindy in a military uniform. To the left of that, there was a photo of Cindy in military fatigues on a battlefield, attending to a severely injured Marine. Cindy deduced Patient Joe's thoughts from the way he contorted his head to inspect the photo.

'He survived. We're still in contact. His wife was expecting at the time, and she called their beautiful newborn girl Cindy-Lou. That's one hell of an honour for someone to name their precious baby after you.' She spun away and ushered him onto the bed to lie down. 'More about you. You get some rest. I'll shut the door and return in a few hours to check on you. I'll be downstairs or nearby outside, sorting out the loungers and sports court if you need me. You'll be fine.'

He nodded his head in response and snuggled down into the pillow. Not as soft as he would like, but beggars could not be choosers as he slipped into the abyss.

Cindy exited the room as his eyes went straight to closure. She returned to her private room downstairs and quietly closed the door so that she could make her private calls. The priority one for her was the medical issue call to the surgery. Her good friend Dr Len Rolle was as ever on duty. The conversation delved into what she had encountered and the procedures she had performed. Len agreed she had taken the correct action and, considering everything, it was the right decision for the patient to rest and be monitored. She could hear him typing up some notes in the call's background. He reminded Cindy that she could contact him on his mobile 24/7 if the patient's condition deteriorated at all. Both content with their decision making, they politely ended the call. Her next call was to the police station. She was acquainted with some officers there, but not as well as the staff at the surgery. Some officers popped into the shack when off-duty.

Cindy also hosted the annual 911 Family Day Beach Party that recognised the all-round efforts of all emergency workers on the neighbouring islands. A day to thank the families for supporting their partners in the servitude. Cindy got to know a few people by their names and faces. They remembered her more than she could recall them. That's the thing about being the charitable host.

As the information was shared, the desk officer typed it into the computer, capturing all the details. For what others may think was a quiet calypso nation, the government had invested into good IT systems. Having confirmed no one was reported missing, Constable Ferguson confirmed he would make some proactive enquiries and bring the report to the attention of his sergeant to supervise. Because of their adult age, their inquiries were limited. With six million tourists visiting the Bahamas each year, finding immigration records would be like searching for a needle in a haystack. Making progress would be more likely if someone called in a missing person. Cindy thanked Ferguson, and they promised to keep each other updated if anything relevant materialised. She disconnected the call on her mobile phone and stashed it away in the pocket of her shorts. Cindy still needed to change into her host clothing, but she had plenty of time. She planned to retrieve her clothes out of her bedroom when she next checked on Patient Joe.

Cindy had to prepare for her day guests. She went through to the bar with her laptop and fired it up from standby mode. Logging into the music streaming service was the first step. Cindy adjusted the volume lower than usual for the guests and connected all her speakers via Bluetooth. Cindy had her playlists in various moods for different times of the day. She loved party music to raise the vibe of the bar during the day. She appreciated all kinds of music, but her world travels had left an impression on her. Her early tours at sea were on naval aircraft carriers stationed around the Mediterranean Sea. There was an abundance of party towns with lively nightlife, bars and discos. Unlike her fellow Marines on shore leave, she wasn't interested in heavy drinking. Cindy enjoyed dancing to the music. She had experienced the bars of Ibiza, Ayia Napa and Mykonos, to name but a few. Her favourite playlist was related to classic 1980s and 1990s songs. She had it on random play just to mix it up a bit. The first to bellow out reminds her of a club called "Tropicana" on one of her more hedonistic nights out. Classic beats filled the air. She picked up her disinfectant spray bottle and micro cloth and went around all the tables to wipe them down. She arranged the chairs and wiggled her hips to the beat of the music. Cindy weaved in between the tables with an increased wriggle as she loosened up. She hoped Joe would stay in her room and she could then dance in wild abandonment. She wandered out to the two lilo lounger areas. The popular one on the beach, then the sensible one in the shade near the large tarpaulin roofed floor area that doubled up as a yoga class area and a dance floor. She neatly stacked the rolled up brightly coloured yoga mats and swept the floor to remove all the blown-in fine sand. The up sale of yoga classes to the day visitors brought her in a bit more revenue, whilst also allowed her to enjoy her passion. A true win-win.

CHAPTER TEN

'Fore!' went the loud shout from Spencer. Damn, he thought as he hooked his drive at the first hole. That complimentary golf ball with a 2 on it had flown true, if you had been trying to play an exaggerated draw. Spencer had not. He had hardly digested his hearty breakfast when he had rushed to the tee for his second round in two days at this prestigious golf course. Spencer needed to get this round underway at the request of Michelle. He had his golfing routine. He had his pre-round drills. Ten balls in the nets, then ten balls on the chipping green, followed by thirty putts on the practice green, and only then heading to the tee. Not today. Michelle made sure of that.

'We've got a lot to discuss this morning, Spencer, before we get anywhere near that ship. You've got to be a sponge for everything I impart to you.'

Spencer was feeling a bit more laissez-faire about things. When you had pre-registered for a golf round under the World Handicap System rules, you had to return a score, or you received a penalty score that impacted on your handicap. Why Michelle could not appreciate the importance of this was beyond him. If Spencer was to maintain his single figure handicap, he needed a decent round. Anything less than a perfect round and he would be in real danger of his handicap slipping into double figures. Will he be able to live this down with his golf buddies in England? The shame of it. He opted for a provisional ball, just in case he couldn't locate his original one on the first hole.

'Provisional ball with a 3, also with a blue line,' he called out.

'Who on earth are you telling that to?' questioned Michelle sat in the buggy, who had never been on a golf course in her life.

'Michelle, please. Just go along with this. You must declare a provisional ball. Rules are rules.' It already peeved Spencer that he had not had the best start to his round. He needed to concentrate and follow the rules and etiquette.

Michelle took a loud sip from a massive plastic beaker of cola with a straw poking out of the top. She placed it back in the holder with a bit of a rattle. Spencer, who was waiting to play his provisional ball, paused and looked over at Michelle. He thought it best to say nothing. He reset himself and played his provisional shot. The humidity was already rising. Looking down at the first fairway, there was not a soul in sight. There was no-one else waiting on the tee box. Millionaires golf, as they called it. Only a select few hotel suite holders enjoy reserved tee times during this time of day. Like Michelle, not everyone played golf. This complimentary amenity was not always in demand. It was very much like shows at the Vegas hotels where the front couple of central tables were left for the high rollers who would seldom be drawn away from the card tables. Empty seats or the odd bored wife or girlfriend sat alone. Michelle was that bored girlfriend. Isn't golf considered a way to ruin a nice walk? Not that Michelle was intent on walking anywhere. Like many top-class golf courses, a buggy was mandatory. Spencer bent down to pick up his tee and strode back to the buggy with purpose. He went to the rear and put his driver back in his bag with the replaced head cover, then jumped into the driver's seat. The buggy bobbed as he took to the seat and fidgeted around a bit. He huffed, stepped on the accelerator to drop the automatic brake, and the buggy jerked forward as it accelerated. Not the smoothest of lift offs, but it was typical of a petulant golfer whose pride had taken a bit of a knock. All too often seen on any golf course you care to mention anywhere in the world.

Boys and their toys, Michelle thought as she squealed, 'Steady on.'

Michelle planned to lay out the ground rules for the coming days back on the ship. She had additional information to reveal to Spencer, beyond what she had already shared the previous night. She was concerned that between the moments of passion Spencer had not fully taken in everything she had told him. Last night, his excitement was comparable to a kid in a candy store. Upon reflection, briefing Spencer at that time was not ideal. Work hard, play hard as they say, but she got the order a little mixed up. Spencer informed her that completing the course would take over three hours. Isn't that sufficient time for her to monopolise him? Michelle underestimated that 90% of Spencer's time was dedicated to concentration. He had to be in the zone. Arriving at the spot where the first ball had landed, Michelle joined Spencer in searching the rough. He pointed out to Michelle the ten yards of area he believed the ball landed in. He did not see it bounce, so presumed it buried itself. They walked in opposite directions, away from the buggy in the line Spencer identified. His provisional ball was sitting in the middle of the fairway. He hoped he didn't have to play it.

'Here it is,' called out Michelle helpfully, as she bent down in the wispy grass and picked it up to show Spencer.

'No, put it back exactly where you found it,' shouted out Spencer from five yards away. Michelle thought they heard that loud comment back in the clubhouse.

'Excuse me.'

'Michelle, you can't touch it. Hell! Okay. Sorry. Of course, you don't know the rules. Fine. Thanks for looking and well done on finding it.'

Michelle guessed that was an apology in golf parlance, as she trudged back to the buggy.

Spencer ended up laying up from the repositioned poor lie and bogeys the hole. Not the best start for a hole that was a lowly stroke index 17, but still better than having to play his provisional ball. Not a disaster by any means, but for a player of his calibre, he knew he had to step it up. This front nine was difficult enough set amongst the shelter of the mangroves interspersed with water hazards and sand traps that on some holes ran the length from tee to green. There was no forgiveness. Having played the previous evening, he anticipated the challenging back nine, with each hole extending into the sea on a peninsula. They filled it with verdant vegetation and there was an abundance of tropical birds nesting in mature mangroves.

It was a challenging championship quality course. They designed it with aspirations for being a qualifying course for the US PGA soon. They had clustered the multiple bunkers around each green to act as obstacles. There were five different tee positions that increased in difficulty and length as they went. Red, white, blue, black and the revered emerald. Playing from the championship emerald tees, Spencer had to be on top of his game. The slope index of 141 reflected just how challenging a course it was. Tee markers were gargantuan conch seashells, spray painted in their respective colours. The buggy was a lifesaver in the humid conditions, with the course being over 7000 yards. A par 72 was not within reach of Spencer, but his target was to break a net 75 shots.

'Spencer, we'll need to pass through security when we return to the ship on the speedboat. I'll give you Theo's ship pass, which I kept as he knew he wasn't going back on board. The ship is expecting him back and is unaware he is off on an assignment. Keep your sunglasses on and your baseball cap down and you'll be fine. Once we are onboard, follow me to our suite. I'll give you a tour around it. Sit back and enjoy being pampered and looked after. Don't forget that at all times, you are Theo and not Spencer. You must do what your brother would do. Everyone will call you Mr d'Vere, so that's easy for you. It's fun. It's a game. But don't drop the ball.'

'Sure. Sounds fun. But you know I've never been on a cruise ship. I won't know my arse from my elbow.'

'Look, just relax. We'll be together 80% of the time. I have some duties to perform that will drag me away a few times a day, but just lie low. Look smart. Be casual. Be yourself, but also be Theo. You can do this. I'm depending on you. Don't let me down.'

'Fine. Hand me that club that has a P on the bottom of the clubhead. It's only 97 yards from here.'

Having played his shot, he replaced the wedge and took out the putter. He removed the cover head and tossed it into the basket behind the seats. Spencer removed the glove from his right hand and tucked it in to his rear pocket, with the fingers sticking out and hanging down. He walked on to the green with Michelle strolling alongside him, still muttering away about the ship. Spencer looked down at the ball, marked it, and repaired the pitch mark four inches to the right.

Michelle walked on and declared, 'I've seen this on the television. I'll hold the flag for you.'

Spencer was still focusing on the slope and falls across the putting green and then looked up to see Michelle walking along the line of his putt.

'Michelle, please move to one side. You're walking all over where I'm about to putt!'

'Oh sorry, I didn't realise. Is that wrong, then?'

'You could say so,' he said sarcastically, with a nod.

Michelle pulled out the flag with a bit of a wriggle. She then went beyond the hole and stood in a straight line to where Spencer was replacing his marked ball. She wanted to examine the putt closely, mimicking what she had seen caddies do on TV.

'Michelle, please don't stand there. You are in my line of

sight.'

'Sorry. It's difficult this game, isn't it? I'll go stand over here.' She took four paces to her left and stood as still as she could.

'Do you see that bright orange thing up there in the sky behind you?' asked Spencer.

Michelle looked over her left shoulder at the sun.

'That's what's casting your shadow over my putting line!'

'Oh. Sorry,' said Michelle as she took another couple of steps backwards.

'Just one more thing, Michelle. Lower the flagpole as the flag's moving shadow still falls in front of the hole.'

Michelle lowered the flagpole and her head. She dared not look now.

Spencer banished any conversation from his mind and took a couple of practice swings in the thinking zone. He took half a step forward, rocked on his legs from side to side, then steadied himself and the putter whilst not quite grounding the club. He was now in the delivery zone. No more thinking about the putt. Just do it. He brought the clubhead back and played the eighteen-foot putt. It bobbled twice through the footprints Michelle had left and the ball came up three inches short. Spencer could not believe his misfortune. Those bloody footprints.

'Damn. That's a chance that's gone begging,' said Spencer, as he wiped the bottom of his putter with his hand to take off the miniscule grains of sand, then tapped down a few spike marks, albeit too late.

'A bad workman always blames his tools,' responded Michelle in jest.

The comment worsened Spencer's mood as he tapped the ball in for another bogey. The thought of enduring a long, punishing round crossed his mind.

'How many hits was that?' asked Michelle.

'Shots Michelle, shots. It was five.'

'Three more and you have my favourite lucky number. That would be cute.'

'Michelle, it would not be cute. It would be a total embarrassment that just may lead me to breaking a club shaft over my knee. Can we move on now, please?' asked Spencer in an irritated tone as he removed the scorecard and pencil from his side pocket and recorded his score. Where on earth on the course was he going to recover some shots? Not anytime soon, with a stretch of low stroke index holes coming up before the turn for home. Keep it steady. See it out until the 10th tee and refocus, he thought to himself.

After the holes played out, they made a quick stop at the halfway hut for two vanilla lattes. The buggy came to a stop.

Michelle placed her hand on Spencer's arm before he could alight. 'So, on board there is this very nosey couple, Cecil and Connie, who are an awful bore. I would say they are harmless, but they are tiresome. They make conversation about things they know nothing about. They just don't let go. Especially her. Just be polite, nod and give the answer she wants to hear, then they'll leave you alone. A woman onboard works with Theo. I'm not sure about her and I'm uncertain if she's remained on board since there's nothing left for her to do now that Theo has finished his talks. I saw her name on a video credit and a book tribute as Suzanne. If she comes near you, be careful, since I don't know what she's up to. Feign a sore throat or something.'

Spencer smirked.

'I'm bloody serious Spencer.'

'Okay, fine. Look, I've got to keep up with play. I saw another buggy coming down the 9th fairway as we left the halfway hut.' Spencer exited the cab and selected his 5-iron club from his bag strapped on to the rear of the buggy. He could feel Michelle's gaze as her head spun around like an owl, following his every move. He looked up and gave her a wink with a cheeky grin. She still did not look happy.

Against expectations, two back-to-back birdies brought Spencer round to where he needed to be. He had played the course the evening before with the assistance of a resident caddy, who for $80 had given him some sage advice. They cleverly designed the back nine holes along the coastal shore. The order was in a figure of eight, which meant that whether you had a fade or a draw, you were neither advantaged nor disadvantaged over all the holes. Ingenious, he thought to himself.

With the golf round about to finish, and the last two holes favouring his natural draw shot into the wind coming off the sea to his right, he fancied his chances. If he was a betting man, which he was not in particular, he would wager that he would beat the course on the last two holes if the challenge was his golfing ability against the forces of nature; the wind, the slopes, the distance, the bounce. With just two pars needed to maintain his single-digit handicap and bragging rights, he aimed to replicate his previous night's performance.

He executed the 17th hole flawlessly. At stroke index one, it was by definition the hardest hole on the course, but with his handicap allowance, he was grateful for the shot he received. With a short approach, he had to get it up and down in two. It was a phrase he had had in his head hundreds of times on other golf courses, and invariably there was only a 25% success rate. This he needed to nail. Did he take a seven iron and run it to the flag, or take a sand wedge and float it all the way? Decisions, decisions. Most golfers preferred one option or the other. Spencer was blessed with either option after years of practice. Take out the slope or run it like a banana? His positive mental attitude kicked in. He was convinced he wouldn't blade the wedge. He could only picture in his mind the flight of the ball one way. "Picture the shot," as the professional at his own club would say. Weight through the left knee, a short backswing and follow through. He took the sand wedge and, with no hesitation, went through his practice drill and approached the ball. With soft hands, he released the shot and saw the ball loop up in the air. It came down gently and rolled the last eight feet towards the hole. It did not quite reach, but it was dead. A tap in for a par. He fist-pumped his left hand at waist height, bent down and retrieved the ball. Saving time, he kept the flag in and returned to the buggy. Michelle stayed close to the buggy on the back nine, not enjoying the experience as much as she had hoped. Yes, game on, thought Spencer. Nothing could stop him.

He stood on the 18th tee and looked ahead at the sculpted fairway, and he felt very composed. As it was the last hole, Michelle thought she would show some affinity to the game and join Spencer on the tee. He had his ball on the tee peg ready to play. He had not lost the ball since Michelle found it on the first hole. It was now his lucky charm. He had out his driver. Spencer stood at the back of the tee, loosening up with a few swings. He positioned himself behind the ball and surveyed the course. A brave choice of club with the narrow fairway, but he was oozing confidence in his own ability. He held out his club horizontally to point it down the fairway, picturing the flight of the ball and where he wanted it to land. Aim past the bunker on the right and fade it left onto the fairway. He took out his course guide with his hand-written notes from the evening before. The left side was the optimum location for the second shot into a tight green. It confirmed it for him. He took his open stance and drove through the ball majestically. The ball flew, skipped, bounced, and stopped on the fairway. Spencer was thrilled with that. It could not have gone better. Sensing that it was an excellent shot and pleased for him, Michelle gave a short clap and skipped back to the buggy like an excited youngster going to school for the first time. Spencer's spirits were lifted. They simultaneously jumped into the buggy cab, giving it an enhanced bounce. They advanced 280 yards towards the ball's resting place. The elevation and contours had helped the ball skip on much further from its original landing spot. Perfect, he thought. Another twenty yards ahead, Spencer pulled up on the left side of the ball and glanced down from the cab. He could not believe his misfortune. The ball was sat down in an unrepaired divot. If he could see 60% of his golf ball, he was lucky. He knew his next shot was going to fly with little control. No panic at this stage, but he felt the tension. Nothing left for it. He could take his eight iron and aim to control it as much as possible. Spencer chose his line and played the shot. He was right about his prediction. The ball flew out at a lower trajectory. The green was guarded at the front by what, in other circumstances, would have been an inconspicuous bunker that should not have come in to play for Spencer. Unfortunately, the ball caught the top lip of the bunker, sending it spinning into the deep rough on the right. It looked like ball eating territory. In frustration, he hit his club into the ground, leaving a chunk out of the grass that he then bent down to repair. Other players or a groundsman wouldn't have been impressed. All players knew better than to take their frustration out on the course. He placed a small red tee peg in the ground in case he had to return to play another ball if he could not find his original. Fingers crossed, he thought. This would not be a buggy ride to savour. He steered a course to where he thought the ball had landed. Keeping your eye on the ball was never more important. Before the buggy had come to a complete stop, he hopped out. Michelle waited until it had come to a complete halt before gripping the window stanchion to aid her exit. She trotted around the front of the buggy to help Spencer find his ball.

Spencer drew an imaginary circle and stated, 'It's in this area here somewhere.'

He held the sand wedge, knowing it was the only club suitable for this terrain. The long grass was already rubbing around his legs at knee height. It was not good. Failing to locate it, he'd be forced to return and play another ball. He would lose a shot and distance. He would have to sink that shot to keep his handicap. A shot in a million. He had three minutes. Not that anyone else was counting, but keeping to the rules and the spirit of the game, he was being true to himself.

'I've got it. It's here!' shouted Michelle in excitement.

A sense of relief came across Spencer. He walked four yards to where Michelle was standing. There indeed, at the foot of the long grass stems was a ball marked number 2, sat right down but just about playable. Here we go again, thought Spencer. Up and down. Up and down. He threw down his baseball cap next to the ball without disturbing it, so he could return to where it was. He strode up to the green about ten yards away. By chance, they positioned the pin on the back left of the green. He walked the entire length of the green to measure the distance he had left. The further, the better, he hoped, as it gave him the chance to get the ball to land a long way short of the hole and let it run up naturally. Coming out of the deep rough, he would have no control over the ball and no check-spin. It was in the lap of the gods. He identified where he wanted the ball to land. Up and down. Up and down. He was now saying it to himself in the same tempo he wanted to hit the shot. Don't decelerate. Play through the grass. Strong left hand. Come on now. He returned to his baseball cap, picked it up and wore it again. The cap's peak shielded his eyes from the sun's glare, reflecting off the bright sand in the bunker ahead. Here goes, he thought. The swing came down nice and steep with an open face in order to take as little grass as possible with the clubhead. He took a divot under the ball, and it popped up like someone throwing the ball underarm. It landed just where he wanted it, but it was now about the speed. Without the spin, it was not stopping quick enough. The line was excellent, though. Could it? Would it? Bloody right, it did. It hit the flagpole flush, kicked up eight inches and stopped dead on the lip of the hole, but still clutching to the surface. He had not sunk it, but job done.

'Michelle, if you would kindly take the flag out, and please don't touch the ball.'

'My pleasure,' she excitedly said whilst lifting the flag out and stepping aside out of harm's way. It was so close to the hole that Spencer did not need to get his putter. He could just tap it in with his sand wedge. Leaning forward with his weight through his front leg, he tapped the ball in for a par, and claimed a handicap-saving total.

'Fantastic,' he called out whilst using his customary fist pump. He took his cap off in the traditional fashion you would to congratulate your playing partners. He leaned forward and gave Michelle a kiss on her cheek. Spencer bent down and retrieved his ball from the cup. He looked at his golf ball and twizzled it in his hand. To his horror, there was a red line on the ball instead of his blue line. Where's the blue line? Jogging over to the buggy, he checked the two complimentary sleeves of balls in the basket behind the seat. In one box, there were balls marked with a 2 and a blue line. In the other box were balls marked with a 3 and a blue line. None of the balls he was playing with had a red line. He had played the wrong ball. He shouted out, 'No. No. No!'

Michelle knew something had seriously gone wrong. She watched Spencer walk over to where he had played out of the rough. Walking in small circles, he found it - a ball marked with a visible blue line and a 2, just two yards to the right. It confirmed to him he had indeed played the wrong ball and, in so doing, had incurred a two-stroke penalty. He had never checked the ball he played before he did so. The red line must have been under the ball as it sat in the long grass. He could have checked it before playing it, but presumed it was his. A costly mistake. A schoolboy error. How could he have been so stupid? He had no one else to blame but himself, and he knew it. He had to take it on the chin. Dejected, he played his own ball and made the up and down again.

'What does that mean, Spencer?'

'It means that I have to sign for a score two shots higher than I needed.'

'But sweetheart, just say that didn't happen. I mean, you played a great shot as it was. Just put down a four instead of a six. Who is to know?'

'I'll know Michelle. I'll know. That's cheating,' he clarified.

'Well, you don't mind cheating with your brother's wife! What's the difference?' Michelle said acerbically.

Spencer found that comment rather crass and hard to digest, on several levels. He always thought she had a charming nature in their university days. He had never witnessed this cutting streak from her. Wow! That was an insensitive thing to even imagine someone saying, let alone hearing it for yourself. Their relationship had its difficulties, but now it could face an even rockier path. He did not answer and instead headed back to the buggy to return in silence back to the clubhouse. His thoughts were swirling through his head. His first job when he arrived was the bureaucracy of completing the scorecard electronically in the clubhouse bar. Keeping true to himself, he recorded the penalty shots, pressed return and walked away. Gone was his chance of entering the annual scratch competition next week at his home club, as he would no longer hold a single figure handicap. The ribbing from his city mates would be unbearable. He walked over to the bar and ordered a pint of gunners on ice. The barman mixed the dash of lime, ginger beer, ginger ale and Angostura bitters, stirred it together and handed it over.

'Anything for you, Michelle?'

'No, I'm fine. I'll head off upstairs to pack the bags and arrange the boat transfer. Take your time and I'll see you shortly.'

Spencer headed towards a large, brown leather-bound armchair in the spikes bar. With his athletic physique, he lowered himself into the comfortable seat. He gave out a deep, audible sigh as he landed. His sulking demeanour over a cold drink was unmissable as he dejectedly retracted into his own shell. The barman walked over with the bar tab on a small black plastic tray.

'Sorry sir, I need you to sign for this so we can charge it to your suite. For your convenience we have already added your suite details on there Mr d'Vere.' They left the tab in front of him, with the pen resting on top.

'I have my own pen, thanks,' said Spencer. He reached into his rear left-hand pocket, extracted his designer pen and signed the tab, then pushed it back across the table towards the barman. The barman was unconcerned about the indistinguishable signature. The point of sales screen was already showing Mr d'Vere's photo, with which he was content. All the sites of Destiny Luxury Group had access to shared software and data.

CHAPTER ELEVEN

Jack proceeded to the gym, as he had a rare chance to enjoy an uninterrupted run on the treadmill. As a gifted long-distance runner, it gave him the opportunity to clear his mind. He set up the machine pace to allow an even tempo warm-up and after completing one kilometre; Jack sped up. He allowed his mind to revert to some of his old memories of how it all began.

***

Never a shrinking violet but also someone who had yet to achieve their true potential. Jack Shaw had lived a life that few people had ever experienced. A junior officer in the Royal Marines and then a former detective of merit in London's Met Police gave Jack the platform that he should have stepped onto, but he had forever felt he could not achieve to the level of his forefathers. One shadow he lived in was that of his father, Danny Shaw; a heroic leader within 42 Commandos in the 1981 battle to retake the Falkland Islands. His father landed at Bluff Cove and led his men across the islands to relieve Port Stanley. There was forever the constitutional pride between the Paras and the Marines on who got there first. The stories of his father meant that in Jack's heart, he knew the accurate answer. A sense of forbearance lived with Jack from a young age. His father spent much of Jack's young life serving away from home. Both Jack and his devoted father, Danny, cherished the early memories of those brief times together upon his return. It all sadly ended too soon when tragedy struck whilst Jack was of primary school age. His impressionable mind would never forget the day he saw his mother return home in tears in the early hours of the night to break to him the news of his father's untimely death. Trying to prevent a street mugging in his local community, Danny Shaw, who had performed military service in the theatre of war on behalf of Her Majesty, was stabbed through the heart needlessly. Jack had kept the newspaper cuttings of the killer's Crown Court trial reporting. At such a young age he could not understand how in the early stage of the reports it recited stories of his father's heroics in far-flung battles, as well as in protecting the vulnerable on the night of the stabbing. However, the countenance by the killer's defence barrister about the alcohol levels in his father's autopsy report insinuated that Danny could have been the aggravator of the incident. The callous minds of lawyers would subsequently shape his life, attitudes, and desires.

He yearned to follow in his father's military footsteps. In the Royal Marines, Jack had showed immense physical strength and fortitude from his early days in training. Before long, they earmarked him as having the potential for a junior officer position, but he lacked the self-belief to go higher. There were still a few Marines who remembered serving with his father, and a few more again that had not served with him but recollected the legacy his leadership had left. Regrettably, there were those that did not fall into either of those categories and looked at Jack as someone who they thought was living on the back of a legend to progress themselves. Jack knew that was as far from the truth that you could get, but why let the truth impede a good reason to niggle at someone? Is it jealousy, character building, or downright stupidity? It did not matter, but for all of Jack's strengths the lingering jibes played on his mind much more than they should have. He thought he would be stronger, and as much as he tried to be, it was the one thing that got him down and arrested his true potential.

After nine years of grit and determination to serve his

country to the best of his ability, it was now the right time to consider another direction in his life. There were varied but limited opportunities to find another job. He had entered the Marines at such a young age, without the opportunity to achieve his true academic capability. On reflection, he was of the firm opinion that he was failing to reach his goals and potential. This was a recurring theme in his life, but he could at least alter that thought through academic self-progression. He enrolled on a three-year Open University course in Sociology. Jack wanted to exorcise the demons from his memories of all those press cuttings. Would society see his father as a hero or villain? Was his father a heroic leader of men in the theatre of war, or were the voices of the nit-picking anti-war brigade's rhetoric louder? Was his father seen as a hero stepping in to stop a knife-wielding youth, or had he brought his demise upon himself by drunkenly challenging someone his father had looked down upon as a total waster? He wanted to know more about the society we lived in and understand the frailties that prevail. Despite attaining a 2.1 degree, he still wondered if he had fulfilled his maximum potential.

It was time to enter civvy street and find a job that suited his skill set. Through his ex-services contacts, there was plenty of work available in the security industry. He was, at the time, still a physically fit man with a panache for enjoying Saturday afternoons playing rugby. His regressive ability to run at speed meant he had edged infield from a gazelle-like winger to a more dogged centre. With that came a sharpness to read the game like a chess grandmaster more than a headless chicken. With this change in tempo, and the academic appreciation and progression later in life than he could have earlier imagined, came a realisation that whilst his physique would waver, his mental ability was still developing. He now wanted a more stimulating profession that could stretch his mental capacity, whilst his physical attributes could also remain a positive element. His uncle Gary had retired as a uniformed inspector in the police. He had early recollections of how his father made disparaging remarks about Gary, his brother-in-law, saying, "Your mum's brother is a 'Plod', as he didn't have the balls to join the military". Jack recalled his mother had a different spin on it but did not want to encourage his father any further to joke about Uncle Gary, as their jobs were not that different. Jack recalled his mother mentioning that whilst his father was serving in the Falklands in a battle against an identifiable enemy, Uncle Gary was being petrol bombed on the streets of London by members of a community he believed he was there to protect. It was with this memory ringing in his head that he took it upon himself to talk to Uncle Gary about the possibilities of joining the Metropolitan Police.

At the time of joining, Gary had to endure two years on the beat as a uniformed constable. Gary spoke of the promises the recruitment department gave him before he himself joined. He was told that he had to carry out a two-year probationary period, but after that the world was his oyster and he could progress to work in any of the specialist departments. He could transfer to the Traffic department to drive the fastest cars, he could join Mounted Branch to police football matches and demonstrations on horses, or he could even become a detective. What they did not say at the time is that over the coming years, you will learn of nepotism amongst the ranks, and that progression was not that easy. Even if you worked your way in to applying for your dream posting, the Personnel department would morph into a HR department, and you would find new barriers put in your way by people who had never been cops but thought they knew best on what a cop should be like. Jack had a sense that they have trapped Uncle Gary in an 80s time warp but acknowledged that even if that was the case, he had moved up the ranks to be an Inspector. Did Gary have any regrets he asked? "Only in never making it into the CID to be a detective". He told Jack how there was the lively banter between uniform and CID. The uniform referred to the CID as "The Suits", whilst in reverse they were called "The Lids". Of course, this did not meet with the approval of the HR department, but then again, whatever did? There was always a lot going on beneath the surface of front-line policing.

The role of a police officer was intriguing to Jack, but the work of a detective was even more so. As part of his Sociology degree dissertation, he had researched the role of policing in a modern society. Gary's stories humoured him, but could feel the appeal of a career in policing. Stuck with him was the overwhelming grief of losing his father before he could get to know him, and the desire to protect the integrity of the innocent. He felt the stars were aligning and that the gravitational pull was growing.

Jack took the plunge and joined the Met. He performed well in the uniform role during his probation, but he hoped to be a detective. As was customary during his training, he went on an attachment to the CID to gather an insight into detective work. He started off with processing low-level crime prisoners for minor thefts, but soon assisted in dealing with prisoners for burglary, robberies and knife crime. The transition brought back memories for Jack, but with that also came a new maturity and the realisation that a police officer has to be professional throughout. They soon realised his potential and encouraged him to apply for the Trainee Detective program, which would require another two years to complete besides the initial two years of compulsory probation. Ironically, the completion of the Trainee Detective program and the elevation to the rank of detective also coincided with the HR announcement that UK Policing was going to recruit senior officers direct to the rank of Superintendent from careers outside policing. Was this his first taste of what Uncle Gary lauded about those HR influences and impacts? Were the Met going out to recruit the local departmental store manager to run a police station just because they have a different outlook on life? Another HR vanity project? Jack recalled Uncle Gary once saying he fancied having a go at a bit of heart surgery, but the Royal College of Surgeons would not like it!

Undeterred, Jack wanted to lead those around him. He desired to move on to the first rung of supervision and become a detective sergeant. Jack already had experience of police examinations through his initial recruitment and then his National Detective exam. He now had to pass the National Sergeant exam paper, which was no mean feat. If he was then successful at that stage, he would have to pass other hurdles such as psychometric testing and in-tray exercises, as well as a structured interview. He wondered to himself how someone with six years of front-line policing experience was being tested to be on the first tier of the supervisory ladder compared to how the store manager was being tested to a position on the fourth tier. Would he have been better served working in the private sector for four years as a pen-pusher and then leapfrogged to a position that would otherwise take him a minimum of another 8 years to achieve? He remembered that Uncle Gary told him that in the early 80s an officer below the rank of superintendent who had a degree was a rarity, and if you came into the police force, they would soon earmark you for accelerated promotion if you had one. Jack looked around at his compatriots and saw that those with a degree were now, as his mother would say, "ten-a-penny".

Jack proved himself and passed the sergeant exams and attained a position just outside the top 15% nationally. He had just missed out on the opportunity to have an interview as a 'High Potential' candidate. HR said that, of course, he could apply if he believed he had the right credentials, but his application would need to be supported by his line managers. Not to put him off, of course, but HR had implemented a filtering process where the local superintendent had to eliminate 90% of the local applicants through a paper-sift. It was a shame that with all their influence they held, that the centralised corporate HR had not spent the same amount of energy on eliminating nepotism, as they had on reinventing the wheel on promotion processes.

They then posted Jack to another central London CID office as a new detective sergeant. Joining him on the same day also as a newly appointed DS was Keith Jameson. Keith's career progression was like Jack's, but more convoluted. Keith had been in "The Job" for 16 years. He had spent the first nine years in uniform but had gradually moved over to the CID through frustrations he found in uniform front line policing. He had been a Response Driver, being the first to arrive at several crime scenes. They put the onus upon him to take on more and more investigations, which he took pride in doing. This meant he was being hampered by the time he was then still being posted to other driving duties and debilitating postings to "aid" whereby he was being sent to central London to police endless protests and the odd football match. The straw finally broke the camel's back, and Keith decided he wanted to undertake a more professional and focused investigative career. Identical to Jack, he also went through the Trainee Detective Constable program and, as he said, "earned his spurs". He then spent the next few years remaining in the DC role, but broadening his experiences through working in the local CID departments, investigating a variety of more complex cases. With this, he built a broader knowledge of investigative skills and especially in forensic advancements.

Jack and Keith had an immediate connection right from the start. They were like chalk and cheese in many respects; however Keith saw this more as Stilton and Port. They complemented each other. A bond grew with a mutual understanding and respect for what each other brought to the party. Forever providing each other with staff from their own teams when there were those inevitable shortages on the other's. The Lids may have those aid abstractions, but often less visible were the times that the Suits spent endless hours reviewing CCTV, submitting detailed case papers to the CPS, and the days spent in courtrooms. Observing a broken legal system, to the detriment of not only victims, but to also suspects and therefore justice. A chord that hit home all too often for Jack.

Nothing would unnerve Jack. He grafted every day. He managed his staff. Jack supervised his own investigations and oversaw other investigations across his team. When he was the Duty DS for the shift, he would supervise all major crimes and incidents across the whole Borough. But then, one day, there was that one call. Just as he was about to take a week's long holiday the next day.

Into the CID office walked a young probationary PC. As is procedure, he informed the CID of a missing seven-year-old girl by the name of Charlotte. She had gone missing once before, but the police quickly found her nearby in a local playground. The previous debrief of that inquiry established that Charlotte was mischievous and adventurous, but aren't all kids of that age? The uniform PS had graded this as a High Risk Misper, with which the uniform Inspector had concurred. Charlotte had been missing for 2 hours and a more detailed and enhanced investigative plan was required. Not that Jack did not have other priorities, but this now would have to take centre stage. Jack could seek the assistance of the Missing Persons Team, known as the MISPER Unit, however it was now early evening and the only two staff on it had long since gone home. No calling them back in to work; Jack had to make do with the scant CID resources at his disposal. He could call upon the CID proactive wing to help in what they classified as a reactive investigation. The problem was they were already engaged on a surveillance operation that the detective inspector had declared before going home that afternoon as the number one CID policing priority that night. The guv'nor was getting his arse chewed by the senior managers on the robbery crime figures, and this was his plan to take the pressure off. Jack felt unable to call upon those extra resources because he believed his hands were tied. He looked across the office at empty desks. He only had three DCs on duty, and they were already dealing with prisoners in the cells.

The detention clock running and Jack had to ensure that the prisoners were all being dealt with "expeditiously". Custody sergeants wanted it. The law demanded it. Low numbers of staff were becoming the new normal. Oh, how he scowled at watching the Prime Minister during the Wednesday PMQs on TV howling on about how the government had that year given an extra £1 billion to policing, yet it's the same person who as Home Secretary forced the Met Police to find £1 billion in savings over three years. The irony of the situation was not lost on Jack. That sociology degree had sharpened his mind to this political drivel. All that pontificating did not make it any easier for Jack to muster the staff. He knew how to create an investigation strategy. The utopian version would be the only one a panel of reviewers would ever be interested in if this investigation went wrong. In the cold light of day with all the time in the world, the likes of these never saw the reality of empty chairs and a backlog of work for everyone. You were always in for a shoeing and potential misconduct investigation just so they could tick boxes for their own career progression. "Officer, why didn't you do this? Why didn't you do that?" would always be the chant they regurgitated. "And where do you think all these staff are coming from to do all these lines of enquiry?" would be the common-sense answer, but they never wanted to hear that. The buck stops with you, and you take one for the team. Now Jack could spend a couple of hours writing up a no holds barred investigation plan, but as he would be the only source available to carry out the investigation, the hypocrisy is that you have wasted the only time you had to get things done. The Professional Standards disciplinary department was forever spouting out the same drivel, "If it wasn't written down, then it never happened".

Really? Get a life, he thought. In reality, the reason they only ever said that was because the more you write, the more they had in front of them to criticise everything you do, and the less they have to think for themselves. It was easy to pick constant holes in what you did, but they never had the gumption to come up with half of your ideas in the first place. Jack had to get the balance right. Yes, he needed to make decisions. Yes, he had to record them. The trick was to prepare a summary of priority lines of investigation, and when the time allowed later, to write a full investigation plan.

Often in these missing person enquiries, the best way to look forward is to look backwards. From reviewing the initial investigation to date, no-one had done that. A disappointing discovery since the initial supervision of the police constable's investigation had been carried out by their sergeant, and then their uniformed inspector. Either of the supervisors had identified not one new lead, nor even a cursory investigation plan. All the Lids wanted to do was pass it on to the Suits. With the shift changeover approaching soon, they were just wanting to get off duty. Seldom did they take their work home with them. Everything got handed over or assigned to someone else. The total opposite to the CID, where you never felt you were ever off duty and kept what you started whilst taking on even more work from others.

Jack utilised his IT skills to search for any previous reports on Charlotte. He was looking for a pattern or reason. It took him a bit of time as there was another previous report, but it was difficult to find. As he was searching for records of any "Charlotte", and getting no hits, he expanded it to different spellings, misspellings and diminutive versions of her name. His intuition led him to discover a previous report on a missing child named "Lottie", who had been found safe and well. Bingo, the same address with her parent's surname of Davis. Lottie's surname as Faye was different. What he could see was that mother was called Sandra. He reviewed the

LAURA HOLFORD

report, but there was a distinct lack of information. The report lacked detail. A rather lazy investigation as the child was found within an hour and safely returned home. That investigation was curtailed as a result. Jack was expecting to find a "de-brief" of the child to establish even the simplest of facts; critically, why did she run away or go missing in the first place? Clues like that would assist in future reports, but not every officer thinks proactively like that. Officers are often too busy jumping from one crisis to the next, without time to stop and reflect.

Jack needed to know more. The uniform team had already conducted a nearby search hoping to find Charlotte but to no immediate success. Jack had to delve into the home life more. Children go through so much development, with each being unique. Some children often carry emotional scars. Families of current generations are now more diverse than ever, with parents not necessarily being married, or are bringing up stepchildren. Jack could have just picked up the phone and spoken with the parents, but in these kinds of delicate investigations he knew it was best to set aside time to look the parents in the eyes and get a feel for them, and importantly, of them.

Jack searched the office for keys to a CID car. As always, they were in short supply. Each station had an allocation of vehicles. It was for the senior management to decide the quotas for each department. With the station's senior management always being top heavy with uniform over CID, it was the norm for a disproportionate amount of the fleet of vehicles to be assigned in favour of the uniform over the CID. Tonight was no exception.

Jack put the address details into the Maps app on his phone. He noticed that the family's home address was on a bus route and just over a mile down the road. As fit as he was, it was not practical for him to jog there. In his kit he could run that in around 5 minutes, but being a Suit he dressed smartly. The TfL live online bus timetable said a bus was due in less than 3 minutes. Just enough time to pick up his briefcase and get down to the bus stop across the road from the nick. In rush-hour traffic, it would be just as quick to walk, but tonight the streets were calmer, and he would be there within a few minutes. On the walk through the station, he looked at the missing person report and picked out the home number for Sandra and called to announce he was on his way to see them. He stepped off the bus and walked towards the house. A tidy looking two up, two down mid-terrace house. An eight-year-old Vauxhall Corsa parked at the front. A moderate family car and in keeping with the local neighbourhood. There was nothing visual from the outside that would draw attention to the house or its occupants.

Jack rang the doorbell, and Lottie's stepfather, Derek Davis, swiftly answered it. Following an expected two-way greeting, he invited Jack in. Jack took a seat opposite both of them around the second-hand pine wood dining room table. Sandra, the mother, looked upset, and to comfort her, Derek placed a consoling arm around her shoulders. Their respective seats were close together, and there appeared to be a tight bond between them. Time was not on Jack's side, and he had to have more clarity on areas that had not been explored or probed by the original investigating PC. Jack went through a whole host of questions. He first discovered what the family would prefer her to be called or what she would answer to if her name was called out, Charlotte or Lottie? The question surprised both parents. How did he know she was also known as Lottie? Jack explained he had already researched the previous report and found that she was referred to as Lottie instead of Charlotte. Sandra elaborated that they all called her Lottie, as that was what she preferred. Derek acknowledged he was extremely grateful that Jack had done his homework and had taken it seriously. Jack already had a description of Lottie on the latest missing person report that enhanced the scant details known about Lottie on the original report a little time before. Jack delved deeper in to the first report to get some background. He established from Sandra the facts as she understood them. It was a sensitive subject, but Jack asked them both to be open and honest with him. Sandra highlighted that before the first episode of Lottie walking out and going missing, she had craved about having a pet, and if there was a choice, a cat. Derek admitted it was at his bequest that Lottie did not have a cat because it was on his own medical grounds, as he was allergic to cats. They caused him severe asthma. He did not want to worry Lottie with that detail, so just kept saying "No", and then as Lottie pushed it more and more, Derek said that having a cat would tie them down and they could never go on holiday again. That, of course, was not true, and Derek regretted saying it ever since. It caused Lottie to go straight to her room and cry. The most recent comment about tying them down was made by Derek just the day before this most recent disappearance. Jack took the time to look at both of them and into their eyes. They were talking to Jack but then bowing their heads in shame after every sentence. Even if something sinister has happened to Lottie, on the face of it, Jack did not believe that Sandra or Derek had anything to do with it.

Sandra explained Lottie was a sensitive little soul and would get upset at sometimes the most minor of things; especially if it was Derek who had to talk to Lottie about a delicate subject. Derek interjected to say that Lottie's biological father was a fireman who, in her eyes, was her hero. He attended a fire in a house where he had to go in wearing breathing apparatus. Sandra turned away to look at the rear dining room wall. Tears welled up in her eyes. Derek finished by saying the suit, the apparatus, together with the heat and humidity, caused him to have a fatal heart attack. They established he had an undiagnosed heart disorder. It was devastating for Sandra and Lottie. Sandra picked up the pieces and when she was ready to date again, met Derek. They had only been married six months and, as a family, they were as happy as expected in the circumstances. To Jack, it was a heart-breaking rendition. It brought back the tragic memories of his own father. He paused to think for a moment. Jack had to be dispassionate but respectful. He passed on his condolences to Sandra and thanked Derek for his insightfulness.

Jack still had to complete some of the basic investigative tasks that the original uniformed initial investigating officers had failed to do. He had to search the house and any cars to which the family had access. Derek confirmed that their only vehicle was the Vauxhall Corsa parked out on the front, and that they had not used it for the last few days. Sandra consented to both the house, the car and the gardens being searched. Derek took Jack outside and unlocked the car, and popped the boot open. There was nothing obviously untoward such as blood or blankets that had been used to hide a body. Derek popped open the bonnet to allow Jack a feel of the engine: it was stone cold. Whilst Derek observed the searches, Jack talked to Derek whilst they were alone. He wanted to establish if it was a happy family household? Derek confirmed it was, but like so many modern families, it was difficult when there were stepchildren involved. It took a long time for him to build trust with Lottie, with him being the new man in the house, but there was no game-play book to teach you how to integrate with a child that biologically was not yours. Jack said although he was not a father or a stepfather, he could appreciate Derek's position and how it must be in reality. Jack studied relationship building in depth during his degree course, so had an insight on it. They both went back indoors to the living room. Derek took a seat whilst Sandra escorted Jack on a tour of the house. He guided where he wanted to go first so that he could end up in Lottie's room. Jack would need to spend most of his time in there searching it. He would have at any other time wanted another officer present to help seize and log any exhibits they found so that Jack could maintain a constant rapport with Sandra. Yet again, it was another luxury he was not afforded. Those that set the minimum staffing levels did not understand the intricacies of policing to this depth. They were too busy balancing the books financially. Tactfully, Jack allowed Sandra to enter Lottie's bedroom first. After all, he was about to enter the inner sanctum of the main character. If the outcome of this investigation ended up having tragic consequences, the condition of how this room was left would forever stay in the memory of the parents.

The first thing Jack noticed was how tidy the room was. It was not even just how everything had been put away, but also the lack of children's toys being visible. It was immaculate for a child's room. Already wearing police-issued latex gloves, he pulled open the built-in white MDF wardrobe doors and unit drawers. Nothing looked out of place. The duvet had a repetitive cat design that matched the pillow cover. A cushion at the foot of the bed had an embroidered feline pattern. A couple of colourful paintings of cats on the wall broke up its beige background. Resting on the small bedside table was a lacquered treasure box featuring an embossed black and white cat on the lid. Jack opened the box to view the contents. He found Andy's fireman badge and a little cat pendant on a silver chain. Sandra confirmed Lottie had always been a lover of cats.

Sandra explained Lottie's psyche was behind this fascination. For whatever reason that no one could explain, Lottie had the misguided impression that when her father Andy died during the house fire incident, he was in there so long as he was trying to find the family's cat. Sandra had never told her anything to contradict this belief. She believed it was the basis of Lottie wanting a cat of her own, so that she could keep that connection with Andy. Jack nodded sympathetically and carried on respectfully but methodically, searching the room. There was no diary, and Lottie's access to a mobile phone was not allowed. There was not a lot more to go on. In the same way that Jack had earlier spoken to Derek in privacy about how cohesive the family was, he asked the same of Sandy. She explained that recently Lottie had not wanted to go to school. Lottie had spoken about being bullied by the other children in the playground. The school had a policy of calling children by their full given first name. For Lottie, they insisted on calling her Charlotte. Children could be spiteful. Charlotte had been an above average achiever at school and that could build resentment. In the playground, some of the other girls called her "Car Lot" instead of Charlotte. Never stopping to think how such a phrase was chosen to mimic her name, Sandy put it down to the saturation of TV with Americanised children's programs. The nickname infuriated Lottie, but kids would be kids.

Jack pulled open a cupboard door that revealed a bookshelf. Reading the book spines, he noticed that there was only one title but a series of books. They were all about a fireman called Sam. Sandy dabbed a tear from her right eye and her hands had a slight tremble. She said that, of course, it was in homage to Andy. Once a week on a Sunday, Lottie would pull out one book and read it in its entirety, and would not leave her room for anything until she had finished it.

Jack had completed his search of the bedroom and wanted to move down to the garden. Sandra led the way down the stairs and through to the kitchen. As they passed the dining area, Jack looked across to see Derek sat at the table with his head in his hands, in what was a mournful pose. Sandra unlocked the door and stepped outside into the garden. The automated lighting came on, which illuminated a rather sparse garden. It was diminutive. He estimated about twenty feet square. It was a lawn with two tiny flower beds. There was no children's play apparatus or anything to play with. Jack expected something there. It was as devoid of children's toys in the same way as Lottie's bedroom.

'Does she play any games or enjoy spending time with her toys?' enquired Jack.

Sandra answered they had brought Lottie up to keep

her bedroom tidy and read books rather than fill her time with playing with dolls and teddies. Sandra then elaborated that Lottie would not stay in the garden for a long period as she could be agoraphobic. She only suffered mildly from this disorder. Lottie would fear outside spaces, but she exhibited traits of the other side of it; of fearing not being able to escape crowded spaces. She did fear leaving home. Sandra believed that her reluctance to leave the house and go to school might have a connection with the bullying. Jack had to ask for two last things, but he thought it would be best to ask at the dining table in the presence of them both. All three of them were reunited at the table.

'I need a photo of Lottie for any public appeals going forward. It's early days, and we hope to find Lottie safe and well soon. I want it to be a photo that resembles Lottie's looks. Not face painted, not in a group. Something that is clear and distinctive. It also has to be a photo that you are content with seeing repeatedly if we need any publicity. I promise you we will return it.'

Sandra went over to a unit drawer and pulled out a large white envelope containing several family and school photos. She spread them out on the table and gave the question due consideration. Derek and Sandra agreed on one in particular; last term's school photo of her posing in her blue and yellow uniform from the waist up. Jack paused for a moment as he took hold of it from Derek. With Lottie not liking school, was it a good idea to select a school photo? Yes, it fit the bill, but could it cause an issue for Lottie if she saw it? Would it bring back nothing but bad memories? Glancing over the other available photos, this one was still on balance, the best one to use for publicity. Jack placed the chosen photo in his faded, brown leather briefcase. They could always review later this should the need for more family-style photos be required to raise the empathy level again. He then sensitively asked for Lottie's toothbrush for DNA purposes. Sandra took hold of Derek's hand and wept. Derek volunteered to get it. He returned with a toothbrush head from an electric toothbrush. He dropped it in to a small bag Jack held open, which he also placed into his briefcase. Jack got up to leave and promised to be in touch. Both Derek and Sandra warmly shook Jack's hand and thanked him for his help. He left and headed around the corner to catch a bus back to the police station.

The uniformed inspector was coordinating the ground search. They had deployed the police helicopter to utilise its heat seeking cameras, looking over parkland and rear gardens. Switching between infra-red and normal cameras with terrific magnification. The police helicopter detected nothing. There was a ground search by foot, calling upon not only staff from the local nick but also from neighbouring police stations. The Territorial Support Group were called upon, but the local overtime budget could not cover their vast expense. The inspector could have asked the Centre for retrospective funding, but she didn't want to take the chance as there was no guarantee senior management would authorise it. So, she released them from the search before incurring any additional cost for them.

Of all the information Jack had gleaned from meeting Lottie's family, the only thing of particular use at this early stage was her photo, so that they could produce emergency flyers. Out of hours, Jack had no support staff to call upon to assist with creating the flyer, so it was another task that fell to him. More time taken out of his busy schedule that would have been better spent using his investigative skills. The stupidity of allowing all support staff to start between 7am and 8am, and therefore them finishing by 5pm at the latest. They spent the first three hours of their day collating statistics for the senior command team and their daily 10am management meeting. Jack had never known a spreadsheet to solve a crime, but they looked pretty good under the arm of the superintendent as he strutted like a cockerel around the station. Jack could do with that support right now, but once again, the civilian support staff were nowhere to be seen. The inspector had already declared the event a Critical Incident, expecting an enhanced response. There was always more Critical Incidents declared across the Met than they could at any one time throw necessary resources at. You had to manage your own disappointment when you saw the barrel was empty and you would not see an infinite number of resources thrown at it.

There was little value that Jack could add to the ground level investigation. Writing up the electronic missing person report and devising a clear and precise investigation strategy would be a better use of Jack's time, as he could then brief the incoming night-duty CID on it. It would also be available for DCI Andy Ness and the other senior management team in the morning. He would have loved to be there to brief them and fill in any other voids, but he would be off first thing in the morning on his pre-booked holiday. He was relying on the inbuilt resilience for the CID to come to the rescue whilst he was off. Jack was not expected to be on-call 24/7. The uniformed officers were quite militant about that, and as relaxed as Jack was about being phoned out of hours, it would not be possible from where he was going to be on holiday.

Jack spent his last hour on duty typing up the investigation plan. The actions he devised were, as far as he was concerned, conducive to best practice and his professional experience. He had recorded verbatim the information from Derek and Sandra, and the searches of the car, house, garden, and Lottie's bedroom. To prevent any potential suggestion of cross-contamination of exhibits in the later stages of the investigation, Jack disclosed the specific forensic fridge where Lottie's toothbrush for DNA had been stored. This allowed for placing any suspect's DNA samples in a different fridge. He had summarised the uniformed officers' work and the voids they had left. Jack devised a plan to search for local CCTV. He included the suggestion of how to word an appeal leaflet that would need to be created and printed, as well as a suggested press briefing that a senior officer should deliver, such as the DI or superintendent. He established initial parameters for the house-to-house enquiry, which could be later revised and expanded if needed. For now, that was as far as he could go. In the morning, the assigned investigating officer should catch up with the action plan and either adopt it in whole or in part, and then keep it running as a live document to record the decision-making process. Jack signed off the report and put his out of office on for his emails. Before going home, he briefed both CID Night Duty officers once they were settled into their shift, causing him to be late once more.

The next morning, Jack had to set off from home early as he was heading into the Snowdonia National Park for some relaxing hiking and rock climbing alone. He took his mobile with him, but he knew the phone signal was sketchy and he would be incommunicado for most of the time. He had no actual contact with the outside world.

A week later, Jack was back refreshed from his break. He arrived in the office for a mid-shift starting at 10am. The early turn sergeant told him that DCI Ness wanted to see Jack in his office at the earliest opportunity. Jack knew the DCI would be in the 10am morning meeting with all the other senior staff, so he would give it an hour before knocking on his door. He used that time to catch up on his 300 plus emails that went unanswered in his absence. No-one else dealt with that whilst you are away. They stacked it up for you upon your return. That along with messages on his own 30 live criminal investigations and the other 150 he was having to read at least once every ten days as he was the assigned first-line supervisor for his own team. That administration alone would take his entire shift. Having set the alarm for 11am on his mobile phone, Jack got up and left at 11am, and headed off down the management corridor to see the DCI. DCI Ness was very affable and happy for the Sergeants to call him Andy. Jack did not mind the more relaxed approach, but on the first address, he always called him sir or guv'nor. Amongst the CID ranks below DCI Ness, they referred to him as "Nessie", but never in his presence.

DCI Ness signalled for Jack to come in. It was not good news. In a drawn-out conversation, Ness had to bring Jack up to speed with the missing Lottie case. The search for her continued, with regional news covering the case and some interest shown by Sky News and the BBC at a national level. As soon as Jack had gone on holiday, Superintendent Matt Brooker decided he would take the investigation out of the hands of the CID and lead the enquiry himself, as it was becoming a high-profile case with media interest. The superintendent had only recently transferred to the police station, and he was determined to make his mark. Before his arrival at the station, there were rumours abound that this new boss was a glory-seeker with a streak of ruthlessness, but not necessarily in a good way. He had reviewed the stance Jack had taken and the direction the enquiry was going, and totally disagreed with it. Jack had ruled out any impropriety by Derek and Sandra, but the superintendent disagreed. He was of the belief that the enquiry should focus solely on the parents and to not prioritise on the CCTV or house-to-house enquiries. In his opinion, they were outdated CID methods. The superintendent had never been a fan of private household CCTV systems like video doorbells, as he thought that their imagery was extremely poor. Instead, he instigated for both Derek and Sandra to be invited into the police station for a video interview under caution. Not under arrest, but a quite daunting experience all the same. It was only one step short of being arrested and detained. All that the interviewing officers gleaned was the same story that Jack had already supplied on day one. The superintendent had the house forensically examined and their family car towed away for a similar examination. The forensic examination outcomes would take some time to come back, but on first analysis, they identified nothing new. They took away Lottie's bed sheets and collected DNA samples from Derek. The superintendent was adamant that Derek had something to do with Lottie going missing, and all efforts were now focused on that. Everything else had to remain on hold, as there were not enough resources to deal with both. Instead of extending the house-to-house parameters, Brooker had decided that the house-to-house would not even be undertaken.

Jack was dumbfounded. This wreaked of gross stupidity from an unqualified officer. The work of an idiot. The problem Jack had was that the superintendent with seniority and supported by his own line management, who were mentoring him along the accelerated promotion scheme, was causing the issue. For Jack, this felt, to coin an old-fashioned phrase, like the blind leading the blind. The superintendent had what they called "top cover" and, therefore, an air of invincibility and authority. Jack could not just sit back and watch this happen. He had to express his feelings and recover the investigation before it was too late. DCI Ness denied Jack the opportunity to speak with the superintendent, and it was for a good reason. The superintendent was so annoyed with the line that Jack had taken; he had directed DCI Ness to serve an official notice of disciplinary investigation on Jack for Gross Misconduct! The outcome of which could be instant dismissal if found guilty. Jack could not believe what he was hearing. The spineless bastard, he thought to himself. He had to keep his composure. DCI Ness pushed the disciplinary notice across his desk.

'I'm sorry, Jack,' he said as he looked Jack in the eyes. 'You're not being suspended, but you are being shown on "Restricted Duties" until they have completed the investigation into your conduct. As you know, it is quite normal for these investigations to take months. Rarely is justice swift. You are not allowed to be involved in the Lottie investigation, either directly or indirectly. The superintendent has also directed that you may not lead a CID team. He is allowing you to be deployed otherwise at my discretion.'

Jack looked up at the ceiling. He felt his career was hanging by a thread. He had done nothing wrong in his own mind, but the nepotistic hierarchy look after their own. Whatever the outcome the superintendent wanted to achieve, nine times out of ten, it would happen. Jack was up against it.

'Look Jack. I've got your back as far as I can, but this superintendent is ruthless. He has no time for the CID, and he wallows in this stuff. I can give you a job here reporting directly to me, reviewing some pony process or something, or you can work "away from the office" at home, keeping outside the line of sight and take a bit of time to reflect on your next move. I expect you to fully exonerate yourself, but the opportunity to do so will be a long time coming.'

Jack leaned back further in the chair and, whilst still staring at the light overhead, clasped his hands behind his neck. He was in disbelief, but not in denial. 'Ok sir, I'll clear my desk and free up the space in the office for whoever will come in.'

'They may replace you, Jack, but to me I think in this team you are irreplaceable. I'm not just saying that, Jack. If this ever got to a disciplinary board, I'd be standing there and telling them. You're a top officer, a great assiduous detective, and an honourable man,' said Nessie.

Jack inhaled deeply, puffed out his chest and let out a slow sigh. He shook his head, got up, and exited the office. As promised, he discreetly packed up his desk and left the station. He had never had a day like this in his life. What now?

**

Two weeks later, Jack picked up enough courage to call Nessie. 'Guv'nor, I need to speak with you. Can we meet somewhere private?'

'Of course,' came back the swift reply. 'How soon?'

'As soon as, would be for the best boss.'

'Look, I can clear my diary for the next couple of hours and come over to your place. Is that ok?'

'Yeah sure. I'll stick the kettle on.'

Within 25 minutes, Nessie was at Jack's door. Once invited in, they both took a seat in the corner of the soft velvet chocolate brown settee on either side of the dividing coffee tabletop. Jack placed out the two porcelain mugs of coffees.

'I've been thinking,' started Jack. 'It's not been easy but as you know I am a decisive guy. I think it's best I hand in my notice and move on with my life. I've suffered disappointments before in my life, but nothing like the equivalent of a Spanish Inquisition. Please don't try to dissuade me, Andy. I need to go, and by that, I mean as soon as is contractually possible.'

'Wow Jack. I wasn't expecting that bombshell. I can tell you are sure, and I'll respect your request to not even question that. What are you going to do with yourself? There's got to be great opportunities out there for you.'

'I'm not 100% sure, but I'm certain that with my CV there will be an opportunity out there for me somewhere, maybe in the security arena.'

'Okay,' responded Nessie. 'I've got a great contact in the recruitment field. He's a talent spotter. I had him lined up, as it's quite conceivable that I'll be taking retirement in the not-too-distant future. He owes me a favour after a bet over a round of golf where he was foolish enough to double or quit on the 18th green, and I think you'll have worked out the outcome. If he can help you out, then I'll call it quits for him. Sounds like a plan?'

'That's quite something. I'll take you up on that. Thank you. One more thing, though. I'm entitled to an exit interview upon resignation, and want that with Superintendent Matt Brooker. I'd like to get a couple of things off my chest, as they say,' Jack smirked.

Nessie smirked back. 'I'm sure I can wangle that. Brooker might think that he'll relish in the opportunity to see the back of you. Arrogantly, I think he'll invite you in and help you on your way with gusto.'

'That's what I was hoping you would say. I look forward to it!'

***

It was a month later and the Directorate of Professional Standards had concluded their unusually expedient investigation into Jack's conduct on the case. They found there was no case to answer and the disciplinary action hanging over Jack had ended. This gave Jack the option to reverse his decision to resign, but his mind was well and truly made up. He had to move on. As long as there were the likes of Brooker running the show, there would be no room for the likes of Jack. The ending of the disciplinary action meant that there were no longer any barriers in his way of being allowed to resign. As arranged, he attended Superintendent Brooker's office at the organised appointment time. It was his last day in the police. He occupied a seat in the room outside. They had shut the door between the two rooms. Out walked the Staff Officer to the senior management team. Like Jack, she was of sergeant rank. Another of the officers being groomed by senior management for accelerated promotion. Once the management had you in their grip, you just hang on to their coat-tails. They take you with them everywhere they go. As a team, they never hang around long enough in any one post. All too often they arrive, turn the place on its head, reverse all the good things their predecessor had in place and declare it was all done in the name of "necessary change". They ballsed it up and moved on. These clowns got promoted while they left the good guys and girls picking up the pieces. They then added the posting to their CV and went around telling their mentors what a success they had been. The cycle carried on time after time and only stopped once a less ambitious boss turned up and put it all back in place to how it used to be. The Staff Officer said that Jack could now go in. Their voice was unemotional and quite blunt. Another that has fallen under the nepotistic spell.

Jack walked into the private office and closed the door behind him. 'Good morning, Superintendent Brooker,' Jack said courteously.

'Sit down, Shaw,' replied Brooker sternly. That set the tone for the rest of the meeting. You cannot say that Jack did not try to be respectful from the start. Clearly, Brooker had other plans.

'Well Shaw, it's your last day working in the police, and as far as I'm concerned, the day couldn't come soon enough. It's about time someone held the CID accountable, and I'm sure you'll be the first of many the organisation will root out. The CID have had it good for too long.'

Jack reached into his rear suit trouser pocket and pulled out his police warrant card. He opened it up and pushed it across the table towards Brooker.

'Sir, you are right knowing that it is indeed my last day in the Met. That day ends at midnight tonight. As my warrant card shows, I have achieved and held the rank of detective sergeant. I would have, of course, expected you to at least hold some decorum for what will be my last official engagement in service; my exit interview. You have, however, let yourself down. It was to be expected. Before you can be respected, you have to earn respect. Your attitude is abhorrent. You are nothing short of being a bully. One day, they will find you out and your career will come to a dramatic end. I'll be totally honest and frank with you. You are totally incompetent and belligerent. The Met may be a large family of 50,000 people, but it is still a family. But it's a family where people know people. The staff at this station know about you and what you have achieved, or should I say failed to achieve. It's well known that the only investigative experience you've ever had was on your way up the promotion ladder. Like when your mentor, as they do, arranged a three-month posting to the Fraud Squad looking at cheque crime. One of the most low-level crimes that is an outdated, low priority crime. That's about your level and gives you no standing. That doesn't give you the right to walk all over the CID and then, at your earliest opportunity, try to make your mark by taking over the Lottie Faye investigation. You've trampled all over the best investigative practices and protocols, thinking your way is the best way. Policing in London is nearly 200 years old. You think you can simply rip up years of progressive learning and throw the textbook out of the window. It would be funny if it wasn't so serious. There are dire consequences here. Your abstract failure is going to potentially cost a small child their life.'

'How dare you, Shaw? You are insubordinate. Therefore, the Met needs to get rid of officers like you,' said Brooker, with a face of rage.

Jack looked beyond Brooker to the shelves on a unit behind him. His attention drawn to the many photos of Brooker shaking hands with the highest-ranking officers from New Scotland Yard. Arranged on the shelf as a badge of honour. There were no framed awards for bravery or detective ability. The lack of such awards, where there was ample wall space to hang them, spoke volumes to him. There was the Bramshill Senior Command Course group photo. All high-flyers loved to show that one off.

'Do the decent thing sir and for the sake of Lottie and her family, step aside from your quest for fame and let a decent, appropriately qualified officer investigate her disappearance. With you at the helm, this can only lead to an absolute disaster and an obligatory organisational review where we'll all hear the same old rhetoric. Some senior officer who is an adversary to your mentor will stand on the steps of New Scotland Yard repeating the same old speech. "As an organisation, we have learned from the failings. Sadly, this will not bring Lottie Faye back, blah, blah, blah." It's the only speech your ACPO mates know.'

Brooker was by now even more enraged. 'You are so wrong, Shaw. I'll never step down from this enquiry. I'll show you and your CID colleagues how a senior officer can lead an investigation.'

Jack looked Brooker in the eyes, but Booker was doing his best to avert his gaze. 'You may lead, but who will follow? Nobody.' Jack shook his head and stood up. 'You can't see the hurt you are heaping on the Davis family. It's shameful. The reputational damage you are causing to this fine service is humiliating. Your incompetence will go down in the annals of history for this great organisation, of which I'll always be so proud.' Jack turned and walked to the door. He took one last look at Brooker, who was speechless, gazing back blankly at him. He had no worthy retort. 'See you next time,' said Jack as he pulled down the door handle. That phrase was lost on Brooker.

Jack walked down the senior officers' corridor and reached the office of DCI Andy Ness. Like all good guv'nors, his door was wide open, and the desk positioned so that Andy could greet anyone coming to the door with direct eye contact and a welcoming look.

Jack knocked on the door in the customary polite way. 'Andy, thanks for all your support. I'm going now. I've got a job interview lined up tomorrow with a company called the Destiny Luxury Group. Jack being Jack, I've done my homework, so fingers crossed. It looks an exciting opportunity. I'll grab it with both hands and give it my all.'

'I expect no less, Jack. Good luck and stay in contact. Don't forget, be good, as the revolving doors here mean that one day, we may be inviting you back. Revenge is a dessert best served cold, as they say,' replied Nessie with a wry smile.

Jack smiled back and walked away, never to look back.

***

Feeling the slight movement of the ship under the pod boosters, Jack reached forward to turn down the pace and decelerated after crossing his imaginary finish line on the treadmill. He hit the walking button and gradually slowed to a halt. He switched off the machine and grabbed his dark blue towel hanging off the bar and wiped the sweat from his face. Time to finish compiling next week's rota and polish his shoes.

CHAPTER TWELVE

Dance classics blared through the speakers by the beach lilos. Cindy used her mobile phone app to tweak the volume down a few notches in this peaceful area. The beauty of modern technology, even on a remote island, was being able to manage the music and speakers. She could isolate each speaker and even change the music in different zones. When taking the yoga classes, she liked to play panpipe music through the speakers just for that room. Tranquillity and relaxation were the tone. Panpipes were not everyone's cup of tea, but it helped to promote amenities in the half hour before the class started. It was a draw not too dissimilar to Greek mythical sirens calling sailors in their boats onto the rocks. Time was tapping on. She could see about 300 yards out to sea that an all-yellow boat was heading straight towards her location. She recognised it even from afar that it was "Yellow Elder", the boat belonging to Billy. Billy claimed he had named it after the native Bahamian flower. Cindy knew Billy would not have been that clever and, without doubt, it was his wife who had been the inspiration. Cindy had her fingers crossed Billy had had a successful morning fishing. The chalk board behind the bar had a blank space under "Catch of the Day" and it needed to be filled with something special. Something enticing. Something plentiful on which she could turn a healthy profit. Her bare feet created deep footprints across the warm, sandy beach before she reached the small jetty. She waited to grab Billy's mooring rope so she could tie it off for him.

Billy had one hand on the wheel, with the other

waving. 'Good morning, my precious Cindy-Lou,' he greeted her enthusiastically. 'Have I got some wonderful things for my beautiful lady?'

She heard the same greeting every day, so it was too early in the conversation for her to get excited. He put the boat into idle, then expertly reversed the engine to let it drift the last couple of feet onto the jetty with minimal effort. He threw Cindy the rope, and she took the tension. She used the wooden upright to draw it in and put on a half turn whilst the boat bounced off. She loosened it and pulled it in again. A perfect figure of eight wraps brought the boat to a tidy halt.

Billy jumped off and did the same to the front. He hopped athletically back on to the boat and stepped down into the well. Billy bent down and collected the two fishing crates. He loved to eke out the excitement. 'Look what I have for you here, my darling.'

The first crate was not the showstopper. It was the usual conch, snapper and grouper. It was going to be the second crate that was going to entice her. Nothing wrong with the first one by any means, but what was going to appear on the menu board? Billy started doing his usual little calypso dance, shaking his hips from side to side and moving his arms backwards and forwards like a steam locomotive. He was whistling a song that made him happy, interrupted only now and then with the lyrics that were only known to him. From his lack of tone and pitch, the only boards he would ever tread were on the jetty. No Broadway for him, thought Cindy. It still brought a smile to her face. It was time for the great unveil. The dark blue battered crate was covered in a cloth. Billy placed the crate theatrically on the jetty side. He remained on the boat beneath where Cindy was standing. With a 'Ta-da,' he yanked away the cloth which revealed eight live lobsters.

'Yes,' said a delighted Cindy. 'Perfect.'

She knew she could create so many dishes from this catch. Things came to mind, such as lobster salad, lobster mac and cheese, lobster rolls and lobster Thermidor. She could cook them in the kitchen out back whilst the music was loud enough to drown out the steam coming from under the shell. People wrongly believed that lobsters scream when boiling them, but that was not true. That lobsters did not possess any lungs should have put an end to the myth, but you can't tell some people. It was the same people that, despite their reservations, still sat and enjoyed lobster accompanied by a heavy amount of drawn garlic butter sauce.

'Time for that cold beer?' enquired Billy.

'Yeah sure.'

Cindy and Billy took a crate each and walk over to the kitchen behind the bar. Billy, as always, allowed Cindy to carry the star crate. They stacked the crates on top of the stainless-steel prep table. Billy then took his seat at his usual stool at the bar.

Cindy reached down to the fridge in the bar and took out a local beer. She popped off the bottle top, which was collected below the bar top. She placed it down in front of Billy. It was far too early for her to have one herself.

'Cheers,' he said as he gave her an imaginary toast with his bottle.

'Billy, I've known you a long time. I need to tell you something in confidence.'

'Oh course. Fire away.'

'I was walking along the beach this morning and I came across someone unconscious with a head injury. I treated him and brought him back here to patch him up.'

'Wow. Are you serious?'

'I've never been more serious, Billy. He's upstairs, resting at the moment. I'm sure he'll be fine. As if that wasn't bizarre enough, he has lost his memory. He hasn't got a clue who he is, where he's from, how he got here. Nothing.'

'Do the police know?'

'Yeah, it's the first thing I did after phoning Dr Rolle. They're cool about it. Unless he can tell us more, the police won't be able to make much, if any, progress. No one is missing him. For now, he's called Joe. He might show his face later today. I can't and won't keep him here like a prisoner, so no doubt you'll see him around here until he gets his memory back, or he just decides to move on.'

'Cool Cindy. Let me know if I can help in any way.'

'Well, there is something I could do with. He's only got a pair of shorts to his name. I could do with some spare clothes for him. From my merchandise stock, I have a few T-shirts that would fit him. I'm sure "Flora's Retreat" emblazoned across the back will look quite fetching,' she mused.

'Beggars can't be choosers, honey. I'll head back home to pick something up. I'll be back within the hour.' Billy tipped back his head to drink the last few sips of his beer and then spun around on his stool. 'See you soon,' and he is off, unmooring the boat himself. The familiar sound of the engine as it fired and gurgled filled the air. The increase in revs signalled his departure.

***

'For God's sake, hurry Spencer. I've booked you in to the barbers in five minutes' time.' Michelle unlocked her mobile phone and found the selfie she had taken with Theo just a few days before. 'For us to pass you off as Theo, you need to get your hair trimmed and that irritating designer stubble shaved off. You need to walk out of the barbers looking as tidy as this.' Michelle passed Spencer her mobile phone.

Spencer used two fingers to pinch the picture to expand on it to get a closer look at his brother's photo. He had not seen him in quite some time. Spencer thought it best not to, in case it raised any suspicions about his affair with Michelle. Theo had not changed at all to how he remembered him.

'No worries. I doubt I'll be in there anyhow for over

fifteen minutes.' He passed the phone back to Michelle.

She airdropped the image to Spencer's phone. 'I'll be back before you know it'.

Spencer was only wearing a golfing polo shirt on his top half. He would swap it over as soon as he returned to the room. He hated it when there were stray cut hairs around his collar whenever he went to the barbers. No matter how much they try to brush it away, he always felt the irritation around his neck. He grabbed his room card and pulled the door closed on his way out. Not that he had had enough exercise for the day, he took the stairs to the lobby area rather than the lift. He arrived next to the reception desk, and it was only a short walk along the polished marble floor to "Niroop's Turkish Berber". It was of mutual benefit to the hotel and the barber to have this concession on the premises. He also provided a generous discount to staff members who also wanted to use his services. The Destiny Luxury Group liked their staff to have an immaculate appearance. It was a win-win all round. Haircuts, clean shaves, beard trims, even manicures. Niroop's had it all.

Looking through the window, it had all the hallmarks of a classical quality barber with the two leather-bound old-style barber chairs in front of two illuminated large mirrors. Among the two mirrors, a shelf displayed sterilised jars containing combs, ornate scissors, and corded electric trimmers with clipper guides. Three symmetrical glass shelves against the back wall showcased male grooming products. Niroop was sweeping the floor with a traditional broom, gathering the hair debris towards one corner where he swept it in to a long-handled dustpan.

As Spencer arrived at the door to the barbers, it automatically opened and triggered a tinkling of a bell above the door, letting Niroop know a guest had arrived in his shop. Spencer noticed the background Turkish music that brought back memories of his time in Istanbul walking through the Grand Bazaar. All the fanfare without the hustle and bustle.

Niroop warmly welcomed Spencer with a wide smile and ushered him towards a vacant chair, furthest away from the window. 'How can I help you today, sir?'

'Well, I need my hair tidied up. I'm off to a cruise ship in a couple of hours and I want to look smart for the other half.' He pulled out his phone and located the selfie photo. 'She took this photo of us and wanted to have my hair as tidy as it was on this occasion. If you make me look like this again, I know she will be ultra-impressed.'

Niroop looked closely at the photograph. 'Sure, no problem. In this photo you were also clean shaven. The same again?'

'Yes, please. I don't wet shave, so I hope you have a steady hand with the blade!'

'Worry not, sir. Less than four times a year do my customers require going to the hospital!' joked Niroop.

'For a moment, I thought you were serious,' retorted Spencer.

Niroop tied a short bib around Spencer's neck and tucked a cloth napkin around his collar. He started with the haircut and styling. He carefully trimmed around the ears and neckline. Niroop thinned out and layered the hair around the rest of his head. He stood back to look at his progress every thirty seconds to admire his handiwork. He made minor adjustments from time to time. Spencer had a habit of raising his head to look in the mirror, only for Niroop to pat his head forward as he worked around the back. As Niroop worked on the front of the hair, Spencer annoyingly kept trying to bob and weave side to side as he looked in the mirror, that was obstructed by Niroop standing in the way.

'Please sir. Just sit still for a minute or else you will have a ski slope across the front.'

Spencer followed the instructions and within a few seconds, Niroop moved aside for Spencer to have a proper look in the mirror. Niroop grabbed a medium-sized mirror set in a wooden frame with a handle on each end. He twisted it behind Spencer so he could have a 360-degree look.

'Good sir?'

'Perfect, thank you,' Spencer guessed.

Niroop then moved on to the close shave. He lathered up some soap that had the aroma of bergamot and lavender. He applied it all over the stubble on Spencer's face. From the back of the chair, he removed a long leather strap and affixed it to his belt, along with a small towel. He reached over to between the mirrors and selected a cut-throat razor. Spencer raised his eyebrows and nervously started tapping his fingers on the arms of the chair.

Niroop reclined the chair and pushed Spencer's shoulders back, and steadied his head. Spencer took a big gulp of air and his Adam's apple bobbed up and down.

'Hold still now, sir. This is my first time.'

Spencer looked down towards his feet and the mirror that was reflecting a big grin on Niroop's face. 'You are joking, right?'

'Of course. Now stay still. I have 911 on speed dial.'

Spencer was picking up on the fact that Niroop had a great sense of humour. He wanted to smile back, but thought better of it. Niroop executed a close shave with the skill of a master craftsman. At the end of his shave, Spencer discovered he had nothing to be concerned about. He could relax again and breathe easier.

Niroop walked over to a clear cabinet near the far corner and returned with a steaming towel. He wafted the towel like a magician for a few moments. When the time was right, he wrapped it around Spencer's face. At first there was a stinging sensation that then reduced to just a tingling feeling. 'That will open and cleanse your pores.'

Niroop unwrapped the towel, which gave Spencer the

first chance to see the results. Glistening skin with no nicks. That was a relief. Niroop put his hand in his pocket and pulled out a zippo lighter. He struck the ignitor, and a large flame appeared.

'What the...!' yelled out Spencer.

'Relax sir.' Niroop loved his party trick of lighting the zippo and it started up like a flamethrower. All part of the theatre. He turned down the flame to a trickle and took a firm grip with his other hand on Spencer's forehead. With a stroke of mastery, he passed it close to each of Spencer's ears and expertly singed away the hair growth in and around them. There was an instant, pungent smell in the air that Niroop waved away. Spencer twisted his head from side to side to see in the mirror if he still had both of his ears in one piece. Niroop could tell he had never had this done before.

'Christ. If this is how you treat your customers, I'd hate to be your enemy,' Spencer quaffed.

Niroop smiled back at him in the mirror as he returned the chair to its normal position. He walked over to the wall and returned with some skin moisturiser, which he rubbed between his hands and applied all over Spencer's face. It left a beautiful sheen on his shaven skin. Spencer smirked at his own mirror image. He appreciated the workmanship as his hazel eyes took in the finished effect.

Niroop dusted Spencer down and pulled off the bib and neck napkin, continuing to brush away at him as Spencer rose from the chair. Spencer continued to brush himself down, although that was more out of habit than need. He reached into his pocket and took out a $100 bill, which he placed in to Niroop's palm. He then folded Niroop's fingers over it in the customary sign he did not want any change.

'You are too generous, sir.'

'Not at all. You've sorted out my Turkish barber virginity. What price can you put on that?'

They both laughed in unison. Niroop had in the meantime set the automatic door opening to manual so that he could open the door, as he did for all his customers as they left. Spencer tipped him a brief salute as he said, 'Thank you' on the way out. With a newfound energy, he bounded up the stairs two steps at a time.

***

Michelle finished the packing for both her and Spencer. She separated things out and ensured that she concealed Theo's belongings in her own luggage. She did not want Spencer to go snooping or to come across anything. What was taking him so long? He said he would be back in fifteen minutes. He could be a gossiper, so she had to take that into account. The bags were now stacked near the door. All she had to do was call the bellboy, and they were set to go. She had already arranged the night before for a speedboat transfer back to the ship. The concierge arranged for her hired speedboat to be collected. She had already tipped them in advance. Moments later, the door lock made that unmistakable two-tone noise as it unlocked. The handle depressed and in walked Spencer.

'Not before time. Are you ready?'

Spencer was still getting his breath back from the bounding ascent of the stairs. 'Just a moment. Let me put another polo shirt on.'

Michelle had already expected this, so left the laundry bag out for Spencer to add his polo shirt. Whilst he redressed, she put the laundry bag into the luggage. She called down to the bellboy and requested their attendance. They did not have to wait long for the bellboy. They had their own staff key card. She would check they had everything when they put the luggage on the speedboat.

Spencer was still self-conscious about boarding the ship. He donned his golfing baseball cap and a pair of very dark designer sunglasses. Now he thought he could look like every other Tom, Dick, or Harry. They took the lift down to the reception to check out. The receptionist confirmed that there was nothing to pay as Destiny had already settled the bill.

'Even the golf?' asked Spencer.

'Yes sir, including the golf. We hope you enjoyed your stay with us, and you'll return in the near future, Mr d'Vere.'

Spencer's smile beamed from ear to ear. He could get used to this.

Michelle pulled him away from the counter by his arm before he had to chance to say too much. She led him to the Concierge Desk where the Concierge gave a little hand gesture to a man smoking outside. The man extinguished his cigarette and entered through the revolving doors.

'Mr and Mrs d'Vere, may I introduce you to your speedboat captain who will assist with your transfer from the hotel to the ship? Please, follow him through to the marina where your boat awaits you.'

The captain offered to take her hand luggage, but Michelle declined. He shrugged his shoulders. Michelle got the feeling that this person was not as professional as those employed by Destiny Luxury Group, but she guessed they had little control over sub-contracted personnel.

The captain walked them over to the speedboat. Scurrying behind were two bellboys with a luggage cart containing all the luggage Michelle expected to see. The captain offered his hand to Michelle to help her down into the boat. She made it inside with one last step and found her seat. Spencer did not wait to be offered a helping hand. With an assured leap, he was also in the boat and took a seat opposite Michelle. The captain remained in the boat, ready to receive the luggage from the bellboys. They handed down the largest suitcase first. Its weight caught out the captain. It was heavier than it first appeared. It landed at his feet with a bit of a thud as his hands released it.

'Steady there. There are breakable things in that one,'

highlighted Michelle. In reality, the case contained nothing breakable, but she did like to admonish people if she got the opportunity.

'What's in it? A dead body?' quipped the captain.

'Excuse me,' retorted Michelle in a loud voice, with a sharp and stern look at the captain.

'Lady, I'm joking. Sorry.'

'You ok Michelle?' said Spencer in a concerned manner, taking hold of her slightly shaking hand.

'Yes. Yes. I'm just not used to being spoken to in that way.' Michelle looked over her shoulder and out across the marina, to not reveal the shock on her face.

The captain could see his service tip disappearing just as quickly as a marlin skimming over the water. He untied the mooring ropes and kicked the speedboat into life. It would not take him over twenty minutes to get to the Destiny Celebration anchored offshore.

***

The rapid eye movements were the first indication that the flashbacks had started. He felt himself rolling from side to side on his back. His head flicked from one side to the other. Images were racing through his mind. It was like a déjà vu moment, with the same images being repeated. He saw the crystal-clear water inches from his face. He was in a boat, looking over the side. The side of the boat was pressed into his stomach. He then saw a man and woman both laughing at him and pointing in his direction, but the man appeared to be himself. He was in the dining room of a college. Now everyone was laughing and clinking glasses together, staring in his direction. Now he saw fish in the water. There was a shoal of fish. Fish of every colour. But now he was headfirst into the water, floating on top of the sea, and the fish were swimming away. He realised why, as bigger fish were swimming towards him. There were graceful and inquisitive stingrays that used their wings to navigate, and then sharks which darted in every direction. He felt in imminent danger and wanted to swim away, but he could not move. A lone sea turtle beckoned him to the shore.

'Come, come with me,' the turtle said. The colourful sea turtle then transformed into a woman, but this was a different woman to the one who laughed at him. She was wearing a scuba diving outfit. She was repeating the words.

'Come, come with me,' whilst she waved an arm at him and pointing to the shore.

Theo's eyes flickered. Beads of sweat dropped off his eyebrow and ran down the bridge of his nose, running into both eyes. He rubbed them hard. His mind still in chaos, he opened his eyes and glanced around the bedroom. It seemed familiar, and he remembered where he was. He got up and wandered out of the room and descended the stairs.

'Can I make myself useful?' asked Theo to a startled Cindy as she stood behind the bar, wiping it down with a cloth.

'Jesus. Don't creep up on me like that. You should be resting.'

'I slept a bit, but I feel like I need to be up and doing something.'

'I've got a boat full of visitors due to arrive. If you're up for it, I could do with a hand.'

'Sure, why not,' answered Theo.

'Wait there a second,' said Cindy as she looked him up and down. Cindy went through to the back room and returned a short time later with a light blue "Flora's Retreat" T-shirt and a one size fits all matching baseball cap. 'Put them on. I reckon they'll fit, but if not, I have other sizes.'

Theo was quite oblivious to his state of dress.

'I've got a friend coming back with a change of clothing for you. He's about your build, so fingers crossed.'

Theo put his arms through the two sleeves and gingerly pulled the neck of the T-shirt over his head, being careful so to it would not rub over his stitches. Despite his best valiant efforts, he inevitably caught the wound. He emitted a little eek, but thought to himself that it could have been worse.

'You've got to stay hydrated in this heat. Help yourself to water and soda in the fridge. If I were you, I wouldn't tempt myself to have a beer at this time of day. If you're a good boy, I'll maybe let you have a couple later, but only if,' said Cindy with a stern look crossed with half a grin.

'What's first?' asked Theo.

'Let's not run before you can walk. Have you ever worked behind a bar before?'

'I don't know,' replied Theo.

Under the circumstances, Cindy realised that such questions were insensitive.

'Fine. Just lie low for a bit. You can collect up some empty glasses and give them a wash for me. We won't be at that stage for about another hour, so for now, take a seat on the sofa. I'll call you when I need you. We'll break you in gently.'

Theo took the hint and went through to the back.

Timing is everything. Cindy was alerted by the two sharp blows on a boat's horn. Just metres away from the jetty was Leroy's boat, "Calico Jack", named after the 18th century pirate who roamed the Bahamian waters. The blows on the horn drowned out the party music on board. The next thing she heard was the well-rehearsed introductory speech by Leroy to the thirty tourists.

'Listen up. The party continues now that we have arrived at Flora's Retreat. Our host is Cindy, who is going to make sure the fun continues.'

Passengers were standing up and move around as the boat neared towards the jetty.

'Just a moment, all. I'm holding the boat here until you've heard me out. Please stay seated so that the boat remains steady.'

Everyone took their seats again. Some are more eager than others. Some tried to snuggle into non-existent gaps closer to the gangway. There were a few "Hey buddy" calls, but nothing too dramatic.

'Now when we get off the boat, Cindy will have a welcome drink ready for all of you. There's a choice of the cocktail of the day, soda or water. Like the lilos, there's enough to go round, so please go easy. If you can all leave your bags and snorkelling equipment on the covered dance floor over there, it will all be safe whilst I give you a ten minutes' orientation walk around the retreat. By the end, you'll all appreciate that we have enough beach loungers, as promised, for everyone, and there's no need to sprint to find one. If you want it repositioned to somewhere else, we'll happily do that for you. Just ask. Okay. Are you ready?'

'Yeah,' went up the raucous cheer.

'I said are you ready?' which invigorated an even louder cheer.

Leroy brought the boat in and tied it off. The guests decanted over to the covered dance floor, where Cindy awaited their arrival. As requested by Leroy, the group left their bags on the floor and made their drinks selection from the tray on a table in the shade. Without further ado, Leroy asked them to drink up from the reusable plastic glasses and to leave them on another tray for washing up. He explained the ecological issues of discarding glasses, cups and plates around the island and on the beach. His little speech received a quiet round of applause. It did not go unnoticed that the younger the group member, the more enthusiastically they clapped. The group, in no time, returned to the dance floor and collected their belongings.

Cindy explained the yoga classes, the pricing, and the start times. She looked for a show of hands, which resulted in nine very willing volunteers, and not all were women.

Leroy picked his moment. 'I will explain the "Swimming with Pigs" tour. If you can get yourself in to three groups of ten, these will be the groups I'll be taking to Pig Beach a bit later. Please make sure you are with other people in your party.'

Leroy then handed out laminated group number cards to everyone, who were then free to wander and then find their preferred spot.

'I'll come around and call the groups. Nobody will miss out, so just chill and relax. I'll be bringing out the drinks and food menus and passing them around real soon. We'll bring the drinks to you, or there are a few stools at the bar and tables in this covered area. I recommend you have a glass of water after each alcoholic drink. Drink sensibly people,' announced Leroy, whilst he also thought that they should also let themselves go a little. After all, they were on holiday.

Cindy used her mobile phone app to increase the volume of the music. She was never sure just how the crowd would appreciate the anthems from Ibiza, but in the main, they went down well. She fell into the multiple roles of host, bartender, chef, chief bottle washer, yoga instructor and the matriarchal figurehead. No rest for the remainder of the day, but she would not have it any other way.

Cindy returned to behind the bar where she mixed the cocktails so that she could display them on the bar top. She had created her own and, after a bit of tinkering over time, thought she had some crowd pleasers. She prepared the cocktails and lined them up in a horseshoe line. "Memorable Mojito" went down a storm and which only sold marginally more than "On Your Back Bourbon". "Detox Daisy" was a ladies' favourite after the yoga classes, whilst the men preferred an ice-cold local brew of Barnacle beer. She chilled glasses in the freezer for those who took a seat at the bar. For a little later on in the afternoon, in the kitchen, she had on the go some salted miniature roast potatoes. If the salty sea air was not enough to quench your thirst, Cindy's roast potatoes were. A cute trick she picked up when visiting a pub in Portsmouth, England, whilst overnighting during naval manoeuvres. She had her

"Catch of the Day" and other fresh fish produce to sell first, so the spuds could wait that bit longer. They would benefit from the extended time in the oven sat in goose fat.

Knowing the routine well, Leroy headed over to Cindy in order to collect the laminated menus and mini-chalkboard to hawk the products.

'Leroy, I need to tell you something that I told Billy earlier. It's in confidence.'

Leroy was all ears. Not one for gossiping. He was, however, always interested when Cindy had something wise to impart. She repeated, more or less, word for word, what she had already imparted to Billy about Patient Joe.

'He's out the back, but I'll bring him through so you can meet each other. So that he gets to know the operation here, would you mind if he shadows you this afternoon?'

'No worries, Cindy-Lou. More than glad to help. I'll show him the ropes, but I'll ask for him to just keep a little distance when I'm pushing the menus. I don't want our kind patrons feeling intimidated at all.'

'Sure, I understand. I'm confident it'll be no problem. I know very little about him, but you can just tell he has a kind soul about him.'

Cindy went through the back and called for him. Theo walked into the bar behind her.

'Leroy, Joe. Joe, Leroy.'

'Hey Patient Joe. Now you're working with me. I think we'll call you Pirate Joe.'

'Er, Joe will be fine,' he replied whilst still trying to find where he drew the line with humour.

'Sure. Joe it is. Any time you want to be called Pirate you just let me know.'

Theo did not think it would be soon.

Cindy went through the menus and food options with the both of them. For Leroy, this was like water off a duck's back. Theo felt he could handle this. Cindy would normally have a few sample bites for Leroy to taste and talk up. Today she did not have the time, what with the morning she had had. Theo and Leroy wandered among the guests, who were sprawled out across the retreat. Leroy took the lead and, after a few tables, offered Theo the chance to have a go. It went well. The drinks sold themselves. The food sometimes needed that extra little push, but once you mentioned there may be a lead up wait time for later orders, it spurred people on to commit to ordering. Counting down the number of specials left also galvanised a response. Once other nearby guests overheard the countdown, Leroy found that orders being placed were more instant and prioritised over the drinks' orders. Had anyone ever heard of a bar running out of drinks? But lobster running out?

**

Jack was about to leave his office in expectation of the daily SMT meeting, before heading to the security point for the day's tendering activities.

Before he could rise from his seat, Kulbir, his deputy, poked his head around the door. 'Something for you, Jack, before you get to the SMT. We've had an Interpol notification about a person found on a nearby island here in the Bahamas. The person has amnesia and can't give any clues about how they are there. They are checking with all local shipping and other landside places out of caution to see if anyone is missing. I've run a check on the passenger manifest and we have accounted for everyone. We have two passengers off the ship overnight, but expect them back later today. Otherwise, there are no reports of a person overboard. All crew are also accounted for. Interpol says they don't need negative returns.'

'That's fine, Kulbir. We'll run a manifest check again before we set sail tonight to ensure everyone is back on board and accounted for. Thanks for bringing it to my attention, but I won't worry the Captain with this for now.'

***

They positioned the gangway on the leeward side of the Destiny Celebration. Two personnel were in blue boiler suits with safety harnesses anchored to carabiners on the inner hull of the ship. The watertight door was on massive pistons that had pushed it out and along the outside of the ship. Emblazoned on the door were the words "No tug". A notification to port tugs not to push on the areas of the many watertight doors around the circumference of the ship when assisting in its movement under the captain's direction in port. The swell and wash against the ship had increased in the last couple of hours. Nothing that would abandon the tendering process, but still enough that it needed constant monitoring. Stood behind the two tendering personnel was a member of the security staff in their smart white shirt and epaulettes. Smart shorts were also the order of the day for those security officers on tendering duty as there was always the real possibility of large water being splashed as tenders pulled alongside. The yacht-varnished speedboat was approaching from around the stern of the ship. Spencer got his first glimpse of the landing pontoon and saw the lifeboat.

'Are they abandoning ship?' he asked Michelle.

'Don't be so stupid. They use the lifeboats to tender passengers.'

'For just a moment, I...'

It held its position about thirty yards off the starboard side whilst one of the ship's bright orange-coloured lifeboats finished loading passengers being taken ashore for an excursion.

One of the lifeboat's three crew members shouted over to the security officer on the floating pontoon, '127'. He confirmed '127'. This log of people who had boarded the lifeboat tallies with the electronic log of passengers who have presented their sea passes for disembarkation. Protocols completed, the lifeboat crew put a chain across the open side door and pulled away. The speedboat replaced the tender lifeboat at the pontoon.

'Please remain seated until the crew confirm we can come on board,' demanded the speedboat's captain.

Two crew personnel held the speedboat in place, and then, once content, tied off the ropes.

A security officer nodded and shouted, 'Okay.'

The speedboat captain, seeing that Spencer was frozen to the spot, beckoned Michelle forward to the side of the speedboat. Michelle, with her trusty sea-legs, judged the bob of the boat and at just at the right moment grabbed the forearm of the security officer in a mutual hand to forearm lock and took the leap of faith. Michelle had nothing to worry about, and neither did the security officer. The years of nautical training and exposure had instilled confidence in her. She took an extra step and the security officer ushered her off the pontoon and towards the metal stairs inside the door. There were no airs and graces in these labyrinthine behind-the-scenes areas. All very industrial looking, clinical and practical. The watertight doors and their mechanisms were there to do a job.

She looked back and saw Spencer rooted to his seat. 'For God's sake, man, get up. Are you a man or a mouse?'

Spencer looked up at her, terrified. 'Do you want me to answer that? My lactose intolerance is no bar to me being a helpless rodent,' he muttered, as he remained stuck to his seat.

'Sir, you need to alight before the next tender comes in,' said the captain whilst offering his hand. 'I need you off so that I can unload your luggage.'

Spencer felt every bit a city boy. Give him the trading floor any day over the polished deck and a heaving boat. He needed to grow balls, and quickly. He gripped on to the rail of the speedboat, and then he reached up to take the offered hand.

'No, don't grab my hand. Grab my forearm like the lady

did.'

Spencer had not been paying attention. Since they had briefed him to avoid being seasick, Spencer was too busy looking at the horizon and had not been paying attention.

'Look, like this,' demonstrated the boat captain, folding his own two arms together and putting them each into a firm grip.

'Okay. Got it.' Spencer tried again, and this time, it was a success. Now to navigate over the luggage, which he just managed to do.

'Now, with your other hand, let go of the rail and reach out to the man in the overalls.'

'But I would have to let go!'

'Sir, just do it. Please.'

With his spare hand shaking, he let go and proffered it up to the man on the pontoon. With no hesitation, he grasped Spencer's hand, and he was lifted onto the pontoon by the man. It took Spencer by surprise. He was expecting to see his arms ripped off, but the captain, in unison, had released his grip at the right time. Spencer's momentum saw him tumble to the metal mesh floor of the pontoon in a crumbled mess. Not a dignified look.

Michelle looked down at him and shook her head. 'Buffoon,' she said.

'Hey, I heard that,' replied Spencer as he dragged his sorry self to his feet. He followed Michelle up the steep metal staircase. He glanced round to make sure the luggage was coming with them. Michelle had no such concerns as she knew the Destiny crew were extremely slick at this kind of thing.

Spencer's thoughts were colliding. There was the sudden realisation that at the top of the stairs, he could make out more people in official white shirts. He was getting the same nervous feeling he had when passing through the "Nothing to declare" green channel at Heathrow Airport, even when he had nothing to declare. The delicate wings of a kaleidoscope of butterflies were beating inside his stomach. How on earth was he going to carry off getting on board as Theo? He pushed his sunglasses high up on his nose and pulled down his baseball cap. That should do it, he reassured himself.

'Welcome back on-board, Mrs d'Vere. It's good to see you back safely. We hope you had a great time away?' enquired Jack.

Who is this guy? He looked officious, thought Spencer.

'Mr d'Vere, welcome back,' said Jack.

What should he say back? His mouth was bone dry. He licked his lips. He nodded his head at Jack. Spencer was like a puppy-dog following Michelle along the roped-off channel towards another man who was standing at the security lectern with a scanner in his hand. Just before she reached the lectern, she handed Spencer a token. She had not told him what to do with this. He would just take her lead. She held it out and the security officer scanned it. It made a single beep and the lectern light changed colour from red to amber. The security officer looked at Michelle's face and compared it to what he saw on the laptop display in front of him. Her facial image was being captured by a small camera and it put her image alongside the one on record for her.

'Thank you, Mrs d'Vere.'

Michelle nonchalantly walked on, came to an abrupt stop, and turned to look back at Spencer.

'Sir, please step forward.'

Spencer moved closer and held out his token.

The security officer again repeated, 'Sir.'

Spencer froze to the spot, not knowing what to do. He copied Michelle and held out his token. What now?

'Sir, please remove your sunglasses and baseball cap,' came the stern request.

He thought to himself that it was all going to come on top. He looked up beyond the security officer and saw Michelle mimicking the removal of his sunglasses and hat, as if she was practicing sign language.

'Yes, yes, of course,' he responded. He removed his sunglasses with one hand and his baseball cap with the other. He then looked around 360 degrees to see if anyone else was taking any notice. It appeared not, but a long queue was forming behind him as a full tender had come in, and it was adding to the pressure.

'Sir, stand still, please.'

Spencer was oblivious to the security officer, who had tried to catch his image with the security camera. The security officer put his hand out to indicate for him to stand stock-still.

'We seem to have a problem, sir. Please wait there.'

The officer beckoned over Jack with urgency.

'What's the problem?' asked Jack.

Spencer's heart was beating even faster. It was thudding in his ears. He felt his insides constrict. It was all going horribly wrong.

The developing situation almost tempted Michelle to take a couple of paces back towards the lectern, but she thought better of it.

'The problem, sir, is the damn internet connection to the laptop. Images are not coming up.'

Jack wiggled a lead on the side of the laptop, and it rebooted the images. The security officer nodded in appreciation. Jack returned to his original position at the top of the stairs. The lectern lights changed from red to amber, then to green.

'Thank you, Mr d'Vere. Welcome back aboard.'

In somewhat disbelief, Spencer walked forward to meet up with Michelle, who was wearing a triumphant smile. Every step echoed in the metal-lined corridor. Still following like a puppy dog, they walked through an internal watertight door. They entered the splendour of the atrium. All Spencer could see around him was eloquence and decadence. The marble spiral staircases were in two different directions with a spectacular, lavishly ornamented chandelier. A coffee shop played relaxing jazz music. A cocktail bar with a solitary barman polishing glasses as he held them up to the crystal lights to check for any blemishes. The barman then re-polished the glasses until he was satisfied, before adding them to the rack of upturned glasses.

Spencer looked left, right, and spun around in awe. 'Bloody Nora!' came out of the side of his mouth.

'Pull your tongue back in and stop drivelling. Shape up man. You can't walk around like this whilst you're on the ship. Don't forget, you've supposed to have seen all this already.'

Michelle walked over to the reception desk and, whilst the two receptionists were distracted with two other guests, picked up a handy ship's guide and passed it to Spencer. He unravelled it and pulled it open. A simple see-through drawing of a ship with public areas highlighted, with a categorised list of restaurants, bars, shops and other amenities.

'Learn the contents and learn fast. You'll be able to navigate around with this in no time. Half the ship is staterooms on corridors. You've only got to find your way around the rest. They have assigned about a third of the space to public restaurants. You don't need to bother yourself with any of that because we have our own dedicated private restaurant for suite guests.'

Michelle led Spencer to the all-glass elevators and called it. Upon arrival, it recognised her token and converted it into an express elevator. It cut through the decks like a hot knife through butter.

Spencer followed the journey on his handy ship guide just so he could appreciate the enormity of the vessel. 'It's like a huge hotel at sea.'

'No, Spencer. It's like a small town at sea. Think of me as the mayor,' said Michelle with a smug-looking grin. She was revelling in the glamour, like a Hollywood star on a red carpet. Upon their approach to the suite, for the first time, she let Spencer go ahead. His look of bemusement turned to one of astonishment as the suite door unlocked without him touching it. He pushed the door and walked in.

'After that experience, I was expecting to be met by mystical monsters barring me from finding the Holy Grail.'

'No, Spencer, it's a ship's cabin, albeit quite a nice one.'

With the door closed behind them, they ended up in the middle of the living room. Spencer turned to face Michelle. He put his hands on her hips and drew her into him.

'How the hell did we pull that off with getting onboard? I honestly thought they had rumbled me.'

'I told you to have faith in me, Spencer. I had it all worked out. Ship's management believes it is impossible to get onboard illegitimately. They think they have all slots covered. No-one's ever thought it's possible, but here we are. If you were just Theo's brother, it probably wouldn't have worked. Luckily, I fell in love with his identical twin brother and here you are. Let the good times roll.' She laughed victoriously.

CHAPTER THIRTEEN

Michelle was living abroad, but her parents had sent her to a boarding school in England. Her parents owned a successful and thriving restaurant. Andrea's father was a small-time hotelier in the same harbour area. He had invested wisely in property and soon his portfolio had grown, which was when he developed the Destiny Luxury Group. Both Michelle's and Andrea's fathers rose in prominence within the local business council in that community. Andrea's father took on the role of chair of the business council, while Michelle's father was his deputy. The bond grew over time, but Andrea's family returned to the UK. The families stayed in touch. Although not that close to Andrea when they lived abroad, things changed when both sets of parents sent their children to the same boarding school in Devon. At eleven, Andrea and Michelle found themselves reunited not only in the same school, but also in the same dormitory. A significant moment in their lives as it was their formative years and the transitional time into womanhood. They had similar academic and sporting interests. They were both selected for the school hockey team, where Michelle exhibited a more aggressive take on tackling. Forever being warned about raising her stick too high and deliberate tripping, Mrs Granger, the PE teacher, put that down to Michelle's enthusiasm. If you were on the end of one of her hockey stick swipes, you may not have had such a benevolent view.

In class, Andrea exhibited an enthusiasm for studying hard. She would often spend the first two hours after classes finished to go to the school library. The librarian always knew where to find her when closing the library at 6pm. Andrea would have her head buried deep in to one of the literary classics, whether it be Shakespeare, Wordsworth or her favourite, Chekhov. Even more remarkable, considering that English literature was not even considered one of her strongest subjects. Technology and Business Studies were where she excelled. Michelle, on the other hand, was more laissez-faire for extra-curricular studies. As the school bell went, and the slamming of desk lids echoed throughout the halls, Michelle would be one of the first out of the door. Back to the dormitory and a quick change of clothes into something far more comfortable. Never waiting for Andrea to return to the dormitory, instead she would be off to the school canteen to get in the queue early for dinner. It ran from 4.30pm until last orders at 6.30pm. She would never be there at just gone 6pm to see Andrea scurrying into the canteen. Michelle would more often than not be in the most remote ladies' toilets with her head over the toilet bowl, trying to force herself to throw up. She wanted to remain slender. If she could pinch an inch of fat anywhere on her body, it impelled her to go back to the toilets and try to make a better job of inducing the vomiting. With Michelle's personal friendships being limited to Andrea, and Andrea doing her own thing after class, it was a secret Michelle kept to herself for several years. No-one was any the wiser.

Ninety-six per cent of the boarders received high enough grades to go to university. Andrea and Michelle's grades were good enough to see them both applying for the Oxbridge colleges. They always earmarked Andrea for Selwyn College, Cambridge. Not that her mother or father attended there, or indeed any university. Her father always joked that they educated him at the university of life, and that hard work and graft made him the successful businessman he had become. The red and yellow college crest also reminded him of his MCC club tie he wore with pride at Lord's Cricket Ground on Test Match days. He thought it was fate that his daughter would go there. Andrea was far more pragmatic than that. That she would study Anthropology and Computer Science, with the new advances around Artificial Intelligence, the prospects for propelling the Destiny Luxury Group well in to the 21st century were limitless. With a student base of 200, it was the smallest and most intimate college in Cambridge. She looked forward to growing her friendship circle, and this college hit all the right notes.

Michelle's outlook on having to go to college was just that. The family expectation was that she had to go. Honour and face were such a big thing back home. After boarding in England for seven years, Michelle's exposure to those traditional values had diluted. Not that she would let her parents know that. At 18, she believed she still had to conform and play the game. She was still having hormonal issues. The mood swings and the migraine headaches. The only blessing she felt was that her soft skin had avoided the blight of acne. Still, that did not stop her from often having a negative outlook on life. She did not want to get dragged into the family restaurant business. She preferred life in the UK. This, therefore, was her last opportunity to make something of her education and shape her employment opportunities. In a couple of years' time, she had to get herself a good job, further her education to PhD level, or get married. Now there was a thought. She had led a celibate life having been at a remote girls-only boarding school. Not that after the age of 16, the school had much to say in mingling with the opposite sex. That the school was over eight miles from the next bastion of civilisation and no public transport to anywhere else. It felt like a penal colony in both appearance and nature. She needed someone to bring her out of her shell. Her hormones were screaming she needed love, a physical touch, and who knows beyond that? She had experienced none of that, but now the urge was there. Yes, she could have followed Andrea to Cambridge. They could have been roommates for a few more years, but Michelle wanted to find her own fortune. Would trying to keep up with Andrea the Swat be the way forward? Going in the opposite Oxbridge direction, it would appease her parents, yet give her the opening she was looking for. All the Oxbridge colleges since the early 1970s were becoming co-ed, allowing ladies into historically all-male colleges and vice versa. Andrea's Selwyn College was one of the first in 1976. Michelle's chosen Keble College was one of the more recent ones, only a few years behind in 1979. She was not too concerned with what subjects she wanted to study. As Selwyn and Keble were sister colleges, it meant that Andrea and herself could stay in closer contact. Sociology had proved to be her best A-level result, so that was a given, especially as the success rate upon application was 93%. She also fancied psychology, but that was based more on finding her inner self, rather than its application in a wider context. The only off-putting thing that concerned Michelle was the tradition of dining together in the halls. There would be no chance of her being able to breakaway with her bulimic issues. She had slowly weaned herself off the ritual and the occasions were less than they used to be. At times of acute anxiety, it would creep back in for a few days, but overall, she was in control. She had recovered her self-conscience by reading self-help books. She had become so engrossed in the articles in her final year at boarding school that the pendulum had swung the other way. Controlling had become her chief preoccupation. It started with being able to control herself, to her wanting to have control over other people. Her thoughts were becoming a tad sadistic when she lapsed into dark thoughts. Self-preservation to her was key. Some of her visions and attitudes turned off potential friendships with both males and females in her first four months at college. She had to teach herself to be more subtle in conversations, especially when speaking to members of the opposite sex. If she saw no initial spark in a potential relationship, she would turn on the other person in quite a nasty way. It may be words, sometimes it was in actions. She didn't give anyone a second chance. If she carried on like this, she would become more isolated. The arrival on scene of Theo changed all that.

For the first couple of months in the Michaelmas term, Michelle was quite oblivious to the athletically built young man sat at the rear right of the lecture theatre during her sociology classes. She sat near the front row to ensure her traditional, timely getaway. A ritual she carried on from her boarding school days. She did not know that from his vantage point, he had full view, albeit from the rear perspective, of all the students. For weeks, he had been studying the comings and goings. Looking and listening to the questions they all raised with their assigned and guest visiting tutors. He could see who was in their normal positions for their regular tutors compared to who was hustling further forward for guest professors. Some days it was like bees around a honey pot, spotting who wanted to be a worker bee and who aspired to be queen bee. Although Michelle came across lethargic and ostentatious, he observed she would craftily step it up a level and throw in the odd clever comment or question. She was looking to be the queen of the hive. He thought he was only getting glimpses of this side of her personality. He wanted to take a closer look. Over the next few lectures, he drifted down the auditorium, getting closer to the somewhat mysterious lady. Theo did not care about sociology. Yes, the subject was of his choosing, but his main academic love was for geography. He had not seen her at those lectures, so he was keen to ask what else she was studying. The study of sociology could take many forms. This lady seemed to err more towards class, social control, and gender issues. Theo was more for the environment and the connections to social media. Being a passionate amateur photographer, he aimed to apply his sociological studies in his future career.

The connection between geography, photography, wildlife and the environment was strong. Michelle, as it transpired, was interested in the social causes and consequences of the behaviour of humans. Two opposite poles in the same subject.

By November, Theo had positioned himself one morning to be sitting in the front row alongside where he knew Michelle habitually liked to sit. Being first into the theatre, he had the whole seating plan from which to choose. He did not need that choice. There was only one place where he was going to sit. He had noticed that Michelle was right-handed, so he positioned himself to be on her left-hand side in order to dictate just how close he could lean in her direction to scrutinise her without freaking her out. Theo had his brown leather briefcase that he had inherited from his father. He put that on the seat to his left as to create a comfortable break between himself and anyone else wanting to encroach. He did not want to be disturbed whilst wanting to get to know Michelle. By studying the class list, he had already established her name. What he did not know was whether, in a more relaxed social setting, he would abbreviate her name to a diminutive form, such as the old English name of Shelley?

As the start time of the lecture approached, the students drifted in with a bit more urgency. It was a total no-no to be late. It was only their regular lecturer today, Dr Phillips. Theo could not imagine a rush for the front seats. The auditorium seating outnumbered the students by about seven to one anyhow. Would that mean Michelle taking advantage of that and, for once, sitting in another row maybe? Last through the door was Michelle. Not looking at all flustered, she entered with a confident, flowing grace. She had tied back her hair into a high ponytail. A full-length flowing dress hid her whole body, with an open-buttoned cardigan over the top. Just enough to take the chill off from the cooling November air. She glanced over to where Theo was sitting. He tried to avert his gaze, but he could not help himself. She was walking straight in his direction, but then ignored her seat of choice and came to a stop in front of Theo. Michelle stood there with her legs shoulder width apart and her hands on both hips. She looked very domineering. Weren't those legs slender? he thought. A thing of beauty,

'Can you move your crusty old bag, please?'

'Pardon?'

'Are you deaf? Remove your bag as I want to sit there,' pointing to the seat to the left of Theo.

That failed, he thought. Now he had no control in order to how far he could lean towards her. If only he was left-handed, like his brother. Even to be ambidextrous right now for even just two hours would be a mild blessing.

He reached over and picked up his tattered briefcase. She had given him no option but to place it on the seat where he had presumed she would be sitting.

'Is your second subject Entomology? I only ask because that bag looks flea ridden.'

Cutting. She was feistier than he had imagined, but her personality and appearance had already captivated him.

'No, it's not Entomology at all. You are mistaken. My other subject is Angelology. My dissertation is on how to catch an angel as they fall from heaven. You look like my new muse.'

She did not know whether to laugh or throw up. She chose the former. Michelle claimed, 'I've heard some corny chat up lines in my time,' which was a lie since she had never been chatted up before, 'but that's quite cute.'

Is this how ladies are supposed to act when passed a compliment? Michelle did not know, but as she liked the look of Theo close up, she rolled with it. But what do you do now? Flirt back?

Luckily, she had no time to think as Dr Phillips went straight into her lecture on Historical Sociology: What did the Romans ever do for us?

Theo and Michelle gave each other occasional glances. Theo thought he had already played his ace card, so now it was time to play it cool. He also wanted Michelle to see him making copious notes, which he knew would never see the light of day again. Analysis of the Roman Empire was not his bag. He knew all he wanted to know about Romans when at primary school as a nine-year-old. Theo noticed Michelle was not making many notes at all, which came as a surprise to him given she was sitting straight in the eyeline of Dr Phillips. He thought that maybe Dr Phillips deserved more respect than that, but each to their own.

Placing herself to Theo's left was a deliberate ploy by Michelle. She had noticed as soon as she walked in that his notepad and pen were to his right, and he would be too close for comfort as far as she was concerned. She was studying psychology, after all. Power either takes the form of compulsion or influence. She saw a quick win by using the power of influence. She could decide where she sat and influence him to move his bag. He would feel the compulsion to do as she asked, and consequently, she would gain the upper hand. He was exhibiting weakness. She had it all figured out in a fraction of a second. The lecture was drawing to a close, so now she wanted to use the power of influence again. She thought it would be a good idea to ask him first.

'Fancy a coffee?' she asked.

Theo's mouth went drier still. She had pipped him to the question. He thought her proactivity was a good thing. 'Yeah, sure. Since you ask.'

He knew from his observations she packed her bag and left quickly. Today was no different. While he was answering, she stowed away her write-on fold-down rest, just like a bolshy air steward would demand during the final approach to a runway. He tried to act casual, but did not know if he sounded cool or not. She headed for the door, but he was still packing his briefcase. She did not ease her pace at all. The good thing was the fact that she was taller than of average height, meaning she was easy to spot up ahead. He thought that the cool thing to do would be to move with the flow of the other students, but he soon found himself bobbing and weaving between people, with his briefcase catching the hamstring of more than one unexpecting student.

'Sorry. Excuse me. Sorry,' was being picked up in the ears of Michelle from behind. Her mind could picture the shenanigans going on back there. She knew the compulsion was driving him on.

Theo joined Michelle in the queue for a coffee. She picked up a plastic tray and handpicked a packed sandwich from the fridge display. Cheese and tomato. That would do fine, she thought to herself. Taking her lead, Theo chose a tuna and sweetcorn on white bread and placed it on the same tray, but at the opposite end. Theo ordered a white coffee without sugar, and Michelle requested a strong black coffee.

The server checked with Michelle if two spoonfuls of instant coffee would make it strong enough for her. Michelle nodded. Once prepared. the nondescript server placed the two plain white, heavy mugs on the counter.

Theo then placed a coffee at each end to balance the tray and to distinguish between their orders. They moved in silence to the paying till.

'Sugar and spoons are on the side. Are you paying both together?' croaked the middle-aged till lady wearing her worn blue pinafore.

Michelle had taken the tray, but looked back at Theo and gave him an expectant look. The way he looked back at her was what she imagined Sir Walter Raleigh looked like when he laid his cloak down for Queen Elizabeth I. It was only a sandwich and coffee, for God's sake, she thought.

All Theo could think was that his monthly allowance from his parents had not come through just yet. He was appreciative that they were funding both him and his brother through university, and so they both had a call on the family coffers.

'Was that a yes or shall I put them through separately?' the lady at the till repeated.

Again, Michelle gave Theo a knowing look.

'Sorry, yes. Just a moment,' said Theo, as besides the correct money he had in his right hand, he was desperately looking for more money. He pulled out two £1 coins. That should cover it, but maybe he would have to go without a pint, he thought to himself. He handed over his two crumpled notes.

'Do you want your 20p change?'

Michelle answered, 'There will be no need. Please put it in the staff tips tin. Christmas is but a few weeks away.'

'That's very kind of you both. Thank you.'

Before Theo could even withdraw back his open palm, the distinct sound of two 10p pieces hit the top of the other coins. Gone forever.

Michelle left the empty tray on the counter and walked off to find a seat. Theo received the message loud and clear. Brutal was what he thought, but what a strong woman. This would be a challenge. He pondered, 'How far can this go?' She still had not even asked him his name, and she had shaken him down for everything he possessed. He hoped that his allowance would arrive soon. The last time he checked his balance at the cashpoint, he was down to double digits only.

Having taken a seat, the next hour went by. Michelle was flirtatious and inquisitive. Beyond asking Theo his name, she soon drilled down into his background and where he was from, and likewise, from herself. She had judged him on his charming chat-up line he used in the lecture theatre. She soon learned he was far shyer than he came across. It was now her taking the lead in the conversation. Having revealed that she was staying in the halls at the college, she discovered Theo was staying in a small bedsit in the popular area of Headington, to the east of Oxford city centre. His mention of having his own rental place independent of other students was a plus point for Michelle. Maybe there were some positives there if this developed into something more than a chat over coffee, she thought.

'Tell me about your family?' she asked.

'We're only a small family. My parents live on the outskirts of Rye, East Sussex. My father worked in the city as a banker for many years. He suffered a mild stroke a couple of years ago, so took early retirement. He still moves around fine, but his speech can sometimes be slow and difficult. Mum puts it down to the stress of working in the city. The early starts and late finishes. The daily commuting. Meeting targets. Liaising with the Far East and Europe offices in the early morning, then into the evening for the United States eastern markets. She had pleaded with him in the two years before his collapse to take his foot off the gas, but some people you can't tell.'

'Do you fancy taking that route, you know, into banking?'

'No, not at all. I'll leave that to my twin brother, Spencer. I'm more focused on making my photography hobby into a profession. Out there amongst the wildlife, reporting on the issues that affect nature.'

'That sounds cool. And you said you have a twin. That must be amazing. Where's he?'

'Oh, Spencer? He's also here in Oxford. He's at Lady Margaret Hall College reading Accounting and Finance, as well as Economics. You might know the college as LMH. That's what everyone calls it.'

'So, you live together?' asked Michelle, in a dampened tone.

'No, not at all. People presume twins are close. That's not always the way. He's my brother and I love him for that, but we are in fact chalk and cheese. Spencer wants to follow our father into banking. He already sees the spoils it can produce, but at what cost? Mum wouldn't like to see him go to work in the city. Yes, he'll be rich, but I would prefer myself to be enriched mentally than rich financially. I know mum thinks the same way, and that being the same for the both of us. Spencer is his own man. He can make his own decisions.'

'That's powerful stuff, Theo. You said he's at LMH, just down the road. My friend Andrea is at our sister College, Selwyn, in Cambridge. Since we have a social exchange arrangement and she can visit now and then for formal dinners, we could arrange for Spencer and Andrea to meet up. If Spencer is your twin and looks anything like you, I know there could be a match made in heaven. Maybe we'll try to hook them up,' she said in a half-mocking, half-serious way, looking to gauge how Theo would react.

'He's my identical twin, so there's half a chance you'll spot him if you see him around town. Well, good luck with the idea of pairing them up. He'll only break her heart.'

'What makes you say that?'

'He's faithful as a boyfriend if you are together as a couple, but it never seems to last long. It's usually him that breaks it off. He can get distracted. If you aren't careful Michelle, you could gain a new friend but lose your best friend. I'm not sure it's wise. We'll see.'

Theo was in no rush to introduce Michelle to Spencer. He hardly knew Michelle after only an hour's conversation. He also wanted to dismiss the idea of Spencer and Andrea meeting up right from the start.

They dedicated the remaining time of their afternoon to comparing their paper diaries, searching for a future meeting time. Theo was mindful that his funds were running low in the short term and, therefore, any social engagement would have to be when he received his next monthly allowance. The only time they coincided was at sociology tutorials, with the next one being another week away. They agreed to see each other in the same auditorium seats next week. A visiting professor was due to lecture on the social effects of the collapse of the Communist Block, should it continue? With events developing in Eastern Europe and the Soviet Union itself, it was bound to be a well-attended event with the front row seats being snapped up. They agreed to be there thirty minutes early. They agreed that the first one there bagged a seat for the other. That would be me then, Theo thought to himself.

As the weeks went by, Theo and Michelle drew closer to each other. Their friendship blossomed into something more than platonic. First a few gentle nudges of each other in the lectures. Then touching and holding hands over coffee. Theo took a part-time position helping in a local pet shop. First stocking shelves and then to helping with the animals themselves. He would bring pets out of their cages and parade them in front of perspective owners. If Theo did not feel happy about the potential new owner and how they approached and handled the animals, he had no hesitation in telling the shop owner and advising that it was better to keep the animal at the shop rather than sell it to the wrong home and owner. The shopkeeper appreciated his work ethic and the care of all the animals. He was unfazed by holding reptiles, spiders, geckos and snakes. Theo was a rare breed himself. He built up his income and managed his allowance from his parents. Theo did not want to appear to Michelle as being too thrifty, but he had things to pay for, like all other hard-pressed students. He would go out with Michelle every couple of weeks, but nothing too flash. Maybe a pub lunch or a Chinese buffet. The buffets were not a favourite of Michelle's, as she did not think they were very authentic. Too much monosodium glutamate, and way too sweet for her liking. Before the meals, they were kissing and petting. The passion of those moments soon stepped up to another level until the afternoon Michelle asked to go back to Theo's bedsit. As one thing led to another, Michelle would stay overnight on a Saturday evening. Theo knew weekends were not only for socialising, but were also for additional study time. He battled with himself to hold back a bit more from spending most of the weekend with Michelle, but his brain was being ruled by other parts of his anatomy. Neither of them needed to be reading biology to know where things were heading.

Theo loved his rugby. He had seen a poster in the common room that said the university was holding trials for the combined colleges team. His sports kit included his rugby shirt, shorts, socks, and boots. He had football boots over rugby boots as he did not feel the need for the additional ankle support playing amongst the backs. He told Michelle that he would go to the trials, and she suggested she would come along to support him. She had the college scarf as a fellow student at Keble, so knew she would look the part. Theo was sceptical, as he could imagine what some of the other rugby players would think of a girlfriend cheering him on from the side-lines. He was not mistaken. There was already enough banter between the forwards and the backs without the screams of "Come on Theo", every time he came within ten feet of receiving the ball. One of the opposing forwards had already pointed him out as "Twinkle Toes", which was met with some chuckles in the scrum. Oh, the banter. On one occasion, as the ball broke out to the opposition's scrum-half, Theo went to charge down the cross-field kick, only for it to hit him full in the face. He hit the ground like a sack of spuds. Two forwards coming out of the scrum were close enough to see the impact and went "ouch". For a forward player to be saying that, Theo, upon hearing that comment, knew it would not be pretty. The Ref came over to check him out. He was conscious, but had a bloody nose. It did not look broken to the referee, and to confirm it in a very amateur way, he pinched the bridge of Theo's nose between his thumb and forefinger.

'Core blimey ref. Leave it out,' bellowed Theo.

He thought to himself that if someone did not break it

before, it bloody well will be if the Ref carried on doing that. Michelle did not help things by running the few yards on to the pitch to help Theo up. Now he looked a right prat, he thought to himself.

'Best you go off, son, as a precaution,' said the referee.

Holding his own nose, he stumbled off and found the bag that could only loosely be called a first aid kit. He found some cotton wool from which he ripped two pieces off and stuck up his nostrils.

'Big girls' blouse,' came the shout from the prop forward.

'Ok gents. Let's play on,' defused the referee.

Theo soon tried to signal to the Ref that he was ready to return to carry on playing. The Ref had his back to Theo, but one of his own forwards got the attention of the Ref and said, 'Pretty Boy is ready to come back on, sir.'

Now the good thing about sportsmanship in rugby and camaraderie at university is that if they gave you a nickname like "Pretty Boy", it was a well-known fact that it never stuck. Well, that was not quite true! Once both teams made it into the clubhouse and got stuck into the beer games, anyone wanting to get Theo's attention at the bar only had to call out "Oi, Pretty Boy". He tried to laugh it off but knew you don't choose nicknames; they were assigned to you. He could look forward to this one for the next three years. Thank God it was not "Twinkle Toes", he thought to himself.

***

It was a formal dinner night at Michelle and Theo's college. They were extremely popular. It was not as if they were a rare occasion, as there would often be three formal dinners in any week. These affairs were for the college students and staff, but it was open to students at the college to invite other student guests. It was strictly by invitation only. Theo did not need an invitation; however, he received one from Michelle and made his way there. What a funny thing for Michelle to do, but he thought he would play along with her game. The first time in the six months that they had been dating that she had also paid the cost of the dinner. Mind you, it was far cheaper for a five-course fixed menu in the halls than in any restaurant in Oxford. The time on the invite was 6.30pm. The letter accompanying the invitation said, "No need to be early, but don't be late! x. M".

Theo learned that if Michelle made such a suggestion worded like this, that it, in fact, was not just a request, it was an instruction. She had a feistiness about her from time to time. He had not quite worked out yet if these feisty moments were before, during, or after her migraines. Theo walked amongst the Victorian-Gothic buildings in the grounds towards the hall itself. He crunched over the autumnal leaves which had collected in the courtyard. He reached the wide stairway and bounded up the steps two at a time with an enthusiastic energy. The dining hall was already very busy. Being the largest dining hall in Oxford, it came as no surprise. With the invited guests from other colleges, it was quite a crowd. It could accommodate over 300 seated diners. The 28 portraits of the Keble Wardens that adorned the walls had looked down on raucous gatherings like this for the last one hundred years or more. The long wooden panelled hall with lengthy wooden tables and benches was a sight to behold. Along the tables were lit table lamps with pale double-lampshades which gave off a dappled light. A few magnificent stained-glass windows dotted the hall, giving very little natural daylight even in the best of times. On an autumnal night like this, they provided no help in illuminating the hall. It looked like most people were already there and had taken a seat. Those that had not already taken a seat were huddled in groups of five or six, chatting away. There would otherwise be enough room to walk between the benches, but with these random gatherings of people, it made the journey through the hall a tad more difficult. Many were recanting the beauty of the pre-dinner tour of the chapel, where a painting that was the pride of the college hung. Holman Hunt's "The Light of the World" was the must see on the tour and the pride of Keble. It was always an easy subject to get visitors to engage in conversation. You did not need to be a history buff to enjoy its splendour. That the painter started then stopped his painting, and then waited until they had visited Bethlehem before they returned to complete it, provided a fantastic backstory to its creation. It was a masterpiece.

The high domed ceiling with the arched beams amplified the noise. Michelle saw Theo wandering amongst the end of the tables looking for her. She remained seated and gave a friendly wave. He waved back, realising she was sitting halfway along the hall. Theo could see an empty seat opposite her. He ushered himself between the groups standing between the benches with the odd "Excuse me" thrown in for good measure. He neared his seat when he stopped in his tracks.

'Spencer, what are you doing here?'

'Brother, brother, brother. Lovely to see you. I've been waiting an age for an invitation from you to the halls here, and it turns out that this fair maid alongside me beat you to it,' as Spencer gripped Michelle's hand on the table.

Spencer was sitting to Michelle's right, showing a hold of Michelle's right hand across her knuckles.

'Been here long, the two of you?' asked Theo with a tone of frustration.

'Michelle was here waiting for me about thirty minutes ago. What a charming and interesting woman you have here. I don't know why you didn't introduce me to her earlier.'

Theo had his reasons and cautions. Looking across the table at how they were performing proved he was right.

'If Spencer's hair was just that bit shorter and tidier, then I wouldn't be able to tell you apart.'

'Not all identical twins are identical in every way

Michelle,' suggested Spencer, whilst giving a cheeky wink.

'That's terrible,' laughed Michelle, nudging Spencer's arm.

Yeah, terrible, thought Theo to himself. Here goes Spencer again. Typical of his star sign; manipulative, intuitive, and shrewd. This did not surprise Theo. He had seen Spencer act this way their entire lives. Perhaps the fact that Theo was more representative of his own star sign allowed Spencer to dominate and belittle him, even though Theo was the firstborn. Being the firstborn, he should have been the leader. Theo was entertaining and charming, but also impatient and irritable. This was starting already to rub him up the wrong way. Yes, Spencer could be crabby and moody himself, but now his tenacious side was coming out for all to see. He was already hitting on his brother's girlfriend. My own brother! What a rat, he thought.

Michelle detected the exasperated strain on Theo's face. 'Come on, sweetheart. Lighten up. Spencer's only joking, aren't you?'

'That's right Michelle. I'm pulling his chain. When you're the younger brother, then that's the only way to tickle your older brother.'

Theo wasn't feeling ticklish right now.

'Talked a lot, you two?' Theo asked as he poured himself a glass of table water and took a long sip. He looked at both of them incredulously.

Both Spencer and Michelle reached for their own glasses of white wine. Theo then looked towards the middle of the table at a near finished bottle of Chablis Premier Cru. It occurred to him that Spencer had flashed the cash again, in typical Spencer style.

'Spencer was telling me about the subjects he's reading at LMH, and the financial markets he studies in his spare time. Quite a little entrepreneur on the side.'

'I wouldn't go that far, Michelle. It's all about understanding what's happening in the world right now. All the social revolutions across the globe eat into market confidence. Sometimes it's the time to be intuitive and invest in chemicals and materials, then sometimes you need to be shrewd and look at investing in the safer bets of gold, the US dollar and government bonds. Right now, I think technologies are the way forward. Computers are moving from being the size of an entire room to now being able to fit under your desk. That's the future, as well as building a property portfolio. People will always need somewhere to live, and with a growing world population that can only boom.'

'You have all this worked out,' said an impressed Michelle as she clinked glasses with Spencer.

Theo joined in to clink his glass to the both of them. 'A toast to the future,' proffered Theo.

'And whatever that may hold,' replied Michelle.

'Indeed,' was the reply from Spencer, 'And to wildlife photography, hey Theo?' in another attempt to belittle him.

'Damn it, Spencer. There's more to life than money. For every mining company you buy shares in, they release more polluting gases into the air. For every gold bar you buy, there are miners working in terrible life-threatening conditions for little pay, and every logging company you profit from, there's an ecological impact from deforestation. I'll tell you now, the future of our children, and our children's children, will be in danger within only a couple of generations because of our greed today. You watch.'

'Melodramatic as always, Theo. You take your little camera and snap away.'

'Guys, come on, calm it down. People are staring at you.'

Both Theo and Spencer looked around. Michelle was right. For a moment, you could hear a pin drop. Why does that always appear to happen at the most inappropriate moment? They both carried on looking around and nodding in acknowledgment, offering their open hands above their shoulders in a proposal of surrender and peace. These people were not stupid. They were the cream of academia. They all had passions and opinions. Maybe Theo and Spencer had just expressed those passions in the wrong way and in the wrong environment. Others may prefer such discussions in the lecture theatres, or the junior common rooms, or even in their private rooms over a spliff. Theo and Spencer had just picked the wrong moment, brought on with that sibling rivalry and inherent jealousy from both sides. Spencer showed his compassionate side by offering a handshake of peace to Theo. He hesitantly offered his hand out in return. As soon as they made the handshake, the atmosphere in the room returned to its boisterous and happy self. You could hear the jovial and more light-hearted conversations abound. Laughter, chat and the scraping of cutlery on plates. Life appeared normal again.

Theo and Spencer remained cordial, even if it was under the watchful eye of Michelle. It had not turned out how she envisaged. What she thought would be a pleasant surprise gathering for three had turned out embarrassing. Nevertheless, it sparked her curiosity. The playful flirting and suggestions by Spencer had her pondering. Was he making a pass at her? Could what he was saying anatomically about identical twins be right? Just because she was not reading biology did not mean she could not express an interest in the subject. After all, she was still experimenting with what she wanted emotionally and sexually. So far, her experiences were limited with her interactions with Theo. He had been youthful, stimulating and sometimes inventive, which she also very much liked about his overall personality. But Theo quickly got bored and there was never a suggestion of committal from him. How often did he say, "I love you?" For her, not enough. He enjoyed the physical passion more so than her. Michelle wanted something more tangible than sex. She had the feeling that even in the short time she had got to know Spencer that evening, that he could come across as more helpful, caring and compassionate. He was the first to try to defuse the tension between Theo and himself. Yes, he instigated the feud at the table, but maybe that was him showing off in front of her. Michelle felt somewhat responsible for causing it by arranging the surprise gathering without asking Theo first. Would exploring more with Spencer compound her guilt? There was only one way to find out.

They consumed the three-course sumptuous meal. The chat between the three of them was steered by Michelle away from any subjects the two brothers could clash on and instead centred on the merits of each other's colleges and what they each offered for undergraduates like themselves. Michelle had steadied the ship. She had looked at the prevailing forecast and navigated a narrower course. Well, for now, at least. Theo ensured that at the end of the night, she left with him, and Spencer could make his own way home. When alone, there was no exchange of apologies from Theo or Michelle towards each other. The walk back towards Michelle's accommodation was short, but silent. The lack of verbal communication and obvious stroppy non-verbal body language showed by a taciturn Theo made the short walk feel longer. There was no "make up" passion that night. He escorted her back to her door and, knowing she was there, he left her to make his own way to his bedsit. There was not even a peck on the cheek offered by Theo to accompany the "Good night". The encounter with Spencer had not gone well for him.

Once inside her room, she opened her handbag and retrieved the note that Spencer had passed to her whilst Theo had popped into the toilet earlier. The address for his flat in Banbury Road, just to the north of Keble, but way west of LMH. It was only a nine minutes' walk to get there. She would never major in Latin but thought to herself, "carpe diem". She grabbed her keys and set off. After a brisk walk, she arrived sooner than she predicted, but a little out of breath. Despite the cool autumn breeze, Michelle did not feel the cold. During the complete walk, she had been looking all around her to see if she was being followed. She knocked on the door unannounced and Spencer answered, wearing just a pair of Paisley patterned boxer shorts.

'Well, you better come in,' said Spencer.

There was no look of surprise or shock on his face. Neither that of embarrassment nor deceitfulness. Spencer escorted her through to his small living room. He turned towards her, and she took hold of his hand whilst with the other placing her index finger upright over his lips as if to silence him. The electricity between them was palpable.

'Best you show me where your bedroom is.'

CHAPTER FOURTEEN

'Did you enjoy?' asked Theo as he collected the used dinner plates on his round amongst the visitors.

'Yes sir, those conch fritters and lobster rolls were mighty fresh. The best darn food I've had this holiday,' came the reply.

'Glad you enjoyed it.'

Theo stacked the four plates collected from the family group's table and wiped it down with a disinfectant cloth.

'Listen up everyone,' announced Leroy. 'All those with group one tickets. Please come and join me over on the jetty. Make sure you've got your swimwear on. We're going swimming with the pigs! Group one, that's group one.'

Leroy was enthusiastic as ever. He was already taking big steps across the soft beach and onto the jetty, all while barefoot. The group one ticket holders had been ready in anticipation. People left, right and centre grabbed their beach towels and bags, and swept up the youngsters in their arms. Kids screamed with excitement and tried to run ahead of their parents in gay abandonment towards the boat. No-one was holding them back. They acted like a mini pack of wolves. Theo had reached the kitchen and was preparing the eating utensils and plates for washing.

'Go on, scoot. Join Leroy. I'll collect the last of the plates,' demanded Cindy.

'Are you sure?'

'Sure I'm sure. If you feel ok, then get out of here. Scram, before I change my mind.'

She was a mother hen. He did not need to think twice. He picked up a bit of a jog and headed over towards the jetty. Leroy was there counting the guests on to the boat.

'Eight, nine, ten. Ok, let's go folks.'

A little boy shouted out.

'Wait. Wait. There's a man running.'

Leroy looked over. 'Brother Joe, welcome onboard. Hey folks, a big cheer for Brother Joe.'

He was proving popular with the guests for his ability to bring out the lunch orders in a timely fashion and making sure everyone had their drinks nice and cold. An enormous cheer echoed around the boat.

'Now listen up. In about ten minutes' time, we'll be at Pig Beach. I've been doing this tour for many years and there ain't a hell of a lot that I don't know about them pigs. Anything you want to know, then I'm your man. If you can hold those questions until I get us to that beach, then I'd appreciate that at this time. The same as on the way here, your buoyancy aids are under your seats. For those getting into the water when we get there, then please put one on now or wait until we get there. Sit tight and we'll be on our way.'

Leroy took a standing position at the wheelhouse. Theo took a stand next to him in a demonstration that they were leading an adventure. In reality, Theo did not know where he was heading.

Leroy steered the boat out into the deeper water and took a beeline for Pig Beach. As promised, they were soon pulling forward towards the beach. Leroy held back about thirty metres and cut the engine to idle. The boat bobbed in the clear water. Leroy's voice projected above the tick over of the engine. The passengers were twisting and turning to get the best view of the pigs on the beach. Cameras and smart phones were being whipped out by everyone who had one.

'Ok. Here we are. Now, in a moment, I'm going to pull in and anchor in the shallow water just off the beach. Now it is shallow and adults will see the water come up to about your waist height. You little ones will have it up to about your chest height. Mums and dads, please make sure your little ones are wearing a buoyancy aid. I ain't lost anyone this week on a tour and don't want to start now. I can't talk about all the ones I have lost in other weeks, as my lawyer has asked me not to.'

All the kids turned to look at their parents.

'He's kidding honey,' soothed a couple of the parents.

'Indeed, I am, ma'am, but let's be careful out there.'

Leroy went towards a large closed cooler box at the rear of the boat. 'Now when we pull in, you'll see the pigs come out towards the boat. Don't panic. We know them for being friendly. They know that you folks are going to have something for them. They see us come here every day. Now, in my box, I have some large carrots. They love them carrots. Now the secret is to hold the carrot by the very top end, here at the thickest bit,' as he raised a carrot and demonstrated with his outstretched arm.

'Can I have a small child come over here that I can feed a carrot to? Folks, I'm joking. If I feed the little kids carrots, we'll have them on peas and brussels sprouts by dinner time tonight. Now don't fear the pigs. They want what you have for them. You just need to be confident in letting go of the carrot sooner than later. Now when we get to the beach, just watch how I drop one in their mouths. You got me?'

A quiet group "yes" is the response from some of the now subdued mouths.

'Come on, folks. You got me?'

A louder "yes" now reverberated around the boat. Kids were clapping. Parents had become pensive.

'Now you folks have a choice. If you are confident enough, please walk down the metal steps at the rear of the boat and into the water when I say so. The engine will be off, and you'll be safe. The pigs will come over to us so those that don't want to get into the water, then you can lean over the side and feed them. However, what is the name of the tour?'

The entire boat, including Theo and Leroy, shouted out in unison, 'Swimming with pigs!'

'That's right, folks. Swimming with pigs. Now, one more thing. We are not alone out here on the high seas. We have many other things out there with us today. When we get in the water, if you look down you just may see many fish, some big, some small. Now, you might just see stingrays. You might even see sharks and maybe a turtle. Don't be scared because these things will not hurt you as long as you don't go prodding them. They'll swim around between us. Now, it gets a little crazy at times. You'll be looking here; you'll be looking there. Please look out for each other in your family groups. Brother Joe and I will keep an eye out for all of you as well. I'll be getting in the water to feed the pigs. Joe will return onboard first to help you get back on the boat. Follow me on to the beach when I call you over and I'll guide you around. Please stay together and do as I ask. That way, we all stay safe. When we get onto the island, you'll see some piglets. Please don't go near them as mummy pig will get jealous. If she doesn't harm us, she may well harm the piglet, and we don't want that, do we?' said Leroy, as he shook his head in unison with Theo.

A unanimous "no" went up.

Leroy handed out the carrots and steered the boat under power towards the beach. The closer he was to the beach, the closer the pigs came to the water's edge. Leroy cut the engine and dropped his small anchor chain. He moved to the rear of the boat and entered the water, followed by all the occupants of the boat. Nobody wanted to miss out on this once in a lifetime experience. He waded around to the front of the boat and the pigs gravitated towards him. He kept a bunch of carrots in his hand above his head, and with the other, brought a carrot down towards the snout of the first approaching pig. Six or seven pigs in variations of pink and brown colours with light and dark tones. Large patches of mud dislodged and dissolved in the sea water. The pigs were soon out of their depth but paddling with all four trotters. Snouts in the air, grunting away. Their curly tails splashed on the water's surface. The children were getting excited, but all hesitated to hold out a carrot. Once Leroy dangled the first couple of carrots which were consumed, the parents attempted it next and as confidence grew amongst the group; the children joined in. It was not long before the children, with increased enthusiasm, became the predominant feeders of the pigs. Screams and whelps of delight could be heard all around. Everyone was spinning around to see from which direction the next pig would be coming. A lady gave out a scream and tried to grab her nearby husband. A stingray had approached and brushed against the outside of her leg. The husband grabbed her to hold her tight and laughed as he looked down. There was now a second stingray swimming with grace amongst them. Leroy held his hand out as the first stingray now passed below him.

'If you are gentle, you can let the stingray swim under your hand. You'll then be able to feel its velvet skin.'

Leroy showed the guests closest to him how to do it. Before long, everyone was holding at least one hand under the water. A couple of children built up the confidence to stroke a stingray.

'How does that feel?' asked Leroy.

A little girl about seven years old with blonde hair in bunches replied, 'Wow, that's smooth. It's the softest thing ever.'

'Okay, follow me on to the beach. Brother Joe will follow from the back.'

Leroy waded through the foamy spray and on to the firm sand. Instinctively, the pigs tailed him, followed by the tourists and Joe. Leroy, as he did most days, felt like the Pied Piper of

Hamelin. He guided them around the small beach and showed the areas fenced off for the piglets.

'I would pick up a piglet for you to hold, but it's just finished weaning from its mother over there and she'll get upset if we do.'

'Is it ok to take some pictures of the piglets?' asked one parent, rattling an expensive DSLR camera in front of him.

'Fire away. Having one of those fancy telescopic lenses is the safest for the piglets, their mother and us,' confirmed Leroy.

The man started snapping away, looking at each picture on the display screen at the back of the camera.

Theo walked up behind him and glanced over the man's shoulder so he could inspect the camera and what it was capturing.

'If you don't mind me saying, that's quite a nice mid-range camera. I reckon it's about what, nine years old? With that lens and the settings you are using, with just a slight adjustment, you can get a sharper picture. Do you mind if I show you?'

The man handed his camera to Theo.

'See this setting here? Change that to single point autofocus and lower your ISO. Remove the lens filter and check the sharpness on your LCD screen. Can you see that here on the screen?'

The camera owner nodded and agreed.

'Ok. You don't have a tripod, so the next best thing you can do is steady the camera and your hands by leaning it against that fence post. Have a go over there.'

Theo handed the man back his camera and led him over to a nearby fence post that was about four feet high. He positioned him at the post. 'Let's increase the shutter speed and shoot in burst mode. Shoot away, my friend.'

The man fired off four rapid shots. Theo took the camera

back from him and demonstrated how to use the LCD screen. 'Look. These are your before photos, and these are your after photos.'

The man was amazed at the difference.

Leroy came over and had a look at the before and after shots.

'Wow. Are you serious, man? I gotta say these fine folk are having a mighty fine time out here today, but when you just make a tweak like that, we catapulted the memories of a lifetime that you captured to another level. They've got to be the best pictures I've ever seen taken on this beach. Folks come and take a look at these photos.'

The group gathered round and gazed at the man as he flicked backwards and forwards through the photos. The camera owner offered to email the shots to anyone who wanted them after the tour had finished.

Theo smiled and returned to his position at the back of the tour. Leroy focused on Theo as he trundled back.

After a few more minutes, the crowd relaxed into the environment, and were getting used to the pigs wandering around between them, still on the hunt for carrot treats. Leroy pointed out the freshwater barrels and food storage. He took some scoops from the large food box and threw it in to the troughs. This became a magnet for all the pigs. How fickle they could be. Leroy explained how the local fisherman and tour guides brought regular water and feed to the island and that a local vet came every month to make sure they were all okay. Once the pigs got distracted by the food and they left the humans alone for a while, the group started asking the questions.

'How did the pigs get to be here?' enquired the inquisitive seven-year-old girl.

'Well, there are various accounts of how the pigs came to be here. There is the folklore version that when the pirates roamed these seas, they had pigs onboard as livestock. One ship hit a rock out there at sea, and the ship sank. As it broke up on the rocks, the pigs escaped and swam ashore to here, where they have lived happily ever after.'

'Wow!' said the little girl, looking wide-eyed. 'Pirates.'

'Well, we know for certain that pirates sailed these seas. It's also possible that there's a story that on one of the main islands the pig farmer had an excessive number of pigs because of a frisky pig, and he couldn't manage them all and didn't want to send them to the slaughterhouse. About twenty years ago, she brought the pigs here to give them salvation. Now I'll let you decide which if those stories, or the many other legends are true.'

The little girl exclaimed, 'So what sort of pigs are they?'

Leroy was unsure on how to answer. 'Well, them are the wild pigs of the Bahamas.'

The answer did not sound that convincing in either content or delivery. There was a danger that the bullshit would overpower the actual smell of the pig shit.

Theo felt the need to interject. 'A good question, young lady. The Latin name for the pig is Sus domesticus. We know them as the domestic pig, swine or hog, depending on where you are from in the world. There are many subspecies but I won't delve into them as you are on holiday and not on a field trip. What I can say is that they can be very heavy. A fully grown adult pig, that's a boar or a sow, can weigh anything up to 350 kilograms, which is the equivalent to 350 bags of sugar.'

It transfixed all the children. They hung on Theo's every word. Is this guy for real? thought Leroy, feeling he could be out of a job at this rate.

Another boy raised his hand and asked, 'Do they just eat carrots?'

'I have this, Brother Joe. We love to treat them with a carrot but a pig eats fruits, flowers, leaves from these bushes, vegetation, fish, and many other things.'

Theo added, 'Leroy is right. They have a cartilage at the tip of their nose that allows them to furrow into the ground. With their 44 teeth, they can eat into anything. The rear teeth over time have adapted in such a way that they can crush anything. Even things as hard as bone.'

The same boy asked, 'Bones! Like other animals, birds?'

'Any bones, yum, yum, yum,' answered Theo.

Together, the children all pulled a disgusting face and went "Err" in unison. The adults joined in as well with the gory details.

Theo's story had the right effect. He turned away from the group and smiled to himself, thinking, where the hell did he dig that up from the back of his head?

This man was a walking encyclopaedia, thought Leroy. He had better pull this back around before the kids threw up in his boat. He did not want to spend the rest of the day cleaning it up as there was a point when cleaning up spew the stench gets you right in the back of your throat and you end up joining the puke party.

'Ok, it's time to get back on the boat so we can get you guys back to the paradise that is Flora's Retreat and Miss Cindy. Now you watch yourselves getting back to the boat through the water. Those stingrays are still out there waiting for you, and you never know you might just see a shark!'

Leroy felt the urge to keep the nervous tension going. He was enjoying this.

The little girl asked, 'Are the sharks dangerous?'

'Well,' answered Leroy, but before he could get any further, Theo interjected.

'The sharks you are likely to see today are the Caribbean reef shark. You know, I mentioned a short while ago that pigs have a Latin name, well the same goes for sharks. The Latin name for the Caribbean reef shark is the Carcharhinus perezi.

They can grow up to three metres long and live as a colony, but I doubt you'll see any that big that close to shore. They lie motionless on the bottom of the sea, which is unusual for a shark that is normally actively swimming. If they see you and it darts from side to side, be aware and don't approach it. It may feel threatened, and it's sending out a warning to let you know. If you respect them, they will respect you.'

'That's right Brother Joe. Exactly what I was going to say.'

Theo enthralled the tourist group with his knowledge of the animal kingdom. They were not alone, as so was Leroy. Unbeknown to the tourists and Leroy, so was Theo. The words had been oozing out, and he didn't know how he had this knowledge.

Theo led the group back to the boat and, as Leroy promised, he assisted everyone safely back on to the boat. Within moments Leroy had upped anchor, started the engine, and they were on their way back to the jetty to offload and reload. Leroy sped up more than normal. The passengers had their arms up in the air in a symbolic victory wave. There were broad smiles and laughter from Leroy and Theo. Leroy glanced over at Theo and shook his head in disbelief. It was the best swimming with pigs' excursion he had ever had, and he had been running the tour for over ten years. Theo helped to moor the boat and then assisted everyone off on to the jetty.

Leroy cut the engine. 'Now don't be go telling the others what you saw today. We want them to enjoy the surprise as much as you folks did. It's been a pleasure taking you and I'll see you all later for when we need to be heading back and leaving paradise behind. For now, you all be enjoying yourselves.'

There was a cheer and a rasping round of applause. The kids were skipping down the jetty as fast as they could, making oinking noises as they went.

'Brother Joe, can you do me a favour and go round up tour group number two? I've just got to pop back to use the toilet by the bar.'

Theo obliged. 'Can you kindly bring me back some still water, Leroy, as Cindy told me to stay hydrated, so I better do as I'm told?'

'Sure thing, buddy. I'll see you back here soon. If you can load those folks on for me, I would be much obliged.'

Leroy needed to use the facilities, but more importantly, he wanted to catch Cindy and fill her in on what had just happened.

'Hey Leroy, how did it go? Same old, same old?'

'Are you kidding me, Cindy-Lou? The man is a walking, talking, living fountain of knowledge. He knows things about animals I ain't ever heard before. He gave us all a masterclass on how to take the best photos I've ever seen. And the way he tells those folks. He had them eating out the palm of his hand. He's doubled my service tips for sure.'

They could both hear him calling out and rounding up group two around the lounger areas.

'Don't let him leave the retreat too soon. I'd make him recoup longer. I'll be a millionaire this time next year,' joked Leroy.

'That will help us and him try to work out who he really is,' declared Cindy.

'I don't care if he's Tarzan of the flipping jungle. You don't let him out of your sights,' continued Leroy.

'Time to get going again. No rest for the wicked.'

Leroy grabbed a bottle of ice-cold water from the bar fridge and enthusiastically sprinted back to his boat. Theo had them all aboard and was ready to go.

'Hey folks, welcome to the swimming with pigs' tour. This afternoon we have Brother Joe with us. I've taught him a few things with the first group today. I'm going to be telling you folks some interesting facts about the wildlife out there. Not just the folklore stories, but also some fine detail about the wildlife. For the young ones studying at school, I might even tell you invaluable things like their Latin names, just so you can have a fountain of knowledge like Captain Leroy. Prick your ears up as we're in for an interesting hour.'

Theo looked and smiled at Leroy. 'Message understood, captain,' as Theo offered a nautical salute to him.

Leroy returned the salute with an even wider grin. 'You're the man, Brother Joe, you're the man.'

CHAPTER FIFTEEN

Captain Nico was on the bridge reviewing the weather forecast with Dani whilst they watched the dark menacing skies. It was not looking good. There was an impending storm approaching across the Bahama Escarpment from the east. It was severe enough to be allocated the name of Storm Josephine. Being ahead of the storm season, it came as a disappointment to the senior officers. Another sign that global warming was having an impact that scientists predicted and politicians ignored. If they received the full brunt of the storm, it would become an even bigger disappointment to the passengers. Some of whom would not have the sea legs for it. At the moment, the ship was feeling only the outer edge of the storm. These things could go either direction. To the north or to the south of them, but God forbid it came straight at them. The Captain had seen a lot worse but the storm would be enough to impact on their itinerary. There were still a couple of excursions out on the islands and the call had already gone out to them to curtail the trips and to return to the ship by the lifeboat tenders as quickly as possible. A call had cascaded down to the pontoon to warn them of the increasing swell and that tours would be returning. Not that the pontoon crew needed the update on the swell condition, as they could feel the movement on the pontoon. The first tender was approaching already. It was obvious from the bobbing up and down and rolling and pitching from corner to corner that the occupants on it were going to be feeling a lot greener around the gills than when they set off in the morning.

Jack's deputy, Kulbir Gurung, made his way down from the security screening area to the pontoon platform. He appeared very distinctive against the blue overalled personnel because of his white officer apparel. As a former Gurkha, he was more used to extreme conditions on land. Over the last couple of years, he had adjusted to the variable conditions at sea. He was the go-to member of security staff for such difficult conditions because of his inbuilt bravery and calmness. It was at moments like this that these critical traits were required and most appreciated. For a scared passenger pulling up in a tender against a moving platform, it instilled confidence that all would be well if there was an officer in charge overseeing the embarkation. Kulbir's presence was there for more than the reassurance of passengers. He shared the concerns of the professional crew that transferred people between two moving items. It always had the potential to go wrong. The biggest danger was when passengers did not follow orders and then dithered. A foot hold wrong here, a hand grip let go at the wrong time there, and it could cause carnage. It was seldom that the passenger ended up injured. More often than not, it was the brave crew member who put themselves on the line by reacting to save the passenger and, as a consequence, placed themselves in danger. It only took a split second to surrender to the forces of nature, as Kulbir knew only too well as he had lost his sherpa brother on Everest back home, who succumbed to an avalanche.

Kulbir was looking everywhere whilst also listening to the communications over his radio. As the tender came closer, its wake caused the pontoon to bob up and down just that bit more. It was becoming more than just an irritation. The tender put on its rear thrust to bring it to a stop. The wash caused the boat to rub against the metal pontoon. There was the unmistakable loud grinding noise that confirmed the heavy contact. The jolt caused the occupants of the tender boat to move in their seats. Three impatient passengers, who did not heed the warning to remain in their seats and had stood up to secure prime disembarkation positions, were sent tumbling to the floor. The loud scream did not emanate from any of them, but from a shocked elderly couple at whose feet they had landed.

Kulbir positioned himself on the pontoon opposite the open side door of the tender boat. 'All, please remain seated. We will call you forward row by row. Stay seated. It's for all our safety. If you need a little more time to disembark because of any frailties, then please inform my staff on the tender. We will take you off last of all. Please be assured that we take people off in these conditions regularly and if you follow our instructions, there won't be a problem. Thank you.'

The two tender crew removed the chain across the doorway as the tender pilot held his position. The crew pointed at individuals and said, 'Please, come.'

Someone brought the three guests who had crumpled to the floor forward to the boat's edge, despite the obvious disdain of the other passengers. Kulbir stepped back a little to allow one of the blue-overalled pontoon staff to offer their hand to pull people on to the pontoon at the right moment.

Just as the tender came up on a rise, the staff member said, 'Now,' as the tender crew gave an encouraging nudge in the passenger's back, who stepped cautiously onto the pontoon. Kulbir directed them towards the metal staircase. They were out of sight and on their way. The same happened to the second person, who went to the bottom of the stairs and stood there looking back.

'Sir, please go. You need to go now,' demanded Kulbir.

'But my wife.'

'She'll be fine. Please go. You are holding us up.'

Without further ado, the man reluctantly took to the stairs.

The next two were a teenage brother and sister. They

saw this as an adventure and thrived in the challenge to leap on to the platform. They both fist pumped the air as they walked to the stairway.

'Come on mum,' went out the call.

'Wait kids.'

In her rush, the timings went awry. With no direction from the pontoon crew or tender staff, she released her grip on the upright rail of the tender and attempted to disembark while it was descending. Her portly frame fell backwards into the tender. The two tender staff had their arms around the back of her to catch her. Inadvertently, one of the tender crew in doing so lost his balance and his right leg stuck out through the boat's opening, precisely at the moment that the tender's momentum was in an upward direction. His lower leg, for a fraction of a second, became trapped between the tender and pontoon. The sound of the snap of the breaking bone was unmistakable. The scream of agony only magnified the significance of what had just happened.

Kulbir disconnected his harness carabiner from the rope attaching him to the safety of the ship. He leapt forward into the open tender door. He could see that the tender was about to make its downward drop, so he dragged the crew member's broken leg into the tender. They both end up sprawled on the floor. Kulbir looked down and saw the protruding bone sticking out of the man's leg to its side, just above his sock.

Kulbir reached for his radio. 'Code Blue. Code Blue. Gangway deck 1. Port side. Compound fracture left leg.'

He had activated the signal for a medical emergency. The bridge acknowledged the call, and a broadcast went out on the ship's tannoy system.

'Code Blue. Code Blue. Gangway deck 1. Port side. Medical team to Gangway deck 1. This is not a drill. I repeat, this is not a drill. Code Blue. Gangway deck 1. Port side.'

They did not restrict the tannoy announcement to just

inside the ship. It echoed around the outer decks. Those in their cabins with balconies on the port side appeared on them and leaning over their balconies to get a better view at the spectacle unfolding below them. From Kulbir's position on the tender floor looking up at the ship, he registered glances as the boat bobbed up of people looking like ghouls watching from over their balconies. He noticed that three or four were holding their mobile phones over the side and were videoing the drama. Nothing ever failed to astonish him.

***

Jack was in the middle of grabbing a light lunch at the top deck buffet. He heard the call and abandoned his plate. Jack put his radio to his ear and turned up the volume. He headed towards one of the crew access doors to the correct behind-the-scenes staircase. He bounded down as fast as he could. If he had done this in such an undignified manner on the passenger side, it would have instilled fear in those watching him react. It took about forty seconds for him to reach deck 2 where his security screening team was already waiting.

'Stay at your posts. I'll call if we need help.'

The ship's security and integrity must be upheld at all times and at all costs. He was not thinking that this could be a distraction event by terrorists, but protocols must be maintained. Jack could see Dr Patel and her two nurses who approached from the door leading from the Atrium. Jack held them with an outstretched arm at the security lectern and got on his radio. 'Sitrep please Kulbir.'

'Sir, a pontoon crew member trapped his leg between the tender and the pontoon.'

A grimace came across Jack's face.

'He is on the tender. We have 12 other passengers on here that we also need to disembark. We are ready for a medical team to board the tender. Shall we get the passengers off first, sir?'

'Standby on that Kulbir. I'll come down with the medical team and stabilise the patient. The passengers will have to wait. Who is the crew member?'

'A young man from the engineering department called Jorge.'

'Ok. We're coming down now. See you in thirty seconds.'

The broadcast on the radio was loud enough for the medical team to hear. Jack handed out buoyancy aids to the medical team. They knew the drill. Pre-cruise, they had played out a similar scenario in training. Doing this in calm waters was one thing. Doing this out at sea for real in choppy conditions was another. Jack led them down the stairs and along the platform. All four entered the tender. Dr Patel and her nurses headed straight into assessment and stabilisation mode.

Jack took control and addressed the remaining passengers and tender crew. 'Ladies and gentlemen. As distressing as this is for you all, you'll have to bear with us whilst we treat this crew member. The safety of all of you is, of course, our concern, but right now we have to prioritise the treatment of this patient. We appreciate your cooperation at this time.'

Nurse Kenny extracted a gas and air bottle from his medical rucksack and put the mask over Jorge's face. The release of the gas into the mask brought some instant relief to him.

'We need a medevac. He's stable here for now. We will gain nothing from transferring him to the ship's medical centre. More movement than necessary may complicate things. At the moment, I can feel a pulse in his ankle, so that is a positive sign,' revealed Dr Patel.

Jack went on the radio. 'Bridge from Medic Team. Request an urgent medevac of patient to hospital.'

'Roger that Medic Team. Standby.'

Captain Nico came on to the radio, 'Jack, request authorised. We are already on to the local authorities requesting a helicopter evacuation. As I speak, I'm being told ETA in 15 minutes. On our port side cameras, I can see there are a lot of onlookers. I'll get a message over the tannoy for all guests in port side cabins to go to the theatre muster station. I'll have the helicopter approach from the port side, which will justify my evacuation to the theatre.'

'Understood, captain. We'll await the medevac crew's arrival before we take any further action. Vitals are good. We have a sedated patient. Please inform the Chief Engineer that the patient is called Jorge from within his department.'

'No worries Jack. We're on it. I'll get Personnel to lift his records so we can inform his next of kin ASAP. With people taking mobile phone footage, coupled with our ultrafast internet, this will be on social media quicker than you can say, boo to a goose.'

Giving the passengers the best of everything came with its downside.

***

The whirling of rotor blades overhead gave some relief to Jorge and those treating him. It was only two minutes after the appearance over the railings above of the helicopter sat stationary on the ship's helipad. A pair of medics in overalls and microphone crash helmets appeared on the pontoon. Stepping on to the moving tender was a breeze compared to dangling out of a helicopter on a winch line. Dr Patel briefed the medevac crew and, following their attachment of sophisticated monitors to various parts of Jorge's body, was content to transfer him to the helicopter above. With the synchronisation of a well-oiled medical team, they conveyed him to the pontoon, and upwards through the ship's maze-like behind-the-scenes crew area corridors and into a lift. The one hundred years of emergency room experience between them delivered them the reward they deserved. Jorge was on his way to the hospital ashore. As the helicopter pulled away and turned over to the port side against a backdrop of fast-moving clouds, there was back slapping amongst the medical team and the other helpers. Eerily in the background, the loud grating noise of the side of the tender boat pressed hard against the pontoon continued to be heard.

Jack pointed out the obvious, 'Kulbir, I'm going to need a full report on my desk please within the next two hours. Once Destiny HQ and no doubt the world's press get hold of this, we'll have headlines all over it.'

'I'm on it now, sir. You'll have it within the hour.'

'And grab yourself a coffee on your way down. You deserve it. You did well.'

'Well, thank you, sir. I was only doing my job.'

'You're too modest, Kulbir, now go.'

It was not as if Jack had not had enough to do already without being burdened with anything else. If the captain changed the itinerary, Jack would have to call ahead and plan for each of the ports or tendering points. He would have to alter the staff rota in the security department; making sure all the paperwork and immigration issues were addressed ahead of arrival. He prayed to the weather gods for some respite from the approaching storm. Please turn north, he wished to himself.

CHAPTER SIXTEEN

There was a customary knock on the door of the suite. The door unlocked and in walked Jose. Ahead of him, he saw Michelle and whom he believed to be Theo, in an embrace that neither of them released. It was a common sight that he was used to seeing. 'Mr and Mrs d'Vere, shall I return later?'

They released their amorous grip from each other, and Michelle rubbed her palms down to her waist to take out the creases in her short red dress. 'You're fine Jose. Please come in.'

Spencer whispered in her ear, 'You didn't mention we have a butler.'

Michelle thought she had, but was now doubting herself. How could she omit telling Spencer that there was another man in her life, apart from Theo, and that was her on-hand butler?

'Please put the canapes on the side, Jose. That will be all. In fact, on second thoughts, it won't be. Can I have two glasses of Champagne?'

'In anticipation of your return, ma'am, I have already placed a bottle on chill in your fridge. Allow me.'

Within thirty seconds, there was the unmistakable pop of the champagne cork. Jose poured the liquid in to two crystal flutes. The larger bubbles distinguishing it from the sister bottle of Prosecco that was also chilling. Michelle loved a glass of fizz, and to stave off her migraines she found Prosecco was better for that than the ten-times the price champagne.

Jose handed out the two glasses. 'And may I ask, how did

you find the Destiny Azzurro Cay Mirage hotel?'

'You can. It was like a home from home. Of course, no one could match the hospitality you showed, Jose, but then again, could anyone ever match it?' said Michelle with a slight grin.

Jose directed his gaze into her eyes, as he was unconvinced whether that was meant as a compliment or a sarcastic comment. He thought he was an excellent judge of character, but in the preceding five days, he was doubting himself. Jose would, of course, remain professional and accept it as a kind compliment. He thought it was also the signal for him to leave the couple in peace. One question from a butler was enough in these circumstances, but he still had a couple of formalities to clarify with her. 'You are too kind, Mrs d'Vere. It's dinner with the senior staff this evening. Shall I confirm your attendance with the Maître d'?'

Michelle paused for thought. Was it too early to put Spencer in front of a pride of lions? She had to break him in, but there was no time like the present. At least she would be there to manipulate the conversations and keep Spencer out of harm's way.

'Of course, Jose. We've missed their convivial intellect whilst away. It would be marvellous to engage them in their wit again.'

Spencer brought down the champagne flute from his lips and let out quite an audible sigh.

'Ignore Mr d'Vere. I think the bubbles got to him a bit.'

'And would ma'am like me to unpack your luggage for you whilst you are at dinner?'

Michelle felt confident that there was nothing to hide and wanted to act as normal as possible.

'Off course Jose. When you've retrieved the bags from the gangway, if you could hold on to them to unpack until we have gone down to dinner. I don't want to be tripping over them in the walk-in closet.'

'Very well. If that will be all, I wish you a pleasant evening.' Jose exited the suite, leaving the guests in privacy.

'Tonight darling, it's best you go to dinner with a massive appetite. I need you eating or slurping your wine all the time so that you can't talk too much, and when you do, you'll have time to think whilst chewing on your fillet steak. I'll speak first with all those seated around us. You listen in to how I address them so you can pick up who they are. You only speak when spoken to. That'll be best for all of us.'

'Chewing on fillet steak! It's that tough, is it?' Spencer joked.

Michelle shook her head at him playfully. It sounded like he was going to be relaxed about dinner. She just hoped that he was not too relaxed.

'Get yourself ready. Your bathroom is over there. You'll find Theo's formal wear in the wardrobe. It will all fit you, I'm quite sure.'

'My bathroom? Bloody hell. I could get used to this.'

***

Michelle rapped at Spencer's bathroom door, and in a loud voice called out, 'For goodness' sake, get out of the shower. We have only ten minutes to be sitting at the table. These are not people you can keep waiting.'

Michelle heard the shower being turned off. A few seconds later, the door opened ajar and Spencer stuck his head out. 'Has everything got to be that prompt? I thought we were holidaying.'

'Maybe for you, but I've got things to do tonight... so get a bloody move on.'

Spencer could tell she was flustered. Michelle was done up to the nines and was trying to finish getting ready by putting the ear-ring hooks through her ear lobes without the use of a mirror. There was a sudden realisation by him, he had better shape up and quickly at that. He tried to lighten the mood. 'I'll be two minutes. Promise. I do this every morning before walking down to Bermondsey tube. Start your stopwatch.'

Michelle was not interested in playing silly games. She had a splitting headache already, and the night was still young. Young; similar to the average demographic profile of women Spencer dated on the numerous apps she had discovered whilst scrolling through his mobile phone when he was in the shower. That was the major disadvantage of using your date of birth as your override passcode. So much for facial recognition and fingerprint technology, she thought to herself with a smirk on her face. She understood that when they started seeing each other again that it was not a monogamous relationship, but she had hoped that when she moved back to London to be closer to him, he would have stopped playing the field. "Exclusivity" was what she was hoping for. Making this discovery combined with what now appeared to be the poison chalice of her godmother role was taking its toll.

Minutes later, Spencer exited the walk-in wardrobe, dressed top to toe in Theo's clothes. He saw Michelle sat on a sofa, legs crossed with her top foot tapping in the air, up and down. He could tell something had displeased her. 'How's this look?' he asked whilst doing a slow 360 degrees turn.

'Fine. Let's go.'

She snatched her matching clutch bag and strode to the door. Spencer followed on her heel like a well-trained puppy.

***

The d'Veres walked into the suites dining room, to be met by Rudi the Maître d'. 'Thank you for joining us this evening Mr and Mrs d'Vere. Tonight, we have placed you with the First Officer and a new couple who joined the ship today, Mr and Mrs Sinclair.'

Michelle was hoping to hear that a senior staff member whom Theo had not met when he was onboard would join her, as well as a couple who did not know about her or Theo. Half her wish had come true. They would have missed his theatre talk as well. To encourage conversation amongst them all, Rudi placed Michelle next to Amber Sinclair, and Spencer next to Richie Sinclair. As Michelle and Spencer were the last to take their seats, Rudi reintroduced everyone around the table to each other, ending with, 'and Mrs d'Vere, who is the godmother of the vessel.'

That last comment received gracious nods of approval from the people around the table of five.

Amber was an attractive woman. She had undergone enhancements in various parts of her body, not limited to Botox treatments on her face. Michelle could see by the glances that Spencer gave Amber that this had not gone unnoticed by him. A bit of a cheek with Mr Sinclair sat within a southpaw strike of Spencer's chin. Spencer was getting the feeling that Michelle had spotted his indiscreet glances at Amber. He deflected by engaging Richie in conversation. Richie leaned over to reach for the sparkling water in the centre of the table. Spencer noticed the designer label on his exposed jacket inside pocket.

'Richie, I see your suit is by one of my favourite golf apparel companies, GITC, Get In There Clothing.'

'No kidding. You like GITC?'

'Absolutely. We were at a Destiny golf resort the last couple of days and I spied in the Pro shop they had GITC on prominent display. I bought nothing this time because at my club back in the UK our Pro shop stocks it as well. I haven't seen a GITC suit before, though.'

'Well, you won't, as I had it made for me.'

'I didn't know you could get GITC suits tailor made.'

'Well, you can if you own the company.'

'Shut the front door. You own GITC?'

Richie smiled and replied in his southern Georgia

accent, 'Yes, sir. I started it 15 years ago and battled with the big names for ten years, but never gave up. Now we're listed…'

'On the New York Stock Exchange. I know. I have shares of GITC in my portfolio. Small world,' interjected Spencer.

Rudi was going around the table placing small bread rolls on everyone's side plates.

Richie replied, 'Small world indeed. Are you having the soup or the king prawns?'

'It'll have to be the soup, as I'm allergic to shellfish.'

Rudi saw and heard everything in his restaurant because it was in his professional interest to do so. He reached into his inside pocket and brought out a small notebook and pen.

'Mr d'Vere. Apologies, but I couldn't help but overhear you are allergic to shellfish. I wasn't aware of this. I thought we served you scallop last week. Did that not affect you?'

Spencer must think. He remembered his brother loved the bloody stuff, but if he had them, his throat could swell up. He needed to think of an excuse.

'Well, when I said I was allergic to shellfish, is what I meant to say is that I have an intolerance to them. I don't want to sound too dramatic. To put chef's mind to rest, it's best that I don't have shellfish. It's easier that way.'

Rudi made a quick note in his small notebook. Whilst it was still out, he asked, 'Are there any other intolerances I need to be aware of, Mr d'Vere?'

To downplay the significance, and whilst interrupting Michelle's somewhat mundane conversation, he could overhear with Amber about makeup, perfume and whatever, Spencer retorted, 'My wife has intolerances, particularly to husbands!'

Michelle overheard this but did not find the comment at all funny. Dani, Amber, Richie and even Spencer all laughed at his quick wittedness.

'Very well, Mr d'Vere. I'll make a note of yours but

graciously leave Mrs d'Vere's comment aside. I'm sure she's not the only one with that intolerance on the ship.'

More light laughter greets Rudi's empathy for Michelle. This time Michelle thought it was diplomatic to join in and that would be the end. How could she forget Spencer had an intolerance to shellfish? When she last stayed overnight at his penthouse apartment in Shad Thames overlooking Tower Bridge, they had walked past the restaurant below that had an adjoining Seafood & Champagne Bar. Oh, how she wanted to visit for the fresh Whitstable raw oysters topped off with a shallot vinaigrette, but Spencer always steered well clear of if it due to even the smallest possibility of cross-contamination.

'Are you a gambling man?' asked Richie.

'I'm known to have a dabble.'

'After dinner tonight, I'm heading down to the casino. I'm on a High Roller programme onboard. Janik, the casino manager, greeted me at the gangway. They are very keen to get me in there. I have a high roller blackjack table booked. Would you like to join me?'

Spencer blew out a gasp. 'I think that's above my playing standard. I'm closer to five cent slot machines than $100 minimum bets.'

'You don't have to join in. You can just observe if you wish. It's a fascinating insight, or at least it is if you are winning. Not so much fun if you are losing!'

Spencer smiled. 'Like the stock markets I play. The good thing is that it's not always my money I'm gambling with. As long as I give my clients a few per cent over and above inflation and their natural money depreciation, then that I see is a win for me.'

'You work in the financial markets, or are you a casual investor?'

Spencer had dropped his guard for just a moment and remembered he was supposed to be Theo, who was a renowned naturalist and photographer, and not a financial broker. He thought and adapted whilst remembering the advice Michelle gave him on how to buy time. He grabbed the second half of his bread roll and chewed on it whilst thinking. Normally one to sing his own praises, he now had to put himself somewhere close to Theo's pathetic life. He had to come up with a compromise of what he wanted to say and what he needed to say. 'In between other pursuits, I'm always online at all hours of the day, looking at the markets across the globe. I'm a broker who is qualified, but after hitting the highs and staying there for many years, I've decided to also pursue other interests in photography and wildlife. It's a happy blend.'

Spencer cannot believe the drivel he had just spouted. Part-time broker! What was he thinking?

'Well, it's good that you have found peace with yourself. Anyone that strives to be successful needs those breaks. For me, it's working hard on our brand with a dedicated workforce that then allows me the time to play blackjack in what is a cauldron. I love not just the game itself but also the psychology behind it. I love to people watch. The look in their eyes. The facial expressions and all the other non-verbal signs. Time-consuming but enjoyable.'

Spencer drew Michelle into the conversation, who was holding her own separate conversation with Amber.

'Psychology. I like it. Michelle read psychology at Oxford University, didn't you, sweetheart?'

'Pardon. Oh, yes. Psychology. The scientific study of the human mind and its functions. I guess you could say that people watching in the arena of a casino could be what I would call a case study in psychology, rather than one calling themselves a psychologist, you understand. You are applying scientific principles, if what I overheard was anything to go by. Playing cards at a high roller table has many mental factors. People do display characteristics that affect their behaviour. Often, it's the characteristics of the opponent or croupier that can dictate the reactions of the player.'

'Exactly, Michelle. You put that across so eloquently. When I'm sitting at the table, especially if it's something like Texas Hold'em poker, I love to manipulate the game with those non-verbal moves. I pretend to have nervous twitches like twirling the casino chips between my fingers. I take a sip from my drink. Sometimes I may slip on a pair of reflective sunglasses or even forsake a hand I know is a winning hand just so I can draw them in later. Do you think manipulation is a good thing, Michelle?' enquired Richie.

'Manipulation has its places, and its graces, Mr Sinclair.'

Richie observed Michelle's steely look as she took a sip from her champagne flute and glanced at Spencer for a few seconds; holding her stare before returning to look at Richie.

She was quite formidable; he thought.

Dani could only look on as an observer. She was not comfortable conversing in academia talk. Talking about the ship itself to the unknowing was more of her level.

Feeling a little left out, Amber asked, 'Can you recommend the spa onboard, Michelle?'

The steely look changed in an instant to a glowing smile. 'I can. You'll find me there every morning being looked after by Maisie. They can do whatever treatment you want. That lady is so talented. We have a one-to-one policy, so Maisie is there for whatever I need. That way, I feel there's a trust and a bond there. I don't get asked the same repetitive questions you would get if you saw a different beautician on every visit. You feel you can carry on with a conversation where you left off. You know ladies like to go to the spa together so that you can have some privacy and openly talk. Being the godmother of the ship, I have a tight schedule that most people wouldn't even realise goes on. When I visit the spa, I have to be somewhere else shortly afterwards. I can't always stop and have extended chats, so having Maisie to talk to, even for the briefest of times, gives me that feminine conversation time that all us girls need.'

Dani listened with interest. She was getting an insight herself as to the pressures felt by Michelle on being the godmother. It was not something that had occurred to her before. Michelle's itinerary was nothing to do with her. That was the responsibility of Cruise Director Olly. She thought it best to visit him after dinner and see if Olly could give Michelle a break from her responsibilities for at least a morning so that she could get to feel more relaxed in the spa.

'I'd love to have a chat with you tomorrow morning at the spa if that's ok? As it's a morning at sea, I believe Richie, my darling, will be at the high roller tables again until they close it as we get close to port. Is that right Richie?'

'Yeah. I'm afraid so, honey. I've got to squeeze a couple of games in before we hit that five-mile limit out there.'

'Would that be ok Michelle?'

'Of course. You can't have Maisie though. She's all mine now.'

Spencer cannot get the correlation between Michelle and being manipulative out of his mind. If it hadn't been for the recent conversation between Michelle and Richie, the chat between Michelle and Amber would be normal chit chat. The look from Michelle had left him feeling chilled to the bone. He had not seen Michelle in this light before. Even the simple off-the-cuff phrase of "She's all mine now" sounded controlling in more than one way. Not only the inference that she had some control over Maisie, but also that she was setting her stall out with Amber. Did she feel threatened by her? Why would she? All he had done was to give an admiring look at Amber when he first met her only minutes ago. Michelle could read nothing into that? Spencer felt he was over-thinking things until he heard Michelle's next question to Amber. It came across as somewhat condescending.

'With Richie spending so much time and money on the high roller tables, you must get ever so lonely?'

'On the contrary. I'm used to Richie being away a lot when he was building up his business. All the time he spent abroad, visiting clothing manufacturers across the far east and Asia. With the advent of modern communication technology, we never felt that far apart. It's helpful when you can video call whenever you want, unless there is an extra time difference. I find things to keep myself busy. For Richie to only be tied up at a casino table for three or four hours is nothing compared to days apart. I find fun things to do,' she explained, brushing her long blonde highlighted hair from around her earlobe as her finger drew down the side of her neck, to her clavicle, and across to a gold pendant around her neck.

Spencer could not take his eye off Amber's movements. Spencer reached inside his shirt collar and felt for his gold chain and star sign pendant. He realised what he was doing and drew his hand away and reached out for his wineglass. Spencer hoped that his non-verbal signs were not picked up by the two people sat either side of him. He also half-hoped that Amber had noticed.

As an observer on the fifth point of the star on the table seating, Dani was in the optimum position to see what was going on and to draw her own conclusions. She was not judgemental. After all, what happened at sea, stayed at sea.

***

The meal ended. They had served all the tables, their Petit Fours, and coffee from the blue mountains of Jamaica. Spencer fell in with the rich trappings of the luxury restaurant and ordered an XO Cognac for Richie and himself. All three ladies passed on the opportunity.

Michelle announced she had to take her place in the theatre for tonight's live show. She had to make a brief speech to the audience, which included the rallying generic battle cry of "Are you all having a wonderful vacation?" No cruise would be the same without it. Of course, it meant she would have to remain present to watch the show. She couldn't be seen endorsing it and then be found wandering around elsewhere on the ship. Michelle had one of the most recognisable faces on the ship. She must pop into the ladies' toilet on the way. She had another migraine coming and needed a couple of pills to help it remain at bay. Dani also had to make her excuses because she had operational matters to attend to. In reality, she wanted to grab hold of Olly before he also had to be in the theatre to introduce Michelle to the audience. She had a few minutes to spare. Spencer agreed to go to the high roller tables with Richie, but he made his position clear that he would only stay a short time, as he wanted to play the tables in the main part of the casino. Amber disclosed that she wanted to go to the spa in order to book in for treatment in the morning to coincide with Michelle's visit. She also whispered that she may pop into the casino for a small flutter if time allowed. Rudi returned to the table to help the ladies out of their seats, followed by the gentlemen. Each went their own way. Spencer and Richie kept their brandy glasses and walked off together, in a jovial conversation about stock markets and Richie's latest golf clothing logo. "Nobody cares you had a...".

'What's that logo about Richie?'

'As a fellow golfer, you know what it's like on the clubhouse patio. The next player, finishing their round, walks over and says "Guys, I had a birdie, an eagle, the longest drive" or whatever. And the first thing that goes through your own head as you sip your drink is "Nobody cares you had a whatever", so I thought that there's a market out there for casual T-shirts that say exactly what you're thinking. I don't care you had a hole in one, etcetera.'

'That's brilliant Richie,' replied Spencer.

'But it doesn't stop there. I've come up with some other golf related quotations to go on T-shirts such as, "don't putt me down", "where did that go?" and "this for the win".'

'How about a flirtatious "I picked up"?' asked Spencer.

'We could try that, my friend, we could try that,'

answered Richie as he smiled at the thought.

***

'Pay 21,' announced the croupier.

Fortunately, Richie had twisted a six of hearts when on fifteen.

Money came to money, thought Spencer as he sipped on the last of his XO Cognac. Time for something else to whet the whistle. Standing behind the three players at the table was an attentive drinks waiter assigned to the high rollers private room. It was a closed room with a curtain across the otherwise clear-windowed double door. They dedicated this room to the enjoyment of privileged guests, not for onlookers.

'Can I get a High & Dry Rob Roy please?' asked Spencer of the waiter.

'Sir. A High & Dry Rob Roy? That's a first for me. Can you explain that one?'

'Yeah. A Highland malt whisky with an extra dry vermouth, on the rocks.'

'That sounds perfect, sir. I'll be right back.'

The three players waiting for the croupier to collect up all the cards overheard the order.

'That sounds great. That's a new one on me as well. The same for me please,' said Richie to the waiter.

'I'd have a regular bourbon & vermouth, so your take on it sounds like far more fun.'

'If you're going to ruin a good scotch, there is no better way than with a dry vermouth,' claimed Spencer with a wry smile.

'If you don't mind, I'll stay another ten minutes after the drinks arrive and then I'll leave you to continue your masterful execution of the hands.'

'You are too kind. I'm on a bit of a run, but I don't want to jinx it. It could be a long night. Right guys?' looking across at the two other high rollers who were fixated on their cards.

Their luck had not come in yet, but both were forever hopeful, as are all addicted gamblers. No-one else around the table had plans to walk away anytime soon.

The two drinks arrived between hands. Spencer and Richie clinked glasses as a salute to lady luck. There was, of course, no chitty to sign. All drinks in the high roller room were complimentary. As promised, ten minutes later, as Richie won another hand with a pair of Queens, Spencer tapped him on the shoulder with his spare right hand and said, 'Catch you later.'

The onlooking casino manager, Janik, went to open the double door in order to allow Spencer to leave. Janik had been monitoring the high roller room in person to ensure that they catered for all their needs, and things were running smoothly. It was now time for him in his routine to return to managing the main floor. It was a busy night in the casino. Everyone was maximising its use now that they have set to sea in international waters. Fortunately, the impending storm had turned north and as each hour passed, the waters were becoming calmer. Janik could keep all the tables and machines open, which would maximise casino profit. The house always won.

Spencer entered the main casino floor, and the sound and excitement were quite deafening. They drew him to the craps table over to his left. It was the end table, kind of out of the way of what he would consider the more serious poker and blackjack tables. There was a large group of around eight already gathered around the table, supported by a row of people stood behind the players, making loud whooping cheers. The player throwing the dice was on a roll. Few were betting against the player, but far into the game, that was about to change. He edged closer and joined the players to the left of the thrower. He could reach in with his left arm and between throws, he put some money down for the croupier to count out in clear sight. The dealer deposited the money through the slot with the paddle. He handed Spencer some chips. Spencer pulled them back to the table's wooden edge and bided his time for one more throw. He decided his opening bet would be against the thrower. The cheers turned to sighs. Right first time. His bet landed him a healthy return. They rewarded him with a few pats on the back and, as each thrower sevens-out, he rotated clockwise around the table until he engineered himself into the thrower position. He took his stance at the end of the table and the Stickman offered him his choice of two dice from the five on show. Spencer exaggerated his choice of dice to amuse the growing crowd. He picked them up with his left hand, and then, using his right hand, he arranged the dice to show a 2 and a 1 upwards in his palm. Spencer closed his fingers around them. He avoided the faux pas of kissing or blowing on the dice. Some people found that quite unhygienic. He did not want to lower himself to that. The cheers rang out. He threw the dice down the table and as they tumbled and turned; they came to a slow stop off the top bank. They were showing a natural 11 with a 6 & 5. There were plenty of winners amongst the feverish pack of gamblers. Spencer went through his same routine with the dice in his palm. He rolled again and produced a pair of 4s, setting the Point at 8. They drew the dice back to Spencer with the stick. He went through the same routine again, with the dice showing a 2 & 1 face up in his palm. Spencer threw them down again, and they stopped with a 6 & 2. A tremendous cheer went up as he has hit the Point before the next throw of a 7. Those that could reach patted him on the back.

What on earth was Theo doing back onboard? asked Suzanne to herself. If they had cancelled his trip, why didn't he come and tell me? And come to think of it, what was he doing on the craps table? He's always called it the devil's cauldron. She was only passing through the casino to find the piano bar after her solo dinner. A moment of serendipity. She was only drawn first to the large gathering around the craps table by the emphatic cheering, and out of instinct looked to see what all the commotion was about. She never expected in a million years to see Theo standing there. The crowd was so large around the table that there was going to be no way until he came off it to get to speak to him. She took a nearby seat with her back to a slot machine and watched the activities from afar.

Spencer felt some arms reach around his waist from behind. He looked down to see a pair of beautifully manicured hands and a bracelet that seemed familiar to him, but he could not recollect from whereabouts. He then heard a whisper in his left ear.

'It looks like it's your lucky night. Maybe in more ways than one.'

He could smell the aroma of a lovely citrus perfume. He tried to twist his neck from side to side to get a look at who was talking to him, as. It was not a perfume he associated with Michelle. Being hemmed in by other players around the table did not make it easy for him. Whoever was keeping their grip around his waist and playfully dodging their head behind his, making it difficult for him to see, didn't help him. He twisted around far enough to see face to face who it was.

'Amber. Have you come for that flutter?'

She whispered seductively in his ear, 'When I said I was coming for a flutter, I wasn't talking about playing the casino.' She raised her right eyebrow suggestively.

'I need to finish this game.'

In a hushed tone Amber said, 'Seven.'

Spencer, being superstitious, knew this was the forbidden call at the craps table and would end his turn abruptly. He screwed up his eyes, just knowing that his luck in one way was about to end. Spencer rolled the dice again but, in his haste, forgot to have the 2 & 1 face up. Without checking, he threw them down and delivered a losing total of 7. The cheers turned to groans. Hardly anyone had bet against him. Amber loosened her grip, and he turned to talk to her.

What's he doing now? asked Suzanne to herself. She was about to stand up and speak to him, but Spencer appeared engrossed with this woman, who had had her arms tightly around his waist. She remained seated and poked her head around the slot machine to focus on what was happening before her very own eyes.

'I think Richie and Michelle have a busy evening. I have a bottle of Champagne chilling in our suite. Fancy a glass on the balcony. It's quite a clear night sky for looking at the stars,' said Amber.

Her intentions were quite clear to Spencer. Even without hearing what they had said, the body language made it clear where things were leading by the onlooking Suzanne, and also by Janik stationed at the cashier's desk. Amber, with a walk of defiance, led the way out of the casino. Spencer followed, looking from side to side to see if he was being followed. He could not look more suspicious if he tried. Suzanne got up and tactfully followed. This was the only discreet thing happening in her immediate vicinity. She slowed down near the exit of the casino and came to a complete stop. Using the skills you would only associate with an experienced surveillance operative; she used mirror reflections around the lift lobby to monitor what was happening ahead, without being seen herself. The angles she got would have been akin to a professional snooker player playing a safety shot from the baulk cushion. Despite her discretion, Janik continued to watch Suzanne's movement across the casino floor. Suzanne looked at the couple waiting alone for the lift. She could see the female had used her hand to grab at the male's jacket lapel and how she had pulled him towards her. The man responded with a passionate kiss on her lips. The doorway of a lift flashed and illuminated. Their embraced stopped with the man straightening his tie before the lift door opened. As the doors opened, no-one exited the lift. As a result, you could see them both laughing, and once again the woman grabbed his lapel and drew him in to the lift itself. The doors closed.

What Suzanne had just witnessed horrified her. This was not the Theo she knew and loved. This was not her lover. She had never seen him do anything like this before; at least not to her knowledge. But then again, she questioned herself on how well she knew him? Theo must know she was onboard. How could he not? How could he be so stupid and disloyal? She turned on her heels and walked through the casino to the far exit. Her head was down, and she looked visibly upset. Janik once again watched her movements. He realised whatever she had just seen had upset her. It was a look he had seen in the casino before, but he associated it with the wife of a player being unable to drag their husband away from the card table very late at night. He witnessed this was something different.

***

It was nearing midnight, and the high rollers were still playing. One had dropped out with significant losses. There was only one player who was up on the house, but even he was waning.

'A couple of more hands guys and I'm calling it a night,' said Richie as he stretched his arms out above his head whilst arching his back as he gave out a loud sigh.

Michelle walked across the main casino floor, looking from side to side. Spencer was nowhere to be seen. She walked over to Janik. 'Have you seen my husband, Janik?'

Janik had a clipboard in hand as he recorded some data from the tables and was in the middle of closing down the select empty tables. 'One moment Mrs d'Vere.'

Janik closed the last blackjack table and returned to Michelle. He used the time to think of a guarded answer without being dishonest. 'I believe that Mr d'Vere retired for an early night.'

'Retired Janik? I've never known him to retire before midnight.'

'I can only report what I see and know Mrs d'Vere. Now if you please, I can help you with the late-night lotto draw that I presume you are here to perform?'

Michelle knew Janik too well. Did those previous intimate moments not count for anything? she thought. She instinctively knew something was not right as Janik appeared so uncomfortable and did not give her eye contact when he eventually responded.

Richie exited the high roller room, looking around for the small late-night buffet. Three hours of continuous sitting at the table made him hungry. He could see a group of about a dozen people gathered around the lotto draw machine, with Michelle holding a horizontal spine of winning ball numbers for all to see. She handed it to Janik and, without another word, made her way through the small gathering. Her hand pinched at the bridge of her nose. These damn migraines just came on from nowhere.

'Michelle, how has your evening been?' asked Richie.

'So-so. Same old as they say. Theatre show, jewellery store, then here for this. I get used to it, but being godmother isn't all it's cracked out to be. Drink?'

'Sure, why not? Anywhere you can recommend? I know you British like to "have one for the road". Is that right?'

'I'm not British by birth, but I know of their idiosyncrasies. The true London Cockneys like to use what they call Cockney rhyming slang. They say frog and toad, which means road. Sometimes they might just say "one for the frog" as a total abbreviation. It's not something they teach at Oxford University, but that's my understanding. As long as you don't call me a frog, we could have a nightcap in the Concierge Lounge. Henrique keeps chilled Champagne set aside in there.'

Michelle led the way, and they took the simple route

via the priority lift call. The displayed hours of operation showed that there were still 45 minutes remaining upon arrival. Michelle unlocked the door with the use of her token. Henrique greeted them as they entered and guided them to two Chesterfield style leather chairs at the far end of the lounge. Michelle requested two glasses of Champagne and an assortment of hors d'oeuvres from the covered side counter. Henrique served the order and confirmed with Michelle if it was convenient for him to clear away the food to prepare for closing service. She confirmed they had all they needed. Henrique attended to clearing away the food service and in doing so left Michelle and Richie alone in the lounge.

'If you don't mind me asking Richie, how are things with Amber and yourself? You seem two quite different people.'

Richie took a long sip from the Champagne flute to find time in his thoughts to think over if he wanted to answer that question. 'Is it that obvious?'

'I noticed she wasn't by your side for the rest of the evening, and I presume she has gone off to do her own thing. It's your first night on the ship and from the conversation you were having earlier, I sort of guessed that you work hard and you see little of each other. I thought in this luxurious environment it would be an ideal place to spend some quality time together. I would be too if I wasn't so tied to my godmother's role on this voyage.'

'We are different people now, Michelle. Being 15 years older than Amber, we are on two different paths of our journey. It's now more like a marriage of convenience, or maybe even inconvenience. I have spent a long time building up my clothing empire. By-products of that are spending time apart, as well as the rich trappings of success. My only real escape is my gambling. But that doesn't always work out the way you would like it to.'

'Something I remember from my psychology studies is that a gambler will often tell you about their winnings, but seldom their losses.'

'You are quite right Michelle, and I'm no different in that respect. Something I have lost that is larger than the money at the table is the love of Amber. I met her in Las Vegas at a casino where she was a cocktail waitress. I was an infrequent visitor to this casino, but then I became attracted to Amber, so I flew over to Vegas and stay more frequently at that resort. One thing led to another, and my heart started ruling my head, and before you know it we found ourselves at a tacky chapel and we end up getting hitched. Sure, things were good for a while, but then things change. The friends she wants to hang out with aren't, as you would say, my cup of tea. We ended up not having that much in common. She went out but refused to dress down if I couldn't be with her. I know she's still a head-turner. After all, that's how I fell for her. Now we look at each other and think we shouldn't be married any longer, but facts are facts. I can't afford to pay her off in any divorce settlement. I make sure I don't fall foul of any reasons that a shmuck lawyer would get her a divorce, and that way I keep my wealth and have a little gamble on the side. Admittedly, I have some gambling debts, and if taken together with a divorce, then I wouldn't be in a place that I would want to be. It's for the best that I let bygones be bygones and allow Amber the freedom she wants. Not being stupid, I know she sees other guys behind my back, and in fact sometimes right under my nose. I'm in a catch twenty-two. I just have to turn a blind eye and don't lose my self-control. The hours sat at a casino table are my medicine. I've just got to be careful not to be addicted to the medication I've prescribed myself. How about you and Theo?'

'Me and Theo? If I told you, you wouldn't believe me. Let's just say we are still discovering each other.'

'Well, it's funny you say that. At the dinner table tonight, the way you spoke to each other and the interaction between you appeared to me, you didn't seem to know each other at all.'

'Maybe none of us knows the people we are with. As they

say, you learn something new every day,'

Henrique returned to the room as Richie and Michelle finished both their conversation and their drinks.

'Well Richie, I'll be off now to my suite to see what else I'll learn that's new. It's gone midnight, so technically it's a new day for learning.'

'Smart move. Maybe I'll see you around tomorrow, Michelle. I'll remind Amber to set her alarm in order to meet you at the spa in the morning. She has the memory of a goldfish some days.'

Richie held open the door for Michelle, and they went their separate ways down the corridor as they bid good night to Henrique and to each other.

Michelle reached her suite door, and it unlocked. As she passed the still open door to Spencer's bathroom, she could see that the shower screen was still misted up from its recent use. She could also see the TV illuminating from the bedroom so guessed that Spencer was in there and awake still. She announced her arrival and in return heard a simple 'Hi, you ok?' from Spencer.

'I'll just get changed and I'll be through,' she replied.

Michelle went through to the shared walk-in wardrobe. She pulled back one of the sliding doors to hang up her dress inside. She slid off her shoes first and placed them underneath where her dress would go. Michelle noticed that the linen basket had been moved, so she took it out of the closet because it was too crowded inside. She would put it back later, after she finished changing. It was unlike Jose to leave it in there, so she presumed it could only have been Spencer. He had his own linen basket, or had he not realised? She removed her underwear and went to place it in the linen basket. Michelle removed the lid and the top item was Spencer's shirt he had worn that evening. She did not want her washing mixed up with Spencer's, so she looked in his closet for his own linen basket. Sure enough, it was empty. She was about to drop it in to the basket when she noticed a slight red smudge on the collar. Her instinct told her it was traces of lipstick. It was not her colour. It was too much of a shimmery bright red. She inspected the shirt and noticed a distinctive citrus perfume aroma on either shoulder and on the front tails where the end two buttons were.

At that moment, she could only imagine how this had happened. Her blood pressure increased and her heartbeat raced faster. She had to get her breathing under control. She thought of a way to test him out.

Michelle undressed herself and went through all the drawers in her wardrobe. She redressed herself and walked into the bedroom. Spencer was lying under the covers, scrolling through the photo gallery captures on the interactive smart TV.

Michelle had not announced her arrival, but she was standing in the doorway. She was wearing a revealing set of matching scarlet velvet underwear with sheer black stockings and a pair of red high-heeled shoes. She had one hand on her hip and another suggestively leaning high against the door frame. 'Are you ready for me, Spencer? I've been very patient and couldn't wait to get back to you.' Michelle wandered provocatively towards her side of the bed. She leant across towards Spencer whilst running her hand underneath the sheets. She reached Spencer's midriff and ran her hand down his torso, along his belly button and to the inside of his groin.

'Sorry Michelle. Hold on there. I think I've had too many of those after dinner cocktails. They sure make them punchy on here. I think they've caught me off-guard. Hey, maybe in the morning, yeah?'

Michelle recoiled her hand. His response had confirmed her suspicions.

'Ahh, Spencer. You disappoint me. Your stamina back in Shad Thames is, shall I say, stronger. Has a little drink turned off the tap?'

'Michelle, those barmen know how to make them strong.'

'Sweet dreams Spencer. Let's turn off the TV and get to sleep. You never know what tomorrow brings.'

Spencer turned over and curled into the foetal position, forming a protective shell.

CHAPTER SEVENTEEN

'So, just to confirm, Storm Josephine moved north of our position throughout yesterday, and as a result, we missed most of it. However, the slight deviation in its course in the last eight hours means it is hindering our itinerary. What options are left to me, please?' asked Captain Nico.

'Sir, we could make progress on our published itinerary and hope the storm moves further away. If the storm remains on its current course and we proceed as previously planned, the ship could encounter some rough sea conditions. Rougher than the passengers have encountered so far. An alternative is that we head to another port or island that can accommodate us at short notice. Range and availability limits us. We have made those preliminary enquiries, and the best place is the island from which we have just sailed. They have offered to accept us back for an overnight stay. We were due back there a day later, but all we need to do now is arrive a day earlier than scheduled. I have checked with the Shore Excursions team and they have secured enough land tours and boat tours to accommodate all our passengers. They are also willing to reduce the tour prices by 30% to entice passengers to book them. I'm sure it will disappoint a few guests to miss out on their scheduled stop, but this island still offers plenty to do.'

Having given her suggestion, Dani thought it best to say no more and let Captain Nico decide on the best course of action.

'Thank you, First Officer, for your report. I think you

have made it quite easy for me. We will return to Azzurro Cay tomorrow. We will enjoy a sea day today in the beautiful calm waters, and then allow the passengers and some crew to enjoy the islands around the cay. Which leads me on to the surprise I promised you earlier in the voyage. The Destiny Luxury Group has a lovely new superior hotel at Azzurro Cay. In two days' time, I have arranged for us to all go landside to the hotel conference centre and have our daily SMT meeting in the hotel. I will give you five hours leave whilst at the hotel. We will have a wonderful lunch in their exquisite dining room, and then you are all free to use the spa services, with the compliments of Andrea, our Destiny CEO.'

A small ripple of applause went around the table, with those present looking at each other with delight.

'I will return to the ship after lunch and retain control whilst you can all enjoy the fruits of the hotel. Thank you for your continued hard work.'

***

'Ladies and gentlemen. A good morning to you all. It's your Cruise Director Olly here. There's been a change to our voyage schedule this morning. Unfortunately, because of the untimely arrival of Storm Josephine on the Bahamas Sea in the last 48 hours, Captain Nico has no real alternative other than to amend our course. Here on the Destiny Celebration we like to ensure your comfort and safety at all times, and in order to do so we are staying well clear of the slowly moving storm to the north of us. We will no longer be anchored off Andros Island tomorrow, so apologies for all those of you that had excursions planned. However, we will instead head back for an overnight stay in the wonderful Azzurro Cay. As an appreciation for the disappointment that no doubt some of you must be feeling, we are excited to announce that not only will you receive a total refund for the excursions on Andros Island, but you now receive a 30 per cent discount on all excursions booked today for our two-day visit to Azzurro

Cay. Please visit our wonderful staff at the Excursions Desk to benefit from this limited time offer. There're loads of exciting things happening across the ship today. Please see the itinerary in your daily Destinations newsletter, which is of course available 24/7 on your state room TV or indeed on the Destinations app, which is available complimentary via your mobile devices. On behalf of Captain Nico and the crew, I wish you a wonderful morning and I'll see you around the ship. Bye-bye for now.'

***

Michelle was already awake from her uneasy night's sleep. Spencer had barely stirred all morning. He had tossed and turned restlessly in the bed. Not once had he reached out to touch or cuddle Michelle. Even these insignificant details were preying on Michelle's mind from first light until she had taken her shower. She exited her bathroom in her soft bathrobe, towel drying her hair. She looked across the bedroom and saw Spencer rubbing his eyes and stretching his arms out with a loud yawn. Michelle hated to think what the cause of his exhaustion was as she knew it was not her. She had little time to dawdle. She must hurry now to get to her spa appointment. Maisie would wait, but not that Michelle cared. She had other worries on her mind. She did not know what Spencer had planned for his day, as they had not spoken that much in the last twelve hours. Michelle felt she would struggle to get a meaningful conversation out of him right now. Even if he tried to be his default charming self, she had neither the time nor inclination for it. She wanted him to lie there and wallow in his self-pity. His body was an absolute turn on, but at this precise moment, she neither desired him physically nor mentally. She brushed back her long straight dark hair and, for the last time, looked at herself in the mirror. She gave herself a long, hard stare into her own eyes. Deep into her soul. Her face was quite emotionless, which reflected how, at that exact moment, she felt about Spencer. What a cad. What a charlatan. If she had not been private school and Oxford educated, there were a few more colourful expletives sitting at the back of her mind that were trying to push forward. She shook her head from side to side, which ruffled her hair. She exhaled and got up from the dressing table chair. Michelle switched the hair dryer to its maximum mode and unnecessarily used it for a full thirty seconds. She had no use of it. She did not use it to dry her hair. It was to create unnecessary noise and cause an annoyance to the sleepy Spencer. If he was not awake before, he would be now, she thought. She turned it off and dropped it on the dressing table. It made a loud bang. Without another word, she drew in her dressing gown as tight as it would go to show the contours of her sleek and sexy body, picked up her tote bag and headed towards the suite door. Spencer watched her glide past the bedroom towards the exit. Michelle was walking very upright with her head held high. She did not even give Spencer a backward glance. She appeared steely and focused. This could have all been yours, Spencer, she thought to herself. She had the air of a defiant woman.

Before Spencer could even say the words "good morning", he heard the door opened and closed with a slam. Spencer shouted a strong expletive in his own head. It was dawning on him that Michelle may have had some suspicions of what had gone on last night. He did not fancy being on the receiving end of Michelle's wrath, so he thought it was best to lie low for a little while. A spot of continental breakfast and then a gentle swim.

***

'No Michelle, no. Suzanne help. Suzanne. The lens. Change the lens. Last of the five. It's a wrap.'

Cindy could hear Joe as he called out from within her bedroom. She pushed open the door to see him lying on the bed, turning from side to side. He was in a state of dream. Should she wake him or let him wake himself up? Everything told her to just leave him and let him come around.

'No, don't. Cut the engine. We're getting close to the beach.'

He pushed the sheets off the bed. Cindy edged closer to him and had a closer look at his face, and tried to catch what he was calling out. He opened his eyes and, with a startle, woke up and sat bolt upright.

'You ok there Marine? It looks like you were dreaming. Get yourself dressed and I'll make you a coffee.'

He realised he was stark naked and hurriedly pulled the bedcovers up to his navel.

'Don't worry, I've seen and had worse,' quipped Cindy.

She closed the door behind her. Theo lifted the sheets and looked down his torso, which confirmed his suspicions that Cindy had seen more of him than was appropriate for his new boss. He pulled on his shorts and yesterday's T-shirt and made a hasty exit downstairs. Cindy had laid out two mugs on a table in the bar and was preparing a carafe of coffee.

'A bit of a heavy night last night, hey Joe?'

'All I remember at the end was three of us guys snorting some liquid from a shot glass. After that, it was lights out.'

'You are no longer a snooter virgin, my man. I can't believe that you outlasted the bar legends, Billy and Leroy. When you boys were playing those drinking games, I put a holdall of clothes from Billy for you by the bed. You'll see them up there when you go back upstairs. I thought I had seen most things, but that beer-pong game was new to me. It looks like you had your eye in as those boys were paying forfeits at the rate of about three to one against you.'

'A sign of my wasted youth at university.'

'University now. Which one was that?'

'Why Oxford, of course?'

'You remember going to Oxford university?'

'Of course. Why shouldn't I?'

'Well, because you haven't remembered diddly-squat

since I found you yesterday morning. Here's something else. I could hear you calling out this morning. I couldn't make it all out, but I heard you shout out a couple of names. A Michelle and a Suzanne. Do those names mean anything to you?'

He paused for thought. 'No, not at all.'

'You also said something about changing a lens, and that's a wrap. Thinking back to what Leroy told me yesterday, you were a dab hand with taking some photo shots for someone, and you had a phenomenal knowledge of wildlife and the animal world. Does that mean anything to you?'

He paused for thought again. 'Something in my mind tells me I like animals, but I can't pinpoint it. I just instinctively knew how to use a camera yesterday. Looking back, it came to me like second nature.'

'I now remember you called out "no" with the name Michelle, and "help" with the name Suzanne. Are there some demons in your head? And what about cutting the engine as we are close to shore? Were you visiting Pig Beach?'

'I honestly don't know, Cindy. Can we leave this for now? I appreciate you asking, but it's foggy in my head. Leave me to think about it and if I remember anything, you'll be the first to know. Promise.'

***

After a short walk, Michelle arrived at the spa and indeed Maisie was patiently waiting. Michelle may be a few minutes late, but there were no penalties or cancellations for keeping Maisie waiting. That was not how it worked with the Destiny organisation. Michelle took her usual seat, and she noticed the other chairs were empty.

"Maisie, I think Mrs Amber Sinclair, my friend, also has some appointments this morning, right?"

'That's right Mrs d'Vere. She phoned down about 15 minutes ago, saying she's running a little late. I'm sure she'll be here soon.'

'That's no problem, Maisie. Just to let you know that Amber quite likes those little extra things that you ladies promote here in the spa. She's a little shy, so you may have to be a little persuasive with her, but she will have no hesitation in buying those products. You have such an excellent range here, but I see most of them are on the shelf next to the sales point. I think it would be beneficial if you placed about six or seven of them here on the ledge below the mirror. Amber is quite modest, so won't tell you she usually buys products at the top end of the price range. If I were you, I would concentrate on their placement over the cheaper end. I'm sure that when she buys them and takes them back to show her husband Richie that he will be overjoyed that she is treating herself. He's a very caring man and only wants the best for his wife. Make sure you brief well the beautician who will treat her this morning. Oh, and please don't say I told you. She's too dear a friend of mine and I don't want to embarrass her. Both of us would appreciate your discretion on this.'

'Thank you for the advice, Mrs d'Vere. We'll do our best to cater to her needs. We welcome clients who appreciate our high-end luxury creams and moisturisers.'

Michelle's timing was perfect. Through the door walked Amber Sinclair. As she walked through the door, Maisie greeted her and guided her to a treatment chair next to Michelle. Maisie gave her excuses and went off to brief Amber's beautician in secret.

'Well, good morning, Amber. Did you have a pleasant night's sleep? You look radiant this morning.'

'Good morning. I could have slept better. Richie got back to the suite and was a little sulky, but things look fine this morning. I guess he had a bad run on the tables.'

'Oh, I'm sorry to hear that on both counts. Did you win last night?'

'I'm sorry?'

'Did you win last night at the casino?'

'Oh, the casino. I didn't have time to play much.'

'You didn't get the chance to play? Maybe there's a next time. What did you do instead? Anything exciting?'

'Well, not really. I headed back to the suite a bit earlier than I had planned. There was something I wanted to do and had little time to do it.'

'And what would that be?'

'Well, I wanted to do some stargazing on the balcony, but I knew that there was a blanket of cloud forecasted and I didn't want to miss the night sky.'

'Ah, yes, of course. I understand. Who wants to be under a blanket when there's something nice to be looking at? Now I must ask you. We were talking at the dinner table last night about makeup and perfume just before Theo interrupted our conversation. It slipped my mind, and I never got the chance to ask you, but what was that gorgeous perfume you were wearing last night? It was divine. Please tell,' quizzed Michelle.

'Oh, I'm glad you like it. Richie wanted to diversify his "Get In There" brand, to be just more than golf apparel. He expanded the clothing brand to include women as well as men. I had this idea that since he was trying to corner the women's market, maybe he could consider a perfume and aftershave range, or even extend it to male grooming products and other ladies' lotions. He has allowed me to be the creative brain behind it. It's like my little side-line.'

'Wow. How exciting! It sounds like Richie likes to keep you busy.'

'Yes, that's true, I would say. It takes up a lot of my time when he is away. So, that perfume last night is Citron 21. The number represents the blackjack score, as I thought it would remind Richie of his favourite card game. I wanted the fragrance to be fresh and exciting; a natural aroma. My favourite scent is orange oil. One of my favourite martini drinks is when the barman peels off a sliver of fresh orange peel and twists it over the martini to leave a distinct smell of oranges. If you look carefully, you can see the orange oils sitting afloat. It reminds me of good times and relaxation; hence this is my favourite perfume.'

'That's fascinating. Does the fragrance last long once it's applied? The reason I ask is that when I buy perfume, I want to know three or four hours later that it's still there. The downside of that, of course, is that if I've applied a perfume around my neck, the fragrance can cling to the straps and neckline of my dress. It needs to go to the dry cleaners in between the times I wear it. Even if it's only been a quick dress change for a couple of hours. How does that work out for you with Citron 21?'

'I get your point. Because we consider our products to be top end, we use comparable quality-based products. One of our top selling points is just how long our fragrances stay vibrant and pungent. I take onboard what you say and that is a potential downside to it, but we do extensive market research before we put a product on the market. The longevity of the fragrance is a great plus point for the audience we are aiming at. I took my inspiration for it from long-lasting lipstick. We don't want to be reapplying it all the time, right? We feel the same with our perfumes. "Get In There" perfumes and similar products have the potential to be in the top ten of all perfumes within the next five years, and the absolute market leaders in golf clubs across the globe within three years. The private golf clubs' market is potentially huge. From my experience, you don't see grooming and beauty products available at these places, but why shouldn't they? Richie's golf club has around 700 members. There are nearly 39,000 golf courses across the globe. Even if you have a third of the membership that Richie's club has, at every course, you are talking about a market potential of nine million golfers.'

'That is astonishing to know. Can I just say something

before the beauticians come back? I know you'll appreciate this after everything you've developed. The ladies here have a fantastic range of products. All the beauty products I have in my suite I have purchased from here. They are to die for. Maisie showed me some products on my first day here. We're all used to beauticians pushing fancy moisturisers, etcetera, but do you know what? I thought for once I would try them. Oh my word, they are out of this world. I know you know the industry inside out, but take my word for it as your friend. Whatever they offer you, snap it up. Take the lot. I did. I haven't regretted it one bit. Oh, and please don't tell them I said so. I don't want them to think of me as a beauty products guru. I'm sure you understand. Believe me, you'll love the entire range. You might even get a little inspiration for a new product for back home. Of course, play hard and initially be a little resistant, but give in at the end. It does wonders for their confidence, and let's not forget for their commission. They deserve it. We all like that bit extra on the side, don't we? I'm sure there's been times when you've fancied a bit extra, hey Amber?'

'You are so sweet Michelle. I'll do that. I love to help other people.'

'I'm sure you do, Amber. I'm sure you do. Look, as a token of my appreciation for you supporting the wonderful staff on board, I would like to send some flowers to your room. What's the cabin number?'

'You are so kind. It's 9001.'

'I'll get that arranged as soon as I've finished in here.'

Maisie returned with a second beautician. Whilst Amber's beautician introduced herself, Maisie proceeded to product place in Amber's direct line of sight.

'Well, that's my cue to leave. Enjoy your day,' added Michelle with a broad grin.

'You too, and thanks for the advice.'

'Believe me, the pleasure is all mine.'

Michelle maintained her fixed grin and headed to the spa exit. She turned and gave a friendly wave. The door closed behind her and her face changed to that of thunder. Now where was that bastard Spencer? ran through her mind. He could wait whilst she organised the flowers. She asked to use the phone at the Spa reception and dialled through to the florist.

'Hi, it's Michelle d'Vere here. Would you do me a huge favour and have some flowers sent over to cabin 9001 as soon as possible, but paid for on my account? You can. Fantastic. I would like an enormous bouquet of black dahlias if they are available? They are. Super. No, it's not because someone is in mourning, though I get where you are coming from. It's nothing symbolic like that. It's just their favourite flowers. Personally, not to my taste, but each to their own. And can you add a card to it, please? Quite a simple message. "You are always in my thoughts," signed M.'

***

Breakfast arrived within 15 minutes of Spencer's order. Jose had delivered it and, without dallying around, he left it to be consumed. Jose thought it was strange that Mr d'Vere ordered it instead of Mrs d'Vere, and that it was only for one. He also did not expect the latte to be served with oat milk. Perhaps Mr d'Vere was on a dietary change and was choosing a healthier option.

Spencer thought he needed to leave the suite before Michelle returned. He checked the ship's layout on the bedroom smart TV and selected "Serenity". He noted they had a small swimming pool there and some hot tubs. Right up his street. He chose this option over using the suite's own infinity pool in case Michelle returned. Spencer selected a pair of lined swimming shorts and a short-sleeved white collared linen shirt. He grabbed his sunglasses and headed for the door. He opened it and then remembered that he needed his token to place drinks orders and to enable him to return to the suite.

With everything he required now in his possession, he hurried along the corridor to locate Serenity. The walk took him longer than he thought. It was not helpful that he initially headed to the stern of the ship instead of the bow. Spencer could have used his phone app, but his mobile was still back in the cabin. He was not the first passenger on a ship to get lost, and he would not be the last. He arrived at "Serenity" and selected a beach towel from the stack. Spencer walked around to find a sunny spot that was also within close reach of a shady canopy. Like everything he believed in, he wanted the best of both worlds. He threw the towel on to a sunbed and looked around for somewhere to get a stiff drink. A waiter passed by and asked if he could help.

'Does this place have a bar?'

'Certainly sir, it's just another ten yards further around, under the canopy. Can I bring you a drink?'

'No, that's fine. I'll see what they've got on offer.'

Spencer walked around past the small swimming pool and hot tubs, finding the bar. He could not miss it as it served as both a swim-up bar and dry-side bar, all as one. Around the pool it was quiet, and no-one had taken the plunge yet. There was a solitary barman filling the ice bucket just below the countertop. Spencer took a seat on a bar stool. He had the entire row of bar stools from which to choose as other guests that have ventured to "Serenity" were just laying out and absorbing the morning sunrays.

'Can I help you, sir?' asked the bartender in the poolside attire dress of the day. Spencer could not see the white deck shoes and matching white socks, but he could see the smartly pressed cobalt blue short-sleeve shirt and Bermuda style shorts. The barman's ceramic name badge showed his name as Millie.

'Sure thing. I love to ask this of barmen. I'll have a cocktail of your choice. Make what you like. I know I'm going to love it.'

Millie looked towards the point of sales till. The system had picked up the token and was displaying the details of the customer. 'Of course, Mr d'Vere. You're only the second person ever to ask me that. Normally everyone just grabs the cocktail menu or asks what is the cocktail of the day. We are both fortunate that our Food and Beverages Director, Angelina, allows us the freedom to create drinks for our revered customers. I'll serve you one that I only reserve for worthy guests. You are without doubt that very person. Are you ok with rum?'

'Sure. Go large.'

'Well, for a start, it is a double shot of spiced rum from here in the Caribbean. I'll keep it that way or else you have an imbalance of flavours. Trust me. This is good. Here, let me show you.'

Millie reached for a long crystal cut tumbler glass from the rack of various glasses above his head. He inspected the glass above his head to ensure it was polished. The plastic glasses for the swim-up pool service were on the other side of the bar. He placed the glass on the bar top and then turned his attention to the array of spirit bottles behind him. He talked to himself as he selected several bottles that he then placed in order on the bar in front of Spencer. The theatrical show was about to begin.

'Ok, now watch closely. We start with a double shot of the spiced rum. Next is this lovely sweet orgeat syrup. I make this myself fresh every day. It's a mix of almonds, sugar and rose water. Let's drop in a splash of maraschino cherry liqueur. Ok, now for a little lime juice and the most important ingredient, a top up to three quarters of the way with apricot soda. Let's get a handful of ice in here. Now for a twist of the orange peel, and to finish it, a simple garnish on the rim here. Here is a long spoon for you. Please give it a stir.'

Spencer duly did as he was told.

'I'm sorry, there are no umbrellas or sparklers. This

cocktail doesn't need it. The marriage of flavours talks for themselves.'

Millie pushed the drink across the bar to Spencer, who, without hesitation, took a meaningful sip.

'Oh, my lord. That is heaven. Do you have a name for it?'

'This drink I call "Millie-on-air". My full name is Maximillian, so this is the first part of the drink's name. The key ingredient apart from the alcohol is the apricot soda, which gives it the invigorating fizz. That part is the air. Put them together and I present to you "Millie-on-air". I think it suits our luxurious Destiny brand and no more so than here onboard Celebration. Please enjoy.'

Spencer savoured the drink and was in no rush to finish it. It was the pick-me-up he needed. Maybe the fruit content could count towards his five-a-day, he joked to himself.

Millie was distracted by two elderly customers swimming up to the bar on the other side. He knew them as regulars, so was prepared to serve them their usual half a pint of stout and a gin & tonic. Creatures of habit these two. Spencer was oblivious to the pair, as the opportunity to engage with other random guests up to now had been non-existent. Spencer finished his drink and gave Millie a wave goodbye in acknowledgement of his wonderful service.

'Thank you, Mr d'Vere. It's a pleasure,' replied Millie with an engaging smile.

Spencer returned to the sunbed he had reserved. He removed his shirt and placed it to one side. He lay out on the sunbed, absorbing the rays on his body. With the dapple sunlight shining down, he did not bother to apply any sun cream. He gave it an hour of turning on the sunbed like a suckling pig on a spit. The intensity of the sun increased as time elapsed, and even with the breeze blowing across the decks from the ship cutting through sea air, pearls of sweat rolled down his body. He felt the need to cool off and took a dip in the now empty swimming pool. He walked over to the single poolside shower and respectfully washed before entering the pool. Spencer thought better of diving in as he would do at his London fitness club swimming pool. He entered down the metal steps. At first the slight chill of the water took his breath away, but once submerged and swimming lengths of breaststroke, his breathing regulated and he acclimatised to feel a lot warmer. He completed five lengths and then at the opposite end of the bar he took a hold of the poolside and slowly treaded water at this deeper end. With his loose left hand, he fiddled with his pendant on his gold necklace chain. He gave it a couple of minutes before he lifted his shoulders above the pool side and placed both arms at shoulder height to extend upward and look around. The entire area was still silent, with few people around. He looked over at the hot tubs and saw that both were inactive. A great time to relax in a hotter pool whilst it was so quiet. Some uninterrupted peace. He swam back over to the ladder and ascended. The wet shorts stuck to his body, and he quickly stretched out the material in a show of modesty. He strolled towards the hot tub and looked around to see if anyone remotely attractive was taking any notice. He would have loved to have seen Amber sitting up, looking at him through the top of her sunglasses, but alas, she was nowhere to be seen. In his haste last night, he left her suite with no discussions about the future. It was what it was and served its purpose for both. He continued to strut, self-assured, like a peacock over to the hot tub. He climbed the short ladder onto the small decking and slowly plunged in, like everyone did when stepping into these contraptions. Spencer pressed the jacuzzi button and the air circulation started. The bubbles made his shorts fill with air. Spencer opened the waist band a little to let out the air and reduced the inflation. He then pressed the button again and accelerated the air flow. He leaned back, sunglasses back on, both arms outstretched with his palms up, eyes closed and just feeling the warmth of the sunlight on his shoulders, arms and face. A pure delight. After about five minutes and a reactivation of the jacuzzi jets, the warmth across his face diminished because of a shadow cast across the tub. He sensed someone beginning to descend into the frothy water and take a seat opposite from him. He nonchalantly opened his eyes and espied an elderly woman opposite in a one-piece chocolate-brown swimsuit. Spencer recognised her as one half of the elderly couple from the pool bar from a little earlier.

'Mr d'Vere isn't it?'

'Yes. Sorry, have we met?'

'You must have a short memory; They sat us at dinner on the first evening with the captain. I've also had the pleasure of speaking with your beautiful wife Michelle in the spa. I'm Connie, do you remember now?'

'Of course, Connie. How could I forget? I'm sorry. This bright sunshine can temporarily blind you and it caught me out. Lovely to see you again. Remind me, what were we talking about last time?'

'Blue-footed boobies, the Galapagos and your love of photography, if my memory serves me right.'

These are all subjects of which Spencer was absolutely clueless. He wished now that he knew more about his brother. He had to turn the subject around. 'Indeed, we did. Enough about all that, as I don't want this to be all about me. Tell me, what interests do you have?'

'Funny you should ask. I need to be off to a poetry workshop in half an hour, but I won't dwell on that. I love predicting someone's star sign. You know, their zodiac sign. Can I ask you a few questions?'

'Fire away. This should be fun.'

'I need to know something about you. Are you good around the home? You know, doing the washing up, tidying up behind you, and things like that?'

Spencer thought this was an easy starter. He just had to avoid falling down the rabbit hole by saying he was single and not married. Back home, he had a cleaner in three times a week, but of course, Theo was married, so guessed that he did his share of the chores.

'Yeah, sure. Our place is pretty tidy. I help wherever I can.'

'So you would say you are helpful and caring?'

'Yeah, I think so. Michelle likes to be cared for.'

This was a breeze. This old biddy knew nothing, he thought confidently to himself.

'It looks like you have come here on your own and not with your wife. Is it possible that we could interpret this as selfish behaviour?'

'Maybe to onlookers, but there are always reasons we are apart and don't need to be in each other's pockets all the time. This is a bit of "me" time. Don't judge a book by its cover, Connie. That's all I'd say.'

'So, that sounds like you are quite protective, whether that be of Michelle or yourself. Is that fair to say?'

Feeling the tide turning in his favour, he agreed. 'Nail on the head, Connie. I knew I would get you around to my way of thinking,' he answered with a broad smile.

'Well, that's fine, Mr d'Vere until you uttered that last response. You getting me around to your way of thinking? Some people would take that as you being manipulative. Would you agree?'

Spencer felt like he was being interviewed by the host of a prime-time talk show. He thought he had the upper hand and had the control.

'I'll let you have that one, Connie,' he said with a face changing by the second, from a broad smile to a sullen one.

'Looking at your face, Mr d'Vere, you look completely different from how you were only thirty seconds ago. Can I ask you this? Because of the last few questions, are you within yourself feeling moody at the moment? Your expressions give that impression.'

He tried to change his expression to a more relaxed one, but felt himself failing miserably. 'Connie, few people gain an upper hand on me, to be honest. I don't give up easily on anything I do. In fact, I can't remember the last time I did. I'm sorry if I do come across as moody as I don't mean to. Especially to someone as astute as yourself.'

'Well, that is nice to hear, Mr d'Vere, and it confirms a couple of things for me. You are sensitive and have an excellent memory, even if it is for remembering your tenacity has no bounds. I think I can now narrow down your star sign.'

'Well, I'm ready for this, Connie. Go on. Blow me away. There's not a cat in hell's chance you will get this.'

'I'm confident you are a Cancerian. And I'll even go further than that and say you were born on the 21st of June.'

Spencer's jaw dropped wide open. 'You worked that all out just from those questions? That's amazing. In fact, that's incredible. I've never been a believer in horoscopes and all that twaddle, but how you've got my birthday right in all that, that's just mind blowing.' He drew his arms down from the side of the hot tub and gave a smattering of a round of applause.

'Well, thank you for your kind acknowledgement, but I was helped a bit. First, you are wearing a Cancerian crab pendant on a gold chain around your neck.'

Spencer felt for it. He had forgotten to take it off when he went for his shower that morning.

'Second, and not instantly spotted by me, is the tattoo on the inside of your left forearm. You have the Roman numerals of XXIVI. It was an educated guess that the numbers 21 and 6 would represent your birthday; the 21st of June. That, my dear, confirmed your birth date for me. For a star sign, I could work out even without your pendant.'

Spencer was in awe and did not realise at that moment

the consequences of taking his shirt off. 'Connie. You are a marvel. Of that, there is no denying.'

'Thank you, Mr d'Vere. How time taps on. I must be going as I have the poetry workshop to attend.'

By now, the jacuzzi bubbles had stopped. Connie stood up, and the water dripped off the pleated extra material around the midriff of her swimsuit. She eased her way out of the tub, along the decking and down the steps.

'I'll leave you with this septet poem, Mr d'Vere;

Fear not the man who says too much

His heart exposed yet free to touch

His tongue a thing to impart a voice

His mind although should make that choice

His soul told him just what to say

I pray he lives another day

And doesn't change in any way.'

As Connie leaned over to collect her towel, it left Spencer soaking in the pool, contemplating her chosen words. Connie reached the main deck and towelled her arms and legs down.

'Pardon me. May I get past please?' asked the lady approaching the narrow steps to the hot tub.

Connie stepped aside and allowed the lady in the matching pink bikini to glide past. Spencer was in the tub with his head leaning back as far as it could go. His face capturing as much sun as was possible. She pushed the jacuzzi button, and the water effervesced as she stepped in at ankle height. The start of the jets drew attention to the woman stood in front of him. He noticed the slender legs, tight waist, enhanced bosom and, last of all, the youthful face behind the broad designer sunglasses.

'Well, good morning, Mr d'Vere,' came the introduction from Amber.

She raised her right foot out of the water and bent over to itch the side of her ankle. Spencer noticed her matching red nail varnish on both her manicured hands and pedicured feet. His gaze went from the Achilles' heel, along her straightened leg and to the rear of her bikini thong-styled bottoms. If he had not been in a public environment, he would have removed his sunglasses. In the circumstances, he thought it was best to keep them on so that no one could follow his gaze. Spencer had the distinct impression that she was starting where she left off from the night before.

'May I?' Amber took a seat opposite him and splashed the frothy water over her shoulders and chest.

'I take it you had a wonderful night's sleep?' teased Amber.

'Like a baby, for some reason.'

Amber slowly pushed her right foot forward under the water, obscured by the milky froth. Her toes reached the shin of his left leg. She playfully rubbed her toes suggestively up to his thigh. Spencer did not flinch at all. His left hand hovered over the jacuzzi jet button in case he felt the need to suddenly reactivate it.

'Where's Richie?'

'Oh, he's taking full advantage of the sea day and the casino being open 24/7. There's a general play Texas Hold'em poker tournament that he's just entered. It has unlimited buy-ins, so I guess that's him done until late-lunch time. I saw Michelle in the spa this morning. Any idea what she's up to?'

'No, not really. We didn't have a conversation this morning, but someone will definitely involve her in some unearthly godmother duties somewhere. I don't know, maybe calling out the bingo numbers or whatever the hell they do on the ship on a sea day. She doesn't know I'm here, so that's cool.'

Amber's outstretched right foot was now joined by her left foot, both between Spencer's kneecaps, nuzzling his athletic thighs apart. Spencer did not put up any resistance.

***

Michelle needed some peace. Olly had granted her a free morning, following Dani's intervention. She wanted to keep those dastardly headaches at bay. She thought nothing better than going to the sensory garden on the top deck at midship. Michelle took the longest route possible to get there. No lifts, only staircases and corridors, miles of corridors. She had heard about the garden from Hugo, as it was close to his firing studio. He liked to spend time there meditating. She reached the bow of the ship on the top deck. She pushed open the heavy external watertight door to exit the inside of the ship. Michelle felt the warm sea breeze blowing against her face. Her slender frame was engulfed by her thin summer dress with an English red rose floral design, which was caught like a kite in the wind. She followed the side rail and walked towards midship. Before she arrived, she could see an eight feet tall green hedge and then an equally high wall of living flowers. As she moved closer, she could see two people in somewhat typical garden maintenance clothing deadheading the pretty flowers. A man was atop of a ladder for the higher blooms, and a woman moving between the ground and a two feet high small platform carrying out the same task. Michelle was fascinated by the care being taken. A burdensome task if you were not a horticulturist.

'Good morning. I'm trying to find the sensory garden. I guess I'm in the right place. What a wonderful display.'

The lady recognised Michelle as the ship's godmother.

'Thank you, ma'am. We do our best. It's been a challenge designing this for Destiny, and then becoming the bespoke maintenance team,' answered the woman.

'You've designed this? That's amazing. So, you're not regular members of the ship's maintenance team?'

'No, not really. A lady approached my husband and me at the annual Hampton Court Garden Festival while we were exhibiting. She admired our best at show award and asked about our formal qualifications. We explained we were qualified through the Royal Horticultural Society and had our own full-time gardening business in not only design but also maintenance. The next thing we know is that they invited us to the Destiny HQ at a hotel in London. They seated us in a boardroom on our own. This lady then came in with three or four members of their executive team. She placed out in front of us blueprints for this ship and then asked us for our ideas. We were not expecting this and are always concerned when people ask for our ideas, only then to bleed us dry and pass our ideas on to their own gardeners and not employing us. This lady, however, made us feel relaxed and seemed trustworthy. There was something about her that made us think she was a highly motivated individual. Once we discussed our concepts for the ship, one of her staff opened a large folder. They placed it over the top of the ship's layout. They had presented a blueprint for a hotel they wanted to build. Then they extracted out a second, then a third. Another member of the team then pulled out a contract for us to be paid a retainer to work for Destiny. My husband pointed out that we are happy to work with the Destiny Luxury Group, rather than for them. All the senior staff members followed the lady's nods of approval. We had to explain that over several years, we had built up a client base and that we didn't want to let go of them. They deserved better. She said she liked that approach and we've worked with Destiny ever since, haven't we, dearest?'

The man pocketed his deadheaded cuttings whilst he descended the ladder. He said, 'You are right dearest. A talented team to work with.'

'A husband-and-wife team that is successful together. That's fantastic. How do you make that work?'

'Tolerance, love, and understanding. Oh, and a lot of hard work,' he replied with a smile.

'That lady of whom you speak is my best friend, Andrea. I'll have to report back on what a splendid job you are doing. I didn't catch your names?'

'That's very kind of you, ma'am. It's Mr and Mrs Burke. Samantha and Robert. She'll know who we are. Not everyone we work with is as delightful as her. Some people see us wearing overalls and look down on us as blue-collar workers. Some comments we've had are so judgemental. Someone once said to us we must have failed at school, as we have both ended up gardening. That couldn't be further from the truth. We both are not only highly qualified in this field but are also extremely skilled in delivering that service. I bet they can't identify over one hundred plants in Latin, then spell them correctly to pass the exams. That's the standards set by the RHS,' she explained.

'Even though I identified the plants correctly and named them in the exam, I got the letters "a" and "e" the wrong way around on two of them, and the RHS standards considered that a failure. Luckily, I spelled the other 113 right,' the husband imparted.

'Couldn't you cross them out and re-write your answer?' asked an astonished Michelle.

'Unfortunately, there was no rewriting. You had to sit there and spell it out from memory, face-to-face with the examiner. If there were any discrepancies, they would reassess you. My lovely wife, I'm delighted to say identified and spelled them all correctly.'

'Boy, that is tough,' admired Michelle.

'The surprise, ma'am, with the sensory garden is that what you see here is only the disguised entrance. Follow the first half of the mini maze here around to the right, and you'll then enter the true splendour. Use all your senses. Pick up the scents in your nostrils. Enjoy the tactile foliage with your fingertips. Listen to the water features pouring over the rocks in the background. View the colours from the full spectrum of the colour-wheel. Pick the indicated edible flowers and taste them on the end of your tongue. Submerge yourself in everything around you. It's very therapeutic,' he advised.

'Why thank you. Have a great day.'

Michelle left the gardeners to carry on with their deadheading tasks and took the recommended walk between the immaculately sheared hedges. She exited on to a gravel courtyard that had two benches surrounded by fragrant raised flowerbeds. She walked alongside the flowerbeds and with her arms outstretched wide. Michelle stroked the susurrating soft heads of the pennisetum ornamental grass. The stalks passed smoothly through the gaps between her fingers. She took a seat on one of the benches. She leaned her head back and stretched out both legs. Michelle inhaled the air of the enclosed space. The irresistible combined scents of aromatic lavender and rosemary filled her nostrils and she felt calmed. It reminded her to order the wildflower with bulgur wheat salad at lunchtime. She selected a spike of the fragrant lavender and picked at the small purple flowers one at a time and then discarded them. She rubbed the perfumed flowerhead remnants into her palms, put her hands to her face, and took a deep inhale. Her mind drifted away. She felt immersed in a world like no other. It would only be minutes before the sound of slow footsteps over gravel interrupted her solitude. She looked towards the maze exit and into the courtyard. Above the hedgerow, she could make out the top of an olive-coloured fedora hat bobbing with every step as it drew nearer. A man appeared wearing a floral patterned open-necked shirt and a paisley-patterned cravat, that was challenging her own floral dress for fashion prizes. The beige slacks and brown leather open-toed sandals completed the look. He was carrying a small bronze cherub statue.

'Hugo, how are you?'

'Very well, thank you, Michelle. Sorry to disturb you, but I'm placing this on the empty plinth over here behind your bench.'

Michelle had not even noticed it behind her, with everything else going on in her mind.

Hugo lowered the statute carefully onto the plinth and

returned to the bench opposite Michelle.

'Are you alright dear? It looks like you've got the weight of the world on your shoulders. You're frowning. You look so tense.'

'Hugo, I'm exhausted. There are things going on that you won't understand.'

'Try me, darling.'

'For a start, this godmother lark isn't all it's set out to be. People must look at me and think I'm treated like royalty. Like I can do whatever I want and be free as a bird. In fact, the opposite is true.'

'Dear Michelle. There are only a few days left, so keep your chin up. You are nearly there with it. You've done amazingly well from what I've seen and heard.'

'Oh, you are too kind Hugo.'

'But that's not all, is it, Michelle? It's written across your face. What else is plaguing you, my dear?'

'You wouldn't understand Hugo.'

'Why ever not?'

'Well, it's about my marriage.'

'And?'

'Well, I mean. The man in my life. You know. I don't expect you'd know how a marriage works, except now, of course, you can have single-sex marriages back home for you in the States.'

Hugo laughed loudly and declared, 'Michelle, my dear. I'm not gay. My wife Barbara and I have three beautiful children, of which I hope are all mine! I dress flamboyantly and present myself mystically, but it's all part of the artistic vibe. It's part of the show. I sell my artwork on the back of it. Oh Michelle, you aren't the first one to presume so. I don't normally reveal the truth. I just go with the flow and let them believe what they want to believe. Never judge a book by its cover, as they say. So, what is it about the man in your life?'

Michelle felt as if she had already said too much. 'Oh, nothing. I'm just being silly and over-emotional. I wished you had said you were gay, then you would understand male partners better and advise me accordingly.'

'For giving advice, do you want me to be bi-sexual for ten minutes?' he laughed.

Michelle laughed with him at the suggestion. 'No, you are fine as you are Hugo. Maybe we'll have a chat another day. Please don't approach Theo about our little conversation, or you finding me here.'

'Why should I? We all need our bit of space. I'll be off. You relax and try to enjoy yourself. Those worry lines have disappeared already.'

Michelle smiled back, and Hugo departed along the exit maze on the other side of the courtyard. Once again, she was alone in peace. Her thoughts returned to Spencer. She knew his game. She thought leopards could change their spots, but obviously not. Theo would have loved that analogy, she thought. She imagined Theo's carcass, or whatever remained of it, laying on the ocean floor. Perhaps the twins could be reunited with each other? Well, why not? They deserved each other. Who would miss them? She won't. Spencer lived alone, but had a cleaner. She was sure she could come up with some sort of cover story. Maybe he was taking a sabbatical for an unspecified amount of time and the cleaner could be released. Her services rendered surplus to requirements. He could disappear on his global tour. These things happened. As for Theo, he was always the first to admit he walked headfirst into the danger zone on his explorations. His own employees knew he headed off into the jungle at the drop of a hat, and who knew what he could encounter when doing so? To her knowledge, the jungles were full of poisonous flora and fauna, and man-eating animals. They had a well-established system to patrol and search the savannahs of Africa. Maybe not so for somewhere like the Amazon. after all, it was vast with some of the deadliest things known to man. Even if it was true and they tried to look for Theo, there's every possibility that he would never be found anyhow. That's two scenarios she could fabricate if needs be. Maybe nobody would miss either of them. Certainly, she won't. Another thought came to mind, and she realised an answer was already at her fingertips. She ignored the exit maze and instead retraced her steps through the entrance maze. The Burkes were both checking the automated watering system that passed through the live plant wall.

'Sorry, can I ask you one thing from your horticultural training? I know common things like ivy and stinging nettles can leave a nasty rash, but to your knowledge, what are some of the most poisonous plants you can find in the wild?'

The Burkes looked at each other. Their own body language and facial expressions towards each other indicated they were both thinking this was a bit of an odd question.

Mrs Burke answered on their behalf as usual, knowing her husband would step in afterwards with a supporting answer if he could think of an equally good one. 'It would depend where in the world the wild habitat is you are talking about. So many colourful flowers are poisonous, especially those that produce a bright seed. The uninitiated can fall for thinking colour equals flavour. In fact, colour could lead to illness and possibly death. Man is often drawn to fungi, which are more commonly found in the wild. People see a mushroom and think, great, I'll pick some and cook them. That can be a fatal mistake if you don't understand what you are foraging.'

'That's an interesting point. I had never thought about that.'

Michelle thanked them and walked off towards the Concierge lounge to find out where Spencer could be.

***

'Henrique, I'm trying to find Mr d'Vere. Would you be a sweetheart and check on your system where he is, please? Hopefully, he should have his token with him.'

Henrique logged on to his computer and typed in Mr d'Vere's details. It showed that he was in "Serenity". He then checked the spending audit for Mr d'Vere's token and established that he had ordered a single drink and two other drinks at the swim-up pool bar. Without giving Michelle precise details of the bar bill breakdown, he informed her that her best option would be to look for Mr d'Vere in "Serenity". She thanked Henrique and made her way there.

***

'Theo, Amber, they look a lovely pair of cocktails. May I join you? I'll sit here on the dry side of the bar.'

Spencer and Amber had vacated the jacuzzi and were now sitting in the pool at the swim-up bar. Upon Michelle's approach, they had both been leaning on the bar, chinking plastic glasses and laughing. Michelle sat a couple of seats away, so she had a clear view of their body language.

'The same for me please, barman. I wouldn't normally be drinking at this time of the day, but hell, why not, hey Theo?'

'One Millie-on-air coming right up, ma'am,' confirmed Millie as he turned to find the ingredients.

Spencer was feeling Michelle's bite in her tone.

'Amber dear. That's a beautiful colour bikini but be careful not to catch your death of cold.'

Michelle's reference and connotation regarding Amber's choice of skimpy swimwear was quite obvious to understand by all three of them.

***

Incident reports covered Jack's desk. They had accumulated over the course of the cruise. He was reviewing them all and deciding if further investigation was necessary or whether they could be closed and filed. He was recording his decision-making rationale on a log via the ship's computer system. It was not as if he had not got enough to do. He was planning to incorporate a similar scenario to the landing pontoon incident into the next round of crew drills. There was a light knock on his office door.

'Come in.'

The door opened and in walked the Food & Beverage Director, Angelina Moore, who closed the door behind her. She took a seat alongside Jack's desk as he quickly tidied the scattered papers and placed a cover over the top sheet.

'Whenever F&B come to see me and there's not a tray of delicious food or a cold beverage, I know it's not good news.'

'Jack, you are an eternal comedian, but as always, right on the money. No, it's not good news. I need your help, as usual, in confidence. I've audited the spirt bottles onboard. You know we do a daily inventory in each place on board that supplies drinks, such as the bars, restaurants, casino etcetera, and things aren't adding up. We are missing several bottles of the high-end whiskies, and by the looks of it, it's all down to one bar.'

'Pray tell me more.'

'The bar in question is "Barrels". Originally, the idea was to hold small-group whisky tasting classes on alternate days. However, because of their popularity, they asked me to allow a daily class. I now believe I know why they are so popular, especially with the stateroom guests who are not on the Suites program. It does not entitle them to have access to spirit bottles in the staterooms, as this is a bonus feature for those that pay for the Suites. I've seen this type of scam before. Some staff members must think we are stupid. The usual ruse is for special "Cabin Promotions" to be introduced towards the end of the whisky tasting sessions, once the participants have had generous pours and are feeling more comfortable, shall we say. A bartender will introduce the opportunity to sell to select individuals a bottle of their choosing at a greatly reduced rate that you couldn't get on landside for anywhere near that price. The attached conditions though is that the passenger must pay cash. They are told it's so that the local authorities don't catch on for duty tax reasons. Of course, that's total bullshit. Duty tax is totally irrelevant to our products in international waters, but the passenger thinks it's a cheeky way of getting their own back on the tax authorities, and so play along. They think that not only are they getting a superb deal on the whisky, but they are also enjoying being part of a tax evasion game. The barman mostly targets those that use the casino. They can look on the point-of-sale system and see what bars across the ship each passenger uses who come to their tasting sessions. The barmen are using a system our company brought in to provide an enhanced service to our clients in anticipating what they may like to drink and manipulate that information for their own dishonest means. They know casino users have access to the cashier's desk and are more likely to have access to cash funds. The barman takes the cash on the spot if they can, or invites them back to another tasting event the next day. Once they receive the money, they have a room service server deliver the bottle to the cabin, in exchange for a little tip on the side.'

'What's the estimated cost to the company, Angelina?'

'Around $300 a tasting session.'

'That's more than we take from the participant's fee for the tasting.'

'That's right, so we need to put a stop to it. Any ideas, Jack?'

'H2andOliquid.'

'Sorry?'

'H2andOliquid. It's a product a security friend of mine deals in. We apply a few drops of the liquid to the outside of the bottles, which leaves a unique colour code on it. As a result, we can then follow the people we suspect of being involved through our CCTV systems and track where the bottle turns up. We recover the bottle from the cabin and check it with a black UV light. We can also consider putting a stooge in to purchase a bottle and hand over dollars marked with the same liquid. What we call a "Test Purchase". Back in the day, we carried these operations out where we had intercepted class A drugs through the mail and rocked up at the suspect's door pretending to be a mail delivery driver, asking for them to sign for the package. Great fun duping a con. For our operation here, we'll then search for those we suspect and see how many have received a portion of the money handed over. Bingo. The job's a good'un.'

'I knew you would have a plan in your back pocket, Jack.'

'When is the next tasting session?'

'4pm today. Can you mark the bottles before then and find a stooge?'

'If you bring me the bottles, we can video them being marked up in here. I'll track you on CCTV, going from here to the bar and putting them in place within view of the cameras for continuity evidence. You can then step back out of it. I have a member of my security team who handles backroom tasks for me, so none of the staff will know him. He doesn't go to the crew bar, so he's a very non-descript, low-profile individual. My team doesn't drink onboard or with other crew members on landside, as I like them to keep their neutrality and integrity. I have some dollars in my office safe that I can mark with the liquid. We can then take it from there.'

'Great. I'll get a couple of bottles of the stuff that appears to be the most popular and will be back soon.'

Angelina departed with gusto, leaving Jack to call in and brief Aryal from the Security back office. Jack made a radio call to Kulbir for him to come and see him in his office. He wanted Kulbir to run the sting operation under Jack's strategic steer. Jack knew it would be good for Kulbir's development and impending appraisal.

***

Spencer stood up from their suite sofa and walked to the sideboard to collect his ship token off the polished surface.

'Where do you think you're going?' asked Michelle.

'It's nearly 4pm and I've seen on the newsletter that it's a scheduled whisky tasting at the Barrels Bar. It looks like being a fun thing to do before we get ready for dinner. Do you want to come along?'

'Spencer. How long have we known each other? You know I don't drink it and can barely stand the smell of it. Of course I don't want to go. I was going to talk to you about tomorrow and if you would like me to arrange a small excursion for us for when we get to Azzurro Cay. I know we've had a bit of a turbulent couple of days, but I'm sure it's not of your making. It's me and the mood swings I go through and the migraines I have. I thought I would make it up to you. What do you think?'

Spencer momentarily felt reassured that Michelle was quite clueless about his clandestine activities. 'Golf?' he enquired with a smile.

'No, not golf Spencer. Something that we can do together in an idyllic location. There's an excursion they do called "Swimming with Pigs". It looks so much fun. You'll love it, I'm sure. It's something to die for.'

'Well, I am intrigued.'

'Leave it to me to arrange. Don't say a word to anybody. I want it to be our little secret.' Michelle gave Spencer an encouraging smile with a slight hunch of her shoulders, with the look of a smitten teenager.

'I'll see you later.' Spencer removed the token and his wallet and headed off to "Barrels".

Michelle waited for the suite door to close. She jumped off the sofa and went to the flower vase. She removed the bunch of seventeen purple chrysanthemums that she had requested Jose deliver to the room in the morning. A special request as Michelle knew the superstition that surrounded chrysanthemums. From her travels in Italy, she knew they presented these flowers on All Souls Day to commemorate the dead. She blended this with the Italian unlucky number seventeen, with the colour that was unlucky. They would dress the theatre curtains in purple and black over Lent, which was associated with theatrical disaster. The thought of a theatrical death for Spencer warmed Michelle inside. She shook the water off the stems and took a seat on the floor. Michelle began her familiar destructive routine of picking each leaf and petal off the entire bunch. She thought this regime would take her until Spencer returned from his stupid whisky tasting. She sadistically hoped that he enjoyed his pathetic little flurry of fun, as she knew it would be his last afternoon on the planet. Well, his last day alive, before the Caribbean wildlife consumed him.

***

'So, out of the ones you have all tried, which one is your favourite?'

Spencer answered Adrian the barman, 'It's got to be the Highland malt, the fifth whisky we tried.'

'So you prefer that one to the first Irish one we tried, which was triple distilled? Do you remember me explaining the distillation process, including how the barrel surface area was increased by double charring, and how the complexities were altered by using additional barrels to incorporate bourbon or sherry notes?'

'I'm pretty sure that the more simplified Scottish one does it for me. Horses for courses.'

The barman reached backwards and brought forward the Highland malt bottle that Spencer was pointing to enthusiastically. He poured out into a fresh glass two-fingers of the scotch.

'Try it once more, sir. If you really like it, I can do a deal for you. The deal I reserve for only our finest guests.'

Adrian went through his entirely well-rehearsed sales

pitch. Spencer fell for it. Overhearing this, another of those participating at the bar asked if he could also make a special purchase? Adrian gleefully served up to Aryal the same one-time-only special offer. Kulbir looked on from the Security CCTV office. The easy bit was done. All he had to do now was follow the bottles and track the money. He set the CCTV monitoring system to advance mode and selected "Follow Face". He clicked on Adrian's face, and all the cameras in the bar focused on Adrian from every angle. A box-in-box opened that kept the rest of the normal camera capture in view. He could see Adrian taking money from both Spencer and Aryal. With his back turned against two of the cameras, Adrian counted out the money close to his midriff. The gamesmanship was all part of Adrian's theatrics to extend the suspense. Adrian turned back to them and asked for their room cabins so that he could scribble it down on a piece of paper for the wine waiter to deliver. Aryal gave a cabin number for what was, in reality, a spare cabin.

Spencer gave the suite number and thought nothing more of it. 'Make sure that it arrives safely and I look forward to having a nip this evening.'

'Mr d'Vere, it's been a pleasure. On behalf of the Destiny Luxury Group, we hope you enjoy your rare cask whisky.'

Aryal heard Adrian's words. What started off as a disciplinary offence with various options open to a panel would now only leave the option of being dismissed for dishonouring the name of the company in an illicit transaction. Aryal's stomach tightened with disappointment for Adrian, but even more so for his employers. As a Gurkha, honour and loyalty are just two of the key mantras he upheld. Adrian beckoned over one of the two wine waiters serving the rest of the bar floor and placed the two whisky bottles onto his tray, handed him a note with the two cabin numbers and a crisp $10 bill. Kulbir monitored the exchange and could tell that this was a well-rehearsed drill. He thought to himself that if only the proper crew drills were as well rehearsed as this transaction, then the ship would be a lot safer. Kulbir adjusted the CCTV monitoring to now also follow the waiter on his journey to the two cabins. Kulbir did not intervene, but he was already calculating when to intercede. Aryal left his seat and made a convoluted route back to the Security Office, ensuring along the way that he was not being followed.

The waiter, Sohal, made his way first to the d'Vere's suite. He presented his token, knocked on the door whilst calling out 'Room service' and entered.

Sitting on the floor was Michelle, surrounded by petals and flower detritus. She expected to see either Spencer or Jose. Taken aback by a waiter unknown to her, 'Can I help you?' she curtly asked.

Sohal did not expect anyone to be in the suite, but they trained him for such encounters. 'Sorry to disturb you. The gentleman of the suite has arranged for this to be delivered in his absence.'

Michelle was both confused and concerned. Spencer could have anything he wanted delivered to the room for free. Yet here was a common wine waiter strolling through her private suite. Sohal looked down at the destroyed flowers with bewilderment, but Michelle caught him looking. She was most displeased. 'Leave it on the side there please, and if you would leave me to carry on tidying up.'

Sohal knew when he had overstayed his welcome, even if he had only been there ten seconds. He left the single bottle on the side and scurried out. With another delivery to be made, he headed down to the lowest deck that contained staterooms. He carried out the same routine upon reaching the door and walked in. Sohal switched on the lights and entered the main living part of the cabin. He was looking at the pristine layout. It was eerily clean and quiet, except for the clanging of coat hangers moving in unison with the ship. He placed the bottle on a side table and felt a little puzzled. Feeling something suspicious was going on, he went into the walk-in wardrobe and pulled open the sliding wardrobe. The rail was empty except for those clanging coat hangers. His mind was racing. What was happening? He checked the handwritten note and went to the cabin door. Sohal had got the right cabin, but no-one was occupying it. He thought to himself he had better get back to "Barrels" and continue his shift as normal. His palms were feeling sweaty as he pulled the cabin door shut. Kulbir looked on as Sohal came into vision on the corridor CCTV. He needed to put the "stop" in soon before Sohal spilled the beans. He radioed Jack to meet him in the CCTV room. Upon Jack's arrival, Aryal was already sitting with Kulbir and briefing him on how the operation went on the ground and the conversations verbatim. Aryal had already typed his report onto the computer system. Kulbir brought Jack up to speed.

'Ok. That's all good. Kulbir, get two of the security team in here now. I'll recover the bottles. Get the F&B Director here as well. She can go to "Barrels" and call the bartender and waiter around the back with our two and have them searched for the money. Have it seized and exhibited. Make sure this is all done in full view of the CCTV camera behind the bar. We presume nothing. We'll piece all the evidence together and as soon as I have it, I'll approach the captain to have them immediately suspended and confined to quarters. No evidence. No action. Let's make this like the ship. Watertight.'

Jack knew to record his decisions in his log, but for now, the admin could wait whilst the intervention went ahead in quick time. He collected from Kulbir the names of the two staff members that were identified from the shift roster and confirmed against the data from their tokens, as well as the facial recognition system. Everything tallied. No-one appeared to be using another staff member's token for access. If so, that would have been a seriously aggravating factor for all involved. Then, he received the cabin data for the delivery of the bottles.

'What do you mean the d'Vere suite, Kulbir? Are we

sure?'

'One hundred per cent.'

'Ok. Keep this under wraps. It could be a major embarrassment. What are they thinking? I need to get over there straight away. Where are the suite occupants now?'

Kulbir toggled the keyboard and retrieved the token data. 'At the moment, it appears Mrs d'Vere is in the suite and has been for a little while, whilst Mr d'Vere is in the casino.'

'Ah, bloody hell. I was hoping to retrieve the bottle whilst keeping a lid on it. I'll have to explain to Mrs d'Vere what's happened. Shit.'

Jack pinched the bridge of his nose and pulled himself together. His staff knew he wore his heart on his sleeve, but seldom did he like to show it in front of them. Jack stood upright from leaning over the desk whilst looking at the computer screen. He planned to retrieve the bottle from the empty cabin before heading to see Mrs d'Vere. Jack could be there for some time, but he hoped not. He went to the office safe and took a wad of dollar notes, which he stuffed in his inside jacket pocket. He felt like he was now a walking ATM. Aryal confirmed that the going rate was $150 per bottle.

***

'Place your bets, please.'

The roulette wheel was still, with the ball landing in the last winning number slot. They displayed the last ten consecutive winning numbers on the highly illuminated tower above the wheel. A streak of red numbers must surely end soon? A solitary figure at the side of the table was Spencer. The casino was predominantly quiet, as most people onboard were getting themselves ready for tonight's dinner service. There was an excitement building across the ship, with the highly acclaimed chocolate buffet being held mid-evening. The anticipation of the creative chocolate artistry had been the talk of the ship all afternoon. Other passengers were intent on charging their cameras whilst Spencer sat with the remaining half of his original roulette chips piled in front of him. He turned a spare chip between his left thumb and fingers. He was unaware of a lady just yards away from him, intensely watching his every move. She had been standing there undiscovered for the last twenty minutes. Spencer looked up at the number's tower and contemplated his next bet. In his distraction, he did not see that the lady had now approached the table and had taken a seat at the end of the table. She laid $100 on the table for the croupier to exchange for different coloured chips to the only other player at the table. The time taken to exchange the money for chips gave Spencer a bit more breathing space to study the numbers and pile his chips in to towers seven high.

'What's that you're drinking?' she asked.

'Erm, it's a Rob Roy on the rocks. If you want to try one, ask for a High & Dry. The waiters here know it. I introduced them to it.'

She looked around for a waiter, but the croupier had overheard the conversation and had beaten her to it and waved over an available waiter. They paused the game while the waiter took the order. She organised her chips and placed her five bets. Spencer, being the gentleman, sat back to let her place her bets first. She could not reach the far end of the table, so passed a chip towards Spencer. He glanced down at it, unmoved.

'Can you place it on the double zero please?'

'Yeah, sure.'

He collected the single chip in his left hand and placed it squarely in the centre of the double zero. The croupier observed the move and waited for him to place his own bets. Spencer lifted a pile of seven chips and eased them forward, somewhat dithering on where to place next. He needed to recover some of his losses, so placed all seven chips on number 21. The roulette wheel was now spinning with the white ball circling around the top edge in the opposite direction. He continued to look up at the number's tower and twizzled a chip in his left hand between all his fingers like a magician.

'No more bets,' came the call from the croupier.

The ball bobbled and clattered around the wheel, then bounced in and out of the numbered pockets. Up, down, left, right, and came to rest in number 21.

'Yes. Yes!' cried out Spencer as he punched the air triumphantly.

'Congratulations,' the lady acknowledged the win.

Her Rob Roy cocktail arrived in front of her. The ice rattled against the side of the tumbler.

'Thank you for your congratulations. Have that on me. Let's see if my luck can rub off on to you.'

'That would be nice. Thank you for the drink. Sorry, I didn't catch your name.'

'Theo, Theo d'Vere. And you are?'

'You can call me Suzanne.'

'Suzanne? Nice name. A pleasure to meet you,' said Spencer, offering his hand for a handshake.

'A pleasure to meet you as well. Have we met before?'

'Umm, I don't believe so.'

'Oh, my mistake. It's just that you look familiar to someone I know.'

'Don't worry, my dear. Lots of people say that. They say we all have a doppelgänger out there somewhere,' replied Spencer whilst smiling at Suzanne.

'Apparently so,' as she took a long sip of her drink whilst staring at his features.

Her intense stare gave Spencer the feeling he had had before when women hit upon him. Quite a pretty thing, he thought to himself. This could lead somewhere, he dreamed. He was right, but for all the wrong reasons. Double trouble was brewing with the unnoticed Janik, also looking on behind his customary clipboard, to the rear of the number's tower.

***

The two bottles of local beer chinked together.

'That was a long and hard day,' recounted Theo to Cindy.

'Aw, you did good today. Leroy's feedback was again excellent. You certainly know your stuff. You came out with even more facts on wildlife today. Your brain is an encyclopaedia of knowledge. Look, I've got something in store for you tomorrow. Leroy has his first tour for a new hotel. A few miles away is this plush hotel and they have a tour for twenty guests arranged. It will be the hotel's first visit to Pig Island. It's a brilliant coup for us. Leroy and I were thinking it would be just great if tomorrow you could be the tour lead. Would you be happy about that?'

'Sure. Why not? So, there is civilisation out there?' he laughed.

'Yes, there is civilisation out there. I'm more comfortable for it to visit me than I am to visit them. Rather than you helping me prep Billy's daily catch after breakfast, Leroy will sail on over and pick you up. Grab yourself another bar T-shirt, maybe the luminous pink one, as that sure is eye-catching, and then board Leroy's boat. For all intents and purposes, you are the skipper tomorrow, and he'll work to your command. He has had no one boss him for about twenty years, except for his good lady. You are my personal representative and I wouldn't let you do it if I didn't think you were capable. I'll check out how your wound is healing and get a fresh dressing on in the morning before you go. Hopefully, smaller so you look presentable but also laid back in equal measures.'

'It sounds fun. I won't let either of you down. Promise.'

***

There was a sharp knock at the suite door.

'Come in,' called out Michelle.

Jack's pass opened the door. 'I'm sorry to disturb you Mrs d'Vere, but I need to have a word. I have something rather disappointing to discuss.'

Standing over the living room bin, Michelle decanted all that remained of the bunch of flowers into it. 'Mr Shaw, what brings you here?'

The bottle of Highland whisky on the side was visible to Jack. He took a step towards it.

'Mrs d'Vere, earlier this afternoon your husband purchased a bottle of whisky, which I believe is this one, during the Whisky Tasting event he attended.'

'Yes, he attended, but what's the problem?'

'It's somewhat embarrassing, but staff at the bar may not sell the bottles. Sadly, they seem to have performed a well-known scam. Knowing it was going on, we kept it under observation and tracked what happened to the illicitly purchased bottles. We know there was a cash transaction for the bottle, so we are happy to refund Mr d'Vere with the money against a receipt. Obviously, it is not a good news story for the ship or indeed the Destiny Luxury Group. It is frustrating that the godmother's husband thought it appropriate to make such a purchase. Now we can, of course, give Mr d'Vere the benefit of the doubt in knowing that he was taking part in a scam....'

'Well, of course he wouldn't know, Mr Shaw. That's preposterous to even suggest such a thing.'

'Except I had a member of my staff undercover at the bar and he heard the whole thing, which unfortunately includes Mr d'Vere believing it was a tax and duties scam and then going along with it. That would, of course, be embarrassing for us all, so we would appreciate both yours and Mr d'Vere's cooperation in how we need to diffuse the situation so that we can all learn from it. We are not being underhand in how we are dealing with this. We believe in transparency and honesty, and of course, we have the final say on how we conclude such disciplinary situations. So, I'll be seizing the bottle for evidential purposes and reclaiming what is rightfully ours. As a sweetener, I can bizarrely give you an entirely new identical bottle for free. They entitled you to any complimentary spirits bottle you desire in your position of godmother. I can arrange for Jose to deliver a bottle here within thirty minutes.'

'Mr Shaw. I appreciate your candid approach. There will be no need to order us that bottle, as it should be a punishment to Mr d'Vere for his sheer stupidity, for which I feel I must apologise. I will accept the bottle and dangle it in front of him so he knows what he will be missing.'

There was the familiar sound of the suite door unlocking. Both Michelle and Jack looked over. His timing was impeccable. In walked Spencer. They could cut the tension with a knife as he traipsed into the room.

'Darling. Mr Shaw is here from security. He was just telling me about this bottle of whisky you purchased. Unfortunately, this little present you bought yourself is not for you to keep. The very kind Mr Shaw is going to take it back. Never mind, though, as he has proposed to refund your money and they will say no more about this. Are you ok with that my sweetheart?'

Spencer looked dumbfounded. He stood there feeling like a total lemon.

Jack reached inside both sides of his jacket pocket. He pulled out some crisp dollar bills from one side, and his small notebook and pen from the other. Jack made out a quick receipt long-hand in his notebook. He presented it to Spencer to sign, offering a pen with his other hand. Spencer took the book in his right hand and the pen in his left and signed the notebook with an unrecognisable scribble. He handed both the notebook and pen back to Jack. Jack counted out $10 bills. '$150 I believe Mr d'Vere.'

'That's correct.'

Jack handed over the cash. 'Right, I'll be off. Thank you

for your time. I'll speak later once Captain Nico has authorised our case disposal. Good evening.'

Jack secreted the offending bottle and added it to the Destiny biodegradable carrier bag, where it joined the other bottle from the sting operation. He left the cabin. He needed to get back to his office and write up the Electronic Occurrence Book; a live system where senior staff record incidents of significant importance for the information of other officers. A real-time 'What's occurring?' log that informed and fed the daily SMT. Reading the EOB before SMT "Morning Prayers" was a requisite. Woe betides those that got found out in not reading it. The 'read receipt' in the background was a bit of a giveaway for Captain Nico.

'We need to talk,' said Michelle sternly as she heard the door close.

***

'Is there anyone available from security please?' asked Suzanne of the ship's receptionist.

'Is it an urgent matter or anything I can assist you with?'

'No, not really. I have a quandary and I think they will be in the best position to assist me.'

'Have you lost your ship's token?'

Suzanne's temper was wearing thin, but she kept her composure. 'No, it's nothing like that. Look, it's personal, so if you can call them.'

The receptionist paged Jack and by chance he was in the lift on his way to the security office. He passed by the reception to answer their page.

'This lady wishes to speak to you in private.'

Jack looked at her.

'Please, it's important. I don't want to take up too much of your time, so I'll be succinct.'

'Ok. That's fine. To be honest, I only have five minutes available right now, so follow me.'

Jack escorted Suzanne through to his private office, closed the door behind them, and offered her a seat. He placed the clinking bag behind the desk. He sat opposite her so he could look at her eye-to-eye. 'I'm all ears.'

'What I have to say to you is going to sound a little crazy, but please bear with me. I'm Suzanne and I came onboard to work with my boss, Theo d'Vere. You probably know him?'

'Funnily enough, I've met him just minutes ago in his suite.'

'No, you didn't. He is not Theo d'Vere.'

'I'm sorry to disappoint you, Suzanne, but I met him earlier in the week and I think I know him pretty well. He's easily recognisable.'

'I'll stop you there, as I know him far better than you. I need to tell you something in strict confidence. Theo is not only my boss, but he is also an extremely close colleague who I have worked with intimately for a long time.' Suzanne took a deep breath to steady herself. 'Ok. I need to tell you something about Theo and I. We are lovers.' She let out a loud sigh.

'Fine Suzanne. That sort of thing doesn't bother me. You've trumped my knowledge of him with that revelation. So, what is it that is bothering you so much?'

'The man you have met is an imposter, but I don't know why. Theo left the ship a couple of days ago and was going on a photography assignment for the rest of the voyage. He wasn't due to come back onboard, but now he was back. I saw him in the casino the night he was back onboard from Azzurro Cay. You could have knocked me down with a feather. I saw him with another lady, being flirtatious.'

'That will be his wife, Michelle d'Vere.'

'But it wasn't. I know who she is. She's the ship's godmother. I've been trying to avoid her all week in case she suspected anything about us. It was another female, but I don't know who.'

'I need to ask. Is this about jealousy and his infidelity with another woman?'

Suzanne looked down at the floor. After a brief pause, she looked back at Jack. 'No, it's not, because that person flirting with the other woman is not Theo. If it was Theo, then my feelings would be so much worse. Obviously, I felt hurt when I saw them together, as I thought it was indeed Theo. That has turned itself on its head this afternoon when I saw him in the casino alone at the roulette table. There are only certain casino games my Theo enjoys. I found it strange at first the other night when he was at the craps table. He can't stand the game. It's all boisterous and all a bit unnecessary. That's Theo's words, not mine, but there he was, playing it to his heart's content. Then came the flirtatious thing, and whatever. My heart was breaking watching it unfold. So when I saw him back in the casino today, I was going to approach him, but took a moment to stand back and watch him. What I saw grew my suspicion that it's not Theo. For a start, Theo is right-handed. When he bets, he keeps all his chips he is playing with to his right, and anything he wins, he banks to his left and never gambles with it. Theo has a habit of passing a spare chip between his thumb and forefinger in his right hand. The imposter, who is left-handed, piles all his chips, including the original stash and his winnings, in front of him. He also twiddles a chip but in his left hand. He doesn't restrict the chip to between just his thumb and forefinger, he twists it over the back of his hand, through all his fingers, and even back the other way again. It's quite bizarre.'

'I'm sorry, Suzanne, but could it be that Theo is ambidextrous and you just never knew it?'

'Look. I can't swear that I know everything about Theo, but I'm certain he is only right-handed. From having watched him shoot photos on his camera and seen him write scripts for his documentaries. I've seen him tuck into bowls of food in the wild and he is right-handed. Listen. After watching him for twenty minutes, I took a seat alongside him at the roulette table. He didn't recognise me or acknowledge me. I had to tell him my name, and it meant nothing to him. I ordered the same cocktail as him. It was a Rob Roy. He called it a High & Dry. I've never heard of it, but I know what a Rob Roy is. It's a scotch whisky with vermouth. Theo drinks Rob Roy's, but his order is very particular. Theo drinks a Sweet & Smokey, using Islay malt whisky and a sweet vermouth. It's the total opposite. Now hear me out. Theo only bets on the number 20 on the nose, but this guy placed several chips on 21. I then placed a chip down in front of this imposter. If that is Theo, he would know to place it on one of the three first row numbers; either number one, two or three. This fool looked at the chip in bewilderment. He then asked me what number, so I said double zero. He placed the chip on the double zero. Theo knows that I never bet on the single zero or double zero, as I consider them unlucky. What was this guy thinking? I swear to you we have an imposter.'

It had gone unnoticed to Suzanne that Jack was not only listening intently, but had also opened a new page on his notebook and was scribbling away.

'Ok, granted. You opened up with something that sounds bizarre, and if I can be quite honest, it's not something I've ever heard of before. I'll investigate it and get back to you. To be truthful, we have other priorities at the moment, but I'll set some time aside to look into this and get back to you. I see on my system here that you are Suzanne Harrington, and we have your cabin number. I'll leave a message for you on your cabin phone to call me. I won't leave a message other than that in case someone else listens to it.'

Jack reached over the table and gripped the back of Suzanne's hand with his in a conciliatory way.

'Stay calm. Don't approach him anymore. Leave it to me and I'll see what I can do.'

With that, Suzanne smiled graciously at Jack and left to

return to her cabin. Jack closed his notebook and pulled out his phone to contact Captain Nico about the embarrassing whisky scam that now needed his immediate attention.

***

Following his dressing down by a furious Michelle, Spencer retreated to the comfort of his private shower. He thought it quite confusing that at the end of her mini-tirade she ended it with, 'But don't worry, we'll get over this and I'll make it up to you'. Not the words he was expecting to hear in all the circumstances. He acknowledged to her he was wrong, but she was the one who was saying she would make amends.

Michelle was on the phone with Jose.

'Mr d'Vere and I had such a great time swimming with the pigs the other day that we thought we would take advantage of our unscheduled return to Azzurro Cay tomorrow. We would love to return and do it all over again. I'm shy to say this. As it was our wedding anniversary that day, we couldn't fully enjoy the swimming experience because we were too distracted, so we would like to do it all over again. We were so overjoyed with the picnic spread you arranged we thought we would have the same again as well. I see on the TV that the excursion desk is advertising swimming with pigs' tours for tomorrow afternoon only, so I take it that the place will be free for a private tour in the morning. If you can confirm that for me, arrange for the speedboat hire again, and prepare the same picnic, then that would be just marvellous.'

Jose noted the instructions and ended the call so that he could make the enquiries and engineer all the components.

'For goodness' sake. Hurry up in there. We've got dinner to get to,' shouted an infuriated Michelle through the closed bathroom door. 'You are so slow, you'll be late for your own funeral,' she added to gee him up further.

***

Cecil and Connie were queuing outside the theatre door for the dancing extravaganza show. It was the late show post-dinner. Connie was frantically looking through her clutch bag for her glasses. With her short-sightedness, trying to watch the show without them would be futile.

'Cecil, wait in the queue. I'll need to pop back to the cabin to pick up my glasses. I think they are on the bedside table.'

Cecil did as he was told, as he always did. Happy wife. Happy life. Connie walked back through the queue, headlong into a throng of people. She called the lift, which was full of people wanting to exit and get to the show. She waited her turn, trying to smile at those leaving the lift. Finally, it was free, and she was ascending alone. The lift stopped at the next deck and in stepped Michelle.

'What a lovely surprise, Michelle. Going up? I'm heading that way to get my glasses for the show.'

'Yes, please Connie.'

Michelle offered her token in order to override the lift, but Connie declined it. She had already pressed the button for their same top deck.

Connie had a slight irritation in her throat, so cleared it with her hand to her mouth before she spoke. 'Can I say, Michelle, there's something strange about your husband?'

'In what regards?'

'Well, if you can remember back to our appointment in the spa one morning. We were talking about the signs of the zodiac, etcetera, and from your husband's traits, I rightly identified him as a Gemini. You agreed and confirmed his birthday as the 20th of June. Anyhow, I was in the jacuzzi with him this morning, and one thing led to another, and we got talking. I questioned him on a few things. All the answers he gave led me to believe he is in fact Cancerian. To be honest, the fact he was wearing a Cancerian pendant around his neck helped enormously, and he had his birthday, the 21st of June, tattooed on his forearm in Roman numerals. What I can't get my head around is why he has told me one thing, yet you have told me another. One of you is lying and I don't understand why? The zodiac signs are important to me. I don't know if you were trying to play silly games with me?'

Michelle pulled out her token to override the lift to stop it as it reached the top deck.

'What are you insinuating? I don't know what your game is, Connie, but it ends right here, right now. I won't put up with this zodiac nonsense. Do you understand?'

'What is it, Michelle? What's your game? Do you think common people like me aren't good enough for the likes of you? Is that it? Your husband one day was a Gemini, yet the next a Cancerian. You don't fool me, Michelle. You can't fool the horoscopes. It's written in the stars.'

'Stop your drivel, you old fool. I don't want to hear another word from you. When these lift doors open, I don't want to see or hear from you again. Do you understand, you witch? Now get out, you stupid old woman.'

Michelle opened the lift doors. A rattled Connie exited in a scurry. Michelle needed to think quickly. She's in a dilemma. She knew CCTV covered the lift but was not sure if it picked up sound, or only when you pressed the button to speak on the intercom? A covering scenario came to mind. She opened her handbag and pulled out a disposable tissue. She wiped down the handrail that Connie was leaning against, as well as the lift operation buttons. Michelle overemphasised the cleaning so that it would be clear on the CCTV. She must do something about Connie and pretty damn sharpish before she became even more than an irritant. She released the lift and exited towards her own suite. Once inside, she headed straight over to the phone by the bed. She used the quick dial to phone through to the Medical Centre. It diverted through to Dr Patel's mobile phone.

'Hello. Dr Patel? It's Michelle d'Vere here. There is something I need to tell you. I was in the lift just now with a fellow passenger. I believe her name is Connie Morgan-Brown. She was coughing, so I asked her what was wrong with her, replying she didn't feel well and thought it might be the dreaded norovirus. She was telling me she felt sick and had a bit of a temperature. I advised her she needs to go to her cabin and stay there. The same would apply to her husband, I told her. She was having nothing of it. She got quite angry with me and ranted about not wanting to miss the show. I told her that her attitude was outrageous and that she needed to call the medical centre. I guess by her attitude towards me she hasn't called you?'

'Mrs d'Vere, I am in the medical centre and haven't had a passenger call in here or phone me. So, in that respect, I can confirm no one has contacted me.'

'Oh, that's what I feared would be the case. How irresponsible is that woman? She'll have gone back to the theatre by now. I guess you'll just have to wait until they are back in their cabin after the show. I just hope neither of them spreads the contagious virus to other guests, or even the crew. It would be disastrous for the Destiny Luxury Group if on its maiden voyage there was a report of a large norovirus outbreak onboard. Anyway, I'll leave it in your capable hands. I did my best to wipe down the lift. Best of luck.'

'Thank you for reporting this, Mrs d'Vere. If only there were more conscientious people like yourself. I will handle this. Goodnight.'

Michelle replaced the receiver to its cradle and smiled to herself. Seed planted, she thought.

***

There was a knock on the cabin door. The occupants had only just fallen asleep. A woman vacated the bed to answer the door. The dimmed clock was showing 11.45pm. Who on earth could be knocking at this time of night? There was now a second and more urgent sounding knock on the door.

'Coming. Hold on.'

She picked her dressing gown off the hook by the bathroom door and wrapped it around herself. 'Hold on.'

She removed the security chain off the door and pulled it ajar to look out. She could not believe that outside in the corridor were three people dressed head to toe in what appeared to be Hazchem white paper suits with pale blue facemasks over their mouths and noses.

'Mrs Morgan-Brown. I'm Dr Patel and these are two of my colleagues. Please, can you return to inside the cabin and let us in?'

Connie was in total shock. She did as she was instructed. The three medical staff entered the room and closed the door behind them. Connie climbed back into bed as Dr Patel turned up the light to a dimmed setting.

The light coming on stirred Cecil from his snoring.

'I take it that this is Mr Morgan-Brown?'

'Who on earth would it be otherwise? Brad Pitt wasn't available tonight. What is all this about?'

'Mrs Morgan-Brown, we've had a tipoff that you and your husband may be suffering from a sickness bug, Norovirus. Are you aware of it?'

'Dr Patel. My husband and I have been on more cruises than you could shake a stick at. Of course we have heard of it, and I can assure you we are not suffering from it. And please, call me Connie. All this surname business is all too formal for me.'

'Connie, often passengers who suffer from the sickness bug hide the fact that they have contracted it. Passengers know they will be subject to confinement in their cabin for at least three days so that the virus can be controlled. They don't want to miss out on their holiday, which I understand. They don't like the thought of being constricted in their cabin. I'll need to examine you both and ensure they clean the cabin down.'

'Look, Dr Patel, we are not sick at all. Is someone playing

a practical joke here? Who's put you up to this?'

'Connie. I am not at liberty to discuss who reports these matters. All that I can say is that my priority is the welfare of the entire ship, both passengers and crew, and I therefore need to make a diagnosis. You may not be showing any symptoms now, but I will need to consider a minimum of twenty-four hours' quarantine to be on the safe side. There is too big a risk if I don't do that. I would appreciate your cooperation in this regard. May I ask, when did you last have a bowel movement?'

'About a minute ago when you knocked on my door when I was asleep! I haven't, well, not since this morning. Cecil and I are quite regular in that department, aren't we, dear?'

Cecil nodded, then pulled the covers over his head out of pure embarrassment.

'No loose bowel movements since this morning?' asked Dr Patel.

'Not in the slightest.'

'Nausea?'

'I'm feeling as sick as a pig right now, but I wouldn't count on that. No, neither of us has been sick.'

'Ok. How were you feeling about three hours ago?'

'Fine. Why three hours ago?'

'Well, that's when we were told you were exhibiting signs of sickness.'

'Three hours ago? I was in the theatre three hours ago, and before that we had a peaceful dinner for the two of us. We haven't spoken to anyone about feeling ill. Did you say three hours ago? That's about the time Mrs d'Vere and I argued in the lift about something unrelated. Did she put you up to this? I bet she did. The evil witch. This is preposterous. I demand to see the captain.'

Connie let out a deep sigh and folded her arms. She stared at Dr Patel.

'Connie. As I've already said. I am not at liberty to reveal who has told us what. We need to look at the bigger picture on the safety of the ship. We cannot call out the Captain at this time of night. I would not put him or the ship in danger in letting you speak with him directly. I will, of course, report back to him your desire to speak to him when I meet him at the management meeting in the morning. Until I say otherwise, I'm afraid you will both have to remain in the cabin. Can I kindly point out that whilst you are not under surveillance in the cabin, we have systems in place to monitor the public spaces such as the corridors? If our systems detect you outside the confines of this cabin, it would have dire consequences for you both. We could consider you for instant disembarkation and for you to return home at your own expense. Of course, that is not a threat. I'm purely pointing out the consequences so that you are fully informed. Now just sit there for a moment, and Cecil, if you can please pop your head out from the covers so that I can take your temperature with this hand-held thermometer.'

Her warning had sharply brought Connie to her senses. Connie and Cecil complied with their head temperature being taken. Both were registering a normal 37c.

'Your temperatures appear fine, but that is not a foolproof conclusion, only an indication. We'll check in on you in twelve hours' time and take it from there. In the meantime, my two colleagues here will disinfect parts of your cabin and bathroom. It will only take them a few minutes. After that, they will leave you in peace. I bid you goodnight and we hope you will feel well in the morning.'

Dr Patel passed the bathroom door on the way out. She doubled backed and investigated the open bathroom. It looked to be in a pristine condition. The toilet roll still had the folded point to the end piece, as left by the room steward once they had finished their cleaning regime. It was another sign to the doctor that there appeared nothing to support the insistence that the norovirus was present. Longing for her bed, Dr Patel made a head start on her colleagues by typing up a quick executive summary on the EOB before retiring for the evening.

CHAPTER EIGHTEEN

It was late, but Jack still had to investigate the report made to him by Suzanne. If he managed as much as five hours' sleep tonight, he knew he would be happy. He sat in his office and dimmed the lights. The light emanated from the computer screen and was enough to illuminate his desk and notebook. Before he became too engrossed in the issues Suzanne had raised, he checked his phone for messages. There was a broadcast from Captain Nico informing the senior staff that tomorrow's SMT would be at Destiny's Azzurro Cay Mirage Hotel. Because of the necessity to get to the landside, the captain had delayed the start time to 11am. It was not as if Jack was going to benefit with an extra hour of undisturbed sleep, as he would lose that and more researching Suzanne's case.

He refreshed his recollection of what she had relayed to him from his notebook. It took him back to his days in the Met Police, where in court you could only use your notebook to refresh your memory of events. You were not supposed to read them out. They were an aide-mémoire and not a verbatim account. Try telling that to the young recruits these days, he thought. Jack had been a dying breed of sergeants who would sit at the back of the court whilst their subordinates would give evidence. No-one had the time anymore to provide that quality supervision and feedback. Most supervisors he encountered before his resignation had never even given evidence in court before. It was a dying art. He flicked back over the three pages of his distinctive scrawl in the A4 notebook. He deciphered the contents and reached for a strong coffee before he pulled together his action plan. Jack recorded his summary of events on the computer and saved it under a version control. He now had a time stamp on the investigation that was irrefutable. He drafted out his action plan for how to prove or indeed disprove the events stated. Jack used this time under the investigative principle of the 'Golden Hour' rule.

He had to identify all the evidential lines at the earliest possible time to prevent the loss or destruction of evidence. He had humans to talk to and technology to secure. Jack thought through what to prioritise. Technology these days had grown year by year. People used to record things like CCTV on VHS tapes that were easily over-recorded. However, now they record CCTV digitally, which allows them to keep it for long periods of time.

Humans could lose their memories in an amazingly quick time, especially in these circumstances where potential witnesses may not have even realised they had witnessed something significant. Considering the average age of passengers, if they were called upon, they may have little or no memory of events. He must first identify which people to whom he would need to speak. From the concept of the cruise ship, he influenced the technology installed in the security infrastructure. He logged onto the technology systems from his computer. Using his experience of Anacapa charts from his attachment days on homicide, he ran a couple of searches. The first was a complete visual history from CCTV of Michelle's movements in all public spaces across the ship since embarking. Jack wanted to see who she had met. The computer produced two pieces of intelligence, with the first being a timeline with captured images of whom she had engaged. The second was a route map around the ship of precisely where she had been and when. Jack then switched his searches to Mr d'Vere or whoever he may be. He performed the identical searches with the additional detail of a breakdown of his expenditure. He checked his notes and amended the search to include all individual drinks purchased or set against the suite account. Jack knew the devil would be in the detail. He went to a cupboard and recovered a second computer monitor that plugged in, allowing him dual screens. The intelligence material at his disposal was too vast to view on a single screen. Harking back to his experience in the HOLMES suite on Homicide, they too used dual screens to read and display the raw data. Known as the Home Office Large Major Enquiry System, it had come on leaps and bounds since its creation following the Yorkshire Ripper enquiry.

The security system that Jack had helped to devise for Destiny made HOLMES pale into insignificance in comparison. The Home Office and the police had limited funds for technology. Not so much the Destiny Luxury Group. They wanted to be at the forefront of technology and were content to invest heavily. The timeline showed not only the faces and interaction but also identified every individual, whether it be a passenger or staff member, through the system's facial recognition software. Jack now had a comprehensive report at the touch of a button. He toggled the report settings to narrow down a list of individuals. He circled the ones that he needed to prioritise. The overlapping crew duties software that highlighted through a RAG system who was available, assisted Jack. The red code was for those that were registered in their cabin and then presumed to be resting and therefore not to be disturbed unless in an emergency. Amber codes showed Jack those away from their cabin, but not working a shift. The green code indicated those currently on duty and working. The RAG report displayed those that either Michelle or Mr d'Vere had interacted with during the cruise. Janik from the Casino was still working, and Jose, the suite butler, was off duty but not yet back in his cabin. Using his common-sense, Jack prioritised contacting Jose first, knowing that he would soon be in his cabin and up early in the morning to deal with the breakfast run. He paged Jose to join him in his office.

At this late hour, the ship was quiet in the public areas with only the night shift cleaners hoovering the main areas, except for the cabin corridors. The monthly chandelier cleaning regime in the main atrium was underway, with two members of the crew harnessed from the safety rail as they delicately polished the intricate crystal teardrops. Jose made quick unhindered progress to the security office.

'Jose, I won't keep you, but I need your help, specifically around your knowledge of the d'Veres. I can't go into detail about what this is about, but I need you to be as open with me as possible. I have little time, so I'll get straight to the point. Have you seen anything different from Mr d'Vere from prior to our stop in Azzurro Cay when the d'Veres left the ship for an overnight stay at the Destiny Hotel, or since their return? Anything at all?'

Jose pondered the question for about twenty seconds. 'It may be something or it may be nothing. You may know butlers unpack and repack the guests' suitcases. Before they left for the overnight stay, Mr d'Vere's underwear was universally Y-fronts. Upon his return, I have noticed that they were Paisley boxer shorts. We are all creatures of habit, Mr Shaw; I don't need to tell you that. I thought at the time this was strange, but thought nothing more of it.'

'Anything about their personality or mannerisms?'

'Mannerisms?'

'You know. Change in habits or how they interact with you or in between themselves.'

'Mrs d'Vere always seems to be strained. The other day and again this evening, whilst they were at dinner, I found several flower petals in the bin and some discarded under the rims of furniture. I know they are from the floral arrangements I organise for their suite. Someone has nothing better to do than pick them apart. I was going to ask Mrs d'Vere if there was something wrong with my displays, as I would replace them if she wasn't happy with them. I'm quite proud of those extra touches we provide here at Destiny.'

'That's fine Jose. Come to think of it, when I was in their suite earlier, I recall seeing some petals on the floor. How odd. Don't mention it to her. Let me work it out. Just carry on with your normal routine. Is there anything else?'

'No. Not that I can think of. The music on the Robyn system has changed over the week. It's now a livelier kind of music at an increased volume. It's noticeable when you walk into the stateroom. Especially so if Mr d'Vere is in the suite. Mrs d'Vere has also arranged another swimming with pigs' tour for tomorrow, even though they only did this the other day. She said that it was such a great excursion she wants to do it again. I understand it is a beautiful experience but to go back so soon?'

'Not such a once in a lifetime experience then as described in the tour excursion brochure, I guess,' smirked Jack.

'One more thing. Mrs d'Vere is the one that usually orders breakfast, but for the first time yesterday, it was Mr d'Vere. That's all I can think of, Mr Shaw. I'm sorry if I haven't been that helpful. I feel like what people say, something of a chocolate teapot.'

Jack laughed out aloud. 'Not at all, Jose. A chocolate teapot, chocolate kettle or chocolate fireguard. You are none of them, but maybe between us we have a suggestion for chef's chocolate bonanza. We'll leave it there. Please enjoy the rest of your evening.'

Jose glanced up at the clock above Jack's desk and realised he had to be on duty in less than six hours. He left.

Jack checked the RAG system again and noticed that Janik was still on duty. He switched to the live CCTV system and dropped into the casino cameras. Janik was easy to locate, as he was in his usual area behind the croupiers. The facial recognition overlay confirmed it for Jack. The casino floor was looking quiet, with only a blackjack and a roulette table in play.

You could count the participants on one hand. There was no time like the present, so Jack called Janik.

Janik saw on the display that the call was from the security office. As was his instinct, whilst answering the call, he looked up at the security camera above the two active tables and across to the players. Jack noticed Janik's motions on the camera and reassured him there was nothing coming to note for him to worry about, but he needed to speak with him, if possible, on another matter. Janik knew his position in the organisation and headed up to Jack's office. Knowing that they closely monitored the casino, he didn't mind leaving his position temporarily.

'Thanks for coming Janik. What I'm about to ask you might appear strange, by any stretch of the imagination. Do you know a Mr d'Vere? On our system, he is a regular frequenter of the casino.'

'Yes. Sure. He is married to the godmother. Why do you ask?'

'I'm not at liberty to say, but what can you tell me about him?'

'Well, he's not a big gambler. By that, I mean he doesn't gamble very much. Maybe near $200 dollars a visit. I can check for you?'

'There's no need to Janik as I have access to that information here. Who does he interact with?'

'Beyond playing with the croupiers and ordering drinks from the table waiters, I have seen him with his wife, and also a couple of different women, should I say.'

'I'm interested in that. Who are these women you have seen him with?'

'I know for sure there is one woman in particular that I saw him with on the early days of the cruise and then again this afternoon. I don't know if they have fallen out in that time, but the dynamics appeared different today.'

'What do you mean?'

'Originally they were talking together, both taking money out at the same time for the same amounts against their respective cabins. You could tell there was a spark between them back then. May I even be bold enough to say they were flirtatious with one and other? That seemed to have changed today. Mr d'Vere was playing at the roulette table. This same lady appeared and sat next to him. There was very little talking between them. Maybe they had an argument, and he was being obstinate towards her. It was as if he was trying to blank her. There was none of the tomfoolery I had witnessed before. All strange.'

'Apart from that, have you seen any other changes in Mr d'Vere?'

'Thinking of it, his persona has changed over the week. He was more of a reserved individual when I first saw him. I noticed his obvious displeasure when there was loud cheering from the craps table. He would look over and physically shake his head. It was so obvious sometimes that I was waiting for him to say something. Yesterday evening, instead of waiting for a seat at the roulette table, he went over to the craps and waited to join in there. When he was on the dice, he was being accompanied by a different female. He was revelling in the atmosphere and applause, and certainly wasn't complaining when this lady was, how can I put it, being more physical and touching him? What was stranger still was that as the two of them abruptly left the casino towards the lift lobby, they were being followed at a distance by the original woman he played roulette with. This woman returned to the casino afterwards and looked upset. I don't know what happened. Maybe it was the chrysalis that made their meeting today seem cold and emotionless.'

'Do you recall either lady's names?'

'The original lady was a Suzanne Harrington. I remember authorising the withdrawal against her cabin. The other lady from last night I haven't seen before. I'm sorry I can't help you with that.'

'No worries Janik. I'll be able to trace her if I need to. Anything else about Mr d'Vere that you can think of?'

Jack was being careful not to lead Janik in his questioning. He wanted an honest recollection, so Jack could later use technology to support his account rather than the other way around. The technology available to Jack was fantastic at securing physical information, but worthless for capturing emotions and feelings. That needed a human touch.

'There is something at the back of my mind. Yes. I have it. Earlier in the week, Mr d'Vere had a particular method of gambling. The croupier would give him his chips, and then he would pile them to his right-hand side. He would only gamble some money at a time. He had a reserved nature. If he won anything, then he would place the winnings to his left. He never gambled with his winnings. I've seen this before in Vegas when I worked there. As you know, the house always wins, but we don't win as much when people don't gamble their winnings. This is just one thing they have taught me to observe over the years. When it came down to it in Vegas, in handing out free buffet vouchers and other perks, we wanted to target those that spent well and will gamble. Mr d'Vere wouldn't fall into that category. He wouldn't be the one that we would chase if he himself wasn't chasing our money. Today, Mr d'Vere had a different approach. He piled all his money in front of himself. He had no money to his right or left. Anything he won, which wasn't much, went back into his pot. A very different approach. One we would give buffet vouchers to.'

'You said he would interact with the table waiters. I don't suppose you know what his preferred drink was?'

'Sure. Rob Roy. The scotch with the vermouth. Yes. He always ordered a Rob Roy. I don't know the drinks as well as the casino floor, but he liked to have something he called a sweet & smoky, or was it a high & dry? I forget now, as I think I've seen him drinking both.'

'Can you remember when that changed at all?'

'I believe he used to have the sweet & smoky, but in the last couple of days, he has been drinking the high & dry. Maybe his palette has changed.'

Jack did not answer Janik's hypothesis so as not to leave that as a definitive in his memory.

'Janik. That's helpful. Please don't discuss this with anyone else. Especially any of those we have talked about. And please, I'm not saying you would, but please don't discuss this even with your staff.'

'Please tell me that none of my staff has performed dishonestly. I drill into them on every shift that it's a long flight home if they act with impropriety.'

'I can assure you, Janik, that we are not looking at either yourself or your staff. It's a delicate matter that needs my attention, but also your discretion.'

'I can promise you, Mr Shaw, that you have this.'

'Just one more thing, Janik. I notice on my timeline that during the crew drill, you are with Mrs d'Vere for a couple of minutes and appear to be talking closely. Is there anything you want to tell me about that?'

'Can I tell you it's about the nightly lotto draw?'

'You can, Janik, but would it be the truth?'

Janik paused and gave a slight smile. 'No, it wouldn't be the truth, Mr Shaw. She approached me as she wanted to know about a lady present in the casino on Masquerade Ball night with Mr d'Vere.'

'And did you tell her who it was?'

'No, I did not, and neither would I. She asked me on the night itself and I told her I didn't know. She approached me at the crew drill, and shall we say, she was slightly threatening me.'

'In what way was she threatening you?'

'I could lie, Mr Shaw, but it's not in my nature. When I was a young croupier on a ship many years ago, Mrs d'Vere and I were briefly lovers. In hindsight, it was something I regret. Of course, I was much younger then and thought nothing like this would come back to haunt me many years later. She tried to use that indiscretion against me to find the name of the mystery masquerade lady. Mrs d'Vere is vindictive and threatening. I refused to be blackmailed and said I didn't know.'

'But do you know who it was?'

'I can't be certain, but ironically, if I was a betting man, which I am not as a casino manager, I would say it was Suzanne Harrington.'

'Janik. Thank you for your brutal honesty. It's best to get these things off your chest. I would rather know that Mrs d'Vere was being manipulative than anything else.'

'Will I get in to trouble for this, Mr Shaw?'

'Janik. I can't give any cast iron guarantees, but look at it this way. When you investigate events, as I have done for several years, there is always the possibility of fallout on the periphery. Knowing what I know, that you had a dalliance in your younger years and have a good disciplinary record otherwise, let's just put this down to one of life's experiences. Let him who is without sin cast the first stone, and all that. Best you close down the casino and get some rest. I'm sure you've deserved it.'

With that Jack gestured towards the door and closed his notebook in a sign that nothing would come of Janik straying off-course all that time ago. As soon as the door closed, Jack reopened his notebook and still made a brief note for integrity's sake. He intended to keep to his promise.

He logged back on to the computer, which had long since gone into standby mode. As soon as it kicked in, there was a pop-up message to show there was a new entry in the EOB from Dr Patel. Jack was now feeling weary and was longing for his bed, but his passion for knowledge led him to click open the EOB entry. The entry was lengthy given that the title was "Possible Norovirus Case". Intending only to skim read the entry, all that changed as he spotted the d'Vere name in the body of the text. Dr Patel had laid out events as she had witnessed them, in a very evidential way. Jack felt there must be more meat on the bones than Dr Patel had alluded to in her report. The entry was only a couple of minutes old, so without even checking on the RAG system, he messaged Dr Patel to call in to his office. Like all SMT, you were never off-duty anyhow.

There was a knock on the door. Dr Patel was half-hoping that Jack would not answer and that she could go to her quarters for some much-needed sleep. She was to be disappointed.

'Come in,' was the reply. 'Dr Patel, please take a seat.'

'Jack, you're using my phrase. That's reserved for doctors to tell their patients. I'll reverse the role-play here to what would be my next question. What can I do for you?'

'Very sharp Dr Patel. I've been reading your EOB entry regarding the norovirus case.'

'Or not. Should I say, Jack?'

'Well, that's what has caught my attention. What do you make of this?'

'It's quite simple. I don't believe this couple is suffering with norovirus.'

'I note with interest in your report that Mrs d'Vere was the informant of the case. What do you make of that?'

'It's all rather odd. I've had to take an air of caution and quarantine the couple for twelve hours. I believe that in eleven hours' time we will be returning to their cabin to sign them off with a clean bill of health.'

'So what do you think is Mrs d'Vere's motivation for this?'

'It's one of two things. Either she has a genuinely held belief that the couple were suffering with norovirus. She said at the time that she immediately cleaned the lift they were in together, which could be an instant reaction to ensure hygienic cleanliness, or alternatively, she was someone wanting to be seen to take those steps for vicarious reasons.'

'Interesting Dr Patel. Let's take your second prognosis there, the vicarious reasons scenario. What makes you think that?'

'Well, I need to marry together the whole episode. The lady in the cabin, Connie, believes that Mrs d'Vere did this out of spite. She told me she had an argument with her that was unrelated to norovirus. I didn't delve any deeper because it was a slight cause for worry, but not my overriding concern at that moment. Preventing sickness spreading was my priority. Connie called her a witch, which was quite a strong put-down, but then again, not if someone has falsely quarantined you.'

'Now we're getting somewhere. Let me put this to you. If you coupled what you have encountered with the same individual, also demonstrating manipulation and blackmailing of crew members, together with destroying flower displays in private in their own cabin, what does that tell you about someone?'

'Possibilities of paranoia, depression, maybe even being psychotic. Some of these appear as low-key symptoms individually but can manifest themselves into severe outpourings of emotions and extreme actions.'

'How severe are we talking, doctor?'

'At the extreme end, it can be verbal assaults, and even physical assaults. Have you any evidence of physical assaults, Jack?'

'No, none. None at all. I was just looking for your professional help so I can understand what I may be facing. It's good to know.'

'Well, that's a relief. If psychotics advance to extremes, you could have your hands full. It could be a slow-burner over days, weeks, months or even years, but when they snap, you'll know about it. Hopefully, we can all rest assured.'

'Yes, let's hope so, doctor. I'll let you be off, as we both have a long day tomorrow. The SMT at the hotel is a bit later than normal. Once you have seen the couple and given them the all-clear, can you contact me as I'd like to have a chat with them in private before they head off around the ship?'

'Agreed, Jack. You'll be the first to know, See you in the morning.'

Dr Patel left whilst Jack was busy scribbling in his notebook. He closed it and logged off the computer. At least he had his own desk now, which was far better than the Met using desk-sharing, as in his days gone by. Time for some shut-eye.

***

The phone rang. 'Good morning, Jack. As I thought would be the case. The room steward and I have been in to see Mr and Mrs Morgan-Brown. Their cabin and bathroom remain pristine. No sign of excessive use of the toilet rolls, which for me is a healthy sign. Their temperatures remain normal and I'm about to sign them off with a clean bill of health. Before I complete that technicality, if you would like to join me in their cabin and I'll hand over to you. The wife is already talking about getting to the spa early, so best you hurry down. I've told them who you are and that you want to speak with them.'

'You're a star, Dr Patel. I'll be right there.'

Without further ado, Jack was knocking on the cabin door within minutes. He entered as Dr Patel signed the release form.

'Mr and Mrs Morgan-Brown. If you don't mind, I need to ask you some questions about what has happened, especially in relation to your interactions with Mrs d'Vere.'

'About time someone is taking us seriously. Let's skip the

formalities. You'll only need me for this. I suggest you let Cecil here be off to his informal bridge social then you and I can have a cosy chat. No more of this Mrs Morgan-Brown nonsense. Just call me Connie.'

Dr Patel, knowing when she was not needed, left the cabin ahead of Cecil.

'I'll cut to the chase Connie. Why did you suggest to Dr Patel that Mrs d'Vere had it in for you?

'I thought I knew Mrs d'Vere, but now I realise I don't know her at all. This spurns from me knowing too much about Mr d'Vere. I told her so in the lift last night, and this is how she rewards me.'

'That sounds melodramatic. Can you expand on what you mean?'

'Let me guess, Mr Shaw. Your star sign is Aries, the ram. You are energetic. A defender of the vulnerable. A leader who accepts a challenge. You continue to strive even when others give up. Am I right?'

'Quite astonishing Connie. I'm not one for horoscopes and all that, but I know others are. As for those attributes, yes, I can relate to them. But isn't that the same for any description of a star sign? It's a manipulation of words and descriptions. You can say the same words for any of the zodiac signs.'

'Yes and no, Mr Shaw. Yes, if I wanted to be on stage as a hypnotist or trying to exploit vulnerable people. But I'm neither of these things. I have a passion for the zodiac signs and am good at identifying them from people watching. I observed Mr d'Vere when I first met him and thought he was a Gemini, the sign of the twin. After speaking to Mrs d'Vere about this as and after a few questions, she identified him as indeed a Gemini. She even confirmed his date of birth for me as the 20th of June. I had nothing to doubt this until a chance meeting yesterday with Mr d'Vere in the jacuzzi at Serenity. I asked him a few questions to pinpoint his star sign, and he gave me a conflicting sign of Cancer, the sign of the crab.

That's only the funny part, and probably the bit of showman in me we all have. In fact, I didn't have to use my intuition or instinct. I only had to use my eyes. There on his forearm is a tattoo of his date of birth. The 21st of June. That makes him a Cancerian and not a Gemini. Furthermore, he has a Cancer pendant around his neck on a chain. As if I needed any more proof. It was as easy as shooting fish in a barrel, Mr Shaw. I approached Mrs d'Vere about this discrepancy, but without the detail, as I thought she was trying to make a fool of me by lying about him being a Cancerian. For some reason, she flew off the handle and started having a go at me. I couldn't wait to get out of the lift. Then I find myself quarantined later the same evening. She called me a witch. Following the signs of the zodiac is not satanic, but the way she reacted you would think it was. If you stand in the Piazza Duomo in Messina, Sicily, at midday everyday you can see hundreds of visitors looking up at the Campanile to watch the figurines moving to the very spiritual and emotive instrumental version of the hymn Ave Maria. If you looked on the cameras and mobile phones of these same people, you would see they had also photographed the image of the twelve signs of the zodiac on the clock tower side that overlooks the Cathedral of Messina itself. That shows just how many people worldwide are influenced by astrology, and its close association with religion. To call me a witch is ridiculous. It's blasphemy.'

'I'm sorry to hear what happened Connie. I can promise you that no matter the relationship between Mrs d'Vere and the Destiny Luxury Group, godmother or not, we will investigate this matter impartially. If what has happened to you is as you have described, it is not acceptable. It sounds like you have built up a rapport with Mrs d'Vere during this voyage. Is there anything else you want to tell me that may be relevant?'

'I don't want to talk out of turn but not so much about Mrs d'Vere than Mr d'Vere. He appears to be a bit of a charlatan.'

'Connie, that's not a phrase I've heard repeated in many a year. What do you mean by that?' asked Jack acting dumb.

'Not one to be a gossip, you understand, but Cecil and I were in the casino one evening and we couldn't help but notice that Mr d'Vere was acting rather adventurously with a lady who wasn't his wife. Just the thought of it,' remarked Connie innocently.

'Goodness gracious,' added Jack.

'Unbelievable isn't it Mr Shaw. Sinning outside wedlock. Well, I never.'

'And when did this indiscretion occur Connie?'

'I can tell you exactly as the moon was in Uranus.'

'I have no doubt of that,' replied Jack, trying not to break out in laughter.

'It was the night of the fireworks outside. Cecil and I were in the casino. Having a little tipple before bedtime. We sat at a slot machine and saw Mr d'Vere with a young lady who wasn't his wife. Of that I have no doubt, Mr Shaw. Mr d'Vere was, shall I say, a little worse for wear. They left the roulette table together and headed off towards the lifts. Well, I didn't know where to look. The cheek of it. Have you ever known such a thing, Mr Shaw?'

Jack tried to remain neutral and non-committal to even the most slewed question. He remained silent and carried on writing in his notebook. The exaggerated slowness, he hoped, would be the prompt for Connie to keep talking. It worked.

'Cecil and I were in such shock that we had to order another nightcap. On the house of course Mr Shaw. A privilege of our loyalty status.'

Jack knew better than that, as it would have been because of being on a slot machine at a quiet period.

'So, when I met him in the jacuzzi, I was taking a chance. Putting myself in the firing line with a man that chases women like that.'

'I'm sure you did Connie,' observing she was no looker.

'So having sacrificed my personal safety, I find myself being treated in this distasteful fashion. I hope the Destiny Luxury Group understands our displeasure and will compensate us accordingly?'

'I'll put in a good word with Customer Services ,Connie. I'm sure they will be understanding.'

Connie obviously had a free cruise in mind, whilst Jack was thinking more like a bottle of Champagne and a bouquet of flowers in the suite within the hour.

'If you would forgive me now, if you have nothing else to add to your account I'll need to return to my other duties. You've been very helpful, so I'd respectfully ask that you keep this conversation to yourself. I'll pop along to customer services whilst on my way back.'

Connie gave a grin as if she had won the lottery.

Jack walked back to his office. He had a lot to consider. There was a fine line for when he had no choice but to elevate this matter to Captain Nico. Having such a bizarre set of circumstances to deal with at any other time would be one thing, but when it involved the ship's godmother, well that was another situation entirely.

When he was back in the Met, officers first on scene were forever calling mediocre events "Critical Incidents". Sometimes out of a misconceived necessity. Other times to pass the buck to someone else so that they could take the flack. After all, he was head of security. Happy to take responsibility, but he needed that top cover.

So, this call fell on him. If he was to elevate it immediately, it would only add another level of interference. He could heed advice from Captain Nico, but in all honesty, the investigation of major incidents like this aboard would fall to Jack to carry out. They employed him for his detective ability and organisational skills. Of course, he could appraise and enlighten Captain Nico as to the existence of an allegation and avoid the minutiae. He still wanted to pour over the electronic intelligence available to piece the jigsaw together with some meaningful evidence, rather than recant a story that might be full of jealousy, hypothesis and revenge. He only had less than two hours until he must be in attendance at the Azzurro Cay Mirage Hotel. This should give just enough time to create a first draft briefing note to present at the SMT, knowing that the entry on the EOB would already alert Captain Nico to an incident of interest. He stopped and thought for a moment. He would call in on Suzanne Harrington and ask a favour of her to assist in the investigation.

CHAPTER NINETEEN

'Joe, if you can assist me in preparing the food for lunch service, then I would appreciate it. We have around an hour until Leroy arrives to pick you up. You don't need to iron your T-shirt. The humidity here should take out any creases.'

Cindy and Theo were walking around the bar area, putting out the chairs and ensuring the condiments boxes were stocked. He was still trying to get to grips with wrapping knives and forks inside the paper napkins. It was clear he had never wrapped Christmas presents by himself.

'So I go to the hotel reception and ensure all twenty guests are all ready to go. I wait to give them a detailed itinerary once we are onboard the boat so as not to cause disruption in the lobby. You want me to upsell the extras we have at the bar, such as daily food specials and cocktails of the day when we land back here? I leave the yoga introduction to you and then Leroy and I arrange the entire group into even smaller groups for a real personal experience for the tour of Pig Island. What isn't there to like?'

'Joe, you are a natural. Once you get your memory back, are you sure you don't want to stay?'

'That would be nice Cindy, but I'm sure somewhere out there I have another life and I need to know what it is. Anyway, I make the place look a mess and I'm sure you need your bed back one day.'

'Don't you worry about that. As long as I still have bragging rights with those fishing boat boys, I have a man in my bed every night. I'll still have the upper hand and their respect.'

Theo laughed heartily at her playful innuendoes.

***

'Jose, is everything arranged and ready for the swimming with pigs' experience today?'

'Yes ma'am. I've had the food hampers prepared as you wished. I've been to the stores and collected the scotch whisky bottle you requested. There's a flask of ice and two tumblers to compliment it. Do you wish me to pack a day bag for you or shall I leave that to yourself?'

'I'll be fine with that myself. Are there any other tours from the ship today doing the same thing?'

'The ship isn't running any tours there today, so you should be alone. Looking here on the Pig Island website, today's calendar is showing it as unavailable. I presume the resort there is closed for the day. Unfortunately, I can only guess, but that would make sense. Even the staff on these holiday islands need a day off.'

'Too right Jose. Although there is no rest for the wicked. If you can kindly ensure my chartered speedboat is alongside in, let's say one hour, I'll ensure Theo and I are both ready.'

***

'This is choppy. Do they have sick bags on here?'

'Dr Patel. After all the years you've had at sea, can't you handle a short tender ride across the cay?'

'Captain Nico. I come from a family of land-based doctors that just so had taken up residence in a famed Indian fishing town, having never set foot on a boat until I joined the merchant navy fleets. I have to confess, when not at front of house in the medical centre onboard, you'll find me in the cabin with seasick patches behind both ears. An appreciation of the condition is why I supply the boutique onboard with a stock of them. I know there will be other sufferers like me.'

'And that's why I stock our tendering lifeboats with sick bags. If we had to deploy these lifeboats in an emergency, it's highly unlikely it would be when the waters are calm,' said Captain Nico.

They dispersed Jack and the other SMT members across the tender. Jack was still reading his draft executive summary that he would soon present to all those around him. The Azzurro Cay Mirage Hotel was emerging in to view like a mirage itself.

***

'Good to see you, Joe. Did you sleep well or were you having those nightmares again?'

'I wouldn't so much call them nightmares, Leroy. More like flashbacks. To be honest, I had my best night's sleep so far. I blame you for that with your idea of a last round of "snooters". If nothing else, it cleared my sinuses. I've nothing new to reveal, unless you count relaxing in my Hollywood pool with a bevy of beauties.'

Leroy laughed at such a scenario.

'In your dreams, Joe, which is exactly where that idea comes from and should remain. If you're ready, we can head off to the Mirage Hotel and pick up our wonderful clients. I hope the tips come pouring in today. Quite a posh lot, I would imagine. Anyhow, before we set sail, I'll need a hand to stock the cool boxes with water, beers and sodas. Time to get those princess hands dirty.'

Theo chased Leroy around the bar like a game of tag as Leroy goaded him.

'You two are like kids. Save it for tonight's after-tour BBQ. I'm treating you guys to tomahawk steak. Now get out of here before I banish you to your rooms.'

With that last lashing from Cindy, Theo and Leroy returned to the store fridge and took some drinks for the boat. The negotiated enhanced tour ticket cost would be enough to pamper the guests whilst onboard.

***

'Why are you always so slow? Bloody hell, hurry or else we'll never get off this ship,' called out Michelle impatiently.

Spencer was still perusing through the swimwear from Theo's wardrobe. He knew he could fit into anything he selected, but what poor fashion sense his brother had. He would not be seen dead in half the choices. The first thing he discarded was a pair of tight fitting "budgie smugglers" that harked back to the 1980s. Thankfully, there was a pair of loose-fitting shorts with an internal net lining. Not that the taupe colour was of his liking, but beggars could not be choosers.

'Has Theo got anything better than this?' asked Spencer as he stepped out of the walk-in wardrobe holding the swimming shorts aloft.

Michelle stood just outside with one hand leaning against the wall. 'They'll be fine. You'll find a pair of bright red shorts that you can wear over them in the bottom drawer. There's also a yellow T-shirt in the drawer above. Put them on.'

Spencer carried out the instructions he was given. He caught a glimpse of himself in the tall mirror. 'I look like a lifeguard.'

'I don't care if you look like a drag artist at the Mardi Gras, just get going as we need to be out of here pretty pronto.'

Spencer stepped out of the wardrobe. Michelle saw a small piece of toilet roll stuck to his skin, where his jawline met his muscular neck.

'What have you done to your face?'

'I cut myself shaving. I think it will stop before we get to the island.'

Michelle could not believe her luck.

'A swim in the cool sea water will help it heal. Let's get you out there and into the sea.'

***

'Fellow SMT members, welcome to Destiny's Azzurro Cay Mirage Hotel. First impressions show how this lovely hotel embraces everything about the Destiny Luxury Group. I'm led to believe our booked conference room is just off the lobby area here. Please grab yourself a coffee from the bar here and I'll meet you all in the room in ten minutes. I'll keep control of the ship this afternoon whilst you enjoy what the hotel offers. The food and beverages are complimentary all day. When you present your token to the servers, they will recognise you on their pay system and bill it back to me.'

Captain Nico had kept his promise of allowing the SMT an afternoon off to grab a bit of rest and recuperation. Jack queued for his coffee alongside Dr Patel.

'Are you feeling better after that trip, Doctor?'

'Thanks for asking. I'm much better now, even if it is a self-diagnosis. That was a longer tender journey than I am accustomed to. Did anything come out of Connie's interview?'

'What she had to say added not only some complexity, but some clarity. I've been reviewing the CCTV since then and it's revealed some interesting things.'

Before Jack could say any more, the barista interrupted their conversation.

'Dr Patel and Mr Shaw, welcome to our coffee shop. Can I take your orders, please?'

Dr Patel looked aghast at the mention of her name until she realised the hotel had the same customer recognition software as the ship. Jack was unfazed, as it was the same system he was interrogating just before the tender shuttle departure.

'Latte for me,' replied Dr Patel.

'Make that two,' added Jack.

'I haven't time to tell you more now, Doctor, but I will reveal all when the item rears its ugly head on the meeting agenda in a minute. I might ask for some input from yourself.'

With that, they both carried their drinks and walked towards the nearby meeting room.

Once everyone took their seat, Captain Nico started the meeting. 'Fellow officers, ladies and gentlemen, welcome. I would go around the room and ask for an update from each department, however I feel we have a more sensitive and pressing item on the agenda. If no one has anything more urgent to impart, I will begin with Jack at security. Please tell us about this incident involving the husband of our godmother Mrs d'Vere.'

'Thank you, Captain. If we were having a casual chat amongst us, it would be one of those things where you don't know where to start, however this has some serious implications for our ship, its security, our systems and likely the integrity of the Destiny Luxury Group.'

Captain Nico interjected, 'Team. It is important that the conversations we are about to have do not leave these four walls. I don't need to tell you the consequences of us discussing the contents outside of this forum.'

'Thank you, Captain. I'll get straight to the point. It's possible that the Mr d'Vere that entered this ship on launch day with Mrs d'Vere is not the same person who is claiming to be Mr d'Vere onboard at this very moment.'

There were some deep intakes of breaths around the oval table. No-one muttered as they knew it was not their place to over-dramatise SMT business.

'Jack, you base this serious allegation on what?'

'Captain, I hope everyone this morning spent some time reading the EOB and therefore have some knowledge so that I can go straight to the salient points?'

Everyone nodded, so Jack carried on.

'You would have read that a Miss Suzanne Harrington came forward to say that she works with Mr d'Vere and is onboard to support him in his presentations on his photographic explorations. I will declare now that she is more than his assistant. She is also his lover. I give you that detail as it provides credibility to what she told me and what I've confirmed by studying CCTV and other data checks we hold on our security systems. She claims that Mr Theo d'Vere shouldn't even be onboard the ship right now. He should be landside on a photographic assignment somewhere else. Following our earlier call to Azzurro Cay, she was shocked to see him back onboard. She observed him for a while and thought it was him, but as time has gone on she has decided this was not the case. This change of mind happened when she approached him in the casino without introducing herself. He did not recognise her at all. Through her observations, she discovered a lot of differences between the Mr Theo d'Vere she knows, and the man onboard claiming to be him. First, Theo d'Vere is right-handed, whereas this other man is left-handed. Theo d'Vere knows her roulette numbers as well as she does, but this other person does not know about them. Theo d'Vere, if he was to make a bet on the nose, it would always be number twenty, whereas this second person always bets on number twenty-one. I don't believe that this is a slip of the hand. I believe that is deliberate, and I'll explain why. Beyond speaking with Mr and Mrs d'Vere's butler, and the casino manager who also observed marked differences in the two men, I had the chance to speak with a guest, Mrs Connie Morgan-Brown. Last night we detained her in quarantine, along with her husband, on suspicion of being contagious with norovirus. And here comes the cream. That allegation of being contagious came from our godmother, Mrs Michelle d'Vere. Connie says that she had challenged Michelle in a lift about the authenticity of her husband. Connie believes that because of challenging Michelle, it ended in the godmother fabricating the illness in order to have the Morgan-Browns confined. This in effect would mean banishing them to their cabin, had it not been for the excellent observations by Dr Patel who found no evidence of sickness in either of the Morgan-Browns. Connie explained to me about the observations and conversations she had with Theo d'Vere and the person I will continue to call the second man, as well as conversations earlier with Michelle. I will summarise the outcome this way. Connie established that Theo d'Vere is born on the 20th of June and is the star sign Gemini. This was confirmed to her by Michelle, and that matches our ship's passenger records and passport scan. She then confirmed that the second man is born on the 21st of June and is of the Cancer star sign. She deduced this from the tattoo of his birth date on his forearm, by the Cancer star sign pendant on his neck chain, and by the congratulations afforded to her by this second man on identifying his star sign and date of birth. I have scrutinised the CCTV close up on both individuals in the casino. Both have star sign medallions around their necks. On even closer inspection, the man we believe to be Theo d'Vere has a Gemini pendent that he twizzles, whilst indeed the second man has a Cancerian pendent as described to me by Connie. He also twizzles this in a similar fashion. As I'm sure you would all appreciate, none of us have ever come across such a thing before, and why should we? This isn't normal. I then went back to when the second man came onboard at Azzurro Cay, as I was there at embarkation point at the tender pontoon. I saw him with my own eyes. Personally, I thought it was Mr Theo d'Vere. I remember one of my security staff asking him to remove his glasses and hat at the security lectern, as is the standard procedure on all cruise ships. It's well known if you have ever boarded a cruise ship. Could it be he was trying to disguise himself to get onboard? There was no reason to suggest foul play as this man had undergone a security check and a successful clear facial scan which perfectly matched the profile for Theo d'Vere. He, therefore, bypassed the most advanced facial recognition software in the world. I've asked myself how on earth can this happen, and I think I have the answer. Mr Theo d'Vere has an identical twin, and that identical twin is the second man we have on our ship.'

There was a long silent pause, of a collective disbelief.

'Jack, is this even possible? I mean, having twins with different days of births and star signs?' asked Captain Nico.

'You would think not, Captain, but yes, it is possible. The d'Vere family is from the UK. In the UK, if you are born on the 20th of June, then you are a Gemini. If you are born on the 21st of June, you are a Cancerian. It is possible for that to occur if the births occurred on either side of midnight that night. It takes a little stretch of your imagination, but it is feasible. I had to get my head around this and it even took me a little while to believe it myself.'

'Ok, Jack. Just for a moment, let's go ahead with your suggestion, but what has become of the first Mr Theo d'Vere? This swapping of male guests would take a long time to concoct. From what you are saying, Michelle d'Vere would have to be central to this,' asked Captain Nico.

'Highly likely, Captain. As for what has happened to Theo d'Vere, I can only presume he has gone on the photographic assignment. I asked Suzanne Harrington to phone his mobile if he has one. She used my office phone so that I could witness any conversation. You can't get through to it. I could ask contacts to trace the phone through triangulation, its recent use and the like, but it would take days and there is no guarantee it would even be authorised. Convincing the team around the table that my theory is possible is one thing. Convincing a foreign policing entity the same would be another leap of faith.'

Jack then extracted the critical timeline out of his briefcase, which he had built using the technologies available to him. If a picture painted a thousand words, this was the document to do that. He laid it out in front of Captain Nico. The others left their chairs to stand behind the captain in order to get the best view they could. Individual sheets were circulated to the attendees. Jack had the foresight to paginate the report before taking it with him, knowing that it would be pulled apart. This meant it could be put back together again and that no-one had taken any piece of it.

'Dr Patel. You are not only an eminent medical doctor, but also I believe you have practiced psychiatry and psychology. If this executive summary is true, what kind of woman do we face with Michelle d'Vere?' asked Captain Nico.

'To be frank, captain, you may have a psychopath on your hands, and a dangerous one at that. I have been through some of Jack's findings before this meeting. There are snippets here and there that shine light on a potentially violent and manipulative individual. She has, on more than one occasion, destroyed the flower arrangements in her suite. Now, to many that may seem somewhat odd and miniscule. To me, it reveals a person who wants to destroy something of beauty and meaningfulness. They have no regard for things like signs of love and affection. Also, they have no concern for others finding the remnants of their destruction. It's like putting out a warning sign that if you know I am like this, and you think you can stop me, then I'll show you that you can't. Repeatedly killing something as simple as flowers could mean a sign that whatever they kill or destroy, they can do so again. Their actions are often based on jealousy, greed, fear, or lust. If triggered, individuals may exhibit these psychological patterns again, even if they have previously received successful treatment. Some passengers can suffer with what we know as cabin fever.'

'Are you saying that if some harm has indeed come of Theo d'Vere, that she could bestow a similar fate on this second male?' asked Captain Nico in a concerned tone.

'I don't want to scare anyone at this stage, but you have asked me my professional opinion. I lectured on psychology at university, so I am aware of cases of psychotic episodes that have resulted in murder. Remember, statistically, women who commit murder are three times as likely as men to kill someone they love. That's all I can say. You need to take all the evidence collectively and conclude. I suggest you err on the side of caution, as history has shown that when mistakes are made and we ignore evidence, grave consequences can occur. When we sit around this table and discuss protecting the brand of the Destiny Luxury Group, you have one of those pivotal decisions to make, right here and right now.'

Captain Nico paused for thought. 'Ok. I need to take a moment to think about this. We will go through some other items on the agenda. In about ten minutes, we will break for another coffee break. Not that I need the caffeine to keep me awake after that topic. Let's go to the top of the page and have reports from each department, please. Engineering?'

***

'This hamper is pretty heavy,' said the ship's pontoon hand upon receiving it from a member of the catering department, as they lowered it into the speedboat.

He got on to the radio and called the embarkation podium.

'The chartered speedboat is ready for launch. Please, can you call down to the guests who have ordered it? We need to clear the pontoon for the next tender launch which is scheduled to go in five minutes.'

At the embarkation security point, the security officer scanned the two passenger tokens. 'Mrs d'Vere, Mr d'Vere, bon voyage. We look forward to welcoming you back on board later. Your speedboat awaits you.'

'Thank you,' acknowledged Michelle.

She had not considered how to explain later why Mr d'Vere had not returned to the ship. Right now, her focus was on ensuring that he did not return and that he was reunited with his brother in the depths of the ocean or devoured entirely by the pigs. They could rest in peace together.

***

'Careful as you go there, Captain Leroy. The moorings at the hotel here are a lot smaller than at Flora's Retreat. If you want me to take over?' Theo quipped.

'You care more about greeting those guests. Leave the steering to me bubblegummer.'

Leroy pulled their boat alongside the pier. Theo jumped off and tied it up. Leroy leapt up on to the pier. Together, they walked into the lobby of the Mirage Hotel, passing Niroop's Turkish Berber shop. Stood inside was Niroop, who was snipping at someone's hair. He spotted Theo and gave him an enthusiastic wave as he headed to exit his shop. Theo was looking around to see if this barber was waving at anyone else.

'Do you know this barber guy, Leroy?'

'Would I have my dreads cut in a place like this? Of course not.'

Niroop stepped into the hotel corridor. 'Mr d'Vere. Welcome. Welcome. Your hair has grown so quickly. Do you want me to cut it again?'

'Sorry, you called me Mr d'Vere. How do you know that?'

'Why, you were here last week. I cut your hair and gave you a traditional Turkish shave.'

'Are you sure you have not mistaken me for someone else? I've never been here before in my life.'

'Mr d'Vere, I never forget a face. Especially not when they tip so well. Welcome back.'

'Well, that's kind of you, but I need to get going, so maybe another time.'

'No worries, Mr d'Vere. You are welcome back anytime. And don't forget, Niroop's is a cut above the rest!'

Theo and Leroy walked towards the main part of the lobby.

'He called you Mr d'Vere. Are you sure that isn't who you are?'

'I'm not sure of anything anymore, Leroy. Looking around, there's quite a few people stood and seated that look like potential boat passengers. I'll join the queue for reception behind those checking in and introduce myself. You standby to round them up. Move around a bit, Leroy. You're making the place look untidy.'

Theo joined the queue.

'Excuse me sir, can we just get past?'

Leroy stepped back to let a line of ship's officers dressed in white with insignias walk towards the coffee shop next to reception. Jack, as courteous as ever, let the female SMT members go first, leaving himself as a tail gunner at the rear of the queue. Simultaneously, Theo walked forward to reception, now that the last of those checking in had moved aside.

'Welcome back to the Mirage Hotel, Mr d'Vere. Will you be staying as well as using the golf course today?' queried the receptionist.

Theo looked at her perplexed.

Jack's head turned 180 degrees to look back from the coffee shop queue at the receptionist and the man stood in front of her. Before Theo could answer, Jack hurried to the receptionist. Upon reaching them, Jack interjected, 'Did you just say Mr d'Vere?'

'Yes, I did, sir. This gentleman was here with his wife only a few days ago. I checked them out before they returned to the cruise ship. I believe it's the same cruise ship. The CCTV on our automated system has identified Mr d'Vere as he approached me.'

Jack needed no introduction to the security system. He helped to design and implement it. Theo stood there looking pale and shellshocked. Leroy could see them meet and overheard the conversation. He cautiously headed towards those stood around the reception desk. He was not one to get too close to those in authority. Ship's officers or not. Theo turned to Jack, and they looked at each other eye-to-eye.

'She's the second person here to call me Mr d'Vere.

What's going on?'

Jack turned to the receptionist. 'I need a confidential chat with this gentleman. Do you have a private room I can use?'

The receptionist pointed to a thick oak panelled door behind her. 'You can use the manager's office. I'm sure he won't mind. He's on his lunch break.'

'Sir, I need to talk with you just so I can explain what's happening. Please come with me.' With an open palm, he guided Theo towards the office door.

'Hey, buddy. Hold on there. This guy's with me. We've given him the name Joe back at Pig Island. He's lost his memory. He doesn't know who the hell he is, sir.'

'Ok. That's fine. Come and join us in the office. I'm sure we can sort this out.'

Theo was feeling nauseous, but remained calm and obediently did as he was told.

'I see you have a cut there on your head. Thankfully, it looks like it is healing. I have our ship's doctor with us in the hotel, so I'll get her to check you out. Come in here and take a seat.'

Jack sat Theo down in a chair and pulled up another for Leroy. He took a seat himself in the manager's chair opposite them. He opened his notebook and drew out his pen. 'I'll let you in on a secret, Joe. We are pretty certain we know who you are, and your name isn't Joe. It's Theo d'Vere. You are a passenger on my ship.'

'Ok. I'll be honest. I don't recognise that, but then again, until a couple of days ago, I didn't know diddly squat about anything. A lady named Cindy found me unconscious on a beach, patched me up, and has been taking care of me.'

'Where was that beach?'

'Pig Island. It's where my newfound friend here, Leroy, runs tours to go swimming with pigs. I've helped on the tour for the last couple days, and we are here to collect a small private party from the hotel and take the tour, as well as taking them to Cindy's "Flora's Retreat" for food, drinks and relaxation. I need to inform them we will be delayed.'

'Theo, please don't worry about that for now. We can sort that out. It's interesting that you mention the Pig Beach and the swimming with pigs' tour. You have a wife back on the ship. Her name is Michelle. She has a role on the ship of the godmother. It's a sort of formal role, but the ship does not employ her. She is the ship's matriarch. A few days ago we have you leaving the ship with her on a speedboat. I was reviewing the CCTV only this morning, and that's why I'm confident you are Theo d'Vere. You were both going on an excursion to Pig Island. Michelle drove the speedboat, as she was qualified to do so. That excursion would coincide with you turning up on the beach.'

'Holy crap!' said Leroy in bewilderment.

'I'm sorry, but it gets worse and even more complexing. Michelle stayed at this hotel that night. She returned to the ship the next day with another man, but that other man looks identical to you. If you were being cared for since being found and can account for your movements, then that man on the ship is an imposter for you. We can only think that this person is your doppelgänger, or your twin brother, if you have one.'

Theo paused for thought. 'Well, that's insane. That can't be. I don't know about any twin brother. I get flashbacks at night and I had a dream that I was at university halls and a man who looked like me but wasn't me was laughing back at me. There was also a woman doing the same. It was as if they were having a laugh at my expense. I know little about myself, except I love photography and wildlife.'

'Theo, that more or less confirms who you are to me. You were not only onboard keeping your wife company for the voyage, but you were also giving a lecture onboard about your photography in the wild. You are Theo d'Vere. The security cameras we have onboard and also here in our sister hotel use facial recognition software. Once our system captures and identifies you, it will flag up your identity when you approach service points. It's for us to acknowledge you upon greeting you. That's why the receptionist recognised you not only from a personal recollection from check-out but also your details flashed up on her system as being known to the hotel.'

'Shut the front door. Are you serious? Is this science fiction?' questioned Leroy.

Jack ignored the question and focused on extracting what he could from Theo.

'I wish I could help you more, sir, but I still can't recall that much. I had a vague recollection of being in the water, but then again I was washed up so I don't want to lead you awry.'

'That's fine Theo. I'll get Dr Patel to check you out quickly and we'll need to get you checked out afterwards at a medical facility. Stay here as I need to speak with our captain.'

'But I have a tour to take out.'

'Right now, Theo, the last thing you need to be thinking about is the tour. Things have moved on in the last ten minutes. Stay here. I'll be back shortly.'

Jack exited the office to see that the coffee shop was empty, and the SMT members had returned to the meeting room. He briskly walked over and re-entered the meeting.

'Sorry I'm late, everyone, but I have found Theo d'Vere here at the hotel. He has a head wound which I need Dr Patel to check.'

'Goodness gracious, Jack. How the hell?' asked Captain Nico.

'Sir, I will explain all soon. He was washed up on Pig Island following his excursion there with Michelle d'Vere. I believe she dealt a blow to his head and left him for dead. I can't think of any other scenario.'

Jack's radio was out of range of the ship, so he used

his mobile phone to call Kulbir back at the disembarkation lectern onboard. They informed Jack that both Michelle and the second man had departed on a speedboat heading towards Pig Island.

'Captain, Michelle and the second man are heading out to Pig Island for their own two-person swimming with pigs' tour on a speedboat. These are the same circumstances that led to Theo d'Vere being viciously assaulted and left for dead. We need to act.'

'What do you propose, Jack?' questioned the Captain.

'I can commandeer the boat Theo arrived on. The skipper, called Leroy, was in on my interview with Theo. He is aware of the circumstances so can come in useful.'

'Well, you have my authority and blessing, Jack. Go with haste. Go now.'

Without further ado, he steered Dr Patel through to see her new patient. After the introduction, Jack led Leroy aside to the lobby.

'Leroy, I need your help. I need you to take me to Pig Island. Michelle d'Vere and this second man are heading there now. I fear she will inflict the same injuries and attempt to leave him for dead. We need to go now. Are you ok with that? If not, I will need to still take your boat.'

'Sir, I understand and will help my fellow seaman. I think it would be useful to stop on the way at "Flora's Retreat" and pick up Miss Cindy.'

'How is that going to help?'

'She is a retired US Marine Surgeon. She is an expert in trauma on the battlefield. Cindy also knows Pig Island and each pig like the back of her hand. They also know her. She's dealt with horrendous things on beaches across the globe. She's modest, so don't tell her. We need her.'

'Right. Ok. I like your suggestion. Get us back to the retreat now. We can see what she says.'

'Can you handle the fast, choppy trip on my boat? It's not as stable as what you are used to.'

'Don't worry about me. I'm an ex-Marine myself.'

Leroy was suddenly finding himself in esteemed company. They boarded his boat and set off. As they cleared the hotel harbour, Leroy upped the revs and watched as the speed dial steadily increased. He was soon at maximum knots.

***

'These fish down here are beautiful, Michelle. The variety in this shallow beach water is amazing.'

'Do you know the name of them, Spencer?'

'Not really. There are some obvious ones, especially the larger ones.'

Michelle cut the engine speed and allowed the speedboat to drift slowly towards Pig Island. As it bobbed on the low ebbing waves, she looked from the cockpit at Spencer, leaning over the front to get a better look at the various fish. She opened the day bag down by her left knee and reached in for the heavy whisky bottle. She continued to look at Spencer whilst sliding her hand up the base of the bottle to find its neck. Michelle took a tight grip.

'What do you see, honey?' she asked.

'Oh, my god Michelle, you must come and see this. There are two stingrays swimming around, and, yes, there are reef sharks. It looks like a colony of reef sharks. Outstanding?'

'Reef sharks. How lovely. They are man eaters, so be careful.'

'Michelle. No, they're not. They are one of the most docile sharks known to man. They are totally safe to swim amongst. Reef sharks only get defensive if they feel they are being attacked. They can swim among people, but you would be totally safe.'

'But what about the stingrays? They've killed people with their barb.'

Still leaning over the front, Spencer raised himself so Michelle could hear him.

'I reckon you are thinking of that poor Australia explorer who got the barb in his chest on the Great Barrier Reef. He was so unlucky. If I'm not mistaken, I remember reading that stingrays have only ever killed about twenty people worldwide, and he was one of them. They are pretty harmless. You can even stroke them. Do you want to come over and try to stroke one as it passes under the boat?'

Michelle lowered the whisky bottle back into the day bag. She felt perplexed. These big fish were deadly. Everyone knew that. Spencer must be mistaken. He could know nothing more than her regarding deadly fish.

'No. I'm fine. I can't even pick a goldfish out of a bowl, let alone stroke a killer fish.'

'Michelle. They are not dangerous. I promise. Here. Watch me. I'm going in.'

With that, Spencer lifted his body and legs over the side of the speedboat and jumped into the sea. Michelle watched as he dropped to the seabed. Spencer was standing upright in the water, which came up to his midriff. Michelle waited for the stingrays and sharks to attack. Nothing happened.

'See. I told you. It's fine. Look, I'm even stroking both these stingrays.'

Michelle left her seat to get a closer look. Spencer was being circled by various fish species, and none were attacking him. She thought that this was not possible. She left Theo in the same waters, but surely the fish and the pigs consumed him?

'Hey, Michelle. Look. The pigs are paddling over towards us. There's four, no, five coming straight for us. Can you check if there are any carrots in the hamper that we can feed to them?'

'Of course, darling. Give me a minute to look.'

Michelle bent down and opened the hamper. Sitting on the top was indeed a bag of large fresh carrots. She got them out and paused for thought. Surely the pigs would get aggressive and attack. For her they resembled life where she was from, where the population was renowned for eating anything with legs except the kitchen table, and anything with wings except the aeroplanes. In a moment of creativity, she threw the carrots into the water all around Spencer. That must draw them in to him.

'Sweetheart, what are you doing? I thought you were going to hand them to me.'

The pigs gathered speed in the water through swimming using their trotters. Spencer still could outrun them in the water, but he just stood there. The pigs approached Spencer and as they got close to him, their jaws opened. Michelle awaited the crunch of pig jaw on human bone and a loud scream, then as Michelle closed her eyes, they ignored Spencer and, with their powerful jaws, gnawed at the carrots. There was no scream. Just the sound of splashing as the pigs buffered each other to get to the carrots. She opened her eyes. By now Spencer had grabbed one of the largest carrots and was hand feeding a medium-sized pig. This was not going to plan for Michelle.

'Come and join me in here, sweetheart. It's fun.'

She paused for thought and came up with an unrehearsed Plan B. 'Hey, Spencer. I'll bring my day bag over with me and you can join me on the beach. Give me a minute.'

Michelle checked the bag and found that the heavy whisky bottle was still inside. She leaned over the side of the boat and dropped into the water at her waist height. She kept the bag above her head and waded on to the shore, towards a secluded pen sat back off the beach, that housed the piglets who were suckling on the sow. The sow emitted a protective, loud grunt as it sensed Michelle in proximity.

'Spencer, you need to come and see these gorgeous

piglets.'

'Ok, I'm coming over.'

Spencer took long strides, and with the incoming tide assisting him, he reached Michelle within seconds, as she lowered the day bag to the soft sand.

'Sweetheart. Let me get a picture of you with these piglets. They are so gorgeous. You would all look cute together, Spencer.'

'Sure, why not? How do you want me to stand?'

'Throw me your sunglasses. I have the bright sun behind me. Face the pigs with your eyes closed, then when I say "go", turn one hundred and eighty degrees to face me and open your eyes wide open so that I can get a surprised look on your face.'

Spencer removed his sunglasses. 'That's quite a bright light without these shades.'

'Stop your moaning and toss them to me.'

He followed her directions.

'Ok. Turn away and close your eyes.'

Spencer turned away and closed his eyes shut. 'What, like this?'

'That's perfect, darling. Hold on. I'll just get my camera out of my bag.'

Michelle reached down and located the whisky bottle once more. She took a tight grip, drew it out, and raised it above her head. She took two steps to be within striking distance of Spencer.

'Hurry, sweetheart. Squinting my eyes this tight for so long will give me wrinkles on my forehead.'

'Nearly there, dear. Steady, and go.'

Spencer spun around to face Michelle and opened his eyes. He raised his left hand to his eyes as the bright light over Michelle's shoulder was blinding him. As the bottle swung down towards his head, it connected with his left wrist. The audible cracking sound suggested his left arm was broken. He screamed with the intense pain. His eyes focused, fighting against the shocking pain, and he looked at his arm. The ulna bone fracture that poked through the skin confirmed it for him. The reverse swing on the bottle caught him above his eye socket. He dropped to his knees, and the blood poured out.

'Michelle, what are you doing?' He tried to look up towards her, but the blood streamed down into his left eye, which he could not see through. His right eye was open, but blinded by the sun.

'That first strike Spencer was for all the women you have seen behind my back when we have been apart. The second was for that slut Amber that you bedded right in front of me. The next strike Spencer will be for all those other women that you would have bedded in the future if I hadn't decided to kill you today. I'll say to you what I said to your pathetic twin brother. Goodbye.'

Michelle aimed her third blow at Spencer's head. His entire torso hit the floor. The blow knocked him unconscious. She bent down to hang over him. 'You are as pathetic as each other. You can spend your eternal lives in death together.'

She washed the blood off the whisky bottle and replaced it in her day bag as her trophy.

***

'How much further to Flora's Retreat?'

'Only a couple of minutes. You can just about make out the jetty,' replied Leroy.

Cindy was at the bar and could hear a boat in the distance. She stepped out from behind the bar and strode towards the jetty. It was a boat approaching at great speed. She recognised it as Leroy's boat. She thought to herself that it could not be the case. The passengers must be seasick, hitting the waves that hard. It came closer and approached the jetty. Cindy could now see that it was Leroy at the helm, and alongside a naval officer dressed all in white. There were no passengers. Leroy cut the engine and slammed the boat in reverse to make the best emergency stop under the circumstances.

'Leroy. What on earth are you doing? Where's Joe and where are my customers? And whilst you are at it, who is this guy?'

'Cindy. I have no time to explain. Please believe me. Grab your trauma first aid bag and jump onboard. I'll explain on the way to Pig Island if there's enough time to do so. It's urgent,' explained Leroy.

Cindy did not hesitate. She knew that if Leroy was having to do this, then it was serious. She rushed back to the room and cupboard behind the bar and collected her emergency rucksack. Cindy sprinted across the beach back to the jetty. Her heart raced because of the drop in her fitness since her Marine days. She jumped aboard and Leroy set off at a pace. The waves crashed against the bow, with Leroy doing his best to ride the waves.

'Thank you. I'm Jack Shaw. I'm head of security on the cruise ship anchored someway offshore. The man Joe that you speak of is really one of my cruise passengers by the name of Theo that went to Pig Island a few days ago with his wife.'

'Oh, my god. Is she still missing out there?' asked Cindy.

'No. We believe she inflicted the wounds on Theo that you treated. She returned on board, just after you found him washed up. The thing is, she returned onboard with someone we believe could be Theo's twin brother. We haven't got down to the bottom of that yet, but right at this moment, the two of them are heading to Pig Island. We can't be one hundred per cent sure, but we believe she may try to inflict the same injuries on him, or even something worse.'

'Wow. You merchant navy boys deal with some strange shit.'

'Well, nothing stranger than this. And by the way, don't let appearances deceive you. Like you, I am an ex-Marine. I've made landings faster than this, but I feel it's a race against time. I hope we are not too late.'

'A brother from another mother. Welcome onboard Marine. Let's get going. Leroy, are you a man or a mouse? Get a move on. My Marine buddy and I have a job to do.'

Jack smirked, but he had nothing to be cheerful about. Just a mark of respect to a fellow combatant. Leroy did his best to squeeze every bit of juice out of his engine. He felt happy if he only got away with an engine refit out of this race. As soon as they rounded the peninsula, Michelle's speedboat came into view. Leroy, Cindy and Jack saw it.

'Keep the power on Leroy. That boat is facing away from the shore and there is someone at the controls. If that boat moves before we get there, let it go. Unless the man is in the boat, we are more likely to find him ashore in the same way as Theo was found. Saving life is paramount, everyone,' barked out Jack over the noise of the engine.

Leroy continued to give it his all. The person on the speedboat had long flowing dark hair blowing across her face in the strengthening sea breeze. As they gained on the motionless speedboat, Jack could make out the familiar body outline of Michelle.

'Cut across the front, Leroy,' shouted Cindy.

She had her medic rucksack on her back. She pulled the straps on her shoulders as tight as she could. The pack was going nowhere. Michelle was having problems starting it. The rear engines were spluttering, but no power was being transferred.

'Leroy, pull us up so I can jump aboard the speedboat. As soon as I'm onboard, put Cindy ashore and both of you look for our man.'

Leroy gave the ok sign. Yards from the speedboat, it

was becoming obvious that even if it started now, it would not speed up enough to get away. Leroy dropped the revs and slammed his engine in to reverse. Cindy and Jack braced themselves for the imminent lurch forward. Jack leapt the five-foot gap to the speedboat and gripped the outer rail to stop his self-propulsion throwing him off the side of the boat. He landed inside. Michelle threw the hamper at Jack, but her action was fruitless. Instead, Jack took advantage and grabbed her arm and put it in to a goose-neck hold. Michelle's slight frame was powerless to fight back. Jack could see that the well of the speedboat was empty. He saw Cindy and Leroy wading through the shallow waters and on to the beach.

'The game is up, Michelle. Do yourself a favour and tell me now, where is he?'

'I don't know what you are talking about, Mr Shaw,' she stated with a sound of arrogance in her voice.

'You've got ten seconds, or I'll make sure the prosecution recommends a double life sentence without the chance of parole, ever. Now where is he?'

'You are too late, Mr Shaw. I've left him for dead. He's by the pigpen. They should be enjoying their unexpectant treat by now.'

Jack shouted across at Cindy and Leroy. 'The pigpen. Go guys.'

'Thirty seconds away,' replied Cindy.

'I hope for your sake Michelle, that he's still alive. Who is he? We know he is not Theo.'

'Bravo, Mr Shaw. Another absolute loser. I wouldn't be surprised if they will find Theo in the pig waste that they wallow in. There would be nowhere more fitting.'

'Stop the games, Michelle. Who is he?'

'His name is Spencer. He is the highly intelligent, identical twin brother of Theo. Although it now appears he won't be looking too clever once they have chewed his face off.'

'We've got him,' shouted out Leroy.

Jack observed Leroy standing up and Cindy kneeling, leaning over what appeared to be a prone torso.

'He's not looking too pretty, but I have vitals. I have a pulse,' shouted out Cindy reaching for her trauma kit.

Jack could hear her call. Leroy repeated it for good measure.

'You look rather pale, Michelle. It seems like it may be Spencer d'Vere's lucky day.'

'The pig deserves to die with the pigs, just like his brother did.' She grinned menacingly.

Jack grabbed some loose rope and tied Michelle's wrists together. He tied the two boats together and lifted Michelle across to Leroy's boat. He sat her down.

'I have some news for you, Michelle. We've found Theo.'

'How did you identify him? I doubt there would be even a tooth left.'

'When someone has more than just a tooth, let's say a complete set of teeth, it's easy to identify them when they smile back at you as you ask them a question. Theo isn't dead, Michelle. He is alive as you and I are sitting here. He's being treated by a doctor and will make a full recovery. But don't worry. Two attempted murders carry the same sentence as two murders. You are going away for a long time, regardless of whether Spencer lives or dies. Theo made it to the Azzurro Mirage Cay Hotel earlier today. Staff at the hotel identified him as Mr d'Vere, as well as by our security systems. How unfortunate for you that you stayed at the hotel the night you tried to kill Theo d'Vere, with an identical Mr d'Vere. You thought it would be ok for him to use Theo's identity. Brilliant Michelle. It nearly worked. However, it will prove to be your undoing. A downfall that you have manufactured all by yourself. The police will want to know why you've done this. When they hand you over to the police, you better hire a talented lawyer.'

'Mr Shaw, I don't fear the police. I fear for losing face for my family. My elderly father and mother. I will tell you why. As a young girl, I moved from Hong Kong to receive a private education. My parents wanted the best for me, but life is not that simple. In those days, being a girl from the Orient, with oriental features, was a unique thing in my school. Soon, my classmates started bullying and mocking me. Only Andrea, your CEO, stood up for me. She tried, but it wasn't enough. First came the headaches, and then the recurring nightmare to self-harm. But I didn't want to stop there. I wanted to hurt others. First, those that bullied me, but then it was anyone. Last, it was the need to hurt those close to me. Especially if they let me down. Both Theo and Spencer were close to me. We were at university together. Everything seemed rosy. But it wasn't. I was looking for love and affection. I could get that from both of them, but never from just one of them. Looking to be a Yin to a Yang, it trapped me in a broken marriage. I wanted to be successful in my own right. Andrea gave me that chance by appointing me as the godmother, but it all blew up in my face. It wasn't of my making. It was them. They both havehad infidelities, yet neither of them thought I knew. Well, I knew Mr Shaw. Call it a woman's intuition if you like, but I didn't even need intuition. It was happening right before my eyes. Theo and I had been through a trial separation before, but now I wanted a permanent solution, and the deaths of Theo and Spencer was the answer I needed. I have no regret or remorse for what I have done. I care nothing for myself.'

'Save it for the police and the courts, Michelle. Your justice will come, but for now, we need to make sure they both survive. This isn't France. Crimes of passion do not differ from cold-blooded murder. You didn't think you could get away with this?'

'I had it all worked out. Who's going to miss them? Not I for one. They were lost souls. They didn't care for anyone else but themselves. Self-centred, that's what they were. Theo was cheating on me whilst on the ship. As for Spencer, he was always seeing other women. And like his brother, he had no qualms about doing it right under my nose. Two peas in a pod from the moment they were born. If I had my way, they would have been two peas in a pig. I wanted them to physically lose their faces, like I metaphorically lost mine to my family.'

'There is no honour in murder, Michelle, only the dishonour you have brought upon yourself.'

Jack shouted over to Cindy and Leroy, 'Is he ok to be moved?'

'In about two minutes,' Cindy yelled back as she wrapped a second bandage around Spencer's face, over the top of the first blood-soaked one. She felt her heartbeat akin to that of Spencer. Steadily, she brought both under control. Spencer gave out a groggy groan and tried to lift his arms to his head. He was trying to take deep breaths, but was struggling to inflate his lungs. He again attempted to catch his breath.

'Leroy, grab those arms for me and try to control them whilst I tie off this bandage. I'll deal with that broken one in a minute,' clarified Cindy.

Leroy, on all fours, did his best to comply with her request. Realising that he needed to take a tighter grip than he first expected. 'He's a fighter,' interrupted Leroy.

'He has no choice as he needs to go the entire distance and not just the first round,' responded Cindy, as she washed blood from around his face with a bottle of sterilised water and wipes.

'Ok, he's ready to move.' She then shouted over to the speedboat, 'Jack, I'll need a hand to get him onboard.'

Jack used the end of the restraining rope to tie Michelle to a side rail.

'No silly ideas, Michelle. Sit tight whilst we get this done.'

He jumped off the stern and waded through the water

onto the beach. He looked around to see Michelle sitting slumped like a rag doll devoid of its stuffing. Her head was facing the deck. A look of resignation on her face. Jack felt comfortable in heading over to assist Cindy and Leroy, crouching a short distance away.

'Jack, you take his upper torso and Leroy, you take his legs. I'll steady his head. Now on three, lift.'

Spencer let out a groan as they levitated him, with his arms flapping on either side. Once more, he tried to reach for his head. He attempted to pull at the bandages, but Cindy gently and slowly pushed his hands back down. Spencer emitted a long sigh. In his dazed state, he tried to open his eyes, but he closed them again as the relentless sun shone on to his pale face.

Cindy and Jack regressed into their former roles in comfortably evacuating Spencer from the beach. Leroy was quite unaccustomed to this procedure, but his brute strength supported the others in their task. They stepped off the beach and into the water's break. The foamy water lapped firstly around their feet and then gradually to above their knees and then up to their waists. An additional heave on the command of three from Cindy raised Spencer's now once again limp body that extra bit above the smooth and regular waves. His hands dangling in the cool water made no difference as he lapsed into unconsciousness.

'Stop a second,' demanded Cindy. 'I need to check his pulse.'

She held his head up and still with her left forearm whilst two fingers of her right hand pushed into Spencer's neck in search of a pulse. She could detect one, but it was faint. Cindy could have taken them all back on to the beach, however she decided they needed to push on and get Spencer on the boat. Once onboard, they could treat and monitor Spencer's precarious condition more easily and consider moving him to a medical facility sooner rather than later. There was only so much she could do to stabilise him. There must be a time where his transfer to better facilities outweighed the stabilisation. This, she felt, was her call to make. He may be one of Jack's passengers, but medically, she had to pull rank. Jack's inner self was already telling him the same thing. All that training with the Royal Marines on the shorelines across the globe overrode the insignificant training he had had in the police. Dealing with severe trauma was a trait of a marine, but he knew ultimately this must be Cindy's decision. If it all went wrong, he was prepared to back Cindy all the way and once more take one for the team.

'We've got to move Spencer. We need to get him flat on that boat deck,' called out Cindy.

Jack nodded. He was facing the boat and saw Michelle looking towards them. She was laughing hysterically whilst rocking backwards and forwards. The respectable guise of being the ship's godmother had been removed, causing her mask of sanity to slip.

'Can you let me deal with her?' asked Leroy.

'You're the skipper, but best you leave her to me,' replied Jack.

'Stick to the task, you two. I'm sure she'll be laughing on the other side of her face for the next thirty years,' usurped Cindy.

They inched towards the boat. Leroy relieved Cindy by holding Spencer's head above the water. Cindy climbed aboard and leaned over the side to grab Spencer underneath his arms and attempted to pull him aboard. Leroy tried his utmost to push Spencer's torso upwards towards Cindy. In unison, Jack pushed Spencer upward from around his thighs and buttocks. Cindy tried to not fall back into the well of the boat. With all her might, she grappled to pull him on board and hold him in limbo.

Jack utilised his knowledge on how to board a boat from the waterline and pulled himself onboard. Without the sound of the waves lapping against the boat's hull, he could now hear the noises of both Cindy straining with her hold of Spencer and Michelle's insane laughing. Michelle's strange reaction to Spencer's unstable condition would not go unnoticed in his report to the police authorities, Jack thought. He joined Cindy and helped heave Spencer onboard. Leroy strode around to the stern ladder and pulled Spencer's heavy torso up each step.

'Jack, we need to get him aboard your ship and arrange a helicopter evacuation from there. Can you organise that?' asked Cindy.

'Sure can,' responded Jack as he fumbled in the wheelhouse to find his secreted satellite phone. He phoned through to the bridge of the Destiny Celebration. The phone was answered by the officer on watch.

'Code Alpha, Code Alpha, Code Alpha. Inbound to the platform on deck one in ten minutes. Code Sierra instructions to follow. Also request a helicopter evacuation for as soon as possible. Male in his thirties, unconscious, with a serious head injury and weakening pulse. Code Sierra. One detained female suspect. Despatch detention team by launch on heading west southwest. Confirm Code Alpha. Officer Shaw over.'

'Confirmed Code Alpha by Destiny Celebration. Code Sierra on heading west southwest. All received. Out.'

Jack looked over at Michelle as he helped to make Spencer comfortable in the boat's well. She was sitting there and trembled as she looked at the floor. Leroy entered the wheelhouse and fired up the boat engines. He applied leverage in reverse to take the boat away from the shore, engaged forward and increased the power.

Jack leaned forward and talked into Cindy's ear. 'I've got a detention team to come out and meet us so we can take her off. I'm not comfortable with her on here with us. She's highly unpredictable. She's the devil in disguise. If she saw an opportunity, she would take us all out.'

Cindy kept hold of Spencer's wrist, checked his pulse,

and watched his chest rise and fall as he took shallow breaths.

'Leroy, increase the speed. This is touch and go,' called out Cindy.

Jack felt there was little more he could do to assist Cindy with Spencer, so went to check on Michelle's restraints. He held on to her arm and lowered her to a seat further down on deck. She sobbed.

'Self-pity Michelle? You should have thought about that. You made some pretty big mistakes. One of the biggest is that you never return to the scene of the crime. In contrast, you have not only revisited the crime scene but also showed up with another victim. You're looking at thirty years for this. You better pray that he pulls through.'

'Asthmatic,' she replied. 'Like me, he's asthmatic. There's an inhaler in my bag back in the other boat. If he becomes conscious, try that.'

Jack looked over at Cindy. They've travelled about two hundred yards from the other boat.

'What do you think? Should we turn back?'

Cindy hesitated for a moment before she decided. 'It's worth a try. It might save him if we can calm his breathing.'

Jack called out to Leroy and gestured his hand in the air at the same time. 'Turn back.'

'Are you kidding me?'

'Just do it.'

Cindy nodded in agreement.

Leroy didn't need telling twice. He put the boat in a 180-degree turn as Jack moved to the bow of the boat.

'No funny business Michelle.'

She sat there with a look of helplessness on her face.

Leroy pulled his boat alongside the other as Jack leapt over. He scrambled around and found her bag. He emptied the contents and a blue reliever fell on to the floor. Jack picked it up, jumped back on to the boat and handed it to Cindy. He then rejoined Michelle.

'That may, just may, knock a few years off your incarceration.'

'He's blood type A positive,' she replied. 'Theo is the same. Maybe he could donate blood if you need it?'

Michelle had come to her senses.

Spencer reopened his eyes and took a couple of deep coughs. His eyes were bulging, and he looked in total shock as they flickered from side to side as he tried to take in what was happening. He endeavoured to take deep breaths, but his lungs were not inflating enough.

Cindy put the reliever in to his mouth. 'Take a deep breath.'

Spencer responded with a half breath as Cindy plunged the button of the inhaler. 'And again.'

Spencer took a deeper breath and exhaled a deep cough. Followed by several other smaller ones. He stared up at Cindy and made small nodding movements with his head. He closed his eyes before opening them again.

'It's working. Leroy, you can go faster. I'll tell you if it's too rough. Go, go!'

Leroy did not need another invitation. Spencer's head had more movement. He turned to look at Michelle. She looked back and mouthed 'Sorry'. He turned and looked away. Cindy and Jack noticed the exchange and looked at each other. Jack's satellite phone rang. It was Kulbir, his deputy, calling.

'Hey Jack. We're coming out to you on heading west southwest. You are in sight with the binoculars. We should be with you in approximately three minutes.'

'You'll be a sight for sore eyes. See you soon.'

'Can they take me straight to the police? Do I have to return to the ship?' asked Michelle.

'You'll be detained on the ship for now. You can see it as your destiny if you wish. Quite profound in many ways. With the riches come the spoils.'

'But that's inhumane.'

'Inhumane? That's the pot calling the kettle black. That's the process Michelle. Deal with it,' replied Jack.

'But they'll be looking over their balconies taking photos of me like vultures. It will be all over social media instantly. My family will see this. I need to tell them first. You must stop this.'

'Little rich girls like you have it your way far too often. You think everyone must sing to your tune. Well, now welcome to the real world. See how the other half live, Michelle? How people in your position milk the occasion when it suits you. Posting your whole life on the web for all to see. But now it's time for warts and all Michelle. No airbrushing today. No stylist to pamper you. It looks like it's time for the entire world to see the real Michelle d'Vere, unmasked.'

The boat crashed down harder on the waves underneath as the ship's tender pulled alongside. Leroy killed the power. Within a moment, Kulbir jumped aboard while wearing his distinctive yellow fluorescent lifejacket, which helped differentiate him from the passengers wearing orange jackets. They tethered the boats together.

'You ok, Jack?'

'I'm good, Sir Lancelot, but I need you to take care of this one,' said Jack as he lifted Michelle to her feet by her arm. He manoeuvred her towards the adjoining tender. Kulbir took over the restraining hold and led her on to the tender.

'She's detained for double attempted murder. Make sure she's searched when she gets aboard and get her in a cell ASAP. And don't put up with any nonsense. The all-inclusive package has just ended. You are now her newly appointed butler.'

Michelle looked down, dreading the ride back to the ship's gangway.

'Got it,' said Kulbir without even looking back.

The crew untied the boats, and the tender pulled away

at ninety degrees to allow Leroy to go ahead without having to ride over a wake. The tender boat paused and bobbled on the ocean. Members of the crew held on as it rolled like a teacup ride at the funfair. All onboard, including the once esteemed guest, handled the movement like the salty seadogs they were. Michelle looked up to see the other boat pulling away at speed. The daunting thoughts weighing on her mind. What had she done?

Kulbir held the tender's position for just a few minutes longer. He used his satellite phone to update the bridge on the movements of the two boats. The bridge had summonsed Dr Patel back to the ship as soon as the severity of the incident had become clear. She had joined her two nurses and the gangway security officer Landon Mason as a reception party on the pontoon. She looked out with a pair of binoculars and saw the boat approaching in the distance. Within no time, there was no need to use the binoculars. It was fast coming in to focus. The detail on the bridge from their elevated vantage point could see events unfolding. The tannoy rang out.

'Code Alpha, Code Alpha, Code Alpha. Gangway port side. This is not a drill. Repeat, Code Alpha, Code Alpha, Code Alpha. Medical team to Gangway port side, midship, deck two.'

Formalities over on the announcement it stirred those on board into action. The crew remained calm whilst those passengers onboard became more excitable. The announcement was a giveaway that something serious was happening at the gangway. Those in their cabins on the port side went out onto their verandas and looked overboard. The bridge suspended over each side of the ship at the bow end. The sight of two officers on the bridge looking out with binoculars towards an approaching boat in-between looking down at the gangway pontoon was unmissable. Passengers in the public area migrated to the port side railings, seeking every vantage point they could manage. Most were reaching for their mobile phones, ready to take photographs and videos. What was it in the human psyche that made people reach for those damn devices at every turn? The bar waiters on deck knew to make themselves scarce in order to avoid the inevitable "What's going on?" questions that guests inundated staff with when tannoy announcements were made.

Captain Nico was at the helm, briefing the deputy first officer on clearing the helipad deck for the expected medevac helicopter. He did not expect the casualty on the incoming vessel to remain on board for too long. As soon as the helicopter arrived, and the local paramedic could assess the casualty, he expected them to be airborne in no time. Until then, his thoughts remained focused on the ship's protocols. In all his naval experience, he had never had a non-passenger being brought on board for medical treatment. The ship's crew had received training to assist other vessels in distress that made SOS broadcasts, so this situation would not be different. A lingering concern was the legal implications if the patient was to succumb to their injuries.

'Can we check please on the status of the medevac helicopter?' he called out to the comms officer in a stern voice.

'On it, Captain,' came back the instant reply.

Nico reached for his radio, dangling from his trouser belt. 'Dr Patel, are you in a position to receive the patient?'

'All set, sir. Myself, two nurses and Officer Mason in position. Life vests on. Carabiners secured.'

Leroy could see the pontoon. The cruise ship, which cast an all-encompassing shadow, dwarfed his small tourist boat. With the loss of the bright sunshine, Leroy felt an eeriness come over him. The enormous ship was very intimidating and domineering. He kept his composure as he lowered the engine speed and brought it to a near idle. He looked back at Cindy to see if everything was ok. Leroy received a thumbs up so turned the wheel hard left as he brought up the revs before knocking them back down again. The boat caressed into the pontoon. Two deckhands both grabbed a mooring rope, each thrown by

Leroy and Jack. After they secured the boat, Dr Patel moved forward.

'I need to assess the patient before we can move him,' she announced authoritatively as she stepped down on to the boat.

Cindy briefed on Spencer's condition with accuracy, brevity, and speed. Dr Patel listened intently without averting her gaze from the patient as she took a pulse reading.

'Thank you. I will take responsibility for the patient from here. You have done well,' as both nurses, Kenny and Nathan, descended on to the deck with a fold down lightweight stretcher. Kenny and Nathan carefully placed Spencer on the lightweight stretcher and strapped him in, to which he gave little resistance.

Cindy handed Dr Patel the inhaler. 'This helped to get him here. It could come in handy.'

Leroy stayed at the helm as Jack helped the nurses lift the stretcher on to the pontoon, slowly up the stairs and into the ship's security boarding area.

Jack shouted down to Leroy and Cindy. 'Cindy, get up here. It's best you join us on here on standby until he's airlifted off in about ten to fifteen minutes. Leroy, circle around for now. You can take Cindy back when you see the helicopter take off. We need the pontoon for the d'Vere's arrival.'

Cindy hopped on to the pontoon as they released the boat from the mooring. The engine loudly roared into reactivation, with Leroy giving a farewell wave. Cindy returned the wave and traversed the metal stairs two steps at a time until she reached Jack.

'This brings back memories. It's the first time I've climbed a gangway since I left the Marines.'

'It's like riding a bike. You never lose it,' replied Jack.

Up ahead, they could see the stretcher team disappearing off towards the crew area and the back door of the onboard medical centre. Jack and Cindy followed and caught up as they reached the trauma room.

'Doctor, Cindy here was a trauma surgeon in the US Marines. I thought it was a good idea that she come onboard to assist you if the need arises. I hope you don't mind?'

'More hands make light work, Jack,' she responded. 'I want to stabilise him as much as possible. When the helicopter paramedics get here, they'll want to assess him as well. That's best done here where we have the facilities. You can do me a favour, Jack, by getting up to the helipad and escort them down here. Secure the crew lift for our use. I don't want any delays.'

Jack wasted no time in doubling back towards the crew lift. Dr Patel began a more thorough examination of the patient, with Cindy looking on. Working in tandem with the nurses, she checked Spencer over for any other severe injuries than those already identified by Cindy. She then tended to the obvious wounds using saline solution and new dressings.

The crew radios crackled into life with news that the helicopter was fast approaching. Within a few minutes, the trauma room door opened, with Jack holding it for a helicopter paramedic. She put her monitoring apparatus to one side and attached monitors to Spencer's torso, whilst listening to the briefing by Dr Patel. Cindy listened in, but did not look to interfere unless anything critical was being missed. Dr Patel's prior emergency room experience ensured the briefing was on point. Cindy nodded in approval. If the patient detected anything contradictory between medical professionals, it would not be good. Professional etiquette remained throughout the briefing. Content with the patient's condition, the paramedic gave the order to evacuate.

Like a well-oiled machine, the patient cortege started their manoeuvre through the back corridors of the ship, emerging from the lift at the helipad. Jack and Cindy used their military experience to guide the team towards the helicopter's open door, keeping everyone low beneath the rotating blades that whirled above their heads. Spencer was conscious as he looked up at the blades. His heart rate increased, but this was to be expected by the medical team surrounding him.

'You're in the best medical care,' said Cindy into his ear. His eyes turned towards her. He nodded and blinked in acknowledgement.

Cindy smiled back at him and told Spencer, 'You'll be ok.'

They secured Spencer inside the helicopter, and the doors closed. The remaining medical party retreated into the deck doorway and watched as the engine idle increased. The helicopter lurched away. With a gentle turn to the starboard side, it was up and away. The noise dissipated as the helicopter flew away into the distance.

'Tea anyone?' asked Jack.

'How very British of you,' replied Cindy. 'Lead us the way.'

Jack reached for his satellite phone and called up Kulbir. 'Bring her in.'

Kulbir had held a position about a nautical mile off the bow. They began the route in. As they arrived closer to the ship's pontoon, looking up, they could see hundreds of people on their cabin balconies. Not the usual sight when tenders were heading back to the ship. Obviously, word was getting around that something significant was happening. It was unmistakable that a handcuffed lady was being escorted off the tender and on to the platform. A dishevelled Michelle d'Vere was there for all the world to see as he tried to shield her face from the unwanted attention and loss of face in front of the growing crowd. The "Welcome back onboard Destiny" sign would prove very poignant. These scenes would have only been for the ship passengers to see, but with the ability to stream live on social media through the ship's high-speed internet, all that had changed. Murmurs from the balconies were getting louder by the second. There was no way that the Destiny Luxury Group could contain this story. A damage limitation strategy was already underway. Jack received a call to meet Captain Nico on the bridge. He took Cindy to the security office and sat her down with a cup of tea.

'I'll be back soon. I need to brief the Captain, as I think I'll be writing reports until my hand drops off. Stay here until I get back.'

Jack headed off to the bridge. He did not look as presentable as much as he would wish, but was sure they would forgive him under the circumstances.

'Jack, I expect your report later but for now are you ok?'

'I'm fine captain, thank you. A bit of an adrenaline rush, but it keeps you on your toes. This won't be good news for the ship or the company back in London, sir.'

'You're not wrong, Jack. I've already briefed the CEO on a very short telephone call. What the hell was Michelle d'Vere thinking?'

'I'll detail it in my report. I need to get it all written down for the local constabulary. Are they aware yet, sir?'

'Not yet, Jack. Can I leave that in your hands? You know those procedures better than I ever will. You speak the law enforcement language.'

'No worries, sir. Looking at those passengers hanging over the balconies when we arrived, I'm sure the cat is out of the bag already. We'll keep d'Vere under lock and key until the locals can collect and transfer her. My security team will keep it as sterile as we can onboard. No one is getting near her. I also need to speak with Theo d'Vere to get an account from him. It will help the island police know what they are dealing with. I'm not knocking them, but these circumstances are a little surreal for even an experienced hand. No one is going to believe this. Where is he now, sir?'

'He was nothing more than walking wounded when he came back onboard with Dr Patel. Once she checked him out, we took him to a spare suite so that he can rest and take stock. He's as bemused as the rest of us. We've locked down the original d'Vere suite. I guessed you would have liked that kept as a crime scene. Hopefully, I haven't been watching too many of those cop shows?'

'You did right, sir. My security detail can help me search it for clues and try to build a bigger picture. There will be some indications of how much planning went on here. I've got several people to re-question. Now we have more of an idea what has gone on. If it's ok with you sir, I'll use my deputy, Kulbir, to assist me and appoint an assistant deputy to maintain the other security operations on the ship?'

'You have my blessing, Jack. Anything you need and we are here for you. Now be off. You have a lot to do.'

Jack nodded and turned about to head back to his security office. Cindy was awaiting him. He had not been long, as she was still holding the cup of tea to her lips and blowing on it.

'If you don't mind Cindy, I just need to take a written record from you on how you met Theo d'Vere and take it from there?'

'That's fine. Shall I write it myself?'

'No, you're fine. I'll take it. We'll keep it as factual as possible but include any background information. We'll give the police authorities as clear a picture as possible and let the legal minds decide how much to redact for a court case. I hope Leroy is happy bobbing away out there? I promised it wouldn't be long, but it might take longer now?'

'He'll be fine, Jack. He's a big boy. Leroy can wait. We scrambled his brain after that little adventure. Let's begin.'

Jack used his police interviewing skills to draw out of Cindy every little fact. Recalling all the conversations she had had with Theo and all the medical conditions she identified him suffering with from the moment she found him. Her medical background made the evidence she was providing very compelling reading. Jack could not have had a better professional witness. Her recollection was unwavering. Once complete, he bid Cindy farewell as he took her down to the pontoon. Leroy had noticed their arrival on the pontoon and steered his boat in close to collect her.

Cindy stepped aboard. 'Well, mister, if you fancy a bit of R & R, you can always head over to my bar for a beer anytime you're passing.'

'I'll do that. Straight from the fridge, right?'

'You've got it. Stay good soldier.'

'It's a Royal Marine, if you don't mind!'

Cindy laughed heartedly back at Jack. He waved her off and headed back inside the ship. No rest for the wicked, he thought to himself.

CHAPTER TWENTY

It had been a mad 24 hours back on the ship. Jack had written a detailed report for both the police and the Destiny Luxury Group CEO. He had examined the d'Vere suite and uncovered other evidence that would assist the police. He had secured all the CCTV evidence and presented a collage of relevant evidence to assist the police. Michelle d'Vere was now incarcerated with the local constabulary. Spencer d'Vere was making steady progress at the hospital, while Theo d'Vere stayed onboard until he recovered enough to disembark and be flown home. Theo was still trying to come to terms with the fact that Michelle tried to kill both him and Spencer. Jack had enjoyed an evening in the company of Dani, who tried her best to bring him back down to some form of normality.

Jack looked at his email inbox. Top of the list was one entitled "Call me" from Keith Jameson. Jack opened the email, but the message was brief. "Jack, call me here in London. I have some good news, so you better be sitting down". Jack looked up at the clock in his onboard office. It was 2pm here in the Bahamas, meaning back in London it was 7pm. The email was only sent two hours ago, so he would give Keith a call and try to catch him. He would contact him on his mobile as it was a waste of time calling a published Met Police number as everyone was hot-desking and was harder than ever to track down. He lifted the receiver on his desk phone and dialled Keith's number. There were enough coffers in the Destiny organisation to cover the cost of this call, he thought to himself.

'Keith, how goes it mate?' he asked as the phone was answered.

'Sit back in your chair, geezer. I've got something big to tell you.'

'I'm all ears. Fire away mate,' replied Jack with heightened intrigue.

'I can't believe this myself, but here goes. There was going to be an office move as yet again, we were going to be downsized and squeezed into an even smaller cubbyhole. I was clearing out the office, and I came across a box that was gathering dust. It looked like it had sat there for a couple of years, at least. I opened it up and found a load of house-to-house proformas that, mostly, someone had completed. I didn't know to what investigation it related, but I saw they were from houses near where that girl went missing called Charlotte. The investigation that curtailed your time here in the Met. I recalled that one of the PCs, Alicia, sent it to us whilst they were on light duties because of their imminent maternity leave. They gave her the task to top and tail the house-to-house enquiries by the new officer in the case DI Clive Maynard. You might recall that he was the snidey one who was quick to stick the knife in your back on the original investigation. The level-transfer from the uniformed side. He couldn't detect his own behind, let alone a major investigation. It looks like Alicia didn't quite finish topping and tailing the paperwork and enquiries before she went into early labour. Useless Maynard should have reassigned Alicia's work, but was not sharp enough to pick up on it. I reckon he thought it was complete, but never checked by asking. That's the dangers of presuming. Like you, I don't like to leave any stone unturned, so one evening I laid out the forms on the cleared table. I separated those that were complete and those that were not to my satisfaction. Recalling you always believed we connected the disappearance of Lottie to the park she was found in before, and the woman we anonymously named "Lady in the Park", I delved deeper. I went with your thoughts on this one at the time, but those mercenary bastards wouldn't listen to you. How they said you took the enquiry in the wrong direction and wasted your golden hour looking in the all the wrong places. They believed the focus should have been on the mother and stepfather. I was determined to bring some closure to the house-to-house enquiries. Maynard obviously thought it was a mundane task that you just had to tick the box to say they had covered it off. Bloody idiot. I found there were five houses near the park where there had been no replies after two visits, but they had left it at that. I went back and revisited those five addresses again. Four checked out. They had always been the residents, and all had been away either on holiday or on business at the time. I verified each one, and they all checked out. This left me with only one address remaining. It was the last one I checked out. It was the fifth priority because whoever filled out the form at the time wrote on it, "No reply to repeated knocking. House looks derelict with cats roaming around". I called at the address and on first viewing that description looked about accurate, but I noticed the waste bins were in use. Calling at the door, I got no reply. I then knocked again and looked through the letterbox. I could hear a TV but could not make out what was on. At that moment, someone muted the TV sound. I called out that I knew someone was in there and it was the police knocking. I saw through the frosted glass a figure come to the door. The occupant undid several locks, and the door opened, only to be stopped by a security chain. I could see a lady in her late fifties looking back at me through her steel-rimmed circular glasses. I showed her my warrant card and asked her to open the door, as I needed a minute of her time. The smell of cats was quite overwhelming. She opened the door, and I explained why I was calling. When I asked her if she remembered Charlotte going missing a few years back, she said she had a faint memory of it. I asked if anyone else lived there then or now, and it was a clear "No" from her. She then tried to excuse herself and close the door. I could see beyond her that there was a pair of children's shoes in the hallway, so I asked her who they belonged to, and she said they were nobodies and that a fox had dragged them in to her garden. I then saw a few teddies strewn around on the floor. She tried to say they were other toys the fox dragged into her garden, and she gave them to her cats to play with. Her story wasn't ringing true to me. I could see a child's bright pink raincoat hanging on a coat peg above the shoes. Looking beyond her, I could see through to the living room. The TV had indeed been muted, but it was playing children's TV programmes. I asked her if I could come in, as something was amiss. She called out, "Rachel, run". I saw a young girl with blonde hair run from the living room towards the kitchen and I presumed the rear garden. I bolted around the side of the house and went into the garden. There was a child's miniature playground. I stood in the middle of the garden and waited. I could then hear a child crying, and I found this young girl about nine years old behind the line of tall conifer trees. Looking at her face, it was Charlotte. Jack, we've found Lottie. She's alive.'

Jack collapsed backwards into his chair. He could not take in what he had just heard. As unemotional as he normally was, he could not help but release a tear of relief. He pinched his eyes together with his forefinger and thumb. He took a moment to regain his composure.

Keith, with concern in his voice, said, 'Are you still there, Jack?'

'Yeah, I'm here. Is there more?' Jack had been listening intently and hardly breathing during Keith's entire monologue.

'Oh yeah, there's more,' answered Keith. 'I called for backup and a specially trained vulnerable person officer to take Lottie for a medical examination and full debrief. The lady in the house was previously unknown to us, but had a sad story of her own. Her name is Marjorie Hennessy. When I went back into the house, she was sat slumped in the lounge, quiet and remorseful. The TV was still on mute but playing a children's TV programme about a fireman. It was just ending, but then another episode played. Someone had recorded the episodes, and they were playing on a loop. I didn't want to question her, but she just wanted to get it off her chest there and then. I cautioned her and let her speak. She wanted to help us and let us have some of Lottie's favourite toys so that we could return them to her. Everything she told us in the house she repeated in the interview at the station. Marjorie first came across Lottie when she went missing in the park. She was sitting alone in the park on a bench, stroking her cat on her lap, when Lottie came over and sat alongside her. Lottie wanted to hold and stroke the cat, as she didn't have any pets of her own. Her stepfather didn't want any pets in the house, but didn't say why. After about half an hour of friendly talking, Marjorie asked Lottie if she should get home for her tea. Marjorie didn't have a phone, so tried to find out where Lottie lived. It was only a couple of streets away, so helped walk her home via the main park gate. When she exited the park, Lottie's mum, Sandra, was frantically looking for her daughter and saw them together. Lottie ran into her mother's arms and at that moment Marjorie told her she was trying to find where she lived and take her home. All Sandra kept saying was, "Thank you, thank you. Thank God she is safe". All the time Marjorie was the "Lady in the Park" we had been trying to identify but couldn't trace. It turns out the second time Lottie went missing, it was in near identical circumstances, but with an end twist. Lottie yet again ended up in the park. Marjorie was alone, but this time without a cat. Lottie went over and again sat next to Marjorie and started asking where was her cat? She was told the cat was at home with the recently born litter of kittens. Lottie asked if she could go back and see them, which reluctantly Marjorie agreed to. It was only one road away. They walked together, but nobody saw them. They arrived at the house that looked very much like a recluse's house, because in many ways it described how she lived. Lottie was innocently playing with the litter of cats and was having a great time. She told Marjorie that she didn't enjoy living at home, as her stepfather wasn't that nice since he had moved in. Her mother had less time for her and more time for him. Being an only child and not being allowed pets, she felt very lonely. Marjorie said she could come and visit anytime, but she must now go home. Lottie wanted to stay and not go home. Marjorie has admitted that she didn't know what had come over her and stupidly allowed Lottie to stay. Lottie was given a spare room. She opened a wardrobe and found lots of toys. She asked Marjorie why she had so many toys. Marjorie sat down on the edge of the bed and explained that once upon a time, she had a little girl called Rachel. Like Lottie, she was only 7 years old when there was a tragic accident. Marjorie's husband, David, and their daughter, Rachel, were driving to a children's party in a nearby village. Marjorie recounted it was a cold and dark night, with frost on the road. As they rounded a bend, a car registered to a family from Belgium was on the wrong side of the road and crashed head-on into their car. Sadly, Rachel and David died instantly at the scene. Marjorie was a primary school teacher and was at a parents' and teachers' evening, having been dropped off on route to the children's party. The headmistress called her in to her office to break her the bad news in front of the two police officers. Marjorie never truly recovered. She moved house to where she lives now, packed in being a teacher and became a recluse. When I searched the house, I found cut out articles from the local papers in the top drawer of Marjorie's bedside unit. Below that were secreted reports from the same papers about Lottie's disappearance. Apparently, by the next morning after Lottie going missing, she realised it could look bad for her. She honestly believed she was doing the right thing for Lottie, whilst also filling a huge void in her own life. Lottie enjoyed staying and not once in over two years asked to go home. Marjorie and Lottie formed a pack of love and friendship. She educated Lottie at home to a higher standard than her own primary school could provide.'

'That's incredible!' said Jack.

'It is,' replied Keith. 'But let us not lose sight of the basic fact that Marjorie prevented the true parental bond between Lottie, Sandra and Derek, and caused no end of worry and grief. They thought she was dead. Now answering to the name of Rachel rather than Lottie or Charlotte compounded this further. That's going to leave a large emotional scar, and not just for Lottie. Our DCI, Andy Ness, had your back on this the whole time. It grieved Nessie to see you resign and leave over this. Unlike the cold-hearted, ambitious Detective Superintendent Matt Brooker, who was at the centre of all your troubles. Brooker was scrambling for evidence to submit in his promotion application by any means.'

'No change there!' sighed Jack.

'It looks like Brooker is for the high jump. Rumour is he's heading for a Central Disciplinary Board where he'll be facing gross misconduct charges. In total contrast however, DCI Ness is immensely proud that the leads you said should always have been followed, ending up finding Lottie alive. Infuriatingly, if the senior brass had followed your entire investigation plan from start to finish, we would have recovered Lottie as soon as she went missing. They lost their nerve and did a mountain of harm. If they spent as much time properly investigating Lottie going missing as they spent having a kangaroo court investigating you, the world would have been a better place. I'll let you go, but you had to know this. I'm equally proud of being assigned as the one to tell you. You were right all along, kiddo, you were right all along. One more thing. Andy Ness wants to have a private chat with you, so expect contact soon. Signing off mate. Take care.'

Jack could imagine Keith beaming at the other end of the phone call. 'Cheers Keith, you take care as well mate, and you did a cracking job, too. Glad I wasn't alone on this. Thanks for having the belief. It means a lot. Just a quick favour. I mentioned I would return Lottie's photo to Sandra and Derek at the end of the enquiry. I don't like to break my promises.'

'Sure thing. Consider it done,' Keith replied.

The receivers went down, and Jack spun around on his black leather office chair to see if anyone else was around. There wasn't. He spun back around 180 degrees to face his desk. He looked at his own dark reflection in the computer screen and softly pumped his fist and arm three or four times as he whispered, 'Yes,' to himself. 'Yes, yes, yes.'

No longer had he put down the receiver that the phone rang again. He picked it up on the second ring.

'Hello, Jack Shaw here. How can I help?'

'Mr Shaw. Good to hear your voice. You are a man in demand, I understand. It's Andrea Kennedy here. CEO of the Destiny Luxury Group.'

'Ms Kennedy. A pleasure to speak with you. How may I help?'

'Oh, I think you have helped more than enough, Mr Shaw. I hoped I could help you. Captain Nico has already submitted your d'Vere report to me. It's an embarrassing time for not only the company but also for me personally. Michelle d'Vere was a close friend of mine for many years. I cannot believe what she has done, but with great sadness I must accept it. I have reflected on the fact that Michelle is a rotten apple to her very core. Here at our Destiny Luxury Group HQ in London, the senior management team is committed to repairing our once great reputation that this episode has unfortunately tarnished. Your professionalism, integrity and utmost discretion have shone throughout, for which I am eternally grateful. Which leads me on to a couple of proposals, Mr Shaw. Please listen and give both great attention and thought about what I am about to suggest. First, this must have been equally traumatic for you as it has been for me. We all deserve a break after a harrowing experience, and you should not differ from anyone else. The first proposal is non-negotiable, Mr Shaw. I would like to offer you the opportunity to take a two-week break, with holiday pay included. I would like to send you and a significant other to any of our worldwide luxury hotels on an all-inclusive basis. Flights, hotel, meals, drinks and excursions all at my personal expense. I have a personal jet on standby here in London to fly yourself and one other to wherever you both wish. This will fly out to the ship in the Bahamas so that I can visit and come to terms with what has happened. I would, of course, like to meet you before you are driven to the jet and on to your holiday.'

'Well, I honestly don't know what to say?'

'Andrea laughed and said, 'A simple thank you would be sufficient.'

'Thank you, Ms Kennedy. Thank you once again,' came back the reply.

'Now the second proposal you can think over whilst on that holiday. It's something that you may want to discuss with your significant other, which is why this is a holiday for two. Mr Shaw, I would like you to return here to your home city of London. Our company HQ is here within our luxury Destiny hotel in Mayfair. I want to appoint you as head of security at the hotel. It brings a bit more prestige than performing that role, as I want you to be my personal security adviser to all things the Destiny Luxury Group controls. It would be a day job and a half, but we would reward you appropriately. Would you be interested?'

'Well, I, er, I think, um.'

'Mr Shaw, worry not. I don't need an answer now. You have time to think about the pros and cons of such a proposal. I would be delighted if you took this position, but don't feel obliged to.'

'I'll give it lots of thought. On the subject of a significant other, that is quite a delicate matter. I'm trying to recover a relationship that I've been in and out of, and I need to speak with someone first. I am concerned that it may complicate things here.'

'Mr Shaw. If you are referring to a certain First Officer Dani Lawson, then I have no concerns.'

There was a stifled silence at Jack's end of the conversation.

'Mr Shaw, don't worry. There's not much that escapes the attention of the Destiny Luxury Group or myself. We have been aware of your relationship for some time. From what we know, it hasn't compromised our brand, and of course we would like it to remain that way. Of course, she can go with you on holiday, but for now, her position should remain on the cruising arm of our business. You never know what the future holds, though. Please, don't let us stop your enjoyment. Be mindful that if you choose to work for me here in London, internal security monitoring would fall under your remit. You'll therefore be the manager of discretion.'

Jack paused to take stock. 'I'm very impressed with your grip on things, ma'am. Your job offer is definitely food for thought.'

'Good, Jack. I'll see you soon. I've got to pack and catch a flight. Until we meet again.' Andrea rung off.

Jack replaced the receiver, then picked it up and immediately dialled an internal number. 'Dani, I've got something to ask you.'

EPILOGUE

Jack Shaw will be returning in "Running with Foxes".

Based in London at the sister hotel owned by the Destiny Luxury Group. Jack Shaw is transferred to be head of security.

The intrigue is wrapped around the comings and goings of the major events hosted at the hotel, its transient population and eclectic mix of employees. Major international criminals exploit the hosted events.

Jack uses all his savvy and life experiences to understand just what's going on. Events become darker and more mysterious as each day goes by.

www.jackshawthrillers.com
jackshawthrillers@gmail.com

ACKNOWLEDGEMENTS

First and foremost to our dear friend Ray McCullagh for proof reading the book. He provided invaluable advice for the draft version of our manuscript, for which we are eternally grateful. Also to fellow authors Geoffrey Start, Gordon Thomas and Jane Davis for their continued encouragement. They have been loyal and supportive throughout the process of writing our debut novel. We appreciate you have endured the journey with sage advice and helpful insight. To other established authors, we thank you for your contributions. For the numerous cruise ship crew members and passengers on our many journeys, who knowingly and unknowingly have inspired our fictional characters and plots. To Maximillian Miller, a talented mixologist and barman, who created a unique cocktail that tastes as good as it sounds. Thank you to the photographers along the way who have perfectly captured the moment, especially Alrio Miller, Lauren and Gareth. A big thank you to Poppy Holford for her assistance with the graphic designs. We are very proud of you.

ABOUT THE AUTHOR

Laura & Alan Holford

 Laura Holford holds a Master of Arts in English Literature. A former personal assistant to the most senior officers at New Scotland Yard, she has a wealth of knowledge on the intimate workings of the Metropolitan Police. Using her vast experience of world travel and cruising, she puts this into good effect in her debut novel "Swimming with Pigs".

Her husband, Alan Holford, served for more than thirty years in the Metropolitan Police, mainly in detective roles. He served ten years on Homicide, seeing out the end of his career in the Counter Terrorism Command as Acting Detective Chief Inspector. His operational and strategic experiences in undercover work come to the fore throughout the series of books.

Printed in Great Britain
by Amazon

38245089R00243